The 2nd

Exodus

By
KingELOTheGod

EBook ISBN - 979-8-9920291-0-9
Paperback ISBN - 979-8-9920291-1-6
Hard Cover ISBN - 979-8-9920291-2-3

(Ecclesiastes 1:9)
The thing that has been shall be, and there is nothing new under the sun.

(Book Description)

What if the ancient prophet Elijah returned to lead humanity through the final exodus of the last days? Elijah's Return is a thrilling, thought-provoking journey that reimagines biblical prophecy in a modern context. In a world on the brink of collapse—flooded with chaos, political unrest, and environmental disaster—Elijah, the legendary prophet of old, reappears with a divine mission: to guide a chosen people through a new exodus, away from a crumbling civilization and toward a promised future.

Through riveting storytelling and rich, spiritual insights, this novel explores timeless themes of faith, redemption, and the ultimate battle between good and evil. As Elijah faces new adversaries—both human and supernatural—his journey becomes a race against time to deliver mankind from a fate worse than death. Will he succeed in fulfilling his destiny and lead humanity to salvation, or will darkness prevail?

Perfect for readers of spiritual thrillers and fans of apocalyptic fiction, Elijah's Return merges ancient prophecy with modern-day suspense, offering a fresh perspective on the end-times and the power of faith in the face of overwhelming odds.

(Chapter 1): The New King

(Chapter 2): Staff Turned Snake

(Chapter 3): The Sand Warning

(Chapter 4): River of Blood

(Chapter 5): The Frogs

(Chapter 6): The Flies

(Chapter 7): New Goshen

(Chapter 8): The Chinese Assassins

(Chapter 9): The attack of the Beasts

(Chapter 10): The Wizards of Italy

(Chapter 11): The Skin boil Outbreak

(Chapter 12): The Russian Spies

(Chapter 13): The Flesh Eating Virus

(Chapter 14): The Magicians of Germany

(Chapter 15): The Great Pestilence

(Chapter 16): The Mexican Assassins

(Chapter 17): The Great Hailstorm

(Chapter 18): The Arab Wizards

(Chapter 19): The Locust Outbreak

(Chapter 20): The African Wizards

(Chapter 21): The Great Darkness

(Chapter 22): The Blood Games

(Chapter 23): The Great Passover

(Chapter 24): The Global Courtroom

(Chapter 25): The Chariots

(The New King)

It had to be around 7:00pm when it happened. Nobody ever would have thought that the United States of America would have come to this. All I know is that a major change in that land was about to happen, and I do not think the people in that land were ready for it. I was looking down at the earth and the first location that I focused on was New York City. And as I focused on New York I noticed large crowds of people gathering in the Times Square district. From what I saw there was a event going on and from what I heard the president was about to give an urgent message that night at 8:30pm eastern time. I don't know what kind of event it was that I saw but all I know is that Times Square looked like the night of the day they call New Year's Eve.

So, I looked closer at what was going on, and then I noticed that the event going on was a magic show. So as everyone looked at the magician I focused my attention on him too "for my first trick I will take this large needle and I will stick it through my chest" the magician said as he held a large needle in his hand, and then moments later the magician began sticking the needle through his chest, and the magician was not harmed by his trick, then the amazed crowd started to cheer for the magician, and I didn't bother to count the magicians tricks, but after a good amount of tricks it was almost time for the urgent message from the president.

"The president will speak in 28 minutes" a policeman shouted to the crowds. It was almost 8:30pm and that's when I noticed many officers with the letters S.W.A.T on their shirts arriving on the scene out of nowhere. I did not know what a S.W.A.T team was but by the reaction of the people it could not have been good. "Why is the S.W.A.T team here" a man yelled as everybody was trying to figure out why they were there. Then I realized that the S.W.A.T team was a special force of police officers. Then those officers started letting everybody know that the president was about to speak, and the people had looks on their faces like we already know that, but the officers were trying to inform the people who may have not known. But anyway, the whole situation just seemed a little bit strange to me because one moment everyone was having a good time then the next moment the S.W.A.T team started surrounding the whole Times Squares district.

Then I looked at the giant TV screen that the crowds were gathering around, and I noticed that there was some kind of broadcast being shown. I guess that Times Square had their TV set for the president's urgent message. Then I thought that whatever the president had to say could not have been good if the S.W.A.T team had to pop up. Then a lady on the broadcast started speaking "this week is looking to be a wet one" said the lady, and the people of New York did not look happy to hear that. So, then I thought to myself these people on this TV broadcast must be trying to play God by trying to predict the weather and people were actually believing in what they were saying and that was just strange to me. Then minutes later the president appeared on the TV screen to speak.

"Citizens of America I'm here today to address some important changes that will be happening in this lovely nation. For one thing I just want to let you all know that tonight I will be stepping down as the president of the United States". Then all I saw was a lot of confused faces in the crowd of Times Square then the ex-president began to speak again. "As a matter of fact, there will be no more presidents of the United States after tonight". Then after the ex-president said that everybody was just looking in disbelief at what they just heard then the ex-president continued to speak. "Yes, you all heard me correctly congress and I mostly I have decided to make the United States a Monarchy government, and I will be the last president of the United States and the first King of America, and this is not a joke people".

Then all of a sudden, I heard some man shout "He can't do that", and then that man was escorted out of the Times Square district by some officers and the New King began to speak again. "You see the old Christian fairytale way was not working anymore that is why I have a confession to make, and that confession is that my people created the bible many years ago and we created it to keep the populations under control you see there never was a Jesus".

Then after the new king said that the whole crowd grew angry when they heard the truth, and they were still in disbelief of what was happening then the New King began to speak again. "Now for my first act as the king I will be issuing The New Constitution today and the old one will no longer exist" Then after the new king said those words, I knew that this was why the S.W.A.T team had to come on the scene that night, then the New King continued. "You see tonight America will be under a new law Martial Law" right after the New King said that hundreds of drones began to flood the sky, and that is all that I saw in New York before I began to focus on Atlanta.

Now as I began to focus on Atlanta, I noticed that the time was set back to 7:00pm on the same night. I guess that I was being shown different areas of that nation during the time frame of 7:00pm all the way to time of the urgent message from the leader of that nation. Now the first thing that I noticed was that I was seeing the downtown area of Atlanta, and just like Times Square the downtown area of Atlanta was very busy and I could tell that a event was going on there as well. So, then I focused my eyes on the crowds, and it looked like everyone was going to the same place, and that place was a sports arena with a big ATL sign in the front of the arena.

"Who's ready to see the celebrity game" I heard a guy say as I listened to the conversations of the people, then after hearing multiple conversations I concluded that everyone was going to see a celebrity basketball game. So, then I focused my attention on the inside of that sports arena, and the first thing that I noticed was all of the bright lights and I noticed how huge the arena was , and I also noticed all of the merchants selling sports item's and food, and people were buying the item's, then I focused my attention on the basketball court because the game was about to start because I heard a guy say that the Tip off was about to begin and I guess that meant that the game was about to start. So, as I looked at the inside of the arena where the court was, I noticed how small the actual court was compared to the whole arena. Then I saw that there were thousands of seats in that arena, and I could not even count the number of seats that I saw, and all the seats were filling up as the game was beginning, and there was a giant TV screen hanging from the roof in the center of the arena, and that TV screen was not the only screen in the arena, but it looked like the main one.

So, then I began focusing on the basketball players on the court and I noticed that the basketball game was an all-star game, and one of the celebrity teams had on red jerseys and the other celebrity team had on blue jerseys. I do not know who these celebrities were, and I did not know what they were famous for, but from listening to the conversations in the crowd I knew that most of the celebrities were either rappers, actors, or comedians. So, then the game began and the celebrity team with the red jerseys won the tip off, then one of the players on the red team opened the game with a 3 pointer and then the score boards changed and reflected the current score that was three to zero, and from what I could hear from the people in the crowd was that the player who made the game opening shot was the most famous rapper on the court. Then after some time had passed the score was now 38 to 42 and the red team was winning then out of nowhere the lights in the entire arena went out and the arena was invaded by the S.W.A.T team and the game was shut down.

"What the hell is going on" a guy screamed as the new king appeared on all the TV screens, then an officer grabbed a microphone and began to speak. "The president is about to address this nation and it's urgent and now everybody must listen up" the officer said. And the people in that arena were pissed off that their game was interrupted because I heard that nothing like that had ever happened before, and when some of the people tried to leave the arena, they were stopped by the S.W.A.T team and the S.W.A.T team made sure that no one left the arena and, then everyone focused their attention on what the new king was saying.

        "Citizens of America I'm here today to address some important changes that will be happening in this lovely nation. For one thing I just want to let you all know that tonight I will be stepping down as the president of the United States". "Stepping down" I heard someone yell in the arena, and everyone else in the arena stood in confusion because there has never been a president in their recent history that stepped down as the president of the United States, so then everyone continued to listen to the new king. "As a matter of fact, there will be no more presidents of the United States after tonight", "he can't be serious" a man yelled, and people really were standing in confusion once the new king said that. Then that's when a S.W.A.T team officer told the people in the arena that if he heard any more outburst from the crowd then there would be consequences, so then everybody in the arena shutted up and kept listening to the rest of the new king's speech.

"Yes, you all heard me correctly congress and I mostly I have decided to make the United States a Monarchy government and I will be the last president of the United States and the first King of America and this is not a joke people you see the old Christian fairytale way was not working anymore that is why I have a confession to make and that confession is that my people created the bible many years ago and we created it to keep the populations under control you see there never was a Jesus … now for my first act as the king I will be issuing The New Constitution today and the old one will no longer exist You see tonight America will be under a new law Martial Law". Then after the new king said those things a riot broke out inside of the arena, but the people were not fighting each other but instead they were fighting the officers because the people new that America was about to become like a country under a dictatorship and these people were not going down without a fight, and that is all that I saw in Atlanta before I began to focus on another city and that city was Washington D.C.

Now I was beginning to focus on Washington D.C and just like before the time was set back to 7:00pm on that same night. And I quickly noticed the crowds gathering around a White House, I was told that all the past U.S presidents lived there while they were in office. Then I saw the statue of Abraham Lincoln I was told that he was the president in office when the slaves in America were so called freed. Then I started to focus on the event that was taking place and I noticed that it was a parade going on, then I thought to myself "it certainly is not a coincidence that there are major events happening all around that nation on the day that the whole nation was getting ready to change certainly the higher up elites must have planned that, and even though there were major events all over that nation I was told that I would be only seeing 5 of them and Washington D.C was the third city I was seeing so far.

Now as I looked closely and examined the parade that was going on I noticed that it was a gay parade happening, and I thought to myself this is kinda weird, and everyone was having a good time then out of nowhere the parade was shut down and the S.W.A.T team locked down the whole entire area of the White House, and they made sure that no one who was attending that parade could escape. Then I noticed that there was no giant TV being viewed like in New York and Atlanta, and that was because I was seeing the actual location were the New King of America was filming his speech and he was on a podium located at the White House area and every eye that was at the White House could see him and the ones that couldn't most definitely could hear him because they had lots of speakers set up for that speech, then the New King started to speak.

"Citizens of America I'm here today to address some important changes that will be happening in this lovely nation. For one thing I just want to let you all know that tonight I will be stepping down as the president of the United States". Then all the happy faces started to change into looks of confusion, then the new king began to speak again. "As a matter of fact, there will be no more presidents of the United States after tonight yes, you all heard me correctly congress and I mostly I have decided to make the United States a Monarchy government and I will be the last president of the United States and the first King of America and this is not a joke people you see the old Christian fairytale way was not working anymore that is why I have a confession to make and that confession is that my people created the bible many years ago and we created it to keep the populations under control you see there never was a Jesus … Now for my first act as the king I will be issuing The New Constitution today and the old one will no longer exist you see tonight America will be under a new law Martial Law". Then I noticed that the gay people were actually cooperating unlike the people in New York and in Atlanta because in the first two cities that I saw the people went nuts and started fighting and some were even killed. So, since the gay people at the White House parade event were cooperating, I was able to here a little more of the New King's speech. "I am ordering Martial Law to contain the people all over this nation who might be disturbed about what I have to address tonight because as you know I am being recorded live right now for the whole nation to see, and I just would like to let everyone know that this act of a new monarchy will not be changed and anyone who rebels against this new order will be put to death", and that is all that I heard before leaving Washington D.C.

Now I was about to be shown another city, and as I started to be shown the next city the first thing that I noticed as I started to focused on this city was a big sign that read HOLLYWOOD on top of some mountains, then I was told that I was seeing the city of LA. Then after I saw the Hollywood sign, I began to focus on a beach area, and like the previous cities there was a event happening there as well. Then I thought to myself what kind of event could be taking place at this time on a beach at night, because the time was set back to 7:00pm again. So, I looked more closely at the event, and I saw that a surfing event was taking place on that beach. Then I saw a huge stage with some kind of big screen behind it, and as I was looking at the stage a guy walked on the stage towards the microphone that was on the stage.

"Everybody I have a quick announcement to make as you all know at 8:30pm President Moore will be going live on the news, and we will be broadcasting it right here on this big screen behind me" the guy said as he pointed to the screen behind him and then he began to speak again. "It is now 7:15pm so we have about 1 more hour before the president makes his announcement until then let the games begin" the guy said, and I could notice that the people there wasn't really paying attention to the guy because they were too busy doing what they were doing. Then I saw a group of people pick up their surf boards as they ran towards the sea. Then I heard a lady with a megaphone make an announcement to the surfers, and I noticed the lady was half way naked wearing what they call a two piece swim suit that was all red.

"Surfers listen up there will be 4 teams of 5 people for this game and I will let you all choose your teams and then once yawl get in your teams I will separate the teams by color so there will be a Red, a Blue, a Green, and a yellow team and if you look at the water you will see that we set up 3 borders for 3 levels with level 3 being the furthest away and the waves get bigger every level and there will be 5 rounds and one person from each team per round and the surfer that lasted the longest on the wave wins that round and the team that wins the most rounds will win the cash prize of $1,000 dollars so have fun" and that was all the lady said and then the 20 surfers started to form their teams. Minutes later the surfers had their teams together as round one began, and as the whistle was blown 5 surfers, one from each team ran towards the sea with their surf boards and were off to the first border. Then I noticed that the waves in the first border were really low so it didn't surprise me that everybody passed that level and none of the surfers fell off of their boards, so then the surfers of round one were

7

off to the second border and I saw that the waves were a little bigger than the waves in the first border.

And then I saw that only the surfers from the red, blue, and green teams did not fall off their boards of the second border and those 3 surfers began moving towards the third border and I saw that the waves in the third border were huge then the 3 remaining surfers from round one started to surf the waves in the third furthest border, and after about 3 minutes of surfing the surfer from the blue team lasted the longest on those huge waves so the blue team won round one as the crowd cheered for the winner, and everyone was having a good time then as round 2 was about to begin suddenly the event was shut down by the S.W.A.T team and everyone stood in confusion.

"What's going on" I heard a guy say as the new king appeared on the big screen, then I began to hear the same speech for the 4th time. "Citizens of America I'm here today to address some important changes that will be happening in this lovely nation. For one thing I just want to let you all know that tonight I will be stepping down as the president of the United States". As a matter of fact, there will be no more presidents of the United States after tonight ... then he made a quick pause yes, you all heard me correctly congress and I mostly I have decided to make the United States a Monarchy government and I will be the last president of the United States and the first King of America and this is not a joke people you see the old Christian fairytale way was not working anymore that is why I have a confession to make and that confession is that my people created the bible many years ago and we created it to keep the populations under control you see there never was a Jesus".

Then the new king took a sip of water then continued his speech. "Now for my first act as the king I will be issuing The New Constitution today and the old one will no longer exist you see tonight America will be under a new law Martial Law ... I am ordering Martial Law to contain the people all over the nation who might be disturbed about what I have to address tonight, and I just would like to let everyone know that this act of a new monarchy will not be changed and anyone who rebels against this new order will be put to death", and that's all I saw in LA. Now I was about to be shown the last city I was told, and that city was the city of Houston Texas, and once I started to focus on the city of Houston I noticed that the time elapsed right to the time of the New King's speech, and I also noticed that the people in Houston were gathering together at a large Football Stadium with a big screen T.V in the middle of the field and the

8

S.W.A.T team was surrounding the whole stadium, and unlike the first 4 cities I was hearing the very end of the New King's speech so I started to tune in.

'Oh yea and another thing that I forgot to say' the king said so I kept listening 'I forgot to tell you all that America will now also be under the united world foundation, and in this united world foundation there will be a new one world currency, and also like I said earlier we made up Jesus people and he does not exist and he never did exist and he is not coming back to save anybody so that is why we must now make our own Heaven on this earth' the King explained. And then I noticed that just like the people in Atlanta and New York the people of Houston were also rebelling against the new constitution that was just announced by the new king, then I heard a guy whisper to his friend as they escaped the police officers chasing them "man I knew that eventually these people was going to get rid of the original constitution because too many people were getting too smart and using their own constitution against them and their system and people were starting to legally fight back so I knew that they was going to put a stop to that and they did" the man said and that made a lot of since to me.

(Snake Turned Staff)

And that was the last thing that I saw before it was time for me to go. Because I was being sent to America by The Most High to free his people, and I was also told that as I entered the earth the time would be different from what I just saw. What I just saw was the first days of the new kingdom of America coming into power, and I was told that by the time that I landed on the earth 7 years would have gone by. Then after I was told that I was then sent to the earth, and as I entered the earth's atmosphere I was put back into my same human body just like before as I continued to fall from the sky.

Then I heard the voice of The Most High "I will still be with you the whole time as I use you to preform my wrath upon this nation". That is all I heard The Most High say as I fell through the clouds, then seconds later The Most High made sure that I had a safe landing. Then when I landed on earth I quickly realized that I was in New York City and that was the first city that I focused on earlier, but it only seemed like 10 minutes since the time that I was sent to earth after I saw the first moments of the change, but now that I was on the earth I knew that 7 years must have went by from what I was told.

So I looked around and it was a clear morning from what I saw, and I did not see anybody on the streets as I looked and looked. But what could have happened in the last 7 years and where are all the people I thought then I saw a guy running through an alley way. This guy was the only living person outside other than me it seemed, so then I began to follow the guy then minutes later I caught up with the guy. "What are you doing outside are you crazy" the guy said to me. "No, I'm just trying to" then the guy cut me off "Just follow me" the guy said so I followed him. "The drones will spot us if we don't hurry up and get out of this district" the guy said, and then moments later we were entering an apartment building. "This is my apartment" the guy said as he pointed at his front door and then we entered his apartment.

"Ok who are you" the guy asked me "My name is Elijah and who are you sir and why were you the only person outside if you don't mind me asking" I replied. "My name is David and I was just coming from the king's

10

tower in the rich district and I was running because people like us are not allowed over there so I was trying to hurry back to this district" David explained. "What do you mean people like us are not allowed over there" I asked then David started to explain. "Well it was just 5 years ago when the king exiled all of the remaining believers so they call us but anyways they exiled my people into what they call the district of believers and we were all exiled here because we did not except the new constitution".

"Oh, ok I see" I said and then David continued to speak. "You see they could not kill all of us, so they just decided to cut us off from all of society with the hopes that we would just die out eventually" David explained further. And then after David finished speaking, I felt that I could trust him enough to tell him who I really was, so I told him. "Ok well I think you should know this" I said, "Know what" David replied, "You should know that I am Elijah The Prophet and The Most High sent me to save his people from this wicked world" I explained. Then David shockingly looked at me "No way if your Elijah The Prophet then prove it to me" David replied "ok I will follow me" I said. So then me and David left his apartment and then we went into the middle of the street that was in front of his apartment building and then I began to spread my hands and I began to say a prayer and then moments later a fire came down from heaven right before me and David's eyes.

"Wow you are Elijah the prophet now I believe you because only Elijah the prophet called fire down from heaven in the scriptures and my people and I have been waiting for your return wow, because in the scriptures if you read Malachi 4:5 it says that in the last days The Most High will send Elijah the prophet back to earth in the last days so if you are not lying to me then that means that we are in the last days" David said. "I don't have to lie to you I am Elijah the prophet now please tell me more information" I replied. "Oh, indeed I will tell you more but first let me introduce you to the others" David said, "Ok no problem" I replied. Then we left to see the others.

After we left I was confused because we just got done from running trying to get indoors. "I thought we could not be outside right now" I said, then David replied, "we are not in the rich district anymore when you saw me running earlier we were on the border line of the rich district and the district of believers now we are in the district of believers and we can be over here just not over there" David explained "ok I see" I replied. Minutes later David and I arrived inside of a big park and then I began to see the people. "This is where most of the people in this district come when they are not home" said David, then I looked around and the people looked tired and hungry and the whole park looked lifeless.

Then David yelled to the people "everyone gather around I have a message to share". Then everyone focused their attention on David and me, and then they gathered around us. Then I noticed that not just a little bit of people gathered around David and me, but it was hundreds of people so in that moment I knew that David was the leader of these people then David spoke. "Everyone this man right beside me is Elijah the prophet and he was sent to free us from this land and some of you might not know this, but Elijah once called down fire from heaven a long time ago, and he just did it again". Then I looked at the people and I knew that they were believers because from the looks of it they knew exactly what David was talking about then David continued to speak.

"I don't know how long it will take for Elijah to complete his mission but I have a hunch that it will not take too long from now", then David tapped my shoulder and whispered to me "we need to go now", then David began to speak to the people "everyone thanks for your time but me and Elijah must go for now but we will be back soon" David said to the people and when David was done speaking everyone stood in amazement, then David and I left the park. Then once we left the park I could not help but notice that the whole district of believers looked like a place of struggle. "What is today's date" I asked David "March 13th David replied, then once David told me that it was march I knew that I was sent in the same season that Moses was sent to free his people out of Egypt I could immediately see the comparison, but I decided to let David know that comparison later.

"So, what was in the New Constitution" I asked David. "Terrible things such as the one world religion being introduced, and no one had the right of religious freedom anymore, and martial law was declared, and also there was a population control act issued, and they started an early age military recruitment program" David explain. "oh, ok I asked you because I did not get to see everything before I left" I replied. "What do you mean you didn't get to see everything, and before you left from where" David asked. Then I began to explain "before I was sent to the earth I was looking

12

down from heaven and I saw the very first moments of when the king of America came into power 7 years ago. I was shown 5 different cities the first city that I saw was New York City, the second city that I saw was Atlanta, then the third city that I saw was Washington D.C, and the 4th city that I saw was Los Angles, and the last city I saw was Houston. And I did not see anything else pass that night.

"Oh, ok well to sum the last 7 years up for you all you need to know is that the New Constitution was totally made to go against The Most High's people" David replied. And as David and I walked through the district of believers I wanted to know more about the early age military recruitment program that David mention earlier, so I asked him, then after I asked David my question he began to explain. "Well in November a few years ago the army started the early age recruitment program because they wanted to raise up soldiers from a young age starting from as young as 10 years old. And they started this program because they believed that if you raised up a solider from his youth that he would be a lot stronger and tougher when he became a man". "I think 10 is a little too young for this day in time anyway" I replied, and as David and I continued to walk in the district of believers we noticed that it was getting dark and I did not have nowhere to stay.

"David do you think I can stay at your place until my job is done" I asked, "Yea no problem of course" David replied, then we began walking to David's apartment. Then minutes later we arrived at David's apartment building "I stay on the 7th floor you might have not noticed earlier because we were rushing to get inside" David said, then we walked into David's apartment building and began to walk up the steps. Moments later we were standing in front of a door with the number 78 on it, I did not notice the number earlier I thought to myself and then we went inside of the apartment.

"So, what did you do in the world before the change" I asked David, then David began to explain. "Well I was born in New York, and I was into sports as a kid so at the age of 10 I started playing football for the park leagues, and I was an all-star running back from the park leagues all the way up to high School and my plan was to get drafted to the NFL one day, but when my football dreams did not work out I became a musician and that is what I set my mind to do so I did it and I was very good at what

13

I did, and on top of being a musician I became a security officer at the age of 23, And years later I became a private security officer, and I knew that things were about to change after this one night when I was on a private security post and I mistakenly heard a conversation that I think I was not supposed to hear.

It was about 1:00am when I heard some agents talking so I listened. "The old way is not working we need to find a new direction for America", then there was a brief pause in the conversation "I got it ok we will set up a new kingdom in America this is our land anyway and we will do it before president Moore leaves office", and that is all that I heard before leaving that night, but I wished that I would have stayed longer because I might have gotten more details". Then after David spoke David turned on the T.V and some kind of broadcast like the broadcast I saw before on the big Times Square T.V screen was on, then moments later David turned the T.V off.

"There is always a bad story on the news there is never any good news on nowadays at least before they would sneak in a little good news from time to time" David said "What is the news" I asked "The news is a show where people report the latest events on what's happening or what's going to happen for an example if someone was murdered then the news will report it, or if there was a earth quake the news will report it, and the news tracks the weather too" David explained. "Oh ok" I replied, then moments later I wondered what David's worse experience during the last 7 years was so I asked him and then he replided.

"Well my worse experience would have to be when the bible raid started 5 years ago just 2 years after the change. Basically, the marital law officers were ordered to find and burn every bible that they could find and if anyone fought against them they were ordered to shoot them. So, one night while I was at a gathering for my normal study routine the door of the building was kicked by some martial law officers, so me and the group I was with ran to the basement and the officers chased us, then when I got to the basement I hid behind a wall and the officers did not see me, but then I peeked behind the wall and I saw the officers lining everyone up on their knees horizontally at gun point,

Then one of the officers walked up to the guy that was Ist in the line the guy happened to be the pastor he was 66 years old. "Stand Up" the officer yelled to the pastor then the pastor stood up and then the officer put a gun behind the pastor's head. "Denounce your faith" the officer screamed "Never" the pastor said "If you don't then I will blow your head off old man" the officer said "I won't do it" said the pastor "Seriously where is your God now" the officer said, and then seconds later the officer shot the pastor in the back of the head killing him "Now dose anyone else won't to be stupid" the officer said, then after the officer said that I just did not have the stomach to keep watching so I escaped the building with my scriptures and now today I have the last remaining scriptures in the world". Then after David told his story I thought to myself well now I see why he was the leader of the remaining believers, and then we both went to sleep for the night.

The Next morning, I remembered my dream and in my dream The Most High told me that today I needed to go to the king and tell him to let his people go, and then I was told that I would receive the ancient staff that Moses once used, and with that staff I was told that I would be able to perform miracles, then lastly, I was told that I would be like a God compared to the king and David would be the prophet. So early that morning I went outside and searched for the ancient staff and then moments later the staff appeared to me behind a tree, and then I went back to David's apartment. Then when I entered the apartment, I noticed that David was now up "Why do you have a big stick in your hand" David asked "This stick is not just a stick it is the anointed staff and with this staff I will be able to perform many miracles" I replied "Oh ok that is very very great news now what's your next move Elijah" David said

"Today we need to go to the king and I will ask him to let our people go in peace" I said "But we are not allowed over there" David said "don't worry not a hair on our bodies will be harmed" I told David "What do you mean on our bodies do I have to go with you" David asked "Yes because The Most High has made you his prophet because you were the only person who managed to keep his word alive during Jacob's Trouble and now you must come with me to warn the king" I explained "But what if the king does not believe that you are Elijah the prophet" David asked "Then I will make my staff turn into a snake right in front of his very eyes so that he may believe" I said "ok I'm wit-cha" David said, and then we left David's apartment.

15

"One thing that you should know is that the lower part of Manhattan is where the king's tower is right in the rich district" David said, "what happened to the white house" I asked "Well the king decided that the white house was just for presidents and he felt that he was above the presidents so he decided to move his district to the lower part of Manhattan, and now Washington D.C is just called The Washington District" David explained. Now after David explained about how the king moved his district to the lower part of Manhattan, I knew why The Most High sent me here. "Ok so we are not too far from the king's tower, so we should be there in no time" I said, "Your right but we are all the way up in the upper part of Manhattan and there are no cars, buses, or trains here like in the rich district, so we have quite of a walk ahead of us" David said, and then we began our long walk to the king's tower.

Then when David and I finally arrived in the rich district it was like life on earth had gone back to normal. All I saw was a lot of rushing cars and buses on the streets and what they call the train system appeared to be working, and everybody there looked really happy, and as I saw people shopping at the stores this society just looked like it was back to normal and it did not look like the district of believers because over here had life to it, but the district of believers looked lifeless. Then I thought what are the other parts of America like, so I asked David, and he replied, "Ok you might want to sit down for this". So, we sat down at a bus stop.

"This whole nation is a rich district as a matter of fact the whole world is a rich district" David said, and as David said that I saw an airplane move across the sky then David continued "as a matter of fact the other cities and towns do not call their cities and towns rich districts everything is still called the name that it was called before for an example Brooklyn is still called Brooklyn, Queens is still called Queens, and L.A is still called L.A and nothing has changed but the only place that actually is called the rich district is the lower part of Manhattan and that's because the king's tower is there, and there is only one district of believers in America and that is the one in the upper part of Manhattan and there is only one because the population of the believers got so low during Jacob's trouble that they could fit all of the remaining believers in the upper part of Manhattan", then after David said that I had a look of disappointment on my face and I shook my head.

"I told you that you might want to sit down for this" David said, and then the bus pulled up to the bus stop then David and I waved our hands to the bus driver and we did not get on the bus. "Don't be too disappointed there used to be 5 districts of believers in America, but the other 4 districts did not survive" David said, "Where were the other 4 districts" I asked. "There was one in Atlanta, Washington D.C, Houston, and L.A" David replied, then I replied what a coincidence because those were the cities that was shown to me plus New York before I came to the earth, "oh yea and I forgot to mention that there is also 1 remaining district of believers in every country in the world," said David.

Then a police officer walked up to me and David "Yawl cannot sit here unless you are riding the bus" the officer said, so we left the bus stop. "You see this is why there is only one district of believers left because with no money or resources it's hard for our people to survive" said David "What kind of currency dose America accept" I asked, "Global Dollars" David replied "Ok" I said, and then I lifted my staff and then piles of cash started coming out of it "Can we use this" I said. Then everybody that saw what I did just stopped what they were doing "Hey that guy is a wizard" a guy yelled "Wow yes, we can use this, but we need to get away from here before we draw any more attention to ourselves" David said, then David grabbed the cash and stuffed it in his bag then we walked away.

"You will get us killed if people start thinking you're a wizard" David said, "I told you that not a hair on our bodies will be harmed" I replied. So now with the money that came out of my staff David, and I could catch the bus, so we stood at another bus stop. "Now with this money we can try to blend in with the rest of this society because the only reason why our people get caught is because of the lack of good clothing and to everybody else they are considered bums and when people see bums they know that 9 times out of 10 that they came from the district of believers" David explained, then the bus pulled up and me and David got on it.

Then after me and David paid our bus fare I noticed that people were looking at me funny "mommy look at that guy with the big stick" a little girl yelled, then David rang the bell on the bus and then we got off the bus. "Why did we get off the bus are we at the king's tower now" I asked "No but we just had to get off the bus because you and your staff was

17

bringing to much attention to us" David replied "Oh ok I'm sorry" I said "No don't be sorry for being you it's just that now we know to not use public transportation we need something a little more private" said David, then David began to brain storm "I know I can get a car with the money that came out of your staff" David said. I did not understand the currency of this time period, but David told me that $300,000 global dollars came bursting out of my staff earlier. So, we went to go buy a car, and then minutes later David purchased a black Camaro for $40,000 global dollars. "Now we can move around and blend in with this society," said David.

Then David got into the driver's seat because I never drove a car before I was just used to riding horses that's how we got around back in my time period so I just got in the passenger's seat, and then David and I was off to the kings tower.

Then minutes later we arrived at the king's tower, so we got out of the car and I noticed that the king's tower was being double guarded, and the tower had a big fence going around it and the tower looked like the tallest building in New York City to me. "This is it big isn't it" David said as we walked toward the entrance of the tower, and then I noticed the first guarded layer was guarded by some lions that were ready to attack anyone who came near the king's tower so then I lifted my staff and then the lions started behaving like little house cats so me and David were able to get pass them, Then when we got to the 2nd layer where the entrance was we were stopped by a guard "Do yawl have a appointment" the guard said "No but can $50,000 global dollars get us in" David replied as he handed the guard the money, then the guard took the money. I guess the guard understood the langue of money, so the guard began searching me and David for weapon's and I guess the guard did not see my staff as a weapon

"The king's office is on the 70th floor and it's the last door on the left" the guard said as he let us in the tower. Then minutes later we arrived on the 70th floor and we walked to the king's office, and then moments later we were standing in front of the king. Then I quickly notice that the king was sitting in a big chair with a gold crown on his head with a few females fanning him. "Can I help you two" the king said "No but I got an important message to tell you" I said "Oh really and what might that be" said the king "I came here today to ask you politely to let my people go" I said "Yea and who are your people" said the king "the believers" I replied "oh those people huh and who are you" the king said "I am Elijah the prophet" I replied "Prove it" the king said, and then I lifted my staff and then it became a huge snake

"Eww" the girls screamed and then the girls ran out of the room. Then the king called his magicians, and he ordered them to make a snake with their staff and with their dark magic they did, but my snake ate the magician's snake, then I picked up my snake and my snake turned back into a staff. "Nice trick, but I am not impressed, and you didn't have to scare the girls away" said the king, so then I made my staff swallow the staff of his magicians to further prove that I was Elijah the prophet, then the king looked out of the window of his office. The window was so big it looked like you could see the entire New York City from his window then the king continued to speak. "Look I don't know if you are a magician or Elijah the prophet, but what I do know is that I will never let your people go now you two can step outside of my office" the king said, then the king's guards told us to leave so we left the king's tower and not one finger was laid on us.

(The Sand)

When David and I left the king's tower I couldn't help but remember how arrogant the king was. "What's the king's name" I asked David as we road through the rich district "Richard Moore is his name" David replied. Then David parked his car "Where are we going" I asked, "To a sub-sandwich shop to get a quick bite I'm hungry what about you" said David "Yea I am a little hungry too" I said. Then David and I got out of his car and started walking towards the entrance of the sub-sandwich shop. "David I have a question for you" I said "sure go ahead" David replied "ok so before I came to the earth I heard the king mention about something called the united world foundation what is that" "oh the United world foundation that is basically the newer version of what was once called the United Nations where all of the nations of the world were united and they just decided to renew their program and they switched the name to the United World Foundation but they call it the United World for short" David Explained.

Then we entered the door of the sub sandwich shop. "I haven't eaten here in 7 years, but I like this place because most of the food nowadays are GMO's or it is artificial, but this sub-sandwich shop is 100% organic" David said as we entered the store and got in line. Then as the line moved before I knew it we were at the front counter. "What can I get you two" said the cashier "just 2 veggie patties that will be find you like veggie patties right Elijah" said David "Yea that's ok with me" I said, then our sandwiches were made super-fast and then we sat down to eat. "Man it feels so good to actually be able to purchase some food it has been years" said David "So let me get this straight society has completely cut off the district of believes right" I asked "Yea, so as the rest of the world is still functioning they left us in our district to die out and we have no money there" David explained "And all because of how you all stood up for the truth" I said "yea it is really a shame, but that's why you have been sent to judge this world" David replied.

Then David and I looked at the T.V in the sub-sandwich shop, and on the T.V there was a lady marring her horse. "wow that's forbidden that is bestiality" I said "yep what can I say this society has gone completely

Moral-less first it started with gay marriage, then pedophilia was legalized meaning that adults were now able to marry children, and now it is legal to marry a animal" David explained "really" I said after I looked at what was next on the T.V "oh yea they even play porn on the regular channels now back in the day you had to order those channels, but now these channels are on basic T.V" David explain "Ok I had enough let's go" I said, then David and I left the sub-sandwich shop.

"So, the king must find pleasure in this new kingdom he has made" I said as we were leaving the sub-sandwich shop "yep and he exiled anyone that was against it" David replied, "How much worse can it get" I said, "oh I'm about to show you" David said as we got in his car, then David started his car and then we were off. Then minutes later David began to park his car again "Where are we going now" I asked, "To a playtime booth" David replied, "what is a playtime booth" I asked, "it's like a lemonade stand but the girls are not selling lemonade yea prostitution is now nationally legal and even out in the open as well" David said. So, once we arrived at the playtime booth I saw a naked girl behind the booth bending over in front of a police officer as the officer was unzipping his pants "let's go before I see something that I don't want to see" I said, and then David and I left.

"I think you get the picture now basically these are the types of things you see inside of a God-less society" David said, and then I saw a fat man with a clown face kissing a little boy that looked about 12 years old in the mouth. Then I saw a street fight and it seemed as if the men were fighting to the death and what made the whole situation worse is that people were encouraging the fight. "Blood I want to see his blood" I heard a man scream while he was drinking a glass of blood. Then suddenly one of the guy's fighting broke the other guy's neck killing him, and everybody clapped for the winner. "Terrible and is this legal" I said, "I'm afraid so" David replied, and then the guy who won the fight cut open the man's chest that he just killed and collected the man's blood and put it into a bag. "Why is he putting the man's blood inside of a bag" I asked "oh because blood is a big business nowadays first it started small with plasma and blood donation centers for the public, but now it's completely out of control" David explained, then we got back into David's car and left that terrible street corner.

Then David told me that his gas tank was low and that we had to drive to the closes gas station, so we began searching for the nearest gas station. Then when we arrived at the closes gas station there was a big sign up, so I read it. $48.50 unleaded gas $52.80 Premium is what was on the signs "gas prices sure are high now I remember years ago when gas was like $2.00 dollars, but now that America is running out of resources gas prices skyrocketed" David said, then David and I walked inside of the gas station "I need 2 blunt wraps" said a kid talking to the cashier, and the kid looked about 12 years old. "oh, yea kids 12 and up can now buy Tabaco products and kids 15 and up can buy alcohol' David said, then after David told me that I saw a 16-year-old looking boy drinking a beer as he exited the store. "yep years ago, you had to be 18 to buy Tabaco and 21 to drink alcohol" David said, "that's so out of line" I said "yea well tell that to the king" David replied.

Then David brought the gas and then we left the store, and then David filled up his gas tank and then we drove off. "So now you see sex is everywhere, people are drinking blood, bestiality and pedophilia is now legal, and now kids 12-15 can buy Tabaco and alcohol, but now I'm about to show you one last thing and this will be the worst thing that I have shown you so far" David said "what are you about to show me what can be worse" I asked " what I'm about to show you is the real reason why you've been sent what you just saw believe it or not was the least of the problem" David said "so how many of our people are left because earlier you told me that our population was so low that they could fit all of the believers that are in America in the upper part of Manhattan" I asked "well sadly after they killed most of us they estimated and said that there is about 10,000 of us left in the district of believers in America but around the world there are about 600,000 to 1 million of us so-called believers in total but no one knows exactly" David said "that is unreal considering that there were 7 billion people on the earth once" I said.

Then David and I drove to the Times Square district "why are we stopping here" I asked "because it's almost 6:00pm" David replied "What happens at 6:00pm"I asked "a T.V show called The Believers comes on" David said "what kind of show is that" I asked "basically it is a show where they are making fun of our people" David said "so they don't even know when to stop" I said "I'm afraid so" David said as he took a deep breath

22

"you know I use to love this season spring it was always my favorite season now it's just more days of trying to survive" said David "Well you know that spring is the real beginning of the year right" I said "yea I do" said David "Good but why did a evil group of men have to invent a calendar that made the new year start in the dead of winter just think for a second what happens in the spring" I said "things grow and blossom" said David "right now what happens during the winter" I said "things start to die" David said "exactly, now why do people really think that our creator would start off a year with everything dying or would he start off a year with everything growing and blossoming" I asked "I think that our creator would start off a year with everything growing and blossoming not dying" said David "Right "Also, another fact that you should know about the spring is that Moses was sent to free the Hebrew people out of Egypt during spring, and I think The Most High was trying to give his people a fresh new start just like the year, and that is also why I was sent now because our people are about to have a new beginning" I said

Then David and I walked and then stood with the large crowd in front of the giant T.V screen in the Time Square district to watch The Believers it was now 6:00pm The T.V show began, and the introduction showed how the believers were living day by day in their district. "And these people say that there is a God" the narrator on the T.V show said, and then the large crowd in Time Square started to laugh at the believers struggles. Then as the show continued I could not believe what I saw they were actually broadcasting officers killing the believers "And this is where their stupidity got them" the narrator of the show said, then one by one they kept showing different kinds of ways that they would kill the believers, and the large crowd could not stop laughing as this T.V show mocked the people of The Most High. "you see this is what they were doing to us before they exiled us into the district of believers and the only reason why they did that is well you are about to see in a second" David said. "come on let's go I don't want to see no more of this mockery these people are evil" I said,

"Hold on wait the king is about to make an announcement that I want you to hear" said David "I don't want to hear it this kingdom is finished" I said, then right after I said that the large crowd started laughing at the T.V show again. Then the king came on the T.V and made his

23

announcement "Today is March 15th and as you all know it is almost time for the annual Blood Games", the king said then the large crowd cheered, "and that is why the remaining survivors of our people were exiled to the district of believers" said David "What is the Blood Games" I asked "it's a game where once a year these people haunt our people in the district of believers like animals and murder is completely legal for 24 hours and who ever collects the most blood from our people wins, and this is the reason why they even created the district of believers for this game" David explained as he shook his head.

"Well let's go I believe I have seen enough you can explain the rest of the game to me on our way back to the district of believers" I said, then we got in David's car and left the Times Square area. Then minutes after we left the Times square area David began further explaining the Blood Games. "Ok well the Blood Games is only for 1 night and it lasts until 9pm the next night, and they made a movie about this years ago called "The Purge" where murder was legal for 1 night, but now it is a reality, so on the night of the Blood Games I would ride around inside of a van trying to save as much of our people as I could" David explained, and when David was done explaining the Blood Games we arrived back in the district of believers. When David and I got back to the district of believers we went to the park where David brought me before. Then we stepped out of the car and everyone that saw David and I was shocked to see us driving a car, and I also noticed how hungry my people looked and I knew they were really struggling after that terrible T.V show that I just saw. Then David started to gather the crowds of people, then he spoke "everyone Elijah just warned the king about letting us go, but the king refused to do so, but don't worry Elijah will get us out of this land soon ... now I'm going to let Elijah speak to you all".

Then when David said that everyone's attention turned towards me, so I began to speak. "The king did not want to let us go the easy way I tried to give him a chance, but tomorrow I will give him one more chance to let us go in peace and I hope that he will listen tomorrow" I said, then I got tired of seeing the hunger in my people's eyes then I continued to speak "I have also seen the hunger in you all, but from now on you will not be hungry any more" I said as I lifted my staff, and then out came piles of bread bursting out of my staff and everyone rushed to eat the bread.

"Thank You Elijah Thank you" is all I heard the people say, then I spoke once more to the people "The next time that you all see David and me things will be different" I said, and then David and I left to go to his apartment for the night.

The next morning David and I got ready to go back to the king's tower again, and we were not afraid because we were being protected. "Elijah what if the king denies your request to let us go again" David asked me "well then there will be a great consequence" I responded, and then we got inside David's car and then we were off to the king's tower. Then 25 minutes later we arrived at the king's tower and of course we went through the normal routine of getting checked for weapons, and then after we were checked for weapons we were inside of the king's tower again.

"You see with The Most High on our side who can be against us" I told David as we made our way to the King's office room. Then minutes later we were standing in front of the king again. "You two again" the king said "yes and today I have come back to ask you again fairly to let my people go" I said "I'm afraid I can't do that still "the king said "The Most High needs his people to be free so they can serve him in the wilderness" I told the king "The Most High what you mean God I swear you believers and your fairytales make me sick" said the king "do not mock The Most High" I said "You know what I have heard enough of this non-sense you two can now leave my office bye" the king said, then David and I were escorted out of the king's tower. "I told you that the king was going to deny your request he is determined not to let us go" said David as we entered his car "oh he will let us go after later today" I replied, and then David and I continued back to the district of believers.

So, on our way back to our district we passed through Times Square and I noticed that I was on the news on the giant T.V screen, and the headlines read "A man claiming to be Elijah The Prophet has come to free his people" that is all that I saw as the car passed by and I also heard the laughter of the people who were watching the T.V. Then 20 minutes later we arrived in our district by David's apartment "we need to go to the roof of your apartment building" I told David, so then we got out of David's car then we ran inside David's apartment building. "This way will get us to the top" David said as he pointed to the steps, then we ran up the endless flight of steps. Then finally after running up the steps we reached the top of the building, and the building had to be at least 10 stories from what I saw because it looked like I could see the whole New York City on the roof top of David's building I could definitely see the king's tower from where I was.

"Why did we come up here" David asked, "because I wanted to be high up for this" I said as I lifted my staff up high into the air, and then moments later a big sand storm hit America, and this sand storm was so big that no storm has been seen like this since the ancient days of Egypt, and the sands continued to flood the land for at least 10 minutes, and the sands covered everywhere but the district of believers. "No way that was incredible everybody in America must be going nuts right about now" said David "I told you that there will be a consequence and the sand did not just cover all the cities in America but the sand also covered all the cities in the world but none of the district of believers in the world were touched" I replied, and then David and I left the roof top.

Then David and I got in David's car and then we went to the park to talk to our people, and as we entered the park there were crowds of people cheering us on. Then David and I gathered the crowds "Everyone settle down Elijah has something to say" David yelled, and then I began to speak "Today I gave the king a second chance and he did not accept my request so as you all witnessed I made a sand storm hit all the lands of this world, now this should be the king's wakeup call and now he should let us go" I said, and then the crowd cheered a cheer that could be heard all the way in the rich district, and then I continued to speak. "The Most High has now come to judge this world because this world has gone too far by killing and then mocking him and his people so now this Era of history will soon be over".

And then David began to speak "as you all may know Elijah is here to destroy this world just like how Egypt was destroyed but only this time Egypt is the whole world because The Most High's people were scattered all over the world this time not just in America so that's why Elijah will be plauging this whole planet, because nothing is new under the sun and if it happened before than it will happen again so now our redemption is very near" David told the people, and then the crowd began to cheer again, then after David spoke to the people the crowd began to clear and as the crowd cleared I notice a woman not moving I think she was waiting on someone

"Ashely where have you been" said David. I guess the woman was waiting on David, so then David and I walked up to the woman. "Elijah this is my wife Ashely, Ashely this is Elijah the prophet" said David "Really is it you ... nice to meet you" said Ashely "nice to meet you too and yes I'm really Elijah the prophet" I said. "My wife Ashely was just spying on the rich district and today is my first day seeing her back in the district of believers" said David "What have I missed while I was away I mean I saw the huge sand storm did you do that Elijah" said Ashely "Yea with the help of The Most High and not just that Elijah has been preforming many miracles for our people, and he has been also trying to get the king to let our people go in peace and he tried twice and I was with him both times, so when the king refused to let us go the second time earlier today that is when he made the sand storm hit the lands of this world" David explain "at last we will be freed I knew the time was coming" Ashely said.

Then David turned his attention to me and spoke. "A couple of days ago when you saw me running it is because earlier that day me and my wife were spying on the king's tower because my wife and I are one of the only people that really spy on the rich district from time to time and we go over there to get new information for our people since they have no idea about what's going on in the world, but anyways I was spotted by a drone, the drones can spot our people somehow that is why we try to stay out of their way, so when I lost the drone that day that is when you saw me trying to quickly get out of the rich district" David explained. "Yea and when my husband got away I had to hide from the drones, and I had to hide out in the rich district because the drones were guarding the boarder lines of the district of believers after my husband made it back" said Ashely, and then me Ashely, David, began to walk towards David's car.

"Wow where did you get this car" said Ashely "This car came from the very first miracle that Elijah did he made piles of cash burst out of his staff and then I brought a car with some of the money because we could not ride on the public transportation system because we were gaining to much attention" David explained "oh ok nice car though" said Ashely "Thanks now did you hear any new information while you were over in the rich district" David asked Ashely, then Ashely began to speak "yes, and they are planning something big. You see both days while I was in the rich district hiding out I would go to Times Square and blend in with the large crowds, so I could hear the announcements on the giant T.V screen, then the king appeared on the T.V so I tuned in.

"Greetings America as you may know the believers are dying out a little bit too slowly first it was the district of believers in Atlanta that died out, then the ones in Washington D.C, then the ones in Houston, and then the ones in L.A, but this last group of believers in New York seems to not want to die, so that is why this year for the blood games the military might have to intervein. We have not done this for any of the previous years, but now I think it is time for me to speed up the process", and that is all that I heard before I came back to our district and here I am now" said Ashely". "So, that means that the king just got done making his announcement he must be pissed off at the sand storm that hit" David said, "Yep and now the king is planning to kill all of us once and for all on the night of the blood games" said Ashely, "goodness that's really soon" David said, and then after David said that we arrived at David's apartment and we all went inside for the night.

The next morning, I went up to the roof top of David's apartment building, and as I looked at New York City I noticed that the sands have piled up overnight. Yesterday when the sand storm hit the sand covered the whole city and the stand stood about 5 feet tall, but today it looked like the sand doubled and the sand was about 10 feet high everywhere and even much higher in some places, after I noticed the sand covered New York City I saw Ashely and David coming onto the rooftop and they started looking around at the sand covered city. "Wow this must be how Egypt became a dessert because I heard that before Moses destroyed Egypt, Egypt was a beautiful city" said Ashely "Yes that is correct Ashely" I said, "so when do you plan to go back to the king" said David "well he must be pissed off right now so I will give him some time to cool down and make the right chose next time I replied.

(River of Blood)

After David, Ashely, and I stood on the roof top of David's apartment looking at the sand covered city I couldn't help but notice that nobody in the district of believers had on lights in their apartment but David. Then after I noticed the light problem the 3 of us went back to David's apartment "So Ashely I guess you stay here too" I asked, "Yea I do of course" said Ashely "oh ok and David how come nobody else has on lights in this district" I asked, "oh that is because the city cut off our electricity, lights, and water so now everyone in this district uses candles" David replied. "So how do you have electricity, lights, and water" I asked David "because I got skills from being in security, so I built a power generator to give my whole apartment electric, then I built a solar panel for my apartment for the lights, a solar panel that harnesses the power of the sun to produce light" David explained. "So, what about the water" I asked, "well for the water I built a long funnel that reaches out to the river, and the water from the river runs all the way to pipe lines under my apartment building, so then I connected the funnel to the right pipes leading to my apartment, and then finally I built a filter to cleanse the water coming in, and I started these processes years ago" David further explained.

"Well, it is a shame that nobody else has Power" I said, "Yea I just didn't have enough resources to help the whole district" David replied, "well let me fix that let's go outside" I said, so then David, Ashely, and I left the apartment and went outside. "What are you about to do" Ashely asked, "I'm about to give this district some light" I replied as the 3 of us walked into the street. Then I lifted my staff high into the air "let there be light" I said and then seconds later the 3 of us started to see the lights coming on in all the apartments in the district. "Wow Elijah this district has been living like it was in the 1600s thanks" said Ashely "it's not just the light, but the electricity and the water is also running throughout the whole district" I said, "but how" David replied, and Meanwhile the workers at the New York Power building just realized that they had made a mistake and they gave the whole district of believer's power. The Most High gave me the eyes to see what was happening "Dam-it we just gave the district of believer's power and this mistake is not irreversible until the day of the

Blood Games" said a New York state power supervisor, and a similar situation was happening at the city's water department building and the workers there made a mistake and gave the district of believer's water. Then I looked at David "let's just say that The Most High handled it" I replied, "Man I haven't seen Harlem like this in years" said David, then suddenly, the 3 of us started to hear T. V's turn on, and radio system's blasting a guy that they called 2pac. "It is like you rose this district up from the dead," said Ashely.

Then I looked around and the district still looked life-less because of the non-movement of traffic outside. "This power and water should last us until we leave and that won't be long" I told David and Ashely "well what should I tell the people" David asked, "Tell them that they will be in good hands while we are still in this land" I said "Ok" David replied as we began to walk the streets of the district of believers. "Where are we going" I asked David "well since the blood games are starting soon I think I should show you how we have been surviving for the last few years" David said. Then we continued to walk the streets of the district "hold on wait why are we walking I am so use to walking that I have forgotten about the car" David said, so the 3 of us went back to get David's car.

Then minutes later we arrived at the car, so we got in it "well let's go shall we" David said and then David took off. "So, Elijah, remember how I was telling you about how I would drive around in a van rescuing as much of our people that I could on the night of the blood games" said David "yes I remember" I replied, "well let's just say that I wasn't the only person doing that" David said as we pulled up to a abandon looking warehouse. Then I noticed that there were lots of vans parked outside of the old looking warehouse with the words "Danger Zone" on the side of them. Then the 3 of us got out of David's car

"Where are we" I asked David "This place is called the danger zone" David said as the 3 of us walked inside of the warehouse. Then when we walked inside of the warehouse I noticed how dusty it was "Years ago our hide out was full of energy and high-tech equipment and our equipment is still here, but after the city cheated and turned off the power in this district we were unable to use our equipment. They turned off the power in this district in the first year that the blood games started, but we would still use our hide out on the nights of the blood games to shelter as much as our people as we could, and plus we still keep all of our weapon's in here" David explained as we walked through the building "Who is we" I asked "Our protection squad, the squad is full of trained military and security veterans like myself who serve and protect our people when danger calls" David replied as we walked to the main room of the hideout. Then David turned on the lights of the main room "I haven't seen the main room lit like this for years now" David said as he went to go check to see if all the equipment was working. "Yes, everything is still working" David said as he turned on the big T.V screen in the main room. "We put up cameras on every street corner in our district, and we use this T.V to monitor to watch our streets wow I have to let the rest of the squad know that our hideout is back fully functioning again," said David.

Then the 3 of us left the main room "now I am about to show you the weapons room" said David, then the 3 of us began walking to the weapons room and I noticed that the weapons room was still on the 1st floor of the warehouse just like the main room, then as we entered the weapon room I noticed all of the weapons on the walls of the room and there was no telling how many guns was in that room so I didn't even try to count them, and also there was a countless amount of bullets and Amor in the room also as well as other things. "This did not happen overnight you are looking at 10 years of weapons when the protection squad formed" David explained "So what do you all use the other floors of the warehouse for" I asked, "well we use the other levels of the building to house our people on the night of the blood games," said Ashely.

Then the 3 of us left the warehouse. Then I saw some vans in the front of the building so we started walking towards the vans, then David opened the back of one of the vans, then when David opened the back of one of the van door I seen all the weapons stored inside "yea we also store some of our weapons in all our vans" David said, then David closed the back of the van door. "You see even with all of this protection we still won't be a match for the whole military" said David, then I looked at David "I don't think we will be needing all of these weapons this year David" I replied "why do you figure that because the king is going to come full force with his army this year" David said "as I keep telling you not one hair on no one's body will be harmed this year" I replied, then we started walking towards David's car and then we got inside the car. "Now we need to alert the Sargent's of the protection squad and there were 5 of them and they were all in charge of about 200 men, and on the night of the blood games the different sets of soldiers would rotate shifts, so then David started up his car and then we left the danger zone.

"You know I like that you have an army of men to protect our people David, but we have The Most High on our side this year and I do not think that we will need your army this year" I told David "I know I understand that but you know just in case we need my army we got them, but don't worry we are never the aggressors we just are all about protecting our people" said David "I see what you are saying, but if I tell your men to stand down they must listen to me that is very important" I said "not a problem you are definitely the head Sargent this year" David replied.

Then minutes later we arrived outside of an apartment building then David parked his car "this is where Michael lives he is one of the protection squad's sergeants and I am about to go talk to him so you two just wait in the car for me I will be back in a second" David said as he left the car, so Ashely and I stayed inside of the car and waited for David to come back. "I like the bravery of your husband, but he seems to not really get that we really won't be needing his army and their weapon's this year because I have it under control" I told Ashely. "Well I know that, but he is just in routine right now because this is how we managed to survive in all the other previous years before you showed up, but once you really start preforming The Most High's wrath on this world oh he will start to understand that we will not need the protection squad this year, you just need to give him some time" Ashely explained, then after Ashely finished speaking we saw David exiting Michaels apartment building. "Michael is informed now" David said as he entered the car, then I looked at Ashely and then we took off back to David's apartment.

Then minutes later the 3 of us entered the apartment for the night, then after the 3 of us got comfortable we sat down and watched the news. "I knew that Ashely told me to give David some time, but I had to open his eyes right now, so I began to talk to David. "David where are those scriptures that you have" I asked David "it is in my room" David replied, "well can you go get it" I asked, and then David went to get his book and then seconds later David returned to the living room with his book and then he handed me the book. Then I opened the book, and I turned the book to Exodus and then I started reading the book starting at chapter 5 all the way to chapter 12, and then minutes later I was done reading. "Now David did Moses use an army to destroy the nation of Egypt" I asked "No" David answered "Ok so how did he do it" I asked "with his staff and with help from The Most High and he definitely did not need a army" David replied "yes correct so why do we need a army because the same Creator that was with Moses when he destroyed Egypt is the same Creator with us today" I explained to David "ok I understand now, so we do not need the protection squad this year" David said "Right" I replied, and then the 3 of us went to sleep for the night.

The next day I decided it was time to go see the king again, because I believe that I gave him enough time to make the right decision I thought, so that morning I remember being the first one up, and then David woke up, and then Ashely woke up. "Today we must go to the king" I told David "ok I will get ready" said David "can I come with you guys" Ashely asked, "not this time, but maybe next time" I replied, "yea stay with the people" David said, and then minutes later David and I left the apartment and walked towards David's car and then we got in the car, then David started the car and then we were off to the rich district.

Then moments later David and I approached the border line of our district and the rich district. "Man look at that mountain of sand in front of us" said David, then David drove his car up the mountain of sand, and then we were in the rich district, and the first thing that I noticed is that we were 10 feet above ground level when we entered the rich district as I looked down at the district of believers, then David and I went to go find the king. So then minutes later I noticed that there were still cars driving around the sandy streets of the rich district, and there was not as many cars driving around like before the sand storm, but there were some. Then I noticed that all the people in the rich district were packed inside of their apartments, and it looked like they were waiting to be rescued, but I don't think that they knew that their whole world got effected by the sand storm and it was not just New York City, so being rescued was not going to happen even though the rich district did get the worse of the sand storm.

"Man look at all of those people on their balconies" said David "I see" I replied, and then as David kept riding on the sand covered streets I noticed that the people who were driving were not using the stop lights they were completely ignoring it. Then I noticed that all the store entrances were covered by sand, but the top of the buildings where people lived were not affected by the sand because after all the sand was only 10 feet high and the buildings in New York City were really tall. "I guess these people will have to adapt to the sand just like how Egypt had too adapt when their nation was covered by sand, and if Egypt could have adapted then America can as well" said David.

Then minutes later David and I were finally in front of the king's tower, and of course the king's tower was not really affected by the sand, but the entrance was still covered with the sand just like everywhere else. "Man, how do people entered these buildings now" David asked, "I guess they pick a window and then they go thru it that's what it looks like to me" I replied. "yea that sounds about right" David said. Then moments later a car pulled up to David's car, then the driver of the car that pulled up next to us rolled down his window "the king is not in his tower he is away on business" said the driver "oh ok thank you" David replied, and then the car pulled off "well the king is not here so let's just go for now" said David, and then David drove away from the king's tower. "I wonder what the king is doing" David asked me "I don't know maybe he is looking at the after effects of the sand storm" I replied. Then moments later David and I road by the Times Square, and all that we saw was large groups of people crowding around the giant T.V, and I also noticed that the sand storm did not affect the power in the rich district, and their water was still working I noticed. So, then David and I pulled up closer to the crowd and we got out of David's car and we began to watch the giant T.V.

"Despise the terrible sand storm that hit our nation no one was hurt" The news woman said, then a guy pointed at me "hey that is the guy who claimed to be Elijah the prophet" he yelled, so then David and I got back in his car "we do not got time for this let's go" David said. So, then we drove away from Times Square and then moments later we were by the Coney Island beach. Then I noticed that there was an extravagant looking boat in the water. "Who can be in that boat" I asked David "That is the king I know that boat" David said, so then David and I got out of the car. Then I noticed that there was a big hill leading down to the beach shore, so David and I walked down the hill, then seconds later David and I were on the beach shore, and we saw the king and his guards on the boat.

"That's the man who claimed to be Elijah the prophet kill him" the king yelled. Then the king's guards pulled out of their guns and they tried to shoot at me and David, but all their guns jammed somehow, and the guns did not work, so then the guards pulled out their swords and got out of the boat, and then they started running towards David and me, but running inside 4 feet of water is a slow process. So, then I yelled to the king "let my people go" "Never" the king replied, so then I walked into the water with my staff. Then I put my staff inside the water, and then all the water turned into blood.

"Eww the blood stinks" the guards screamed as they swam back to the boat, and then since the king and his guards were defenseless, they just left. "You just turned all of the water into blood" David said "yea and not just this water but all of the water in the world even the oceans were turned into blood, and even down to every last river and stream that runs through the world" I replied "wow" David said "And even the water that was inside of the pipe lines throughout the whole world was turned into blood so if somebody was taking a shower their water was instantly turned into blood, and if someone was washing their dishes the water was instantly turned into blood, and even the water in people's cups and refrigerators were instantly turned into blood, so now basically anything that was water is now turned into blood and everywhere in the whole world is affected by the blood well everywhere except all of the district of believers throughout the world of course anywhere where The Most High's people are was not affected by this plague" I said as we made our way back to our district in New York. So then minutes later we arrived back in our sand and blood free district, then moments later David and I went into his apartment. Then David ran to his sink, then he got a glass cup from out of his cabinet, then he turned back to the sink and then he cut on the water and made him a glass of water "well our water is all good still just checking" said David, and then Ashely came rushing into the kitchen. "You guys come quick and listen to what they are saying on the news" said Ashely, so then the 3 of us rushed into the living room to listen to the T.V. "we don't know why suddenly all of the water everywhere in the world has turned into blood, but scientist are saying that some kind of a bad virus is spreading rapidly throughout the world, but all I know is that if there was a God then he should help us" said the news woman. Then I grabbed the remote and then I turned the T.V off

35

"people man they only call on The Most High when disaster strikes, but when everything is all good they say there is no Creator, and the scientist always have excuses for everything" I yelled. "You know they had to make an excuse so that they could calm down the public Elijah" said Ashely "and your right they only call on The Most High when disaster strikes, but they are not fooling me" said David. Then minutes later it became dark outside so the 3 of us went to sleep for the night.

Then the next morning I saw David getting ready to go somewhere he was up before Ashely and I. "Elijah I am glad that your awake quick get ready and come with me to address the people" David said, so then I got ready, and then minutes later David and I were in his car, and Ashely stayed in the apartment. "Some people might have saw the news and believed the whole virus explanation, so I want to go clear some things up" said David, then David put the car into drive and then we were off to the park.

So, as we arrived in the park everyone was outside as usual I noticed, so then David parked his car and then we got out of it, and then David started to gather the people, then once David gathered the people everyone became silent, and then David began to speak. "Yesterday if you saw the news they were saying that some kind of a virus is spreading around the world and they said that this virus is turning all of the water into blood well that is a lie because I was with Elijah yesterday and I saw him put his staff into the waters of Coney Island turning all of the waters into blood when the king refused to let us go I seen it with my own eyes, and this very same thing happened to The pharaoh of Egypt when he refused to let Moses and his people go, so do not buy anything that you heard on the news last night", then David pulled out his scriptures and then he continued to speak "If you read Exodus chapter 7 verse 20 it explains that. Now I am here to tell you that it won't be long before we are delivered, and from now on all of the plagues that happens to this world just know that Elijah is making it happen and nothing that he does will affect any of our districts or dwellings throughout the whole world" David explained to the crowd, then after David was done talking to the crowd everyone went back to what they were doing, and David and I went back to his apartment.

Then the next morning David, Ashely, and I woke up to a loud noise, and the noise sounded like a bus entering our district. "What is that sound" said Ashely "It sounds like a bus" I replied. So, then moments later the 3 of us went to go see who was in the bus entering our district, then when we arrived at the bus we saw the king exiting it. "Elijah don't worry I come in peace" the king said, "what do you want" I replied, "well I came to make a deal with you because my people simply cannot survive without any water, so if you tell your God to take away the blood and return the water I will let your people go" said the king. "Ok I will" I replied "Thank You" the king said as he got back inside of the bus, and then the king left, so the 3 of us went back inside of David's apartment

(The Frogs)

The next day I noticed that the waters everywhere were still turned into blood and nothing could be done about it for 3 more days, because I was told that the waters would stay bloody for 1 whole week, But the waters near every district of believers though out the world was of course not affected. "Time to go get some food I am hungry" said David "where are we going" I asked, "You know that park that we always go to well if you haven't noticed that park has a huge riverbank running right on the side of it, and that's where are people go to fish because that is the main source of food in our districts" David Explained.

So, then David and I left the apartment and went to the riverbank park to go fish, and after walking down the steps of the apartment building we were outside, so then we started walking towards David's car, then when David and I got in his car David put the car in drive and then we were on our way to the riverbank park. David did not live too far from the park, so we got there in like 5 minutes, so when we got near the park we left David's car and then we started to enter the park. Then the first thing that I noticed was how the water near the park was normal water and right next to the normal water was the blood water, and even though the blood water was next to the normal water the blood water did not mix with the normal water it was truly divine intervention that separated the blood from the normal water. Then I noticed how the people of our district stood to see the great divine sight as we walked through the entrance of the park.

"We all share fishing poles there is a fishing pole closet in the park, and it's for the people who may not have their own fishing pole" David said. So, then we walked to the fishing pole closet, then when we got to the fishing pole closet David grabbed a fishing pole and a bucket. And before David and I started fishing a guy walked up to me. "Hey you are Elijah The Prophet thanks for all of the work that you are doing" the guy said "Its my pleasure because the time has come for this human era to end" I replied "Right and it is such a divine sight to see that all of the water in our district was not affected by the blood plague but everywhere else was I mean the blood water is right next to the normal water but yet the waters are not mixing" the guy said, then David jumped in the conversation "that's because the thing that has been shall be you see when Moses led the original Exodus way back in the Egypt days all the plagues that he preformed did not harm the Israelites that were in Goshen and these districts of believers around the world are like little Goshen cities because they are full of the children of The Most High" David explained "Well thanks for that information David we should catch up later" the random guy said as he grabbed a fishing pole and walked away to go fishing.

"Now it's time to catch some fish" said David, then we began walking to the river docks, then when we arrived at the river docks I noticed a lot of our people fishing. "These are the most fish that I ever caught in my life" a man screamed, then I noticed that everyone that was fishing was catching a lot of fish. "Wow it's like all of the fish swam to our part of town today" said David "well that is because the fish cannot live inside blood so all of the fish had to migrate to the normal waters" I explained to David, then we both looked at the divine separation between the blood water and the normal water again "yea so in that case I see why everyone is catching so many fish, so that means that we all will be having plenty of fish this week" David said.

Then David began fishing and of course seconds later he began to catch plenty of fish "oh yea all of the fish are right here" David said. It was like every time David threw the fishing pole into the river he caught like 4 or 5 fish at a time "yea we are going to need some more buckets" said David, so then David gave me the fishing pole and then he went to get some more buckets. So, when David went to get some more buckets I decided to give this fishing a try, so I did and moments later I was catching plenty of fish and I never used a fishing pole like this in my life. Then minutes later David came back with the buckets "Wow I didn't know you could fish" David said, "well I never used a fishing pole like this before, but I guess anyone can come out here and catch some today" I replied, then we started to load the buckets with fish "this should last us for a whole week" David said as he looked at the buckets that were full of fish.

Then after David and I filled the buckets with fish we began to exit the park. "We need to bring these fish to my wife, so she can prepare our meals my wife sure can cook" David said as we exited the park and approached his car, then when we got to David's car we started loading all the fish in the trunk of the car, and then we got inside the car. "yea my wife can cook so I can't wait to bring these fish to her" said David "how much younger is she than you" I asked David "she's 3 years younger than me" David replied "well how did she learn how to cook" I asked "well she got real good at cooking from my mom who she calls her mom, then she went to college for cooking" David replied "your mom you never talk about your parents where are they" I asked, then David paused for a second "I don't like to talk about what happened, but since you are the prophet I will tell you, and then David began to explain.

"It was a quiet day in New York and the whole state was on lock down, and I was at my parents' house in RockChester New York where I grew up after we moved from Atlanta when I was little. So, I remember the last time that I saw my parents, and my parents were both around 65 years old when it happened. If I remember correctly my dad was in the backyard working on his car while my mom and I were watching the news. "I am in my sixies and I never would have thought that this would happen to America in 1 million years" my mom said as we watched the news. On the news they were talking about the new population control act, and they were saying that this act was necessary, and my mom was born back when population control was nothing but a joke to people because no one took the rumors of population control seriously in those days, so then my mom turned up the T.V in disbelief and they were saying that elderly people 65 and up had to be obtained, and very soon, so I guess my dad heard the T.V because that's when he walked into the house "what over my dead body" my dad said as he listened to the news.

My dad was in very good shape for a man of his age and he was a very strong guy too. "They tried that years ago" my dad said, "they did" I said "yea, but that does not matter right now" my dad replied. Either way my parents were old, and they did not quite grasp the change that was happening like I did because I knew that the system was never really made for people like us. Then my dad walked into his room, and then he came back into the living room with his AK-47 in his hand "Look if anyone comes into this house trying to harm me or my woman then their dead" my dad said "yea we have rights they cannot do that" my mom said, then when my mom said that all I could think is what rights because they took all of our rights away, but I did not want to tell my mom that because it would have broken her heart so I remained silent. So, to make a long story short

40

the next week when I came to my parents house there was a note on my parent's front door so I read the note "the residents of this house are in our custody because they qualified for the new Act" the note read, and at the bottom of the note it was signed by martial law, and till this day I still do not know if my parents are alive or not" David explained

"Man I am sorry to hear that" I told David after he told me about the last time that he saw his parents, and after he told me the story we arrived back at his apartment. Then we got out of his car and then we took the buckets of fish out of the trunk of the car, then we began to bring the fish into David's apartment. Then when we got inside of David's apartment Ashely had a surprise look on her face when she saw all the fish that David and I caught. "Wow how did you two catch so many fish today" Ashely asked, "oh because all of the fish were in our district" David said, "oh that makes sense because the fish cannot live in blood" Ashely replied, then after Ashely said that she took the fish into the kitchen and began cooking some of the fish, then after about 2 hours the food was ready, so Ashely began placing the plates on top of the table in the dining room. "Come and get your food guys it's ready" Ashely said, But david did not eat the fish. "You guys go ahead I am fasting this week "you know today I told Elijah about my mom and dad" David said "wow you never tell people about them it must have been hard" Ashely replied "yea, and every day I still hope that they are alive still in custody somewhere" David said, then minutes later the 3 of us went to the living room to see what was on the news.

"Many people are dying from the lack of water we now can confirm that 1 billion people worldwide died from this virus so we need to hurry up and find a" said the newswoman before David cut off the T.V I think she was about to say we need to hurry up and find a cure. "So when our people die it's all jokes and they mock us, but then when there people start dying they expect The Most High to have some mercy on them" David said "well The Most High is judging them right now, but not all of them will die from this" I said "yea and I bet they are not laughing now" David said, and then the 3 of us heard a loud noise so we went outside to see what it was, and when we got outside we saw that it was the king entering our district with his big bus again. "what does he want now" said Ashely "don't worry I got this" I replied, then the 3 of us walked up to the king's bus, then when we approached the bus the king got out of it with his guards.

"Guards stand down" the king commanded "what is it now" I asked the king "my people are dying did you not ask God to take away the blood" the king replied " I'm sorry, but I was told that the blood would last for 7 days and I could not do anything about that, so the blood will still be here for a couple of more days I'm afraid" I explained to the king "well when the blood goes away I will let your people go in peace" The king said, and then him and his guards got back into their extravagant looking bus, and then they left our district, So then Ashely, David, and I went back to David's apartment because it was getting dark. "I hope the king does not try any funny business because we cannot control how long The Most High wanted to plague his waters it is not our fault" David said, "all I know is that we are in good hands so let him try" I said. "yea I know it, but where will we go after the king lets us go" David asked me "well we will have to go back to the land of The Most High and just like in the Ist Exodus we will go back into the wilderness until The Most High makes his new everlasting covenant with us" I explained "Right because in the book of Ezekiel it tells us that the children of The Most High will go back into the wilderness" David replied "Correct because we all was there before you just don't remember because in every persons regeneration the memories of their past lives are forgotten" I further explained to David, and then after I got done explaining the regeneration process to David the 3 of us went to sleep for the night.

Then 2 nights later I spoke to The Most High in a dream "the king agreed to let your people go if you take the blood away" I told The Most High "ok I will take the blood away tomorrow, but then the king will harden his heart and he will not let my people go" The Most High said, "why would he do such a thing" I replied "because the King's heart is wicked that's why "The Most High said "ok so what do you want me to do when the king doesn't listen the next time" I asked "next time I will help you by making millions of frogs appear from all of the water all throughout the earth" said The Most High "but why even take away the blood if you know that the king will hold back on his deal" I asked "because I want to multiply my wrath upon the world, so the more he lies the worse it will get" said The Most High, and then I woke up.

That morning I ran to the T.V to listen to the news to see if The Most High took the blood away, so I grabbed the remote and I turned the T.V on. "Scientist have finally found a cure to reverse the blood virus and the waters are back to normal, it turns out that science was right again and there is no God" the news woman said "what" I yelled, then I turned the T.V off. I could not believe that these people actually thought that scientist reversed the blood plague, then David stepped out of his room I think he heard me yell "What's with the noise" David said "I just got upset because the news is saying that scientist have found a reverse cure for the blood plague, and that's why the blood is all gone now" I replied "the blood is gone" David said "yes" I replied "so last week when they were crying to who they call God on the news it was just for show I knew it they didn't fool me I knew that they was not going to give The Most High the credit" David explained, then David and I got ready to go see the king.

Minutes after we were ready we were in David's car "finally we will be freed today" David said as he put his car in drive. But I didn't want to tell David that the king was going to hold back on the deal because the conversations between The Most High and I are only between us, so I stayed silent as David pulled off in his car. Then minutes later David and I was in the rich district and indeed the blood was gone I noticed, then before I knew it David and I was at the king's tower. "Pick a window" David said as we got out his car, and then we climbed through one of the windows of the king's tower, then when we got inside of the tower we were met by some of the king's guards. "It's Elijah the prophet" one of the guards said, then the other guards backed off in fear as David and I walked towards the elevator, so we got on the elevator and went to the 70th floor. So, when we got off the elevator we saw a lot of the king's guards, but none of them came near us as we made our way to the king's office, then moments later we were standing in front of the king. "You two again how can I help yawl" the king said "I did what you asked and The Most High took the blood away so now it's time for you to keep your end of the deal and let my people go" I replied, then the king smiled and said "well I lied I will never let your people go" the king said "are you serious you liar" David yelled, then the king called his guards to escort us out of the building, but his guards did not listen to him.

43

"It looks like your guards are smarter than you, but don't worry we know our way out" I said, and then David and I left the king's tower. David was disappointed because he thought for sure that we were going to be freed today "man I can't believe the king lied" "don't worry because it will only get worse from here" I replied that was all that I could tell David, then moments later we approached David's car, so we got in. "Man, what are you going to do now" David asked as we pulled off in the car "you are about to see" I replied. "That's the empire state building" David said minutes into the car ride "alright let's get out here" I replied, "here why here this is so random" David said, "No it is perfect" I replied, and then David and I got out of his car. Then I looked around and people were outside, and cars were driving around the sand covered streets I noticed, and this was a busy area that's why I chose this spot, so then I lifted my staff and then seconds later frogs appeared from out of all the waters all throughout the world, and even peoples drinking water produced frogs so when someone drank some water even there bellies would get filled with frogs, and to top it all off even the sweat produced from people out of fear started to produced frogs.

Then later on the frogs started to flood the streets of New York, and there were so many frogs that you could barely see the sand anymore. Then I noticed how the frogs were filling up the cars that were driving on the streets making those cars crash, and everyone who was walking outside started running as the frogs started terrorizing everyone in the city, and on top of that the frogs made the whole city stink of a really bad odor. Then I looked, and I saw how people's apartments were being filled with the frogs, and the frogs were terrorizing the city so much that people were jumping out of their windows to their deaths to escape the frogs, and I also noticed that there were so many frogs that the frogs covered whole buildings, and even the empire state building was covered by frogs.

So as David and I watched the frogs terrorize the city around us The Most High made it so that the frogs could not touch us, so everywhere we stepped the frogs would move out of our way, and then seconds later the frogs left and for a moment everyone thought that it was over, and then suddenly more frogs started to fill the New York streets, but these frogs were not normal they were different colors and they were poisonous frogs, and they began licking everyone on the streets, and everyone who was licked died, but some people got indoors and were safe because the poisonous frogs did not go indoors for some reason. So, then moments later the

44

poisonous frogs were gone, but then the regular frogs came back, and this time they doubled in number as if they weren't already a lot of them in the first place and this happened all throughout the world.

"Ok let's go" I told David, and then we got in his car and left the rich district. "It's a living hell in the entire earth right now" David said, "it's just The Most High's judgement that's all because just like how The Most High judged his people for 400 years now they must be judged" I replied, then minutes later we were in our district and not one frog was over there. "How long will the frogs be terrorizing the world" David asked, "Only The Most High knows the answer to that question not even me" I replied, "I would not want to be them" David said as he opened his bible and read it a little. "Well Exodus 8:6 shows that the frogs came after the blood, and it doesn't say for how long" David said as we got out of David's car "I want to get a high view of the city so let's go to the top of your apartment building" I said.

Then we ran into David's building and rushed to the top of the building. Then when we were on the rooftop the first thing that I noticed was that the frogs were still terrorizing the rich district, and the next thing that I noticed was the king's bus entering our district. It's been 30 minutes and the rich district was still being terrorized by the frogs as well as the rest of the world. So, then David and I went to the king's bus, and then the king and his guards came out of it "Elijah there you are" the king yelled "What do you want because The Most High is not done punishing the world because you held back on the deal you made" I said "well I am ashamed, but if you tell your God to take away the frogs then tomorrow I will let your people go" the king said "Ok it shall be done" I said, and then seconds later the frogs stop appearing out of every water source in the world. "thank you" said the king "don't thank me just be ready to let my people go tomorrow" I replied, and then the king got back into his bus and left our district, and then David and I left and went to David's apartment. "When will the king learn Elijah so are you telling me that it took for some of his people to die for him to listen" David said as we sat down in the living room, and then Ashely walked into the living room "The king did not learn his lesson I'll believe it when I see it" Ashely said "you have a smart wife" I told David, "so if the king refuses to let us go again what will you do Elijah" David asked "then there will be another consequence" I replied

(The Flies)

"Elijah" I heard someone say then I realized that I was still dreaming so I replied "Master is it you" I asked "yes it is me" The Most High replied "Yes master" I replied "Elijah the King will not let my people go tomorrow, but listen closely the king is going to invite you to a dinner party and the royal family will be there "why is the king going to invite me to a dinner party" I asked The Most High " Because he's going to try to get on your good side by offering you money, women, cars, and everything that he can give you so you can stop bringing the plagues on his world" said The Most High. "but he does know that its not me bringing the plagues but it is you that is bringing the plagues right" I replied to my master "he does not know that it is me bringing the plagues because he does not believe in my existence, but he thinks that you are just one very great powerful magician still" said The Most High "he still thinks that wow "I replied "that's why I will harden the King's heart again and he will not let my people go and this time I will send insects and files to terrorize his whole world Elijah and I will wait on your signal to do it" said The Most High, and then I woke up from my dream.

It was 8:00am when I woke up from my dream and immediately after my dream I began to have a vision The Most High was allowing me to see what the King was doing so then I began to pay attention. "Are you really going to let those believers go today" said one of the king's wives "of course not April because if I do let them go if their God really does exist then according to their scriptures their God will destroy America, because their God will not destroy a nation if any of his people are in it that is why all of the kings of the earth do not release his people" the king replied to his wife as they laid in there all gold double king sized bed.

Then the king's other wife started to join the conversation "oh so you do read the bible huh" "not any more Kim but when I was a boy years ago my parents would make me go to church with them and I do remember the story of Sodom and Gomorrah" the king replied "what do you remember from that story" Kim asked the king "well I remember that Abraham asked God if he would destroy a city if there were 50 righteous people in it, and then God said he would never do that and God said that he would never

47

destroy a nation even if 10 righteous people were found in it that's why since 1619 we have been keeping Gods people in captivity and not giving them their reparations but instead we try to fool the masses by convincing them that we were sending Gods people back to Israel in 1948, but the people we sent back to Israel were not God's chosen people and we knew that we just did not want to take any chances of God destroying America so we hid the truth from God's chosen people all these years so that some of God's righteous people would remain in this nation so that God would not destroy it and the plan has been working for years, but now we must get this Elijah guy on our side because he's trying to take God's people out of our land" the king explained "you sound very educated in the bible" April the kings wife said with laughter "yea but I can't forget the day that I learned the big secret, then the king started telling his wives' a the story. It was the year 1999 on the night of New Year's Eve when my parents came into my room, and before they said anything all of a sudden, I started hearing fireworks exploding all over town, and in my head all I could think was in 5 minutes it would be a new millennium, but anyways I never will forget this rainy night because my parents told me something that would change my life forever. "Richard your mom and I have to tell you a secret because we think it is time that you should know this" my dad said "he's too young joe" my mother said to my dad "he has to know one day" my dad replied to my mother then he began telling me the big secret and I could not help but think to myself what is the urgency.

"Look Richard me and your mom are not Christians in fact Christianity was made up 2000 years ago and in fact the whole New Testament of the bible is not holy scriptures but a group of people who are our direct ancestors wrote the New Testament because they hated the God of Israel and his scriptures so they stole the real Holy scriptures out of the temple that was in Jerusalem and then they put their made up book behind the real Holy Scriptures and then they called it the Holy Bible and then they even separated the real Holy Scriptures from their book within what they called The Holy Bible and they called the real Holy Scriptures the old testament and then they called the book that they made up the New Testament and they made up a new religion out of it to try to keep God's chosen people ignorant and in the dark, and they gave them a false god called Jesus" Then after I heard my dad say that my jaws dropped

"What are you kidding me this must be a joke" I said "I'm afraid not Richard see me you and your mother we are gentiles and our ancestors planned this 2,000 years ago and we did not think that our Christianity cult or some call it a religion would last this long, but it did and we've been able to conquer lands and eventually the world with this false religion that we gave the world" my dad said further "so why are you telling me this now out of all days" I replied then my dad said "Because it's about to be a new millennium and this new millennium is the third day in Gods eyes and he said that he would raise up his people in this day "what do you mean in this day" I replied then my dad said "son 1,000 years is like 1 day in the eyes of the most high so we will be beginning to see God's chosen people start to rise up starting this year and son me and your mother are getting older so we might not be around to see this all take place but you are the future of our family and the gentiles and you must make sure with all of your power that God's chosen people never ever leave America ok promise me that son" "ok I promise dad" Richard replied

And that was all that I saw in my vision before it was over after I heard the king's story about when his parents first told him about the truth of The Most High, and all I could think was wow that's why the king has a strong desire not to let my people go well that and the fact that The Most High is hardening his heart, then I walked to the living room and I saw David. "Your finally up sir and are you ready for today" David asked me "yes we must go out to the king's tower later today to have a word with him" I replied "ok and the king better let us go now" David said "All I can say is that if he doesn't something way worse will hit this world" I said to David, then we prepared to leave his place. Moments later we were in David's car "I hope the king gains some common sense because how can you fight the creator" David said as he started up his Camaro "I hope so too David" I replied "and Elijah I know what I'm about to ask you is off topic but how do you know how to speak English I mean I know that back in your time you spoke something different" David ask me so I chuckled under my breath a little then I replied "You are right I did speak something other than English because I don't even think that English existed back in my time but I know English now because one of The Most High angels taught me English before I came down to the earth David" I explained.

Then as David and I drove through the sand covered streets of New York City we decided to turn on the radio to hear what was on the news so we did. "Good morning America we have some brand-new world news for you all today about what is happening in Israel and currently the black man who started the Back to Israel movement is now closing his borders and locking his gates and he is saying that no strangers are allowed in his city at this time because he says that he and his people are now preparing for their God who they call Yah to return". And that is all that we heard before the radio station put on some music, but I had to turn down the music because I had some questions about what I had just heard. "David who is this man that the radio was just talking about" "you don't know … he's talking about a man who thinks he is King David" David replied "Are you talking about the same King David who was the 2nd King of Israel and the son of Jesse" I replied "Yea him that's what people are calling him because he is fitting the end time prophecies about King David, so people think anyways but I think he's the anti-black messiah

"Because prophecy shows that King David would be raised up in the last days according to the book of Jeremiah chapter 30 verses 7-9, but this man just is not sure about if he is really King David" said David "So when did this so called King David start that Back to Israel movement that was just mentioned on the radio" I asked David "Oh he began the Back to Israel movement 10 years ago that is when his wall surrounding what he calls the true location of Jerusalem was finished, and then after he built the walls to his city him and his army started to gather some of The Most High's people all across the world with his false doctrines and they started bringing them back to Israel one by one and country by country something like what happened years ago when a man gathered some people out of Chicago and brought them to Israel and they called their city Dimona and, this fake King David is doing that on a bigger scale but it is not the real thing" David explained "hold up so if this so called King David already gathered The Most High's chosen people then why are you and the believers still in New York and in other parts of the world and why did I have to come to save you all" I asked David "My point Exactly that is why that man is not King David but he is the anti-King David because the real King David will be successful at gathering all of The Most High 's people and he will lead them into the wilderness whoever he is anyways and I am pretty sure that he is in the earth right now as we speak" David replied

After David finished telling me about the so-called King David and his movement we arrived at the kings tower. "I know you know if the king will let us go or not today and I also know that you can't tell me, but I hope the king is not lying this time" said David, and I really wanted to tell David what the king was going to do but I knew that I couldn't then I heard the voice of The Most High "it's ok you can tell him Elijah" The Most High said, and I guess The Most High was only speaking to me through my mind through a vision because David didn't seem to hear when The Most High spoke only I heard him. "The king will not let us go today" I told David "man he is a stubborn guy" David replied "I think it's more than him being stubborn" I replied as David parked his Camaro outside of the king's golden tower "well here goes nothing" David said as we walked towards the entrance of the king's tower.

Then after David and I were checked by the king's guards we got on the golden elevator and then we headed up to the king's office "you know Elijah back when America had presidents and they stayed in the white house the president's office was called the oval office but now in the king's tower it is called the Royal Office I noticed" said David as we were moving up in the elevator, then right after David said that we heard a loud "Ding" from the elevator and we were on floor 70. Then moments later we were standing in front of the king's office, and this time I noticed the words "Royal Office" with a eagle image at the top of the king's office door, then David and I were stopped by the king's guards that were guarding his office "Elijah I will let the king know that your hear" one of the guards said, and then the guard went inside of the king's office.

Then moments later the king stepped out of his office "Elijah and what is your name again" the king said as he looked at David "My name is David" David replied. "Oh ok but anyway Elijah before I keep my promise we must go over some things" The King said "what things" I replied "Oh nothing much I just would like to make you an offer" "What kind of offer" I replied "Well I'm having a dinner party at my royal mansion and I would like to discuss it there" said the king "ok no problem" I responded "Ok let's go and we will be taking one of my limo's there and sorry David he can't come only you can Elijah" said the king "well sorry because David goes wherever I go" I told the king "Well I cannot argue with that" The king said, so then the king, David, and I were escorted to one of the king's limo's by one of the king's guards.

So as the king, David, and I approached the king's limo I immediately noticed that the limo was made of pure silver and Gold "so where is your mansion" I asked the king "It is in upstate New York in RockChester" the king replied as the 3 of us entered the king's limo. Then when the 3 of us entered the limo, I noticed that the inside of the limo was made of pure leather mixed with Egyptian cotton, and then we were off to the king's mansion. " So Elijah are you really Elijah The Prophet from the biblical times" the king asked me "Yes I am" I replied "so was you born before or after the great flood" the king said in a joking way and I guess that was the kings little way of testing me "I was born way after the flood why do you ask" I replied to the king "oh there's no reason it's just that I remember studying the old testament because in the Christian church they use to tell us to stay out of the old testament so I read about you and I see what you are doing to this earth now and I know that God is with you, but you see I can offer you the whole world Elijah and you can be whatever you want to be in it" the king said as the limo stopped "We are here sir" The driver said.

So, when the limo stopped the King, David, and I got out of it and we started walking towards the King's mansion. 'This is where I live, I call it paradise' said the King as we entered the mansion. Immediately I noticed that there were a lot of people attending this dinner party. 'Walk this way' said the King as he pointed towards a dining room area, then seconds later we were in one of the many dining rooms in the mansion. 'This is the main dining room and I would like you to meet my wives Elijah', then after the King said that his wives stood up out of their seats then the King continued speaking 'I have 4 wives Elijah, 'this is Kim' the King said while pointing at Kim, 'and this is April and Jill' the King also pointed out, 'and her over there that's Jane' the King said while pointing at Jane 'and these are the wives of the Royal Family' said the King, then the King and his wives and David and I sat down at a large golden table.

'What would you like to eat Elijah anything you wish' said the King 'Nothing I am ok but thank you' I replied 'ok that's fair but what about your side kick' the King also asked referring to David 'he's fine too

52

we don't need anything sir' I told the King because I did not really trust his food anyway. 'Ok that's fine and Elijah I want you to meet the rest of the Royal Family I have 3 sons and 3 daughters but they're not here at the moment but they will be here shortly' said the King 'Ok no problem now what did you want to speak about sir' I ask the King 'come and take a walk with me and leave your sidekick in the dining room please' the King said 'he goes where I go' I told the King as I was referring to David 'ok he can come too' the King said as we began to walk through the mansion 'do you like what you see Elijah and I have 10 more mega mansions and you can have one of them and even your sidekick could have one plus do you see those women over there by the pool' said the King while pointing at the half way naked women 'yea I see them' I replied ' well I can give you any of them they are my servants matter fact I could give you more women than you could ever dream about Elijah plus I can give you all of the money and gold that you could ever want and I can make you a very rich man Elijah what do you say' the King asked me 'I cannot except those things from you but thank you' I replied 'Elijah do you know that most men would kill for this opportunity' said the King 'yea I know and that's the problem' I replied.

Then the King's phone started ringing 'Hello' said the King and then the King paused for a second to listen to the caller then he continued speaking 'ok we will be there in 1 minute' said the King as he hanged his phone up. 'That was just my son on the phone, and he said that him and his siblings are here so let's go to the main dining room again and Elijah please think about the offer' said the King as we started walking back to the main dining room.

Then minutes later we was at the main dining room and I noticed 6 more people who were not in the room before and I figured that those people had to be the King's children but they were no kids because they all looked like they were in their 30's 'These are my children well their all grown but there still mine though' the King said as he pointed to 2 of his sons ' that's Kevin and James and Kim is their mother, and that's Peter over there and his mother is April' the King said as he pointed at Peter ' and then he continued speaking 'and that's my daughter Jessica and April is her mother and this young lady is June and her mother is Jill and my youngest child's name is Melissa and her mother is Jane' the King said while pointing at Melissa ' and now you have met the whole Royal Family and please if I can do anything for you let me know' said the King 'That's ok sir but thank you for your time but David and I must go now' I replied. Then after the King finished trying to bribe me David and I left his mansion, and we were escorted back to New York city with one of the King's guards.

The drive back to the city was not that long and when we got back to the city we was sent back to the King's tower and as we approached the King's tower I saw David's car still sitting in the front of the tower then David and I got out of the limo then seconds later me and David saw a helicopter in the sky 'look at that golden helicopter said David as soon as we stepped outside of the limo. Then the helicopter landed in the front of the tower and I saw that it was the King 'Elijah did you enjoy the dinner party' the King asked 'it was ok but will you let my people go now' I replied 'I just can't do that the King said but I wish that I could" the king said as he walked inside his tower and I already knew that he had made a promise to his dad a long time ago.

'What Now' said David 'I have no choice, but I have to send another plague 'what kind of plague this time 'said David 'I have to send the insects and lots of them' I replied as David and I got in his car 'so where are we going Elijah' David asked 'well its almost 6pm so let's go to the Times square area' I replied so then David started the car and we left the King's tower. Then after a few minutes David and I approached the giant TV screen in Times square and immediately I noticed the large crowds gathering around to watch the TV show the believers. I knew this TV show was a big mockery of my people and I did not want to see it the last time David showed me it but this time I thought I might stay because this time I was going to shut down there little gathering.

So, I lifted up my staff and then The Most High send trillions of fiery serpents, hornets, and other insects throughout the whole times square area and even throughout the whole world, and the insects started terrorizing everybody it was like hell was on earth, and it was so bad that even the flees and flies started entering the eyes and ears of people and it was so bad that it was like people were in hailing and exhaling insects throughout the whole earth. People all over the earth was coughing up insects as well. A lot of people started to die over this plague as well. So then minutes later me and David went back to the District of Believers, and we were not harmed by one fly

(New Goshen)

"Elijah now I am fully convinced that you are really Elijah the prophet from the days of old but I must admit that I was a little bit skeptical" I heard David say "I understand why you were a little unsure" I replied. "But anyways now that I am sure I have a secret that I want to tell you "Said David "Ok what is it" I replied then David began telling me his secret.

"Ok so years ago I started a organization and it was basically kind of a secret organization because it wasn't really public and in this organization we were basically trying to stand in the gap for the rest of The Most High's chosen people but in order to properly stand in the gap for our people we had had to leave America so that we could worship The Most High on Islands as it is prophesied because we could not properly serve The Most High in polluted lands so my secret organization found a Island that was completely untouched by the rest of mankind and on that Island we hid from the rest of the world for years and when I say we I am talking about the leaders of my organization plus the people of the Elite tribe that we created and there was only a little bit of people in that Elite tribe because it had to be that way so that we could stay hidden from the rest of the world so that we could properly stand in the gap for our people, and we called our secret Island New Goshen but anyways to make a long story short by us serving The Most High properly we were able to make special prayer request and our number one special prayer request was for The Most High to send you back to the Earth as it is prophesied so that you could plague all of the evil and curse this evil world so that the evil doers would be forced to let our people go and The Most High eventually answered our request because here you are" David explained

"That makes a lot of sense but this is no secret to me because I knew that a Elite group was going to have to request me in order for me to return" I replied "Right I knew you might" David said "But I do have one question" I said to David "ok anything" David replied "Alright I just would like to know how did you end up here in New York City if you were on that Island for years" I asked David "well after the leadership of my organization established New Goshen we would elect a person or sometimes a few people to go back into the world to prophesy to our people and for other missions, and these were very risky missions because everybody in New Goshen knew that if you left the Island then you might not return back, so to make a long story short I volunteered to go back into the world 7 years ago and I just happen to go to New York City and when I came to America that was exactly the year when the first king of America was placed in power and declared martial law and that made it very difficult for me to return back to New Goshen because when the beast system so I call it was created it made escaping America virtually impossible I guess it had something to do with the new advanced technology that was made so if you didn't leave America before the beast system was set up then you were stuck where ever you were at but if you fled from the world before the beast system was set up as prophesied then you were safe and that's how I know that New Goshen is still hidden from the rest of the world until this very day" David explained "hmm ok so if the beast system were to stop working right now could you take me to this New Goshen place" I asked David " Yes of course that would be great" David replied

So then I thought to myself well The Most High did make me a god to the king then I grabbed my staff after resting it on a rock and then I lifted up my staff with the thoughts of crashing the beast system. Then moments later I heard David say something so I tuned into what he was saying "Wow I just got a alert message one of my tech specialist and he said that the beast system is down but he doesn't know for how long" "That's good news" I replied "yes it is its great news actually but we got to hurry and leave because I know that the king is addressing this technical issue of the beast system as we speak and we don't know how much time we have" Said David.

So after I crashed the beast system David and I began to leave New York City " So where is this New Goshen Island and how far is it David" I asked " New Goshen is between the pacific ocean and the Indian ocean that's all I can say right now and only me and a few other people know the exact coordinates of the Island and that's because we are trying our best to keep the location of New Goshen a secret so not even the common people on New Goshen know where the location of New Goshen is only some of the leadership knows and that's only because we do not hold anybody hostage on New Goshen so if a person wishes to leave we will let them leave and

they would have no way of giving away the location of New Goshen"
David explained " So how are we going to get to this New Goshen Island
because it sounds very far away and how long will it take us" I asked David
" your right New Goshen is far away so we will just have to take the New
Goshen Private Jet but first I need you to do something very important"
said David " What is it what do you need me to do" I responded " I need
you to destroy all of the satellites systems in the world so that no satellite
can detect the New Goshen private jet" David replied "that does not sound
like a issue for me at all" I responded as I lifted up my staff with thoughts
of destroying all of the satellite systems in the world then just like that The
Most High gave me the insight to see that all of the satellites across the
world were being destroyed by meteors. "It is done meteors have just
destroyed all of the satellites in the world" I told David "That's great news"
David replied.

"Now what is our next move" I asked David "Now we have to go to Coney
Island you know the same place where we saw the Kings boat and where
you started to turn the waters into blood there, we will meet the New
Goshen private jet one of my chiefs is on the way now as we speak" David
explained. So then David and I left his apartment moments later and as we
walked to David's car we saw David's wife Ashley "hey where are you guys
going" Ashley asked "where on our way to New Goshen and I need your
help" David replied "what is it" said Ashley "I need you to come with me
and Elijah to Coney Island so that once we leave you can drive my car back
to our district" Said David "So basically your telling me to stay here in our
district" Ashley replied " I told you your wife was smart" I commented
then David replied " yes I need you to stay in our district so that you can be
my eyes and ears in our district once I leave" David explained "oh ok"
Ashley said.

Then the three of us hoped in David's car and then moments later we were
on the sandy streets of the rich district. " I have good news to tell you
Ashley" David said as he drove " what is it" Ashley asked "Elijah was able
to crash the Beast system and he destroyed all of the satellites in the world
so that means no more drones or satellites for now" David explained "
that's great now I can easily spy on the royals without worrying about the
drones" said Ashley " and then minutes later we arrived on Coney Island
and the New Goshen private jet was already there waiting on me and David.

58

So then David and I got out of his car moments later and we started to approach the New Goshen private jet "you can drive back to our district now and I will see you when I come back" David said to Ashley as Ashley got in the driver's seat of David's car "see you soon" said Ashley and then seconds later Ashley was gone.

So then after Ashley left David approached the New Goshen private jet then the doors of the jet opened up and a guy stepped out of the jet "wow it's been 7 years since I've seen you in person chief" the guy who stepped out of the jet said "Elijah this is Jordan and Jordan this is Elijah The Prophet and I know it's been a long time man but let's all talk later on the ride to New Goshen because we will have plenty of time then but now we must hurry" David said. So then we all got in the New Goshen private jet and then seconds later after Jordan who was the pilot of the jet started the jet engines we were gone.

So as we were in the mist of our flight I heard David speak "Elijah this flight will take about 12 hours so if you want to ask Jordan anything well now you have the time" David said " ok so Jordan you called David chief earlier why is that" I asked Jordan "that's because David is the head chief of our organization and I am the vice chief so that would make David my chief and it's been years since me and the rest of New Goshen saw our head chief the one who brought us out of our captivity but when David did not return I stepped up as the acting head chief until David's returned" Jordan replied " Oh ok" I Said "And David New Goshen has not changed one bit and it is still hidden from the rest of the world" Said Jordan. "That's good to know and I can't wait to see everybody again" said David "Yea and everybody misses you and they all already know about what happened but we knew that you would pull through and I'm happy to see that our special request to The Most High has been answered because here he is right beside me now Elijah The Prophet" Jordan said "Yea I was glad to see Elijah myself but I had to make sure that it was really him before I could tell him about our organization and New Goshen because as you know there are a lot of witches and warlocks in the earth nowadays" David said "you got that right" Jordan replied "So how long has New Goshen existed" I asked then David responded almost 20 years at least this one that I started anyways because who knows there could be other New Goshen's out there and I left New Goshen in the 13th year of its existence" David Explained

"Oh ok so New Goshen is pretty new at least your New Goshen right"
"Yes it is pretty new" David replied "And I know that you miss your other wives David because they miss you" Jordan said "yes I do and I can't wait to see them again" said David "wives how many wives do you have David" I asked "I actually have seven wives back on the Island and Ashley is actually just my concubine and I met her back during the seven year trouble you see because when I left New Goshen I left by myself and yes Ashley knows about my other wives" David explained "so how was life in New Goshen" I asked David "well for the first time in millennials a small group of my people tasted true freedom as we hid from the rest of the world with no drama and it was truly like heaven on earth just like how it will be" Said David

After David gave me a brief description of New Goshen I realized that only 1 hour went by so that meant that we had about 11 more hours left of flight time. "I wonder how the world is responding to your last plague of all those frogs" David said as he turned on the T.V that was inside of the New Goshen private jet "Millions of people around the world have died because of that terrible frog infestation and we did our best at trying to treat all of the patients but the hospitals were to full" The News Reporter said "so you guys know that none of the plagues that Elijah preformed affected New Goshen right" said Jordan " yea I pretty much figured that and also the plagues did not affect none of the lasting districts of believers that are still remaining in the world" David replied

Then after some time and rest we were now 6 hours into the flight and we were basically flying over Africa now. "Something tells me that once the world army finally fixes the beast system and the satellites then they will improve their systems to the point that they will be able to locate New Goshen because now after all of the plagues that you preformed Elijah that most likely will motivate the world army to now play some offence and attack us because before we was no threat to them but now there people are dying by the millions so we must get ready to fight" said David

Then after some more time went by we were now approaching a small Island " This is it New Goshen" Jordan shouted and I could see the joy on David's face as we approached New Goshen "Home sweet home" said David "well temporarily until the chariots come and bring us to our true home" Jordan replied "yea of course I knew that" David replied jokingly as the New Goshen private jet was landing on the New Goshen beach shore and I noticed that besides the sandy beach the Island was covered with lots of trees "all of these trees where are the houses and buildings" I asked "there are a lot of homes all throughout the Island plus a Altar and there is what we call the Black House and the Black House is where all of the chiefs stay and that is also where we handle all of the tech and government stuff" David explained " Well why do yawl call it the black house" I asked " Well because it is similar to the old white house that was in America but it is just black oh yea there is one more thing that you should know about New Goshen Elijah" said David "and what is that" I replied "The Altar in New Goshen that I mentioned earlier has a copy of the laws of Moses written in stones word for word located in it" David said " that's good because that is a requirement of a true altar of The Most High" I replied "right and years ago when I was a young man I was the one who made this idea to write a copy of the laws of Moses and to write them on stones in fact that was the first step of creating New Goshen because my team and I had to establish the New Goshen tablets before we could start going on expedition trips to find an Island for New Goshen "David further explained "wow that must have been a lot of work" I replied "It sure was my team and I went on multiple boat trips before we found the perfect Island to start building on and the first thing that we built on New Goshen was can you guess" David said "The Altar" I replied "yep correct we built the altar first before anything else and then we placed the New Goshen Tablets with the laws of Moses around the altar" David explained "great because that is the most important structure on this Island I was told" I replied " indeed and then the next structure that we built was the Black House now the black house is the 2nd most important structure because that is where we planned to govern the whole Island and The Most High had to establish his government before anything else and we molded the black house after the old white house that was once in America but it is just not as fancy though because we didn't have a slave labor force to build it like America did to build its kingdom but we did our best with the resources we had' David explained "Yea and then after we built the black house we started building homes all throughout the Island for our residents which was about 150 people" Jordan added to what David said "yea so you see that the population of

New Goshen is very very small and we consider ourselves the Elite of The Most Highs chosen people" David further explained.

Then after David and Jordan explained the creation of New Goshen to me I was informed that we landed on the Island on the six day so we started to prepare for the 7th day worship ceremony and this was a tradition on the New Goshen Island. Then I couldn't help but notice that most of the people on New Goshen were vegans and a small few of the people ate fish occasionally and the only time that meat was mandatory to eat was only on one of the feast days that required a meat sacrifice according to the laws of Moses other than that no meat was consumed on New Goshen.

So after everybody prepared for the 7th day everybody went to their homes to sleep and I slept in the Black House with the governing body of New Goshen because they gave me my own room and they told me that I automatically had a governing position of New Goshen because of who I was as a matter of fact David told me that back when they built the Black House they built a room just for me with the hopes that one day The Most High would have pity on his people and send me back to the earth. So that night I slept like royalty in the Black House with a king-sized bed and everything and in my head I assumed that David's room was as luxurious as mine with being the head chief and all, and the best part about the whole night was that the beast system and the satellite systems were still down and not working so the whole New Goshen slept in peace that night.

The next morning when everybody woke up to the 7th day I noticed that everybody in New Goshen was preparing a morning offering to bring to the altar that morning. "Elijah since this is your first time in New Goshen I will help you with your morning offering" said David. Then after everybody was finished preparing their morning offering everybody then started going to the altar to make their offering. Now once David and I started to approach the altar I noticed that there was a wall circulating the altar area that was made out of stone with gates attached to the walls that lead inside to the altar area and there was a roof on this wall so that if it rained or if the weather was bad that day everyone would be safe to me it really looked like a very huge pavilion.

Then once everybody was inside the altar area the gates of the altar area had to be shut before the worship ceremony could begin, then once the ceremony begun everyone including me and David had to offer their morning offering on the altar and then everybody gathered around David and his podium then David started teaching the people and it was like how a church service looked but the only difference was that it was a true worship service and between David's teachings there were rotations of different people singing and dancing and worshiping The Most High and then when evening came everybody including me and David had to make a second offering to the altar and then after that David taught until the sun settled.

Then after the long 7th day ceremony everybody went back to their homes for the night and David and I went back to the Black House. "Elijah come with me to the Black room" David said as we stepped into the main entrance of the Black House "I have to give you a proper tour of the Black House" David said so then we walked the halls of the Black House and David was showing me different rooms in the Black House all the way up until we came across the Black Room "this is it the Black Room aka the tech room and years ago my tech team wired the room to make it completely untraceable so that nobody could trace back to this room and that helps keep the location of New Goshen hidden from the rest of the world" David explained and as David kept explaining I took a look around the room and it looked very high tech with lots of computers and monitors everywhere. "We can detect any threat towards New Goshen in this room and nothing can get pass us and plus we do have The Most High on our side so that helps as well and so far we have not had any issues or threats since the creation of New Goshen but if or when anything dose happed my tech guys would be right here on it" David explained and then we left the Black Room and then David and I resumed the tour of the Black House. "Now I got one more room to show you Elijah and that is the flight room and that is where we keep the New Goshen private jet" David said so we began walking to the flight room then minutes later we arrived to the flight room and I quickly noticed some people working on the New Goshen private jet. "Yea those guys are just making sure that the New Goshen Private jet stays functional," Said David. "That's good" I replied "I'm glad you think that because we are about to get on the jet" David said "wait we only been in New Goshen for 1 day and a half" I replied "I know but we have to get back to New York and finish pleading with the King and

Jordan is already on the jet waiting for us but don't worry we will be back" David said.

So, David and I began to board the New Goshen private jet and in my head I already knew that the flight was going to be 12 hours and then Jordan started up the Jet and then we were off to New York City. And for some reason the flight back seemed a lot shorter than on the way to New Goshen because after a while we were landing on Coney Island and I quickly noticed David's car so I assumed that Ashley was in it waiting for me and David. "This is it guys I will see you later chief I know that your mission here is still not done" Jordan said to David "Yea but it soon will be" David replied and then me and David exited the New Goshen private jet, and then after me and David was off the Jet the jet took off. "David and Elijah yawl are back" Ashley yelled and then the 3 of us hoped in David's car and we drove back to David's apartment in our district for the night.

(The Chinese Assassins)

The next morning when I woke up, I went to the living room in David's Apartment, and I saw David and Ashley watching the news again right after the world suffered from a fly infestation. "Just yesterday we suffered from a fly infestation what is going on and when will it stop I hope it dose soon maybe it's some kind of weird global climate change that's making theses creatures act oddly" A American news reporter said and then a Chinese news reporter came on the air right after the American news reporter "The global fly infestation has hit the world by a surprise but China was affected the worse because China had the most recorded deaths recorded at 10 million deaths in one day" the Chinese news reporter said and then David turned off the T.V.

"Wow Elijah this is the worse plague that you preformed so far because now world leaders are starting to really take notice" David said to Elijah then right after David said what he said David's phone beeped then David started reading a message on his phone then David looked at me and Ashley with a shocking look on his face "man I got some bad news yawl" David said "what is it" I replied "I just got a message from one of my chiefs in New Goshen and he said that the beast system and the satellite systems across the world are back up and working and not only are they working again but they made some improvements" David explained "what kind of improvements" I replied "Enough improvements for the Chinese government to locate New Goshen" David replied "wait what New Goshen hasn't been located in almost 20 years this cannot be true" Ashley said "I'm afraid so it is true and not only is it true but I got a second message just now and it said that there is a Chinese assassin roaming around New Goshen right as we speak and nobody can find the assassin" David said "so what are we going to do about this" Ashley said "Well me and Elijah are going to have to go back to New Goshen and find this Chinese assassin before this assassin hurts anybody plus we cannot have a foreign spy roaming around New Goshen so you guys it's about to get real" said David.

Right after David finished telling us the terrible news me and David was informed that the New Goshen's private yet was on its way to come get me and David. "David, I have a question so if the Beast system is back up then won't the American Government see it coming" I asked "You know your right Elijah I didn't even think about that so let me call my chief pilot and tell him to stay put until I can think of something eles. So that is what David did and shortly after he made the call David shouted "I got it" "so you must have a idea what is it" I asked "we are going to have to go deep" David said "deep what do you mean David" I said "Elijah the ocean is a very big place and lots of the ocean still has not been discovered till this day like a little over 80% of the ocean has not been discovered yet" "Ok what is your point" I asked "my point is that the beast system cannot detect the deep deep depths of the seas yet but guess what" "what" I asked "Years ago the New Goshen's submarine team invented a High Tech submarine that can reach the deep deep depths of the sea without breaking and we kept our discoveries to ourselves so what I'm trying to say is that we will have to use the New Goshen submarine to travel throughout the world from now on until you complete your mission" David Explained "Sounds good" I replied.

Then moments later David called Jordan who also operated the New Goshen submarine "Jordan is on his way, and we will meet him in the Coney Island waters," said David. So, then David and Elijah left David's apartment and after they walked down the long flight of steps they left David's apartment building then they got in David's car. "So have you ever been to the deep deep depths of the ocean" I asked David then David replied "Yea I have actually" "So what is down there because in the heavens everyone but the most high is only allowed to see the surface of the earth and not the deep depths of the ocean ... well there might be higher angles that are allowed to see those ocean depths but I am not aware of them but me and most of the host in heaven can not see the deep depth of the ocean so what I am trying to say is what is down there David" I asked then David replied "Well me and the New Goshen team have not discovered every thing but what we did discover is that all of the water dinosaurs that use to roam the earth still exist in the deep deep depths of the ocean let me explain ... ok so when that meteor that wiped out the dinosaurs and dragons hit the earth it only wiped out all of the land dinosaurs and all of the water dinosaurs and creatures escaped by going deep deep into the depths of the ocean and they later adapted to their new way of life so they remain at those deep deep depths of the ocean till this day that is why nobody ever has seen them but however I believe that once in a blue moon that these ancient creatures swim up to the top of the ocean and this is why I believe that the stories of planes and boats that go missing at sea is because of theses ancient creatures that pop their heads up every now and then.

So, after David got done explaining the deep ocean discoveries, we were approaching the coney Island beach. "I can see the submarine head from here" David shouted. And then David parked his car and then we both stepped out of it, then David got a beep on his phone "I am approaching Coney Island I will be sending the lifeboat towards you and Elijah soon so get ready" Jordan said. So, then moments later a lifeboat appeared on the beach shore and me and David got into it then we started paddling to the submarine head that was peaking out of the oceans surface, then after some moments went by me and David was in the New Goshen submarine and at first glance it looked very futuristic and high tech because in my era this did not exist. "You two made it congrats" Jordan said while reeling in the lifeboat and then minutes later the 3 of us where deep under the water heading towards New Goshen. "I'm glad you warned us not to fly the New Goshen jet because we would have been spotted because this beast system came back with vengeance" Jordan said to David "no problem" David replied then I asked David a question "David how is the New Goshen submarine not harmed by the creatures in the deep deep depths of the ocean" then David replied "well the New Goshen sub team was able to create a technology that can make the New Goshen submarine invisible to the creatures in the deep deep depths of the ocean that's how we've managed to stay safe all of these years".

Then after many hours flew by the 3 of us were approaching New Goshen, then there was a message alert that popped up on David's phone and David read it. "We have to go to the Black House immediately after we get off this submarine I was just told" said David. Then moments later Jordan released a lifeboat then me and David started climbing the ladder that led to the to exit of the submarine' then once we reached the top we hoped on the lifeboat and then we paddled our way to the beach shore of New Goshen. It was nighttime when we finally set foot on New Goshen but David still knew the way to the Black House so we started hiking, then in no time we was standing right outside of the Black House. "I wonder if the Chinese assassin was found yet" I said to David "well we are about to find out"

David replied as we walked into the Black House, then suddenly we heard shouting "David Elijah quick we must view the cameras because one of our elders has been kidnapped and I'm guessing that it was that Chineses Assassin," said a random New Goshen Sargent.

So, me, David, and the Sargent went to the monitor room to view the cameras then after some time we did not find the elder on the cameras "No luck so we must go search for our missing elder on foot" the sergeant said as he called for backup then a 100 man search team were ordered to search the island for our missing elder "David do you know the elder that is missing" I asked then David replied "Yea I do his name is Elder Moses and he is one of the elders that helped build the foundation of New Goshen" and then after me, David, and the sergeant approached a open field with a lot of automobile looking machines but I didn't know what they were so I asked David "those are 4 wheelers" David said as me and David and the other 100 men hoped on different 4 wheelers and the 4 wheelers seated 3 people so the sergeant who we first bumped into came with me and David. "Ok lets all split up and search different parts of the Island" David told everyone and then the 100 man search team started their engines and were off searching for Elder Moses.

Minutes went by and the night grew darker and it looked like it was about to start raining "I hope we find Elder Moses before it starts raining" David said and then a incoming video message alert came on David's phone then a Chinese man appeared on Davids phone screen "We have your Elder if you want to keep him alive you must give us Elijah and meet us at the far left docks of your Island in 10 minutes" the Chineses man said then he ended the message "First of all what dose he mean by we because I thought that there was only one Chinese assassin and secondly he must be crazy if he thinks that we are giving you up to them" David said "Don't worry I will be find they can't harm me but they can harm Elder Moses so let's just meet them at the far left docks" I replied "we will meet them but I'm calling backup and no one is going nowhere" David said as he send out a message to the head captain of New Goshen telling him to send 25 soldiers to the far left docks in 10 minutes, then the sergeant from earlier had something to say "Elijah were this wire so that if you are taken we can still communicate with you" the sergeant said as he gave me a small wired cord "ok no problem and what's your name I forgot to asked" I replied as I put on the wire "My name is sergeant Jim" sergeant Jim replied.

So, after 10 minutes Me, David, and sergeant Jim were approaching the far-left docks of New Goshen and upon arrival we saw 25 armed New Goshen soldiers surrounding the area then we saw some helicopters with Chinese men approaching the docks and then seconds later the helicopters with the Chinese men landed on New Goshen. Then a armed Chinese man stepped out of one of the helicopters with Elder Moses at gun point "give us Elijah or he's dead" a Chinese man shouted then I whispered to David "its ok I will go with these Chinese men because they will regret it "are you sure" David replied "I'm positive" I replied back to David, so then David responded to the Chinese men "ok Elijah will go with y'all but first let go of Elder Moses then tensions grew in the air because no one wanted to make the first move so I did the noble thing and I let the Chinese men take me then right after they took me the Chinese men released Elder Moses and instantly Elder Moses ran towards the New Goshen soldiers and the Chinese helicopters quickly took off into the air with me inside.

Then minutes into the flight I heard a voice in the wire speaker that was given to me and it sounded like David "Elijah are you ok" David said and then I whispered "yea I'm ok" I replied "good and do you have any clue where those Chinese men are taking you" David asked me then I replied "I over heard them talking about how they were taking me to some laboratory in Hong Kong, China but remember when I told you they will regret taking me well there first warning to release me will be in 2 minutes "what will happened" said David then I replied "All of the helicopters will start falling out of the sky one by one crashing into the ocean but the helicopter that I'm on will make it to a Hong Kong airport" I explained to David "ok so me and some New Goshen spy's will spy into the Hong Kong airport and rescue you" "great but y'all will have 2 hours to get to China" I replied "ok we will find a way there" David replied, and then after I finished talking to David on the wire The Most High gave me some insight into what was happening in one of the helicopters that I wasn't on "Great we got Elijah some prophet he is" a Chinese man said jokingly to one of his men then all of a sudden the flies from the last plague returned and engulfed the helicopter and there were so many flies that the pilot of that helicopter lost control of the helicopter and then that helicopter started spiraling out of the air and then seconds later the helicopter crashed into the ocean killing everybody onboard, then my insightful vision continued and I saw that their were 3 more helicopters left other than the one I was on, so with my insight I saw what was happening in the next helicopter that I wasn't on. "You fool I told you capturing Elijah was a bad idea" one of the Chinese men shouted to his men then suddenly that helicopter burst into flames burning everybody alive on board of that helicopter and then seconds later that helicopter crashed into the ocean and blew up, and then there were 2 more helicopters left besides the one I was on so with my insight I saw what was happening on the next helicopter. "2 of our helicopters have crashed mysteriously maybe we should turn around and return Elijah" a Chinese man said to his crew and then suddenly a large water twisted formed that was only designed to destroy that next helicopter appeared out of nowhere and swallowed up that helicopter drowning everybody that was aboard that helicopter and then the water twister that was specifically formed to destroy that helicopter disappeared and then there was one more helicopter left besides the one that I was on then with my insight I saw what was happening on that helicopter "I never seen a water twister in my life that was crazy let's surrender to Elijah and his God" a Chinese man cried out to his crew when all of a sudden one of those ancient creatures from the dinosaur age that David told me about jumped out of the ocean opening his mouth to swallow that helicopter and then seconds later that helicopter and everybody in it became that creatures food and they all died instantly. "Oh my we must hurry to the main Hong Kong airport before something happens to us" the Chinese pilot on the helicopter that I was on said, then after some time we were landing in Hong Kong.

"David can you hear me" I said into my wire "Yea I hear you and me and some of the New Goshen spy's had to take the New Goshen submarine to the main Hong Kong airport and luckily there main airport is not to far from a beach shore so we were able to make our way to the Hong Kong's main airport so when your ready let us know when your hear" David said "I'm already here with the last helicopter and they are ready to surrender and release me" I replied to David "ok good" David said and then minutes later David and his spy's were approaching the helicopter that I was on and they didn't have any trouble because the Chinese men on the helicopter that I was on alerted there authorities and told them that they were willing to release me, and not to harm David and his Spy's. "Here you go Elijah" a Chinese man said while releasing me to David and his spy's, and then me, David, and his spy's quickly left the Hong Kong's main airport. "Finally now that that little interruption is over now we can get to the bigger issue of pleading for our people" I said to David "right so I guess we have to go back to New York now" David said "Correct because the king over hear in China is not the head king of the world and I must only plead with the head King over the world and that's the one in America, so after some time we approached one of China's beach shores and boarded the New Goshen's submarine then we were on our way to America.

So, after some time me, David and Jordan were deep deep under the ocean on our way back to America when we saw a prehistoric creature out of one of the submarine windows but we was not harmed because the creature could not see us and it appeared as if it didn't even know we were there. "So Elijah what will the next plague be if the King does not let our people go" David asked "All I can say is that it will get much worse everytime the King refuses to let our people go" I replied "well what if the King never lets our people go because you know how The Pharoh from Moses's time never let Moses and his people go" David said "right and what happened" I replied "Pharoh and his army drowned after The Most High parted the Red Sea for his people" David replied "right so this time there will be a final judgement and trust me you definitely will find out what it will be even after I'm gone you will" said Elijah, and then after some hours flew by we were approaching the beach shore at Coney Island.

"Coney Island we are here guys" Jordan shouted "Thanks for all of your help and we might be needing you soon" David replied as me and him climbed up the submarine ladder that led to the exit of the submarine, and when we got to the top of the submarine we got in a lifeboat and started paddling our way to the shore, and then minutes later we were walking on Conley Island, Then David waved goodbye to Jordan and then the submarine disappeared into the sea. "Ok now let's make our way to the King's tower" I said to David "Ok let's go" said David and luckily his Car was still nearby and unharmed, so we started walking towards it, then in no time we were in Davids's car. "After that Fly plague the King has to let us go know I mean that last one was so bad that even China tried to intervein" said David "well the thing that has been shall be so you should know what the King's answer will be next" I said as David started his car and drove off. Then after some minutes went by, we were approaching the King's tower, and then David parked his car, and then we got out of it then started walking towards the entrance of the King's tower. "Elijah, I think that by now the whole world knows that you are really Elijah the Prophet and even the King" David said "I think you might be right" I replied and then as usual me and David were approaching the lions infront of the Kings tower so I lifted my staff and then the lions began to behave so well that unlike the other times this time they let me and David even pet them. "I see that you two are making friends" the guard guarding the King's tower said as he pat down me and David, and then after me and David was patted down we then entered the King's tower.

"David even though we both know that the King will not let our people go by now we must still plead with him and give him a chance to do the right thing because humans are still given free will and who knows maybe the King might do the unthinkable and actually listen this time because that timeline is still possible" "elaborate on that please" David said "well if you ever heard of the multiverse and I'm sure you have then I'm here to tell you that its true and in this timeline that we are in right now ever since the Pharoh of Moses time all of the Kings of this earth hearts have always been harden oppressing the masses to this day but there is a timeline that exist were the Pharoh in Moses's time actually listened and the earth actually went into a golden age earlier than expected" I explained to David "wow so the King is not doomed to fail then" David replied "right but if the King remains to have a hard heart the earth will still reach a new Golden age it will just be the hard way and it will take a little bit longer and like I said even if I'm gone you will find out" I further explained to David, and then we got on a golden elevator that went to the seventh floor.

So, after a few seconds the elevator opened and we were on the seventh floor, so we started walking towards the Royal office, then as we walked towards the Royal office the doors automatically opened. "You two again I knew y'all were coming what is it this time" the King said "You already know" I replied "You still want me to release your people right" the King said "right" I replied "well I do really want to but I just can't" said the King "sure you can everybody can change" I said "well just give me a little bit more time to release your people but right now I just can't sorry" the king said, then I shook my head and I didn't go back and forth with the King, and then seconds later me and David just left the King's tower untouched, So after me and David left the King's tower we got in David's car and drove to the district of believers. "lets go get some rest and then tomorrow there will be a new plague that will hit the earth unfortunately" I said to David, and after some time we were approaching David's apartment building, then we entered David's apartment "well I'll see you in the morning" David said as he walked into his room and I laid on the coach that was in the living room.

(The Attack of The Beast)

Later that morning I woke up to a loud rumbling sound "Elijah do you hear that" David shouted "yes I hear it" I replied to David and then I began to have a insightful vision about the noise I was hearing and I was being showed different areas of New York City and the first area that I saw was the Lower part of Manhattan, then out of nowhere a large herd of Rhinos started to appear and these Rhinos were wild Rhinos I could tell "Stampede" a guy yelled to warn everybody around him, and then the Rhinos started flipping over cars and damaging buildings and thousands of people started running for their lives but they were not fast enough so the Rhinos stated attacking people and many people were killed "This is crazy call the military" I heard the King say as my insightful vision focuced on him, Then minutes later army tanks and military soldiers started to flood the New York City Streets. "Elijah I'm about to send in some more animals and they will be under your command" said The Most High, then out of nowhere a stampede of wild lions, tigers, and bears started to appear and there were even some other animals mixed in the stampede. "Kill them all" the King said so the military soldiers started shooting their weapons but that just pissed off the animals because the wild animals stated ripping people apart limb from limb including the military soldiers and it seemed like the more shots that were being fired the more animals appeared so some people started to run underground into the subway system for cover but the animals followed and continued to attack people.

"Elijah what's going on in New York right now" said David "New York is under attack by the beast of the field right now and from the looks of it the military was not prepared for such of an attack" I replied "well lets go down to the park to let everyone else know about what's going on" David suggested, so me and David left his apartment and jumped in his car "this must be the next plague you mentioned yesterday" David said "Yes it is" I replied and then David started the engine of his car and we were on our way to the main park of the district of believers and then my insightful vision started again.

Their was blood and human remains everywhere and hardly anybody on the streets and the people I did see were high up in the buildings trying to escape the wild animals "Now that everyone is off the streets they should be safe because lions, tigers, and bears cannot climb up the buildings so ha" The king said under his breath then out of nowhere a stampede of wild monkeys and chimpanzees started to appear and they could climb up the buildings unlike the other animals, so the wild monkeys started climbing into people's apartments biting people and some people tried to fight back but they were unsuccessful. "Get those apes" the King yelled at the soldiers around him then as the soldiers started running towards the buildings they were met by some wild hungry lions and when they shot their weapons their guns started to jam then the lions began ripping their heads off then my insightful vision ended and by this time David was parking his car in the main park in the district of believers.

"Ok let me go address our people that may have been alarmed by the loud noise this morning" David said and then the both of us got out of the car and started walking inside of the park. "Hey, look its David" someone yelled alerting everybody so David got on a podium and began speaking "Elijah is currently Plaguing not just New York but the whole world right now with a bunch of wild animals and that was the noise that you all heard this morning but as I said before not one wild beast will come into our districts" David explained and as David continued to speak I started having another insightful vision.

This time I saw a whole lot of dead animals in the New York streets but not all of the animals were dead "Their almost all dead" the King said to his soldiers, then out of nowhere a stampede of wild hyenas and wild scavenger birds started to appear in the what looked like a deserted New York and this was like the final level because even the sharpest shooters in the military were going to have a hard time shooting those large swift scavenger birds that I saw but they tried anyway and while trying to shoot down the scavenging birds they also had to worry about the stampede of hyenas on the ground so this battle appeared to be an impossible task, then the scavenging birds started swooping down and plucking out the eyes of the soldiers that were trying to shoot them and one guy had it so bad that after his eyes got plucked out by a scavenging bird he bumped into a hungry hyena, and not being able to see the hyena ate that man alive, then my insightful vision ended.

"The land animals are almost done stampeding" I told David "What do you mean" said David "What I mean is that this is only the first wave of this wild beast plague" I further explained "so their will be a second phase" David asked "yes but this time it will be the wild animals of the seas" I replied to David. "When will this phase happen" David asked "around evening so later on" I replied then I noticed that it was still morning around 11:30 am and then I had one more insightful vision for that morning. "In a couple of hours we will have an emergency meeting with the Italians" the King said to a couple of his captains" then one of the Kings captains responded "why the Italians" "Because they believe that they have a solution to our little Elijah problem" the King explained and then my insightful vision ended and then me and David went back to his apartment.

"Elijah since we have a little while before the second phase of the beast plague, I want to inform you more about the 7 years that you did not get to see in my perspective starting with year one" David said "ok that would be great" I replied then David continued. Well I was in New Goshen before the New King of America came into power and I remember it being a cold stormy day in New Goshen then Jordan approached me "David today is the day that we pick someone to go back into the world" said Jordan "I wonder who it will be this year" I said then me and Jordan made our way to the Annual sendoff meeting located inside of the Black House, and after sometime we were in the meeting. "Today a brave soul will be going back into the world, and everyone here knows the risks of leaving New Goshen but we have had no problems yet since the start of New Goshen and every year has went smooth now are there any volunteers to go this year" said Elder Moses, and after Elder Moses said that all I can hear was a long long silence because nobody wanted to leave New Goshen that year so I stood up "I will go this year" I said "David you are the head sergeant we can not risk something happening to you" Elder Moses said "I appreciate that but as the head Sergeant I must lead by example so I will go sir" I said "Ok the New Goshen jet will be ready for takeoff tomorrow morning David so be ready" Elder Moses said and then everyone left the meeting.

So, when the next day came I went back to the Black House and Jordan came with me "David the Elders just promoted me to be the top New Goshen jet pilot so I will be taking you back today" said Jordan "that's good news" I replied "so where do you want to go in the world" "hmmm take me to New York City" I said "ok no problem that can be arranged" said Jordan then we arrived at the Black House shortly after I told him where I was going, and once we entered the Black House we immediately went to the New Goshen Jet room and Elder Moses was in there to send me off "David did you decide where you are going when you leave this Island" said Elder Moses "Yea I will be going to New York sir" I replied "ok and make sure that you stay in contact with us here in the Island" Elder Moses said while handing me one of our special headsets, then me and Jordan went into the New Goshen jet and moments later were in the sky. "This trip might take a while so if you want to get some rest feel free" Jordan said so I rested and after some hours flew by, we were approaching New York now unlike now back then was more normal so we flew to the Newark airport in New Jersey because our jet was registered with that airport, and they had a area made for private jets to land. So, after landing in the Newark airport I said my goodbyes too Jordan and then Jordan took back off into the sky.

Now the purpose of somebody coming back into the world every year was so that that person could inform the rest of New Goshen about what was going on in the world and little did I know that I was in for a surprise that year, so after my air train ride I got in a taxi "Where too" said the taxi Driver "Take me to a hotel in New York City please" I replied "ok no problem" the taxi driver said and then we left the Newark airport, then after about 30 minutes we arrived in New York and the city was just like I remembered it then when the taxi stopped at a red light I saw a flyer on a light pole nearby and it read "The Annual NYC Magic show will be happening in Times Square this year" and the date on the flyer was the same day as today I thought so I also thought about going and then we arrived at a Hotel "This is one of the finest Hotels in this city sir" the taxi driver said "ok this will do" I said and then I left the taxi. Now the NYC Magic show was scheduled to happen at 5:00pm and it was around 3:00pm so I went inside of the Hotel and checked into a room. Then when I got inside of my hotel room I called up a old friend by the name of James then after the phone dialed James answered "hey who is this" said James "its your old friend David I was just calling to let you know that I was in New York" I said "oh it's you David what's up I didn't recognize this number" said James "Yea this is the hotels phone" I replied "Oh ok cool" James said then I replied "I don't go out much but since I just got here to the city I was looking for something to do and I heard that there is some kind of a magic show happening in Times Square this evening do you want to go" "Sure what time is the show" James replied "it's at 5:00pm" I said "ok I'll be there" said James and then the conversation ended. Now if your wondering why I was interested in going to a Magic show well its because I wanted to update New Goshen on if the Dark Magicians were improving, so after a few minutes I left the hotel lobby and I got into another taxi "where to my friend" said the taxi driver "I'm on my way to Times square for a magic show" I replied "ok Times Square it is" said the taxi driver, and then we left.

Now when we arrived in Times Square I immediately started watching the magic show acts and minutes flew by like wind and then it was 7:00pm and the president of America came on the giant screen T.V with a important message shutting down the magic show so I tuned in to what the president was saying. "Citizens of America I'm here today to address some important changes that will be happening in this lovely nation. For one thing I just want to let you all know that tonight I will be stepping down as the president of the United States as a matter of fact, there will be no more presidents of the United States after tonight". Then after the ex-president said that everybody was just looking in disbelief at what they just heard then the ex-president continued to speak. "Yes, you all heard me correctly congress and I mostly I have decided to make the United States a Monarchy government and I will be the last president of the United States and the first King of America and this is not a joke people". Then all of a sudden I heard some man shout "He can't do that", and then that man was escorted out of the Times Square district by some officers as the New King began to speak again. "You see the old Christian fairytale way was not working anymore that is why I have a confession to make and that confession is that my people created the bible many years ago and we created it to keep the populations under control you see there never was a Jesus now for my first act as the king I will be issuing The New Constitution today and the old one will no longer exist" Then after the new king said those words I saw the S.W.A.T team approaching the scene then the New King continued. "You see tonight America will be under a new law Martial Law" then right after the New King said that hundreds of drones began to flood the sky.

After the countless number of drones in the New York City skies went into the air the giant T.V in Times Square went black and the S.W.A.T team started ordering people to go indoors. That is when I saw James "David what is happening with president Moore talking about how he is the King now is he crazy" James said when he saw me "I don't know but he must be up to something BIG" I replied then I tried to contact the Elders in New Goshen through the head-set that I was given but for some reason it did not work as a matter of fact it wasn't just my head-set that didn't work but it seemed that most of the technology like the internet and radio and peoples phones stop working all of a sudden after the King's speech so I was stuck in America with no way to get back to New Goshen, Then me and James ended up going to his apartment by force and his apartment was in upper Manhattan which later became my apartment, then me and James went on the rooftop of his apartment.

As me and James stood on the rooftop of his apartment building at the time, I could hardly believe the sight before my eyes. New York City, once a bustling metropolis filled with life and energy, now lay draped in an eerie mist that clung to the streets like a shroud. Red and blue lights flickered in the fog, casting ominous silhouettes of armored vehicles and soldiers. Martial law had been declared, and fear hung in the air like a palpable presence, and the streets were devoid of their usual chatter, replaced instead with the distant hum of helicopters and the occasional thud of boots on pavement. Families huddled in their homes, too afraid to venture outside, and communication with the outside world had been cut off. We were isolated, disconnected from the rest of the nation, and left to wonder what had caused this devastating turn of events, then a heavy sense of dread gnawed at my insides as I remembered the news that preceded the arrival of the mist. Rumors of a deadly contagion, a virus with no cure, had spread like wildfire that was the excuse that President Moore gave in order to start up more confusion, so panic swept through the city as the government struggled to contain the outbreak, and ultimately, the decision to enforce martial law was made.

From my vantage point, I could see soldiers patrolling the streets, their faces hidden behind gas masks and helmets. They were the enforcers of an authority I didn't fully understand, and they said they were here to protect us, or was there a more sinister motive behind their presence? The lines between truth and propaganda had blurred, leaving me with an overwhelming sense of unease. So as the days turned into weeks, the mist persisted, becoming a symbol of the uncertainty that now dominated our lives. I ventured out occasionally, unable to resist the pull of the unknown, but each step beyond the safety of James apartment was fraught with danger. Supplies were scarce, and the few shops that remained open were heavily guarded by the military. And during one of my excursions, I stumbled upon a group of resistance fighters, ordinary citizens who had banded together to seek answers and restore freedom. Their bravery inspired me, and I joined their cause, hoping that together, we could unravel the truth hidden beneath the veil of mist.

Minutes later in the heart of the city, we discovered an underground network of scientists who had been secretly working to find a so-called cure for the virus. They revealed that the outbreak had been more severe than the government had let on, and the mist was a byproduct of their attempts to neutralize the contagion, and the revelation left me torn between despair and hope. On one hand, we now knew the truth behind the mist, but on the other, the price of that knowledge had been immeasurable suffering. The cure was still elusive, and the city remained trapped in a state of fear and uncertainty, so as weeks turned into months, our resistance grew stronger, and we began to chip away at the oppressive regime that had descended upon our beloved city. Our efforts were not in vain, as whispers of change spread through the ranks of the soldiers, some of whom questioned their role in this unfolding tragedy, then to make a long story short James was eventually killed by the Military for resisting arrest, and that's how I ended up with his apartment and after the United States of America became The Kingdom of America rent payments stopped and what was known as capitalism ended and The Kingdom of America became a socialistic country like China, and that pretty much explains the first year of the 7 year tribulation.

By the time David finished explaining the first year of the tribulation it was now time for the second phase of the beast plague "David let's go to the riverbank in our district so we can witness the 2nd phase of the attack of the beast" I said "ok no problem" David replied, and then we left David's apartment and walked to the riverbank. "It is time" I said then I lifted my staff then out of nowhere thousands of GIANT sea creatures appeared at the surface of the waters of the Houston river even some ancient prehistoric creatures appeared as well, then The Most High gave me another insightful vision of what was happening in New York so I tuned into the vision some more, and I saw creatures swallowing up every boat in their path and the citizens of New York were terrified by the sight, and then it was so many giant sea creatures in one spot that they started a huge tsunami flooding everywhere in New York besides the district of believers.

But then my insightful vision continued, and the tsunami continued into the next day and it was a dark and bustling morning in New York City, and the streets were filled with different unique sounds. But unknown to its inhabitants, a devastating force of nature was lurking in the depths of the ocean. As the sun began to rise, an ominous shadow appeared on the horizon. The monstrous tsunami got bigger and in the likes of which no one had ever seen, was rapidly approaching the city. Panic ensued as the news spread like wildfire. People rushed to higher ground, desperate to escape the impending disaster, and as the sirens wailed outside, New York City citizens peered out their windows, seeing the waves growing larger and closer with each passing second, and without a second thought, the New York City citizens grabbed their most treasured belongings, and they all rushed downstairs to the street. The water was already starting to flood the area, and New York City citizens knew they had to find higher ground quickly. Along their ways, they encountered others struggling to save their belongings and find safety and amid the chaos, New York City citizens' gaze fell upon elderly people stranded on benches, unable to walk on their own. Determined not to leave anyone behind, New York City citizens rushed to the elderly people's side and helped them up. Together, they limped towards a nearby building that seemed somewhat elevated.

But my insightful vision continued some more, and as they reached the building's entrance, the tsunami's first wave struck the city with a deafening roar, engulfing everything in its path. The force of the water was immense, causing buildings to crumble and vehicles to be swept away as if they were mere toys, and with the water rising rapidly, New York City citizens and the elderly people made their way up to the higher floors. They found refuge on a rooftop, surrounded by others who had sought safety there as well. The scene was surreal; New York City, a symbol of human accomplishment, now lay submerged beneath an unforgiving ocean as the waves receded, leaving behind devastation and destruction, New York City citizens couldn't help but feel heartbroken for the city they had come to love was being destroyed. But amidst the ruins, something remarkable happened. Strangers from different walks of life came together to help each other, demonstrating the strength of human spirit even in the face of tragedy, then days turned into weeks, and the city began to rebuild. The process was slow and arduous, but a newfound sense of unity and camaraderie prevailed among the survivors. The artwork of New York City citizens had also survived the ordeal, and they found solace in expressing their emotions through their artworks.

So as my insightful vision began to end New York City rose from the depths, stronger and more resilient than ever before but this was all The Most Highs plan of course. The tsunami had changed the city, but it hadn't broken its spirit. It had taught its people to value one another and cherish what truly mattered in life. As New York City citizens continued to be productive and do business as usual, and they often found themselves gazing at the horizon, remembering the day the tsunami had struck. The image of the enormous wave crashing upon the city would forever be in their minds. But more importantly, they would never forget the lessons of strength, compassion, and community that the disaster had taught them. and so, in the heart of the rebuilt New York City, the sand from the first plague remained and the stories of countless others became a testament to the resilience of the human spirit and the Kingdom of America started finding its strength and began to rise again.

(The Wizards of Italy)

The next day I woke up to the sound of David's voice "Elijah today there is a major issue happening in Italy" said David "what's happening" I replied "There is a group of some evil Italian wizards attacking the people in the District of believers in Italy and we need you to stop them ASAP but this mission may take a little while because we are dealing with some evil advanced wizards" David explained "ok that should not be a problem" I replied "great and the New Goshen Jet made some major technical advancements so we do not have to worry about any government detecting us from now on and until we leave up out of these countries, and it is already in Coney Island waiting on us" David said, and then the both of us left David's apartment and went to Coney Island. And after some minutes flew by, we were in Coney Island and I could see the New Goshen Jet waiting for me and David, so after some moments me and David got on the New Goshen Jet "What's up you two and the next stop is Italy" Jordan said while starting up the jet engines. So after some hours flew by the 3 of us arrived in Italy and Jordan found a safe place to land, so after the jet landed I stepped out of it but I noticed that David did not step out of the jet with me "David are you coming: I said "I can't on this one because I am needed back in New Goshen but once this mission is complete we will meet back up" David explained, then moments later the New Goshen Jet was in the sky and I was in Italy.

And as I walked through the bustling streets of Italy, I couldn't shake the feeling that something unusual was happening. In the midst of the city's vibrant energy, I sensed a dark force gathering strength. Italian wizards had emerged from the shadows, using their ancient arts for malevolent deeds. Their wicked magic threatened to disturb the peace and harmony of the believers, so guided by the divine light, I embarked on a journey to confront these sinister sorcerers and their sinister plans, and their stronghold lay hidden in the heart of the ancient Colosseum, where they had harnessed the energy of the past to amplify their powers.

So as I approached a grand amphitheater, I felt an immense surge of magical energy emanating from within. Drawing upon my faith and the strength bestowed upon me by the Creator, I pushed open the creaking gates and stepped into the arena where the Italian wizards, draped in dark robes and surrounded by arcane symbols, were waiting for me, and their leader, a cunning sorcerer named Lorenzo, sneered at my presence. "So, you've come to challenge us, prophet?" he taunted, then I raised my staff, my heart resolute, and answered, "I have come to vanquish the darkness that corrupts this city and The believers."

The battle commenced as lightning crackled across the sky, symbolizing the clash of ancient powers with modern magic. Lorenzo conjured flames, trying to engulf me, but I stood firm, using my divine gifts to protect myself, and with each incantation and counter-spell, the Colosseum trembled under the magical tension. Our forces seemed evenly matched, but I knew that my strength came from a higher source—a power beyond the grasp of mere wizards, so as the battle raged on, I could feel the dark energy weakening, for evil cannot withstand the might of righteousness. Channeling the words of the Almighty, I cast a mighty storm upon the wizards, drenching them in holy rain.

Then the power of the divine washed away their malevolence, and Lorenzo's magic faltered. Realizing the futility of their efforts, the other wizards surrendered and retreated into the shadows, and with the threat dispelled, I breathed a sigh of relief. The believers was safe once more, and the Italian wizards had learned the folly of their ways, so as I stood amidst the ancient ruins, I knew that the battle had only been the beginning. There would always be those who sought to exploit dark powers for their own gain. But I was determined to continue my mission, bringing the light of truth and justice wherever darkness lurked.

And so, my journey as a prophet continued, traveling through time and space to confront the forces of darkness wherever they may rise. For the Almighty's will is eternal, and I, Elijah, am His instrument in this ever-changing world, so after the confrontation at the Colosseum, word of the prophet who battled the Italian wizards' sinister plans spread like wildfire across Italy. The believers, once living in fear, found comfort in the belief that a divine force was watching over them. They shared tales of my encounter, embellishing the details with each retelling, and as I walked the streets, I was met with warm smiles and grateful nods. Some even bowed in reverence, mistaking me for a heavenly being. However, I humbly reminded them that I was merely a mortal chosen to serve the Almighty's purpose.

So after some time in the days that followed, I continued my journey through Italy, drawn to Florence by whispers of dark magic that had surfaced once again. The Italian wizards, now humbled by their defeat in Italy, had gathered in the shadows, seeking to regain their strength and prove their powers again, so upon reaching Florence, I discovered that the wizards had taken residence within the ancient catacombs beneath the city. The dark and winding tunnels were filled with an eerie silence, broken only by the faint chanting of the sorcerers were guided by an inner light, I ventured deep into the catacombs, knowing that my confrontation with these dark forces was inevitable. I felt the presence of evil growing stronger with each step, but my faith in the Almighty shielded me from fear.

So as I approached the heart of the catacombs, I encountered the wizards once more. This time, their leader was a formidable sorceress named Isabella, known for her mastery of ancient spells. She regarded me with a mix of curiosity and disdain. "Another prophet seeking to challenge us?" Isabella said with a smirk. "Your divine powers won't save you this time." I responded with a calm but firm voice, "It is not my powers alone that protect me. It is the righteousness of my cause and the guidance of the Almighty" then the battle began, and the catacombs started echoing with the sounds of clashing magic. Isabella conjured illusions and unleashed a barrage of curses, attempting to weaken my resolve. But I knew better than to succumb to such trickery, so as I drew strength from the Almighty, I countered with the power of truth and justice, dispelling her illusions and breaking her curses. With every passing moment, the evil influence waned, and the catacombs filled with an ethereal glow.

So as our confrontation intensified, the walls of the catacombs seemed to tremble, threatening to collapse upon us. But the Almighty's protection shielded me, allowing me to stand steadfast against the dark forces, and seeing that her efforts were futile, Isabella finally surrendered. The other wizards followed suit, recognizing the superiority of a power greater than their own. They vowed to renounce their wicked ways and embrace a path of redemption and with the darkness banished once more, I emerged from the catacombs to find the sun shining brightly over Florence. The believers rejoiced, their hearts filled with gratitude for the divine intervention that had saved them from the clutches of evil.

So I bid farewell to The believers of Florence, knowing that my mission as a prophet was far from over. As long as there were forces seeking to exploit dark magic, I would continue to journey across Italy, guided by the Almighty's will. And so, my legend of, the biblical prophet who battled Italian wizards, spread far and wide. The tale of divine intervention in the modern world became an enduring reminder that even in the darkest of times, the light of righteousness would always prevail, and as I continued my journey, I remained ever vigilant, for the forces of darkness knew no boundaries. But with unwavering faith in the Almighty and a heart filled with compassion, I would stand strong against any evil that dared to challenge the balance between light and darkness.

So minutes after my triumphant victory in Italy again, the news of the prophet who vanquished the Italian wizards again reached far beyond the borders of Italy. People from all corners of the world began to hear the tales of the enigmatic figure who wielded divine power against dark sorcery. My name, Elijah, was spoken in hushed whispers, revered as a harbinger of justice and hope, so as I traversed the Italian countryside, making my way to Florence, I encountered villagers along the way who sought blessings and protection from the miraculous figure they believed me to be. Children eagerly approached with bright eyes, hoping for a touch of divine magic. I couldn't deny their requests, as a simple touch on their foreheads brought them solace and joy.

Then the journey to Florence was arduous, but the will of the Almighty sustained me. Upon reaching the edge of city, I found the streets abuzz with rumors of the reemergence of dark magic. Italian wizards, having been humbled in Italy, were determined to prove their supremacy once more and I thought to myself "These dark wizards have no chill", so as the catacombs beneath Florence were a labyrinth of shadows and echoes, hauntingly beautiful yet shrouded in an ancient malevolence. The air was thick with an energy that sent shivers down my spine, but my faith was my shield, keeping me from faltering in the face of danger, and guided by an inner light, I pressed on, the sound of my footsteps echoing through the eerie silence. I could hear faint whispers of incantations as I neared the heart of the catacombs, signaling that the wizards were aware of my presence.

So as I emerged into a vast underground chamber, the Italian wizards stood before me, led by the formidable sorceress Isabella again. Her eyes glinted with a mix of arrogance and determination, and I could feel the intensity of her magical aura. It was clear that this battle would be no less challenging than the previous one. "Prophet, you dare to challenge us once more?" Isabella sneered, her voice dripping with disdain. "I seek not to challenge, but to protect those who may fall prey to your dark intentions," I replied with a calm yet unwavering tone, Then the battle commenced, and the catacombs roared with the clash of powers. Isabella's mastery of illusion magic proved to be a formidable weapon, as she conjured nightmarish visions to weaken my resolve. However, my unwavering faith in the Almighty allowed me to see through the illusions, dispelling them with a mere wave of my staff, and as the battle escalated, the catacombs seemed to react to the unleashed magical forces. The walls trembled, and stalactites fell, threatening to bury us alive. Yet, the Almighty's divine protection enveloped me, ensuring I remained unharmed, then with each spell, I countered Isabella's attacks, using the might of truth and justice to weaken her dark magic. Her forces wavered, and the other wizards began to doubt their allegiance to evil.

Then in a moment of revelation, Isabella dropped to her knees, her magic faltering. "I see now that darkness cannot conquer the light of righteousness," she confessed, her voice tinged with remorse, and with their leader's surrender, the other wizards followed suit. They realized the futility of their pursuit of power through dark means and vowed to seek redemption, so as I emerged from the catacombs, I found Florence bathed in the warm glow of the morning sun. The city's believers greeted me with tears of gratitude and renewed hope, for they knew that the divine had intervened to save them from the grasp of darkness.

So as my journey as a prophet continued, traversing the Italy to confront malevolent forces wherever they lurked. Each encounter brought its own challenges, but my faith in the Almighty and my desire to protect the innocent fueled my determination, And so, my legend of, the biblical prophet who battled Italian wizards, spread like wildfire across the world yet again. Tales of divine intervention and the triumph of light over darkness inspired countless souls, reaffirming their belief in the goodness that lay within every heart, so as I moved forward, I remained vigilant, knowing that evil would forever try to sow discord in the world. But the Almighty's guidance and the love and support of those I encountered along the way filled me with the strength to face any darkness that dared to defy the balance between good and evil.

So as my reputation as the prophet who triumphed over the Italian wizards spread across the globe, tales of my encounters took on a life of their own. People from distant lands spoke of the enigmatic figure, a vessel of divine power who stood against the darkness that threatened to engulf Italy. The name "Elijah" became synonymous with hope and salvation, and throughout my journey, I encountered countless individuals seeking solace and guidance. Mothers brought their sick children, hoping for a miraculous touch to heal their ailments. The impoverished begged for blessings to lift the burden of destitution from their lives. I could not deny their pleas, for I knew that the Almighty's divine grace flowed through my actions.

So as I made my way to Florence, rumors of the resurgence of dark magic grew stronger. The Italian wizards, having learned from their defeat in Italy, and they sought to regain their pride and prove their mastery over ancient sorcery agin. Their influence had spread like a web, ensnaring the hearts of vulnerable souls, and upon reaching Florence, I found the once vibrant city shrouded in an air of trepidation. The catacombs, a nexus of both beauty and malevolence, beckoned me with their haunting allure. They whispered of secrets buried beneath layers of history, and I could feel the weight of ancient sorrows, so guided by an inner light, I delved deep into the catacombs, my every footstep echoing through the dimly lit passages. The air was heavy with the scent of earth and the lingering essence of centuries past. As I ventured further, I could hear faint murmurs of incantations, signaling the wizards' awareness of my presence.

Finally, I entered a colossal underground chamber where the Italian wizards stood, led by the formidable sorceress Jasmine this time. Her eyes burned with a fierce determination, and her ethereal cloak billowed like a dark mist around her. "Prophet, you dare to challenge us once more are you crazy?" Jasimine said, as Jasmine's voice reverberated through the chamber, carrying both arrogance and malice, and in my head I thought to myself this Jasime chick must have not learned from the defeat of Isabella , then I responded out loud "like I said before I do not seek to challenge, but to protect those who may fall prey to your malevolence," I replied, my voice resonating with unwavering conviction, Then the battle commenced, and the catacombs erupted with the cacophony of clashing magic. Jasmine's mastery of illusionary spells was unparalleled, and she conjured nightmarish visions to break my spirit. Yet, my unwavering faith in the Almighty allowed me to see through her illusions, dispelling them with a mere flick of my staff.

So as the battle intensified, the catacombs seemed to react to the unleashed forces. The walls trembled, and stalactites threatened to fall, but the divine shield enveloped me, ensuring my safety, and with each spell, I countered Jasmine's attacks, utilizing the power of truth and justice to weaken her dark magic. Her forces wavered, and uncertainty flickered in the eyes of the other wizards, and in a moment of revelation, Jasmine dropped to her knees, her magic faltering. "I see now that darkness cannot conquer the light of righteousness," she confessed, her voice tinged with remorse. Witnessing their leader's surrender, the other wizards followed suit. They realized the emptiness of their pursuit of power through malevolent means and vowed to seek redemption.

So as I emerged from the catacombs, I found Florence bathed in the warm glow of the morning sun. The city's believers greeted me with tears of gratitude and renewed hope, knowing that the divine had intervened to save them from the clutches of darkness once more, so my journey as a prophet continued, taking me to far-flung lands of Italy and facing diverse adversaries. Each encounter brought its own set of challenges, but my unwavering faith in the Almighty and my desire to protect the innocent fueled my determination.

And as my legend of, the biblical prophet who battled Italian wizards, spread worldwide again and again, countless hearts found solace in the tales of divine intervention and the triumph of light over darkness. The stories inspired hope in the goodness that lay within every human soul and the power of redemption to transform even the most malevolent hearts, and in my continued travels, I remained vigilant, knowing that evil would forever seek to sow discord in Italy. But the Almighty's guidance and the love and support of those I encountered along the way fortified my resolve to face any darkness that dared defy the balance between good and evil again.

So as my legend of, the biblical prophet who battled Italian wizards, continued to spread across the globe, it became an enduring testament to the power of faith and the triumph of righteousness over darkness. The tales of divine intervention offered hope to countless souls, instilling a renewed belief once more in the goodness that resides within every heart, so through my journey, I encountered both the beauty and the struggles of the human experience. The weight of responsibility as the vessel of divine power often felt overwhelming, but the love and support I received from those I encountered continued to fortified my resolve again.

So in every village, town, and city, The believers gathered to witness the miracles they believed me to perform. I healed the sick, comforted the afflicted, and offered guidance to those seeking direction. Yet, I remained humble, acknowledging that it was not my power alone but the Almighty's grace working through me, and then to my surprise I learned about another evil attack gaining its evil strength, and I thought to myself these Italian wizards need to give up so I can go back to New York, but as I faced the Italian wizards in the catacombs once again in Florence, I found myself immersed in an ancient realm where echoes of the past intertwined with the present. The catacombs' hallowed silence seemed to whisper of forgotten lives and untold stories, reminding me of the interconnectedness of all existence, Then the confrontation with a new witch who was named Amber and her coven was an intense clash of forces. Her illusions sought to ensnare my mind and soul, but my unwavering faith in the Almighty shielded me from her dark machinations. The catacombs trembled as the unleashed magic threatened to disrupt the balance of the world, but the Almighty's divine shield protected me from harm.

Then in the moment of surrender, Amber's realization of the futility of darkness was a profound turning point. The Italian wizards renounced their malevolent ways once again, vowing to seek redemption and mend the wounds they had inflicted upon Italy, then as I emerged from the catacombs, Florence bathed in the golden light of the morning sun, the city's believers rejoiced, their hearts filled with gratitude and hope. The story of my intervention became a symbol of hope again, reminding people that even in the darkest times, the light of righteousness would always shine through, and as my journey as a prophet continued, I traveled across diverse landscapes, facing adversaries that challenged the very fabric of existence. Each encounter deepened my understanding of the delicate balance between free will and divine guidance, reinforcing the belief that goodness resides in the hearts of all living beings.

Then my legend of, the prophet who battled Italian wizards, became a beacon of hope and inspiration for generations to come I was told, then It transcended time and culture, reminding humanity of the eternal struggle between light and darkness and the power of redemption to transform even the most malevolent hearts, and in my final reflections, I realized that my purpose was not merely to vanquish evil, but to inspire people to find the light within themselves. It was through love, compassion, and understanding that humanity could rise above darkness and embrace the divinity within.

And so, my journey as the prophet continued, traversing time and space to confront the forces of darkness wherever they may have raised. Guided by the Almighty's will, I carried the eternal message of hope and righteousness, a reminder that goodness would always prevail in the tapestry of existence, so as my legend of a man who battled the Italian wizards, continued to resonate across Italy and the world, and a new chapter unfolded. Rumors spread of a Grand Italian wizard, known as Aurelio, who had risen to power with a level of mastery that surpassed any other sorcerer before him. His name sent shivers down the spines of those who dared to utter it and I later learned that he was the teacher of Isabella, Jasmine, and Amber, and the tales of his magical powers spread like wildfire, and word of Aurelio's reign of terror reached my ears as I journeyed through the Italian countryside, prompting me to investigate the source of this newfound malevolence. Villagers whispered in hushed tones, recounting the stories of Aurelio's malevolent deeds, from dark curses that blighted crops to twisted enchantments that turned loved ones against each other.

So as I was being Guided by an inner sense of duty, I followed the trail of dark magic to the heart of an ancient forest, where Aurelio had established his stronghold. The forest seemed to hold its breath, as if aware of the impending clash between the forces of light and the encroaching darkness, so as I ventured deeper into the heart of the forest, I found Aurelio's lair, a fortress of ancient stones and mystical wards. The air crackled with the power of his malevolent magic, and the ground trembled underfoot. It was clear that this confrontation would be the most formidable yet, so inside the fortress, I faced a grand chamber where Aurelio stood, draped in a cloak of shadows and surrounded by an aura of darkness. His eyes gleamed with an unsettling brilliance, and the power that emanated from him was undeniable. "Ah, the prophet Elijah," Aurelio said, his voice carrying a sense of arrogance and disdain. "I've heard tales of your so-called divine power. Let's see if you can withstand mine." And Without warning, Aurelio unleashed a torrent of dark magic, the force of which threatened to overwhelm me. His mastery of the arcane was unparalleled, and his spells were infused with a malevolence that seemed to mock the very essence of goodness.

So I called upon the Almighty's protection, my staff emanating a radiant light that clashed with Aurelio's darkness. The chamber trembled with the intensity of our magical duel, each spell seeking to overpower the other, and in this clash of grand sorcery, I sensed the weight of not only my own purpose but the collective hopes of all those who had found solace in the tales of my encounters. The battle was not just against Aurelio but a test of the very ideals I represented.

So as we exchanged spell after spell, it became clear that this confrontation would decide the fate of the balance between light and darkness in Italy. The forest seemed to hold its breath, waiting for the outcome of this epic duel, and in a moment of divine clarity, I summoned the power of truth and justice, channeling it into my staff. With a mighty roar, I unleashed a burst of radiant light that engulfed Aurelio's dark magic, dispelling it with a resounding force. Aurelio staggered back, his confidence waning. He had never encountered such a force of righteousness before, and it left him shaken. The believer's belief in the Almighty's grace had fueled my resolve, making me an instrument of a power far greater than Aurelio's malevolence, then in a rare moment of vulnerability, Aurelio dropped to his knees and I thought to myself wow, because even his grand dark magic started waning. "I never thought I would encounter a force greater than my own," he admitted, his voice tinged with a hint of remorse.

So as the darkness lifted, I extended a hand to Aurelio, offering redemption. "There is always a path to the light," I said, my voice filled with compassion. "Renounce your malevolence and seek redemption, and you shall find solace in the divine." Then with a nod, Aurelio accepted my offer, realizing that there was a different path he could tread. From that day forward, he vowed to use his magic for good, to heal the wounds he had caused and become an ally in the battle against darkness, then as the tale of my encounter with the grand Italian wizard Aurelio spread, it served as a reminder that even the most formidable adversaries could find redemption. The people of Italy found hope once more in the transformation of a once malevolent sorcerer into an ally for good, a testament to the potential for goodness that resided in all beings.

And so, my journey as the prophet continued, traversing throughout Italy to confront malevolent forces wherever they may have risen. Guided by the Almighty's will, I carried the eternal message of hope, righteousness, and the power of redemption to transform even the darkest hearts, and then out of nowhere I received a call from David "mission complete great job Elijah we will be coming to get you now in the New Goshen Jet in the same spot where we dropped you off so be ready" David said and then the call ended.

(The Skin Boil Outbreak)

"David I'm glad you called because now it's time to plead with the King of America once again" I told David as soon as he arrived in Italy to get me with the New Goshen Jet "Right and that won't be an issue" David said as the New Goshen Jet took off into the sky. Then after hours flew by, we were in New York landing in Coney Island, then me and David got off the Jet "see you two on the next mission" said Jordan and then the New Gosen Jet took off into the sky. "Now let's go to The Kings Tower" I said so we did and after some minutes flew by, we arrived at the Kings tower, then we went through the same usual procedures and at the end of them the King refused to let my people go once more. So, me and David left the Kings tower after the King denied my request and then we made our way back to the David's apartment. "Let's go up on the rooftop its time to start the next plague, so we did and once we were on the rooftop, I lifted my staff and then after I lifted my staff, I began to have an insightful vision.

So, when my insightful vision started I saw a strange and mysterious outbreak occurring. People across the city of New York began experiencing an alarming and uncomfortable phenomenon: major skin boils were spreading like wildfire. Nobody could explain the sudden and simultaneous appearance of these painful lesions on the skin, and panic began to grip the city. News of the outbreak spread like a virus, and people started flooding hospitals and clinics seeking answers and treatment. The medical community was baffled and struggled to understand the cause of this peculiar epidemic. Experts from around the world were called in to investigate, but even they were stumped by the unprecedented scale and severity of the outbreak. As the situation escalated, New York City declared a state of emergency. Public health officials urged residents to stay vigilant, maintain good hygiene, and avoid close contact with others. The fear of contagion was so pervasive that New Yorkers started wearing masks and gloves to prevent potential infection from the mysterious skin boils.

And as my insightful vision went on the media coverage of the outbreak was relentless. Reporters flocked to the city from all corners of the globe, and speculation ran rampant. Conspiracy theories circulated, attributing the outbreak to everything from a new bioweapon to a government experiment gone awry. Fear and paranoia gripped the population, exacerbating the already tense and uncertain atmosphere. With the city in turmoil, businesses suffered, tourism dwindled, and daily life ground to a halt. The already sand covered streets of New York City, once bustling with energy, now resembled ghost towns as people stayed indoors, fearing the unknown. Meanwhile, scientists and medical researchers worked tirelessly in laboratories, trying to analyze the boils' samples and identify the cause of the outbreak. As the days went by, hope waned, and despair settled over the city like a heavy fog.

So as news of the major skin boil outbreak in America spread internationally, the world watched in alarm and disbelief. Governments and health organizations around the globe closely monitored the situation, realizing that this was no ordinary outbreak and could potentially evolve into a global health crisis. The World Health Organization (WHO) immediately convened an emergency meeting of experts and representatives from affected countries. The meeting aimed to share information, coordinate efforts, and develop a unified global response strategy to contain and control the outbreak. Reports of skin boil cases started pouring in from various countries, and the scale of the outbreak became apparent. From Europe to Asia, Africa to South America, no continent was spared from the reach of the mysterious infection. Countries implemented stringent travel restrictions and quarantine measures to prevent further spread across borders.

The global scientific community rallied together to study the mutated bacteria responsible for the skin boils. Researchers from different countries collaborated virtually, sharing data and findings in realtime to accelerate understanding and vaccine development. The WHO led an international vaccination campaign, distributing vaccines to affected regions and countries. Mass vaccination centers were set up in major cities, and healthcare workers faced the immense challenge of vaccinating millions of people to build herd immunity and curb the outbreak's progression. Global leaders addressed their nations and the international community, emphasizing the need for solidarity, compassion, and adherence to public health guidelines. Governments encouraged their citizens to remain calm and vigilant.

Meanwhile, as the outbreak continued to spread, the global economy suffered. Industries reliant on international travel, such as tourism and aviation, were particularly hard-hit. Supply chains were disrupted, leading to shortages of essential goods and medicines in some areas. The outbreak tested the resilience of healthcare systems worldwide, with some countries facing overwhelming numbers of patients. Health workers demonstrated unparalleled dedication and bravery, working tirelessly to care for those affected while risking their own well-being. So as time went on, the Boils began to disappear. The number of new cases gradually decreased, and all the countries of the world were declared free from the outbreak.

"Wow theses last few of days were crazy and the King probably will still refuse to let our people go next time even after what just happened" David said as the two of us sipped our tea "yea well things will continue to get worse if he keeps on refusing" I replied "Well on that note let me tell you about year 2 of the tribulation" David said "Ok" I replied and then David began telling his story.

I thought it couldn't get worse but, one day everything changed again. The countries of the world decided to unite under a new one world religion, while simultaneously banning the freedom of religion. As the news spread, anxiety filled the air. People clung to their beliefs, not willing to let go of centuries-old traditions. It was a time of uncertainty and fear. The city's once diverse and vibrant places of worship now stood silent, and their doors chained shut, And in the face of this radical change, I couldn't bear the thought of abandoning my beliefs. So I sought solace in secret gatherings with fellow believers, who like me, refused to let go of what we held dear. In the hidden corners of the city, we gathered in hushed whispers, sharing our faith and our hope for a better tomorrow, But even in the shadows, it was evident that the authorities were cracking down on any semblance of religious practice.

So as the days went on the pressure mounted as I navigated the complexities of this unprecedented time. My heart ached for those whose beliefs differed from the new norm, knowing they faced persecution and ostracization. Amidst the chaos, I stumbled upon a group of individuals advocating for unity and understanding. They believed that embracing diversity was the key to a harmonious world, where different faiths could coexist without conflict. Drawn to their message of hope, I joined their cause, then together, we clandestinely shared our stories of faith and compassion, planting seeds of empathy in the hearts of those we encountered, and as the movement grew, the darkness of the new world religion got worse, and in the midst of adversity, people began questioning the oppressive dogma enforced by the new world religion. Our movement inspired others to stand up for their beliefs and defend their right to practice religion freely.

And as the days continued our journey became harder, and we became a beacon of hope in the midst of a now dark world, So I remember turning on my T.V and as the news spread like wildfire across the globe, anxiety filled the air and things began to get even worse. The masses were taken back by this monumental decision that seemed to challenge the very core of their identities, but people still clung to their beliefs, not willing to let go of their religions. It was a time of uncertainty and fear, as families and friends found themselves on opposing sides of this radical shift. And in the heart of New York City, the once vibrant and diverse places Synagogues, churches, mosques, and temples — were all silenced under the weight of the new world religion's decree globally, and the atmosphere was suffocating, the spirit of unity that once celebrated the rich tapestry of faith now overshadowed by an iron-fisted rule, so as things progressed and in the face of this oppressive change, I continued not abandoning my beliefs. because my faith was an integral part of who I was, a compass guiding me through life's trials, so as the secret gatherings with fellow believers continued, the authorities started making arrest at levels that I have never seen before I mean it was even worse than Joe Bidens 1994 crime bill. The once bustling streets now had an eerie stillness, as people treaded cautiously, afraid of expressing their convictions openly. Informants lurked in every corner, ready to report any deviation from the new world order's decrees.

I thought this nightmare was going to end but the pressure continued and mounted as I navigated the complexities of this unprecedented time. My heart continued to ache for those whose believed different from the new world religion, knowing they faced persecution and ostracization, and then things started to heat up as the news of the one world religion spread throughout the world yet again, and the atmosphere in New York City became increasingly even more tense, and now even the NYPD started to get involved because so many people were rebelling against not having the freedom of religion anymore like in the old constitution of the United States, so The NYPD, once seen as protectors of the community, began enforcing the new religious decree on the citizens.

And in the beginning, the police officers were met with resistance from the people they were supposed to serve. Protests erupted across the city, with citizens demanding their right to practice their faith freely. However, the NYPD, now acting under the orders of the one world religion's leaders, showed no leniency. They responded with force, using tear gas and batons to disperse the crowds, and sadly some people were even killed for resisting, and now the streets were starting to slowly divide, with officers patrolling neighborhoods to ensure strict adherence to the new religious norms. Places of worship now getting demolished and at first, they were just locking the doors, and the NYPD were erasing the rich tapestry of religious diversity that once defined New York City.

So as things escalated the NYPD started conducting surprise raids on homes suspected of harboring religious artifacts like bibles and that is when the world wide Bible raid began, but I was still able to keep my bible hidden, but sadly families were torn apart as their loved ones were arrested and taken away, accused of defying the new world order, And Fear continued gripped the hearts of the people, and trust in law enforcement decreased rapidly, and along with the group of individuals advocating for unity and understanding, found themselves at the forefront of the resistance. They became a beacon of hope for those struggling to maintain their faith in the face of oppression.

And as the movement grew stronger, the NYPD intensified its efforts to crush any opposition by increasing surveillance and now infiltrating the secret gatherings and even the gatherings that we thought could not be infiltrated, but by using undercover agents to gather evidence against the groups their infiltrations were successful, and me and my friends knew that we were putting ourselves at great risk, but we believed in the power of The Most High, and then things got worse and a wave of propaganda flooded the media, glorifying the new one world religion while demonizing any dissenters and now good truly became evil and evil became good, And as the NYPD, portrayed as loyal enforcers of the faith, became increasingly isolated from the communities they once served. Some officers grappled with the moral dilemma of enforcing such oppressive measures, while others embraced their new role wholeheartedly.

But still in the face of adversity and as tensions increased as the NYPD's role in enforcing the religious decree on its citizens even created new and deep divisions within the department itself. Some officers found it increasingly difficult to reconcile their duty with the oppressive measures they were ordered to carry out, and me and the group of individuals advocating for unity and understanding continued to stand at the forefront of the resistance, and we found more secret places to meet and our gatherings became more frequent, drawing people from all walks of life, united in their defiance against the imposed religious norms. They held discussions, shared personal stories, and fostered a sense of camaraderie among those who refused to let go of their individual beliefs.

So as the days continued to go by the resistance was met with even harsh consequences, as the NYPD intensified its efforts to suppress any form of dissent. Officers patrolled the streets with newfound fervor, raiding homes at new levels than before and arresting individuals suspected of practicing their faith in secret and the cities around the world were now all out battlegrounds for a clash of ideologies.

But despite of the escalating oppression, the resistance did not waver. me and my friends knew that standing up for our beliefs came at a high cost, but we were driven by the belief that unity and empathy could bridge the divide that had torn the world apart, and then something surprising happened, some members of the NYPD started questioning their loyalty to the one world religion's leaders. Whispers of discontent spread among the ranks, as officers privately expressed concerns about the infringement on personal liberties, and a few brave souls even joined the resistance in secret, using their positions to provide vital information and support, and some officers who started to join the believers were working as spies against the new world religion and they helped us believers with finding even more secret locations, and the media played a crucial role in shaping public opinion, so while the majority of outlets propagated the narrative of the new world order, there were a few courageous journalists who risked their careers to report on the resistance's fight for religious freedom. Their stories shed light on the human cost of blind obedience to an oppressive system.

So as the year progressed in the midst of the tumultuous enforcement of the new one world religion in New York City, an unexpected element came into play with the wizards of New York that were hidden in the shadows for centuries, the secretive group of New York wizards emerged involving their magic intertwining with the unfolding events because even they were starting to disagree with the new world religion, and these wizards possessed ancient knowledge and abilities that had long been kept away from the praying eyes of the world. However, their principles were guided by a deep-seated belief in unity, understanding, and empathy, so as the city grappled with the new religious norms, they saw an opportunity to make a difference by harnessing their magical skills, the wizards embarked on a clandestine mission to foster acceptance and respect for diversity. Disguised as ordinary citizens, they mingled among the people, silently influencing conversations and guiding individuals towards embracing compassion and understanding.

So as time continued and through their magical means, the wizards subtly countered the propaganda propagated by the one world religion's leaders. They planted seeds of doubt, encouraging people to question the oppressive measures and seek broader perspective. Whispers of hope and unity filled the air, circulating like an enchanting breeze through the city streets, And as me and my friends continued to lead the resistance, we unknowingly found allies in these New York wizards. The two groups formed an unlikely alliance, united by their shared belief in the power of empathy and unity. The wizards' magical abilities, combined with the resilience of the resistance, presented a formidable force against the oppressive regime, so in the shadows, the wizards conducted secret rituals that amplified the emotions of empathy and compassion, creating an aura of understanding that touched the hearts of even the most hardened enforcers. Some officers in the NYPD began experiencing visions of the past, recalling memories of harmony and coexistence that had been forgotten under the new world order. And these magical interventions challenged the loyalty of many within the NYPD. Some officers began questioning their role in enforcing the oppressive measures. And a few that did not secretly join the rebelling officers before even started secretly aiding the resistance, providing invaluable information and support, all while concealing their identities with wizards.

So as the momentum of the resistance grew, so did the magic of the New York wizards. Their spells were now focused on revealing the leaders of the one world religion the true consequences of their actions. Visions of a divided and broken world haunted the leaders' dreams, reminding them of the importance of embracing diversity, so the once unyielding leaders of the one world religion were now torn between their desire for control and the unsettling visions they could not ignore. The wizards' magic was proving to be a powerful catalyst for change, making the leaders realize the error of their ways, then in a moment of reckoning, the leaders of the one world religion addressed the city. They acknowledged their past mistakes and vowed to amend their approach, embracing a more inclusive and accepting ideology. The oppressive measures were lifted but now looking back I know that they only lifted the one world religion temporarily because of the influences of the wizards, and religious freedom was restored at that moment anyways, and the New York wizards and the resistance had achieved the unimaginable – unity prevailed, and the world started to heal. New York City, once divided, now stood as a symbol of the triumph of empathy over oppression, and as the days passed, the New York wizards continued to safeguard the city's values of understanding and compassion. And their magic became a protective cloak, shielding the city from future threats so they thought at that time because then something unexpected, happened months later.

It was unexpected and it caught even the wizards off guard because just when the wizards thought that they solved the issue of the new one world religion that effected even them, after months went by the spells of the NYC wizards began to ware off of the leaders of the one world religion and now a new group of evil wizards that sided with the leaders of the new one world religion emerged and these wizards were stronger than the other wizards that were against the new one world religion, so as I'm telling you this Elijah, a shiver is running down my spine, for the events that I am about to recount are as unbelievable as they are sinister, and I find myself compelled to share the tale of a world gripped in the clutches of this new group of malevolent evil wizards who sought to enforce a single, malevolent religion upon us all, but this is how it began on an ordinary day after the new world religion was lifted something was amiss in the air, a sense of foreboding that I couldn't quite shake off. Rumors started to spread like wildfire, whispers of powerful sorcerers congregating in the shadows, plotting to reshape the very essence of our beliefs once more.

So one by one, cities across the globe began to fall under their sway. Ordinary men and women were transformed into zealous followers, their minds twisted and their hearts bound to this newfound faith. The once-diverse tapestry of religions that had adorned our world for centuries was systematically dismantled again and replaced by the doctrines of this one world religion once more. Its tenets were eerie and unnatural, advocating a devotion to an enigmatic deity that demanded absolute obedience some called this deity the Anti-Christ, and I witnessed it firsthand in my own town. Once a place where people of all faiths coexisted peacefully, it soon became a haven for those who embraced this sinister religion. Statues of the enigmatic deity sprung up in every corner, and the very air seemed to hum with an otherworldly energy. Fear gnawed at my insides as I saw friends and neighbors turn into unrecognizable zealots, and their eyes glazed over with an eerie fervor and the wizards themselves remained hidden, and their identities shrouded in mystery. But their presence was palpable in every street, every whispered prayer, every iron-fisted decree. They wielded their magic not with benevolence, but with an iron will to control and dominate. Those who dared to question were swiftly silenced, made examples of by getting beheaded.

So I found myself torn between the desire to fight back and the fear that had become a constant companion. It was then that I encountered a small group smaller than before of individuals who still refused to succumb to the enchantment that had ensnared our world. They spoke of ancient prophecies, of a time when heroes would rise to challenge the darkness that had descended upon us, so I was guided by their words, and I delved into hidden tomes and relics, seeking a way to break the hold the malevolent wizards had over us. And together, we uncovered forgotten rituals and arcane lore that held the potential to counter their magic. And as our numbers grew lower, our strength and determination still fought back, but the final confrontation was a maelstrom of magic and courage. It felt as if the very fabric of reality trembled as we faced the wizards on top a desolate mountaintop. Their power was vast, their spells like torrents of darkness crashing upon us, but united in purpose, us believers stood firm, wielding the ancient prayers that we had unearthed, but as the days went by the numbers of believers fell as many people were deceived by this Anti-Christ figure because of all of the so-called miracles that he presented to the world, and that wraps up what happened in year two of the tribulation.

"I'm sorry that all of that happened to y'all but I'm glad that a small few of you believers stood up for the truth in the mist of all of that craziness" I said as David finished telling me about what happened in year two of the tribulation. "we had to stand up even if it meant the end of our lives" David replied "So is that Anit-Christ figure still around now" I asked David "yes he is and you won't believe who he is" David said "Who is he" I replied "he is and yes like you may have thought the King of America" David said "but how when the Anti-Christ guy was introduced in year 2" I replied "Because when the Anit-Christ guy as they called him arrived with the evil wizards he always wore a mask to hide his identity at first but then in year five he revealed himself and everybody in the world knew who he truly was" David explained "oh ok that makes since now" I replied back. "Yep, and I will fully tell you about year five another time but for now let's go to the park and address the rest of the believers" David said as the night grew darker and as time passed David did address the believers by informing them about the last plague of the Skin boils and then after he was done we went back to his apartment for the night, then David began to speak "the world will truly never forget the last few days" David said "that's the plan" I replied "but you got to know that with these plagues getting worse you are making a lot of enemies just like China and Italy" David said "I know but I also know that I will be fine" I replied and then after we went our separate ways and went to sleep for the night.

(The Russian Spies)

The next day I woke up to the sound of David's voice again "Elijah wake up quick there is now an issue in Russia and it must be stopped" David said to me "Ok when should I leave" I replied "right now and this time I'm coming with you and the New Goshen jet is waiting for us in Coney Island already" David Replied as we left his apartment, and minutes later we were boarding the New Goshen Jet "Where to now" said Jordan "We have to go to Russia to solve a issue over there" said David "ok no problem" said Jordan and then the New Goshen Jet took off into the sky, then after some hours flew by we were in Russia then Jordan found a safe place to land, and then me and David got out of the jet "I will pick you two up from this exact spot when y'all are ready" said Jordan, then the New Goshen Jet took off into the sky and Me and David were now in Russia.

So, as we stood on top of a Russian mountaintop, with the wind howling around us, I could feel the weight of history changing again. I was called upon once again to face a new challenge and this time by my side stood David, eager to prove his worth in the battlefield, and in the distance, we spotted a group of mysterious figures clad in dark attire, speaking in hushed tones. Russian spies I thought, as I could sense their intentions through the spiritual wisdom bestowed upon me. David and I exchanged a knowing look, acknowledging that we must act swiftly to protect our people from potential harm. "David," I said, "Stay close and follow my lead. This enemy is not to be underestimated, but with the Almighty's guidance, we shall prevail", then with hearts ablaze, we moved stealthily towards the spies, concealing ourselves amidst the rocky terrain. Using the cover of nightfall, we closed in on them, their conversation growing louder as we approached. "Ivan," one of the spies said, "We must gather the information quickly and transmit it back to our superiors. This place holds secrets that could change the course of history."

I felt a sudden surge of righteous anger within me. How dare they desecrate this sacred land with their sinister plans! I raised my hands to the heavens, calling upon the power of the Almighty, and a fierce storm began to brew above us. Thunder roared, and lightning danced across the sky. "What is this sorcery?" one of the spies exclaimed, fear evident in his voice.

"We are not ordinary men," David declared, his voice firm and resolute. "We are chosen by The Most High to protect our people and safeguard His divine will," and with a flash of divine intervention, the storm unleashed its fury upon the spies, disorienting them. David and I advanced with unwavering determination. With his mighty sling, David took aim and struck down two of the spies, and their dark intentions.

So as the remaining spies scrambled for cover, I confronted them with my prophetic wisdom. "Your treacherous plans end here so repent and turn from your wicked ways, and perhaps the Almighty will show mercy," then one of the spies, trembling with fear, dropped his weapon and raised his hands in surrender. "We never meant to bring harm to your people," he confessed. "We were misled by greed and power." Then David and I exchanged glances once more, recognizing the potential for redemption in this man's heart. "If you seek forgiveness and truth," I said, "you must reveal the full extent of your mission and any other plots against our land." So through tearful eyes, the spy divulged their nefarious intentions and pledged to abandon their wicked ways. And David and I knew that the battle was not only physical but also spiritual, and that the seeds of righteousness we sowed in this encounter could bear fruit for generations to come.

So together, we escorted the reformed spy back to our people, where he shared his newfound convictions, leading to the dismantling of the spy network. The land once again stood protected, and the Almighty's presence was felt strongly among us. Then in the days that followed, David and I continued our journey, knowing that our partnership was destined to bring about peace and prosperity for our people. So we emerged from that battle with a bond forged in fire, and as we walked side by side, we were guided by the eternal wisdom that transcends time and boundaries, uniting us as one, then suddenly as the storm raged above us, the Russian spies came back but they struggled to regain their footing, and their technology rendered useless against the divine forces we commanded. David and I moved with grace and precision, making our way through the chaos with an otherworldly calmness, and the remaining spies had their faces masked by fear and desperation, exchanged frantic glances, so as we were unsure of how to confront adversaries imbued with such power, I approached them slowly, the weight of my responsibility as a prophet heavy upon me, but also knowing that this moment demanded both strength and compassion.

"Tell us why you have come to this sacred place," I demanded, my voice carrying an authority that seemed to echo across the mountainside. "We were sent here by our superiors," one of the spies stammered, "to uncover ancient artifacts that could grant immense power. We were promised riches and influence beyond our wildest dreams," Then David stepped forward ready, but his eyes softened with a glimmer of understanding. "You were deceived by false promises," he said, "but there is still hope for redemption. You can choose a different path, one that leads to righteousness and truth." Then the spies hesitated, torn between the allure of their former ambitions and the opportunity for a new beginning. So as the storm grew above us, the lightning retreating to the horizon, as if nature itself were awaiting their decision, and with tears in his eyes, the spy who had spoken before dropped to his knees. "Forgive us," he pleaded, "we have lost our way and brought harm to this sacred land. We are willing to cooperate fully and make amends."

Then David started, recognizing the sincerity in the man's words. "Your repentance will not go unnoticed," he said, "but you must reveal all that you know about your organization and their plans. Only then can we truly ensure the safety of our people." Then the spy revealed everything he knew, providing vital information that exposed the depth of the spy network's infiltration. With newfound determination, he pledged to assist David and me in dismantling the operation from within, so we returned to our people, and the former spy became an integral part of our efforts to safeguard our land, and together, we uncovered hidden plots and prevented further harm, all the while teaching the man the ways of righteousness and the path of the Almighty.

And as time passed, the former spy's heart transformed, and he became a devoted protector of the land and its people. He was welcomed into the community, and his past forgiven, and his redemption celebrated, and the bond between David and me grew stronger with each victory against the forces of darkness passing by, and our partnership became a symbol of unity and courage, inspiring our people to stand firm in the face of adversity, and in the days that followed, the Russian land of the believers prospered, and the tale of our battle with the Russian spies became a legend, and a testament to the power of forgiveness and the triumph of good over evil.

So as the storm subsided, leaving behind a breathless silence, and the former spy, whom we now knew as Ivan, looked upon the aftermath of our divine intervention with awe. His eyes widened as he beheld the power of the Almighty, and a newfound reverence filled his heart. "I have never seen anything like this," Ivan whispered, his voice barely audible. "Your God is truly mighty and just." So I laid a reassuring hand on his shoulder, "Indeed, He is. The Almighty is not a force to be trifled with, but rather a loving and guiding presence for those who seek truth and righteousness." Then David smiled, extending a hand of friendship to Ivan. "Your past does not define your future," he said warmly. "You have chosen to embrace the path of redemption, and that is a testament to your inner strength."

So as we returned to our camp, Ivan shared more about the origins of the spy network and the sinister plots they had intended to carry out. The scope of their operations was far-reaching, targeting not just the believers in Russia but many others as well. Our hearts swelled with gratitude for the opportunity to dismantle such an evil force.

Then over the weeks that followed, Ivan proved himself to be an invaluable ally. With his knowledge of the spy network's inner workings, we strategized and countered their advances, foiling their plans at every turn. He was a man transformed, driven by a newfound purpose to atone for his past deeds. Then one evening, as we sat around the campfire, Ivan spoke of his life before becoming a spy. He had been a humble scholar, passionate about history and culture, seeking to uncover the mysteries of the ancient world. But he had fallen into the clutches of greed and ambition, blinded by the promise of power and wealth. "My hunger for knowledge turned into an insatiable thirst for more," Ivan confessed. "I became blind to the consequences of my actions, convinced that the end justified the means. "so I empathized with his struggle, knowing all too well how even the noblest pursuits could be tainted by selfish desires. "We all stumble on our journey," I said, "but the true measure of a person lies in their willingness to change and seek redemption."

So as the bond between David, Ivan, and me deepened, rumors of our triumphs against the spies spread far and wide. People came from distant lands, seeking guidance and protection. Our unity had become a beacon of hope in a troubled world, inspiring others to rise against the darkness that sought to engulf them, and in the midst of battles and strategic planning, David and I found moments of solace. And we would climb the same mountaintop where we had encountered the spies, gazing at the vast expanse before us, and reflect on the journey that had brought us together." We are bound by more than destiny," David said one evening, and his eyes fixed on the horizon. "Our hearts beat as one, guided by a higher purpose." And I nodded, feeling the same connection. "The Almighty's plan is often beyond our comprehension," I replied. "But it is evident that He has intertwined our paths for a reason."

So as we stood shoulder to shoulder, the weight of the world on our shoulders, we knew that our journey was far from over. The battle against the spies was just one chapter in the epic tale of our lives, and we were ready to face whatever challenges lay ahead, and so, me and David continued, our alliance with the reformed spy, Ivan, an embodiment of redemption and hope, and together, we forged a legacy that would echo through eternity, and a testament to the resilience of the human spirit and the power of righteousness to conquer even the darkest of forces.

Then as the days passed, a new group of Russian spies emerged, and our encounters with this new group of Russian spies became more frequent. They were determined to reclaim the lost ground, and their ranks seemed to multiply with each passing night. So our battles with them became more intense, testing our strength and resolve, And on one moonlit night, as David and I stood vigilant on a cliff's edge, we spotted a convoy of heavily armed spies approaching our camp of the believers, and their numbers were greater than anything we had faced before, and the ground beneath us trembled with the weight of their presence, "This won't be an easy fight," David said grimly, his grip tightening around his sword. "But we've faced worse odds in the past." And I nodded in agreeance and steeling my heart for the battle ahead. "The Almighty has not brought us this far to abandon us now. We will stand firm and protect our people."

So as the spies drew closer, we devised a plan. David would lead a small group of warriors in a frontal assault, drawing the attention of the majority of the spies, while I would take a select few on a flanking maneuver, so with a battle cry that echoed through the night, David charged forward, his bravery inspiring those around him, and the spies, taken by surprise, scrambled to defend themselves against him. As, David led his small group of warriors silently through the shadows, seeking to neutralize the spies' communication and support systems. And with divine guidance, we managed to disable their technology and sabotage their vehicles, plunging their ranks into chaos, But the Russian spies were skilled adversaries, and they regrouped quickly. And as I stood amidst the tumult of battle, the weight of my prophetic duties felt heavier than ever. With prayers on my lips, I called upon the Almighty for strength and wisdom.

Then the night erupted in a clash of swords and gunfire. And I could see David's mightiness in action and felling spies with remarkable precision. Yet, the sheer number of enemies threatened to overwhelm us. So, in the heat of battle, I caught sight of Ivan, our reformed ally, engaged in combat with an old comrade. Their eyes met for a brief moment, and Ivan hesitated. The conflict within him was evident, torn between his past loyalties and newfound principles, But Ivan's heart had changed, and he chose righteousness over darkness. With a swift move, he disarmed his former ally and extended a hand in forgiveness. "Join us in our fight for good," he implored. "There is still a chance for redemption." and to my surprise, the former spy hesitated for a moment, then dropped his weapon and took Ivan's hand. Then the act of mercy had touched his soul, and he chose a new path. He was inspired by Ivan's actions, so other spies began to waver, questioning their allegiance to the malevolent cause. One by one, they laid down their arms and surrendered and the battle had turned, not just in terms of the physical clash, but also in the realm of hearts and minds, and with the tides turned, the remaining spies retreated, leaving the battlefield strewn with the remnants of their defeat. We had prevailed once more, not just in terms of military might, but in our ability to inspire change and show compassion.

So in the aftermath of the battle, we gathered the surrendered spies, granting them a chance to mend their ways and embrace on a new life. And they would be under close watch, of course, but we recognized that the seeds of goodness we had planted might yet blossom, And so, the encounters with the Russian spies continued, but our alliance with Ivan proved to be an unexpected turning point. We faced each new challenge with the knowledge that righteousness, forgiveness, and the power of the Almighty could overcome even the most formidable foes. Our bond as a trio, united by destiny, grew stronger with each passing day, proving that sometimes, the most unexpected allies could bring about the greatest victories.

Then something unexpected happened when we saw a even newer group of Russian spies "how many spies do they have" said David "there's no telling and now it appears that the Russian military is now involved" I replied then as the intensity of our battles with the Russian spies escalated, we found ourselves facing an even greater challenge when the Russian military had taken notice of their fallen comrades and the repeated setbacks, and they were determined to crush the resistance that dared to defy them, So the word had reached the highest echelons of their command, and a battalion of well-trained soldiers was dispatched to reinforce the Russian spies. Their arrival brought a chilling coldness to the air, as if the very elements were bearing witness to the clash of two formidable forces.

"We have a new enemy on the horizon," David said, his gaze fixed on the approaching army. "Their numbers are vast, and their determination unmatched." And I nodded, my heart heavy with the burden of the task ahead. "but this is a test of our resilience and unwavering faith," I replied. "But we must stand strong and united, for the Almighty is with us." Then with the Russian spies bolstered by the military's presence, The believers camp became the target of relentless attacks. The night sky was painted with the fiery trails of rockets and the sound of explosions echoed through the mountains, but David led our people with unparalleled bravery, rallying them to defend their homes and families, and together, we devised new strategies to counter the combined might of the spies and the military. It was a dance of life and death, and every move held the fate of our people in the balance.

But amidst the chaos, Ivan proved to be a valuable asset. His knowledge of the spies' tactics and military maneuvers allowed us to anticipate their actions, giving us precious moments to prepare our defense, so as the battle raged on, I stood at the heart of the conflict, calling upon the Almighty for divine protection and guidance. The storm that had once aided us in battle now served as a shield against the enemy's attacks, deflecting bullets and their advances, But the odds were against us, and casualties mounted on both sides. And we faced the harsh reality of war, witnessing the loss of beloved friends and fellow warriors, and each life taken weighed heavily on our hearts, and yet, we knew that our cause was just and worthy.

Then in a moment of desperation, the Russian military launched a full-scale assault, attempting to overpower our defenses guarding the district of believers in Russia, and the ground shook beneath us as tanks rolled forward, their cannons primed for destruction, but David and I rallied our troops, urging them to hold their ground, But just as the tide seemed to be turning against us, an unexpected alliance emerged from the shadows. A faction of the Russian military, disillusioned by the cruelty of their superiors, chose to defy orders and stand with us, and their leader, Captain Alexei, approached us with a sense of determination and regret in his eyes. "We cannot bear the burden of our actions any longer," he confessed. "We see the righteousness in your cause and the cruelty in our commanders' hearts." Then David extended a hand of friendship to Captain Alexei, "Your bravery in defying your superiors speaks volumes of your character so together, we can create a new path, one that leads to peace and understanding."

So now with Captain Alexei's unexpected defection, the dynamics of the battle shifted once more. And the ranks of the Russian military fractured, and some even turned against their former comrades, and in a moment of unity, we joined forces with the renegade faction, showing them the mercy and compassion that had led Ivan to his redemption and through our actions, we revealed the transformative power of righteousness and forgiveness, planting seeds of hope in the hearts of those who had been blinded by the allure of power, and with the ranks of the Russian military divided, the remaining spies and soldiers found themselves at a disadvantage so they retreated in disarray and their sinister alliance was broken. And as the dust settled, the Russian military faction that had chosen the path of righteousness pledged their loyalty to our cause and they vowed to protect our people in the district of believers in Russia and fight for justice and peace.

Then in the aftermath of the battle, we mourned the fallen but celebrated the newfound allies who had defected from the Russian military. Their act of courage and conscience had changed the course of the war, and our alliance grew stronger with each passing day, And so, me and David continued, with Russian spies and their divided military adding unexpected twists to the epic saga, but through it all, we learned that even in the darkest of times, goodness and the power of redemption could shine through, forging alliances and inspiring change that would echo through the annals of history.

But then another challenge approached, when the impact of the battle reverberated far beyond the boundaries of the opposing forces. News of the resistance and the Russian military's division reached the ears of ordinary Russian citizens, and their hearts were stirred by the call of duty and the allure of a cause greater than themselves, when Amidst the Russian spies and the loyal military, a group of passionate citizens emerged, fueled by a sense of national pride and duty to protect their homeland. They saw the resistance as a threat to the stability of their country, and their desire to quell dissent led them to join the ranks of the spies and the military, so these certain citizens, united by a misguided sense of loyalty, and added yet another layer of complexity to the battle. Because they were civilians turned soldiers, motivated by a fervent belief in the righteousness of their actions with weapons in their hands, they joined the Russian spies and the military, ready to defend what they perceived as their nation's honor.

But in the midst of the turmoil, David and I found ourselves facing an enemy that included not just trained spies and soldiers but also civilians who were caught in the midst of a conflict they did not fully understand, and we were challenged to see beyond the face of the enemy, to discern the humanity beneath the hardened exteriors, so as we engaged in skirmishes, we found ourselves confronting these citizen-soldiers, who fought with a zeal that could only come from a deep sense of duty, and their hearts were heavy with conviction, and we knew that simply defeating them on the battlefield would not address the root cause of their allegiance.

So in the heat of one particularly intense confrontation, I stood face to face with a young Russian citizen turned soldier and his eyes were filled with a mixture of determination and fear, a reflection of the inner struggle he must have faced to reach this point. "Why are you fighting against us?" I asked, hoping to connect with the human beneath the uniform and he hesitated for a moment before answering, "I fight because I believe in the strength and unity of my nation I fight for what I believe is right." The Russian citizen-soldier said, then David stepped forward, with his gaze unwavering. "We too fight for what we believe is right," he replied.

"But the path to righteousness must be paved with compassion and understanding." So I reached out my hand in a gesture of peace. "Join us in seeking a resolution that benefits us all because the Almighty's path is one of mercy and justice, and we can still find a way to coexist without further bloodshed." Then to our surprise, the young soldier hesitated, his grip on his weapon loosening. "I never thought it would come to this," he admitted, tears glistening in his eyes. "I wanted to protect my homeland, but I did not expect to face such a dire situation."

Then with compassion in our hearts, we continued to speak with him, bridging the gap between adversaries with words of understanding and empathy. Slowly, the young soldier's defenses softened, and he lowered his weapon. "I never imagined I would find myself in this position," he confessed. "I thought I was doing what was best for my country, but now I see the consequences of my actions." And with an act of compassion, we embraced the young soldier, offering him a chance to find a different path. He chose to lay down his arms, and we welcomed him into our camp as a symbol of hope and transformation.

Then in the days that followed, more citizens joined our ranks, drawn by the promise of redemption and the chance to contribute to a noble cause. Their presence brought a new dimension to our alliance, reminding us that even amid conflict, there was still room for compassion and understanding, then as the battle continued, the lines between friend and foe blurred. The once distinct divisions between Russian spies, the military, and the citizens faded, replaced by a collective desire for peace and unity. Our fight became a beacon of hope, inspiring people from all walks of life to stand together against the forces of darkness and me and David's mission in Russia was now really complete and then we headed back to that Russian mountaintop that Jordan dropped us off at.

(The Flesh Eating Virus)

"David it is time to visit the King of America once again" I told David "Ok so let me call Jordan so he can pick us up" David replied and then after his reply minutes later the New Goshen jet appeared and landed so me and David boarded the jet "We need to go back to New York and plead with the King" David said "ok no problem" Jordan said, then the New Goshen Jet took off into the sky leaving Russia. Then after hours flew by, we were in New York landing in Coney Island, then me and David got off the Jet "see you two on the run" said Jordan and then the New Gosen Jet took off into the sky. "Now let's go to The Kings Tower yet again" I said so we did and after some minutes flew by, we arrived at the Kings tower, then we went through the same usual procedures again and at the end of them the King refused to let my people go once more. So, me and David left the Kings tower after the King denied my request again then after some minutes flew by we made our way back to the district of believers, then we approached David's apartment so we got out of Davids car and started walking towards his apartment "wait before we go inside because I must start the next plague now" I said to David as I lifted my staff then immediately I began to have another insightful vision.

So as my insightful vision began I saw a dormant nightmare, waiting to be unleashed upon its unsuspecting inhabitants. A new virus, once sealed away in the depths of a secretive laboratory, found its way into the hands of a clandestine organization. Intent on wielding the power of the virus for their own nefarious purposes, they inadvertently set in motion an apocalyptic event that would plunge the city into chaos. The virus, known as the "Veil of Desolation," was unlike anything the world had ever seen. Its origins traced back to a remote corner of the Amazon rainforest, where it had silently coexisted with nature for centuries. Ancient tribes revered it as a curse from the spirits, a plague capable of devouring the flesh and soul of its victims. Little did they know that this curse would one day find its way to the concrete jungle of New York. Then the Veil of Desolation was cunning and insidious. It spread through various vectors—airborne, waterborne, and even through contact with contaminated surfaces. The first few cases went unnoticed, mistaken for common illnesses. But as the virus's potency increased, the city descended into anarchy. News outlets tried to quell the panic, but misinformation spread like wildfire, fueling fear and mistrust. Authorities scrambled to contain the outbreak, but the virus was always one step ahead. Hospitals overflowed with victims, desperate for treatment. Quarantine zones were established, but the Veil of Desolation found its way beyond the barriers.

People barricaded themselves in their homes, hoping to avoid the clutches of the flesh-eating virus. Society fractured as distrust grew between neighbors and friends. In a city known for its relentless spirit, despair seemed to take over, then ordinary citizens trying to survive in this dystopian landscape. Families sought refuge in abandoned buildings, forming makeshift communities to protect one another. Others became nomads, traveling through the wreckage of a once-thriving metropolis, looking for any signs of salvation. Amidst the devastation, hope flickered like a dying ember. Scientists, driven by a sense of duty and curiosity, relentlessly pursued a cure. Working day and night in makeshift laboratories, they faced the terror head-on, risking their lives for a chance to save humanity but, even the scientist met their demise from the flesh eating virus and as this outbreak continued on millions of people around the world were killed by the flesh eating virus and as I looked over New York City thousands of people's skin was just falling off of their bodies it looked as if their skin was just melting off of their bones, then after days went by the tide turned. The Veil of Desolation began to wane and hope once again breathed life into the city. As the sun rose over the reclaimed sandy streets

"The world just went through hell these last few days but I bet that the Kings of the earth are pissed that none of the district of believers were harmed by the flesh eating plague" David said "Yea and hopefully they will understand that they must let the believers go now but only time will tell" I replied as me and David sipped some coffee "well in the meantime let me tell you about year 3 of the tribulation" David said and then he began telling his story.

After year 1 and 2 I didn't think it could get much worse but, then news of population control acts reached us from every corner of the globe and the governments of the world decided to enforce these population control acts as a desperate measure to combat overpopulation and its consequences, but fear and uncertainty spread like wildfire through the city as people tried to make sense of the new restrictions placed on them, and in the beginning, life in New York City was a chaotic whirlwind and public services were overwhelmed, and tensions ran high. Families were divided, and friends separated by quotas and regulations. It seemed like a dystopian nightmare had become a reality, then as weeks passed, I watched the city evolve and the once crowded streets grew eerily empty. And those who remained faced challenging choices about their future. And amidst the turmoil, I found solace in a community of like-minded individuals who banded together to face the new challenges head-on so we formed a support network, sharing resources, skills, and knowledge to navigate the changed world.

Then that's when I met Ashley, a kind-hearted woman who had lost her family to the population control acts. Her story touched my heart, and we became each other's pillars of strength. Together, we pledged to create a world that valued unity and compassion over division and fear. In our quest to make a difference, we discovered an underground movement fighting for a more humane approach to population control. They believed in empowering people with education and resources rather than enforcing draconian measures. As the movement gained momentum, we realized the power of unity and collective action. Through protests, advocacy, and the support of some courageous politicians, we managed to bring attention to the plight of those affected by the population control acts but still the governments of the world decided to enforce these acts as a desperate measure to combat overpopulation and its consequences. friends separated by quotas and regulations. It seemed like a dystopian nightmare had become a reality.

Then as weeks passed, I watched the city evolve. The once crowded streets grew eerily empty as some citizens left in search of new opportunities and freedom from these acts, but their was nowhere to run because these new population acts were global. Then Ashley and I got married, and together we founded a nonprofit organization dedicated to promoting education and sustainable living. We traveled the world, sharing our story and collaborating with other change-makers to create lasting impact. Then things turned for the worse when the governments of the world decided to enforce these acts as a desperate measure to combat overpopulation and its consequences once more. Fear and uncertainty continued to spread like wildfire, not only in New York City but also in other major cities around the world, and In Europe, the policies led to heated debates and protests across capitals. Some countries opted for voluntary family planning programs, while others implemented strict birth control measures. Families were faced with difficult decisions, and migration patterns shifted as people sought refuge in more lenient regions.

And meanwhile in Asia, the population control acts had varying impacts. China, having previously enforced the one-child policy, modified its approach to encourage smaller families voluntarily. In India, education and empowerment initiatives were prioritized, ensuring women had more say in family planning decisions. And Africa faced unique challenges, as different countries grappled with diverse cultural norms and resource constraints. Some nations embraced community-based solutions, emphasizing sustainable development and women's empowerment. Others faced resistance due to concerns about cultural imposition. And in South America, the population control acts sparked debates about individual rights versus societal well-being. While some countries emphasized education and family planning services, others resorted to stricter measures, leading to unrest and migration towards more accommodating regions.

So Amidst this global upheaval, the New Dawn Collective's message resonated far beyond New York City. As stories of compassion and empathy spread, similar community-based movements began to emerge worldwide. People across continents were inspired to form support networks, recognizing the strength in unity. And the underground movement that Ashley and I had joined forces with became an international coalition. They worked with governments and organizations to promote sustainable development, equitable access to healthcare, and empowering women to make informed choices. And As the movement grew, so did its impact. Governments started to listen to their citizens' voices, realizing that top-down approaches weren't the solution. Instead, they embraced more holistic strategies, focusing on education, resource management, and socio-economic development, but still news of population control acts reached us from every corner of the globe.

The governments of the world decided to enforce these acts as a desperate measure to combat overpopulation and its consequences. So in secret, the movement that sought to challenge the population control acts with grew stronger. Our mission was to expose the flaws in the policies and advocate for more compassionate and sustainable alternatives. Together, we devised ways to raise awareness without attracting the authorities' attention. We used art, literature, and clandestine gatherings to share our message of hope and change. Our graffiti appeared on city walls, carrying messages of unity and freedom. Ashley, my steadfast companion, was the heart of our movement. Her unwavering determination and passion fueled our efforts. We knew we were taking a risk, but we couldn't bear to sit idle while our world descended into fear and control. So together, we devised ways to raise awareness without attracting the authorities' attention. We used art, literature, and clandestine gatherings to share our message of hope and change. Our graffiti appeared on city walls, carrying messages of unity and freedom. And Ashley, my steadfast companion

So as time went on our rebellion went beyond just defying the laws; we aimed to build a network of support for those affected. We established safe houses for families struggling under the burden of population control measures, providing them with resources and protection. As our movement grew, so did the risks. The authorities cracked down on dissenters, and the consequences for rebellion became more severe. But we couldn't back down; we had come too far to let fear silence our voices. In a daring act of defiance, we organized a large-scale protest in the heart of New York City. People from all walks of life, irrespective of nationality or background, joined our cause. We marched, chanted, and held up signs demanding a world where individual rights were respected, and families weren't torn apart. The authorities tried to disperse us, but our spirit was unbreakable. The world watched as the rebellion in New York City became a symbol of hope for those fighting for change in their own countries.

Our movement sparked conversations at an international level. It put pressure on governments to reconsider their approaches and engage in open dialogues with their citizens. While some resisted, others started to listen, realizing that unity and understanding were the keys to a sustainable future. Over time, our rebellion grew beyond New York City, spreading to other cities, countries, and continents. It became a global movement, challenging the status quo and advocating for a more humane and inclusive approach to population control. As we continued our stand, we faced hardships and sacrifices. Many of us were arrested and endured periods of imprisonment, but that only strengthened our resolve. Our commitment to building a world based on compassion and empowerment remained unwavering. In the face of adversity, the Harmony Foundation evolved into a formidable force for change. Working alongside governments, organizations, and communities, we sought to implement sustainable practices that uplifted people rather than oppressing them.

So Ashley and I had continued as two individuals rebelling against injustice, but our journey had inspired millions to join the fight for a brighter future. The Harmony Foundation became an institution, fostering change and supporting communities worldwide. Together, we devised ways to raise awareness without attracting the authorities' attention. We used art, literature, and clandestine gatherings to share our message of hope and change. Our graffiti appeared on city walls, carrying messages of unity and freedom. We knew we were taking a risk, but we still couldn't bear to sit idle while our world descended into fear and control. Our rebellion went beyond just defying the laws; we aimed to build a network of support for those affected. We established safe houses for families struggling under the burden of population control measures, providing them with resources and protection. As our movement grew, so did the risks. The authorities cracked down on dissenters, and the consequences for rebellion became more severe. But we still couldn't back down In a daring act of defiance, we organized a large-scale protest in the heart of New York City. People from all walks of life, irrespective of nationality or background, joined our cause. We marched, chanted, and held up signs demanding a world where individual rights were respected, and families weren't torn apart. The authorities tried to disperse us, but our spirit was unbreakable. The world watched as the rebellion in New York City became a symbol of hope for those fighting for change in their own countries.

Our movement sparked conversations at an international level. It put pressure on governments to reconsider their approaches and engage in open dialogues with their citizens. While some resisted, others started to listen, realizing that unity and understanding were the keys to a sustainable future. Over time, our rebellion grew beyond New York City, spreading to other cities, countries, and continents. It became a global movement, challenging the status quo and advocating for a more humane and inclusive approach to population control. As we continued our stand, we faced hardships and sacrifices. Many of us were arrested and endured periods of imprisonment, but that only strengthened our resolve. Our commitment to building a world based on compassion and empowerment remained unwavering. In the face of adversity, the Harmony Foundation evolved into a formidable force for change. Working alongside governments, organizations, and communities, we sought to implement sustainable practices that uplifted people rather than oppressing them.

Through perseverance and the support of millions, we achieved significant victories. Several countries revised their population control policies, embracing voluntary family planning, education, and women's empowerment. As the movement gained momentum, influential figures from various fields joined our cause. Celebrities, activists, and scientists amplified our message, using their platforms to advocate for a more compassionate world. Despite our progress, challenges remained. Some governments and factions continued to resist change, holding onto outdated ideologies. Yet, even in the face of resistance, we persisted, knowing that we were on the right side of history. With every step forward, we nurtured a generation that valued empathy, unity, and global cooperation. Schools around the world integrated lessons on sustainable living, cultural understanding, and the importance of respecting individual rights.

As the days passed, I watched the world transform before my eyes. The once-bleak future now held the promise of hope and harmony. It wasn't just a world without population control acts; it was a world where compassion and understanding were the driving forces behind every decision. New York City, once a symbol of chaos, emerged as a global capital of unity and innovation. The city's revitalization became a testament to the power of collaboration and the resilience of humanity. But The governments of the world Continued and decided to enforce these acts as a desperate measure to combat overpopulation and its consequences and as the impact of the population control acts began to unfold, even the Elders of New York found themselves directly affected. The respected leaders of the community faced challenging decisions about their families, traditions, and the future of the city they held dear.

I, along with the New Dawn Collective, learned that the Elders of New York were troubled by the division these acts caused within their families. The policies left them torn between their love for their children and their sense of duty to the greater good. It was in one of our clandestine gatherings that I met Elder Jameson, a wise and compassionate figure. He spoke of his sorrow over the measures that forced families to separate and how the population control acts threatened the very fabric of their community. Elder Jameson confided that the Elders of New York were grappling with a dilemma - to support the government's decisions in the hope of securing a better future for the next generations or to challenge the oppressive policies that tore families apart. In their wisdom, the Elders of New York recognized the importance of dialogue and unity. They called for a meeting between the government officials and representatives of the various communities to find a middle ground that would ensure a sustainable future without sacrificing family ties. As the New Dawn Collective, we joined forces with the Elders to mediate the discussions. Together, we worked towards a solution that emphasized compassion, education, and voluntary family planning over coercive measures.

Elder Jameson emphasized the importance of acknowledging cultural diversity in the decision-making process. He believed that policies that took into account the unique values and traditions of each community would be more readily accepted and respected. The government officials, initially resistant to any alterations in their policies, were swayed by the words of wisdom and empathy shared by the Elders. Slowly, the tone of the negotiations shifted, and the Elders' influence began to shape a more humane approach to population control. The New York City model became a beacon of hope for other cities around the world. Other Elders, inspired by the resolve of their counterparts in New York, began advocating for similar dialogues and open discussions with their governments.

Over time, the policies evolved to consider the insights and experiences of local communities. The harsh measures of population control gave way to a collaborative effort that prioritized education, access to healthcare, and sustainable practices. As the Elders of New York and the New Dawn Collective continued their collaboration, New York City transformed into a haven of harmony, embracing its cultural diversity while striving towards a sustainable future, then in a world gripped by environmental catastrophe and overpopulation, governments worldwide implemented desperate measures to regain control. The Population

Stabilization Act, a grim solution to an unsustainable crisis, came into effect, authorizing military forces to enforce strict population control. The elderly found themselves ensnared in a merciless web woven by a government that believed sacrifice was necessary for survival.

So As the sun cast a dim light over the city, elderly citizens became targets of a relentless operation. The military, armed with lists detailing age and medical conditions, conducted raids that sent shockwaves through communities. The first wave of detentions saw bewildered seniors seized from their homes and streets, their feeble protests falling on deaf ears. Resistance brewed in quiet corners, where whispers of rebellion spread among the youth who couldn't bear the thought of their elders suffering such a fate. Underground networks formed, exchanging information and strategies to evade the military sweeps. Yet, the government's grip tightened, and the elderly population dwindled. Elderly individuals were held in makeshift facilities, their once-timeworn faces now etched with fear and confusion. Attempts at resistance were met with cold brutality, and escape was nearly impossible. In these grim places, the elderly traded stories of their lives, their loves, and their experiences. Each story was a fragment of history that the world was slowly erasing.

News of the detentions reached the international community, sparking outrage and protests. Some countries condemned the actions, while others watched in silence, wary of similar measures being imposed on their own soil. Despite the global outcry, the government remained unyielding, resolute in its belief that drastic measures were needed to secure a future for the remaining population. Days turned into Months, and the once-vibrant elders languished in captivity. With the world's attention shifting to new crises, their plight slipped further into the shadows. Families mourned the loss of their loved ones, not only for the physical absence but also for the invaluable wisdom and stories that had been silenced.

As the sun set on the horizon, casting a somber glow across the now-empty city streets, the echoes of the past lingered like ghosts. The elderly who had once lived through decades of joy, pain, and change had become symbols of a world that had turned its back on its own history in the name of survival. And so, the story remained untold, buried beneath the weight of a dystopian reality where no heroes emerged, and no redemption was found. The Population Stabilization Act had achieved its grim purpose, leaving a scar on humanity's conscience that would never fully heal. Then after David finished telling me about year three of the tribulation the night grew darker and we rested for the night.

(The Magicians of Germany)

The next day I woke up to the sound of David's voice yet again "Elijah today there is another major issue happening in Germany" said David "what's happening" I replied "There is a group of some evil German magicians attacking the people in the District of believers in Germany and we need you to stop them ASAP but this mission may take a little while" David explained "ok that should not be a problem" I replied "great and the New Goshen Jet is already in Coney Island waiting on us" David said, and then the both of us left David's apartment and went to Coney Island. And after some minutes flew by, we were in Coney Island and I could see the New Goshen Jet waiting for me and David, so after some moments me and David got on the New Goshen Jet "What's up you two I heard that y'all are headed to Germany so lets go theres no time to waste" Jordan said while starting up the jet engines. So after some hours flew by the 3 of us arrived in Germany and Jordan found a safe place to land, so after the jet landed I stepped out of it but I noticed that David did not step out of the jet with me "David are you coming this time: I said "I can't on this one because I am needed again back in New Goshen but once this mission is complete we will meet back up in this same location" David explained, then moments later the New Goshen Jet was in the sky and I was in Germany.

So as the sun set over the horizon, I found myself standing atop the ancient Mount Carmel. And A powerful coven of dark magicians had risen in Germany, wielding forbidden arts that threatened to plunge the believers of the world into chaos. Guided by my divine mission, I set forth to confront these malevolent sorcerers and put an end to their nefarious schemes. Armed with the staff of my ancestors and the unwavering belief in the Lord's protection, I approached the entrance to the dark lair where the magicians were said to practice their wicked crafts. As I stepped inside, a chilling aura enveloped me, but I steeled myself against fear, knowing that my purpose was righteous.

The magicians, sensing my presence, emerged from the shadows with their sinister grins. They taunted me, casting spells and hurling dark energy in my direction. I called upon the Lord for strength and wisdom, feeling His divine power course through me. Bolts of lightning and fire

124

erupted from the tip of my staff, clashing with the dark spells unleashed by the magicians. The battleground trembled with the intensity of our battle, the echoes of ancient prophecies colliding with the forces of modern-day sorcery.

With every spell, I recited verses from the Scriptures, reminding the magicians of the consequences of their actions. Yet, they remained defiant, their hearts consumed by darkness. As the battle raged on, I could feel my energy waning, but I knew that I could not falter. I mustered the last of my strength and unleashed a blinding ray of light upon the dark coven, invoking the name of the Almighty.

The magicians were overwhelmed by the brilliance of the light, their malevolence crumbling under its divine power. One by one, they fell to their knees, surrendering to the might of the Almighty. With the dark coven defeated, I offered them a chance to repent and find redemption in the light of righteousness. Some heeded my words and chose a new path, forsaking their wicked ways. As I departed from the lair, I knew that my battle with the dark magicians of Germany was just one chapter in the ongoing struggle between good and evil. The world would continue to face challenges, but I was reassured that the Lord's guidance would be ever-present.

From that day on, I remained vigilant, knowing that my duty as a prophet was to stand against the forces of darkness, wherever they may arise. And so, my journey continued, as I embraced my role, ready to face whatever trials lay ahead. As word of my triumph over the dark magicians spread, I became a beacon of hope for those who sought protection from the malevolent forces that lurked in the shadows. People from all walks of life traveled to seek my counsel and aid, believing in the divine guidance that flowed through me.

Then One day, as I wandered through the bustling streets of Germany, a weary traveler approached me. His eyes held the weight of the world, and he spoke of a sinister sorcerer who terrorized a small village in the heart of Bavaria, Germany. The villagers' cries for help reached me, and I knew that I could not turn a blind eye to their suffering. With a heavy heart, I embarked on a new journey to confront the malevolent sorcerer. Guided by the Almighty's grace, I arrived in the quaint village nestled amid lush greenery and picturesque landscapes. But the air bore an oppressive aura, indicating the sorcerer's presence. The villagers huddled in fear as I made my way through the narrow streets. I assured them that the Lord's light would shield them from harm and pledged to put an end to the dark wizard's tyranny.

Reaching the heart of the village, I discovered an ancient castle, adorned with sinister symbols and dark magic. A chilling wind whispered tales of the sorcerer's heinous deeds, fueling my resolve to vanquish evil once more. As I stepped inside the castle, an eerie silence greeted me. My senses heightened, alert to the dangers that lay ahead. I ventured deeper into the labyrinthine corridors, my staff held firmly in my grasp. Soon, I encountered the sorcerer, a malevolent figure cloaked in darkness. He sneered at my presence, mocking the power of divine intervention. His spells were swift and powerful, aiming to overwhelm me with dark energy. But I stood firm, reciting verses from the Scriptures and invoking the Almighty's name. The staff crackled with holy energy, repelling the dark forces that assailed me. Our battle raged on for what felt like an eternity, the walls of the castle shaking with the magnitude of our powers clashing.

As the sun set and the moon rose, casting an ethereal glow over the castle, I felt the sorcerer's defenses weakening. His malevolence began to waver, and I seized the opportunity to extend an offer of redemption, imploring him to turn away from the darkness that consumed him. In that moment of vulnerability, I saw a flicker of remorse in the sorcerer's eyes. His heart torn between the path of evil and the glimmer of hope I offered. The Almighty's mercy knew no bounds, and with His guidance, the sorcerer chose to relinquish his dark arts, embracing a life of penance and redemption. With the sorcerer's dark reign over, the village rejoiced, and I returned to Germany, my faith in the Almighty's compassion reaffirmed. My journey continued, seeking out those who needed protection from the forces of darkness, offering hope and a path to righteousness for all who crossed my path.

And so, my the legacy, as the prophet of old, lived on through the months, as a symbol of unwavering faith and a beacon of hope against the darkness that forever sought to engulf the world. As my reputation as a champion against darkness grew, I received a summons from a mysterious order of magicians, known as the Guardians of Light. Intrigued by their request, I journeyed to a hidden sanctuary deep within the Bavarian forests.

The Guardians of Light were an ancient brotherhood dedicated to preserving the balance between light and darkness. They sought my counsel, as they were troubled by a rising threat that even their ancient powers could not fully comprehend. Dark forces of unknown origins were gathering, and the world stood on the precipice of a cataclysmic clash between good and evil.

Embracing my role as a chosen prophet, I joined forces with the Guardians to investigate the gathering darkness. Our journey took us to sacred sites across the globe, where ancient prophecies hinted at the impending doom. In the heart of Egypt, we deciphered hieroglyphs that foretold of a shadowy figure seeking to harness forbidden magic to plunge the world into eternal night. In the icy lands of Scandinavia, we encountered an ancient being who wielded elemental powers, threatening to unleash a devastating winter that would engulf the earth. As we delved deeper into the mysteries of the darkness, I began to experience vivid visions, granted by the Almighty Himself. These visions revealed fragments of a forgotten past, a time when dark magicians once tried to harness the power of the divine for selfish gains. The past and present intertwined as I realized that the rising darkness was a manifestation of an age-old struggle, a cycle of light and dark that transcended time itself. The forces that plagued the world now were descendants of ancient malevolence, seeking to reclaim power lost through centuries of banishment.

Armed with newfound knowledge, the Guardians and I stood united against the dark forces gathering strength. We strategized, honed our skills, and forged an unbreakable bond, ready to face whatever lay ahead. The final confrontation awaited us in a forgotten temple atop the Andes, where the shadows thickened, and the skies rumbled with dark energy. The malevolent beings we encountered were relentless, testing the limits of our endurance and faith. In the heart of the tempestuous battle, I remembered the teachings of my ancestors and the strength of the Almighty's love. With renewed conviction, I called upon the powers granted to me, combining ancient prophecies with the magic of the present age. Together, we unleashed a cascade of light, a brilliant display of divine intervention that pierced through the darkness. The malevolent beings howled in agony as they were vanquished, their dark powers shattered by the overwhelming force of righteousness.

With the darkness dispelled, a serene calm settled over the world. The Guardians of Light and I knew that our battle was not the end but a continuation of the eternal struggle between light and dark. As long as evil lurked in the hearts of men, our fight would persist, for darkness could never truly be eradicated, only kept at bay by the unwavering light of hope and faith. From that day forth, the bond between the Guardians and me remained unbreakable. We continued our vigil, standing as beacons against the encroaching darkness, offering hope and protection to all in need. And as the sun set on one chapter of our journey, we embraced the unknown future, knowing that the Almighty's guidance would forever light our path.

As news of the malevolent forces spreading across Germany reached the highest echelons of power, the German military took notice. Unbeknownst to the public, a specialized division within the military, known as the Occult Defense Unit (ODU), had long been keeping a watchful eye on supernatural activities. Recognizing the gravity of the situation, the ODU dispatched a team of elite soldiers to assist Elijah and the Guardians of Light in their battle against the dark magicians. Their mission was to provide tactical support and neutralize any potential mortal threats posed by the malevolent sorcerers. The alliance between the Guardians, the ODU, and me marked an unprecedented collaboration between the forces of light and the human world. The soldiers brought with them advanced weaponry and specialized training, complementing the Guardians' ancient powers and my divine guidance.

Together, we embarked on a series of covert operations, tracking down dark covens hidden within the depths of the Black Forest and the remote corners of the Bavarian Alps. With the ODU's expertise, we gained access to valuable intelligence, enabling us to plan our moves with precision and accuracy. However, as we delved deeper into the heart of darkness, we encountered formidable adversaries. Some dark magicians had formed unholy alliances with malevolent spirits, granting them enhanced powers that defied comprehension. The battles became more intense, with the ODU soldiers skillfully combining modern weaponry with the Guardians' age-old spells. The collaboration also led to cultural exchanges, as the ODU soldiers learned about ancient rites and rituals while the Guardians gained insights into modern warfare strategies. Bonds formed amidst the chaos, as soldiers found camaraderie with the supernatural beings they once considered mere legends.

In the midst of the struggle, we faced a moral dilemma when we discovered that not all dark magicians were inherently evil. Some had been misled and coerced into serving malevolent entities, while others were victims of ancient curses beyond their control. Our alliance became not just a fight against darkness but an opportunity for redemption. We sought to free those who could be salvaged from the clutches of evil, offering them a chance to atone for their past deeds. As our combined forces continued to thwart the malevolent forces, the world took notice of the unique alliance between the supernatural and the military. Governments from other nations approached us, seeking assistance in dealing with their own occult threats. Our actions transcended borders and ideologies, uniting the world against a common enemy. Nations set aside their differences and joined forces, acknowledging the need to protect humanity from the encroaching darkness. In the final confrontation, our alliance faced the most formidable dark magician yet. The battle tested our strength, both physical and spiritual, as the malevolent sorcerer unleashed ancient spells of unimaginable power. The fate of the world seemed uncertain as we fought against overwhelming odds. But it was in that moment of peril that the unity between the Guardians, the ODU, and me shone brightest. United in purpose and determination, we harnessed the power of ancient prophecy, modern military might, and divine intervention.

Through a combined effort of strategy, sacrifice, and unwavering faith, we emerged victorious. The darkness was vanquished, and the world breathed a collective sigh of relief, but As the collaboration between the Guardians of Light, the German military's Occult Defense Unit (ODU), and me continued, our efforts expanded beyond Germany's borders. Reports of supernatural threats emerged from different corners of the world, demanding our attention and expertise. The alliance became a well-coordinated international task force, pooling resources, knowledge, and skills to combat the rising tide of darkness. Governments from various nations acknowledged the expertise of the ODU and sought assistance in dealing with occult threats within their territories.

Teams of Guardians and ODU soldiers were dispatched to various trouble spots, where malevolent forces threatened innocent lives. Our joint missions took us to haunted castles in Transylvania, remote temples in Asia, and ancient ruins in South America. The German military's advanced technology and tactical prowess proved invaluable in facing enemies that transcended the bounds of conventional warfare. We faced entities from ancient mythologies and encountered creatures thought to exist only in folklore. In the heart of the Amazon rainforest, we confronted a powerful shaman who had turned to dark magic, seeking revenge against the modern world for the destruction of his ancestral lands. His mastery over the forces of nature proved a formidable challenge, but the ODU's cutting-edge equipment provided a much-needed advantage, allowing us to temporarily disrupt his magical abilities.

The Guardians' ancient wisdom also played a vital role. Drawing power from the land's spirits and channeling the Almighty's grace, we found a path to reason with the shaman. Our shared respect for the earth's harmony ultimately led him to abandon his malevolent quest, choosing instead to embrace a life of healing and preservation. As our missions continued, we discovered that certain occult threats had been unleashed through the exploitation of ancient relics. A race to secure these artifacts ensued, as dark organizations sought to harness their power for nefarious purposes. The ODU's intelligence and expertise in covert operations proved critical in locating and securing these artifacts. The Guardians used their connection to the divine to shield the relics from falling into the wrong hands. One such relic, hidden within the depths of a Himalayan monastery, held the power to manipulate time itself. As we journeyed to secure it, we faced a powerful cult of dark magicians, sworn to protect the artifact at any cost. In a climactic battle, the ODU soldiers fought fiercely, employing a combination of modern weaponry and tactics. Meanwhile, the Guardians channeled ancient spells, forming a protective barrier that repelled the dark magicians' malevolent energy.

United in our purpose, we overcame the cult's defenses, securing the artifact and preventing its misuse. In a moment of triumph, the alliance's bonds strengthened, and our commitment to safeguarding humanity deepened. As the the months passed, the alliance between the Guardians of Light and the ODU continued to be a beacon of hope in the face of darkness. Nations across the globe recognized the need for collaboration and established their own defense units to confront supernatural threats. Our combined efforts ensured that malevolent forces remained contained, their influence weakened by the unity and resolve of the international task force. We couldn't eliminate all darkness, for it was a part of the world's balance, but we managed to tip the scales in favor of light and protect the innocent from harm. As the supernatural threats escalated, some brave German believers began to step forward, offering their support in the battle against darkness. Drawn by stories of the alliance between the Guardians of Light, the German military's Occult Defense Unit (ODU), and me, these individuals sought to play their part in protecting their homeland and the world. Among them was Anna, a young archaeologist with a deep fascination for ancient artifacts and folklore. Her expertise in deciphering cryptic symbols and ancient languages proved invaluable in uncovering the origins and weaknesses of the malevolent forces we faced. Max, a former special forces soldier, felt compelled to join the fight after witnessing the devastation caused by dark magic firsthand. His military training and combat experience made him a valuable addition to our task force, and his strategic mind helped us plan our missions with precision.

Alongside Anna and Max, a diverse group of German believers with unique skills and talents came forward. Among them were historians, scholars, engineers, and even artists who believed that their contributions could make a difference in the battle against darkness. As more citizens joined our cause, our alliance expanded into a formidable force. We formed a network of individuals, each committed to safeguarding humanity from the malevolent entities that lurked in the shadows. In a remote village in the heart of the Black Forest, we encountered a particularly sinister coven of dark witches. Their powerful spells had ensnared the villagers, causing illness and despair. Anna's understanding of ancient rituals and symbols helped us identify the source of their power, and together, we devised a plan to break their enchantments.

Max led a team of ODU soldiers, working in tandem with the Guardians and the believer volunteers. With swift and stealthy maneuvers, they neutralized the coven's guards, allowing us to confront the dark witches at the heart of their lair. As we faced the coven's leader, a chilling aura of malevolence surrounded her. But our unity remained unshaken, our resolve unwavering. Anna's knowledge of ancient counter-spells allowed us to disrupt the dark witches' ritual, weakening their powers. In a climactic battle, we unleashed a coordinated assault. The ODU soldiers provided cover while the Guardians channeled their divine energy, and the citizen volunteers assisted in protecting the villagers who had fallen victim to the witches' dark magic. With each passing moment, the coven's influence waned, and their hold over the villagers loosened. One by one, the citizens regained their senses, liberated from the witches' enchantments.

In a final surge of divine power, the Guardians incapacitated the dark witches, leaving them vulnerable to justice. Instead of resorting to violence, we offered them a chance at redemption, hoping that they, too, could be guided back to the path of light. From that day on, the citizens who had joined our cause became a permanent part of our alliance. Their diverse skills and unwavering determination added a new dimension to our fight against darkness. Max and his fellow soldiers forged strong bonds with the citizen volunteers, fostering a sense of camaraderie that transcended the boundaries of their individual roles.

As we continued to face supernatural threats around the world, the involvement of ordinary citizens became an inspiration to others. Reports of similar alliances forming in different nations began to emerge, a testament to the power of unity and the belief in the greater good.

Our alliance became a symbol of hope, a beacon of light in a world grappling with darkness. The combined efforts of the Guardians, the ODU, and the citizen volunteers showcased the strength that could be found when individuals came together to protect humanity from malevolent forces.And so, the legend of Elijah, the Guardians of Light, the German military's Occult Defense Unit, and the citizen volunteers grew, etched into the annals of history as a testament to the extraordinary power that could be unleashed when ordinary people united to stand against the encroaching darkness. As time continued to pass, the alliance between the Guardians of Light, the German military's Occult Defense Unit (ODU), and the citizen volunteers grew stronger. Together, we faced countless supernatural threats, leaving an indelible mark on the world's history.

Our task force expanded its reach, forging connections with other nations and cultures. We exchanged knowledge and expertise, learning from each other's traditions and fighting styles. The bonds of friendship and mutual respect that formed between our diverse group of allies became a testament to the power of unity in the face of adversity. As the world witnessed the tangible impact of our efforts, ordinary citizens across the globe found inspiration in our alliance. Reports of people banding together to face supernatural threats began to emerge from various corners of the world, creating a global network of defenders dedicated to preserving the balance between light and darkness. Anna, Max, and other German believers who had joined our cause became influential figures in their own right. Anna's research on ancient artifacts and folklore led to groundbreaking discoveries, shedding light on hidden aspects of history. Max's strategic mind and military experience inspired new generations of soldiers, instilling in them a sense of duty and dedication to protect the innocent. The alliance continued to grow, attracting beings from various mythologies and supernatural backgrounds. Creatures once considered adversaries found a new purpose in protecting humanity, realizing that their destinies were intertwined with the world they inhabited.   The news of our alliance reached the highest ranks of governments and supernatural councils alike. World leaders recognized the significance of our efforts and offered support, establishing global treaties and accords to unite nations against common supernatural threats. As the balance shifted, the darkness fought back with renewed vigor. The malevolent entities sought to break our unity, to exploit the chinks in our armor. They targeted the hearts and minds of our allies, sowing seeds of doubt and discord. But our alliance proved stronger than any individual, as the power of unity transcended the boundaries of myth and reality. Through perseverance and unwavering faith, we weathered every storm, standing firm against the onslaught of darkness.

Our final confrontation came in the form of a dark sorcerer who had amassed an army of malevolent spirits. He sought to open a gateway to a realm of unfathomable darkness, unleashing chaos upon the world. The stakes were higher than ever before, and the fate of humanity hung in the balance. In a climactic battle, the full force of our alliance was unleashed. The Guardians' divine energy clashed with the ODU's advanced technology, while the citizen volunteers drew upon their individual skills, each playing a crucial role in the fight.

Anna's knowledge of ancient rituals provided the key to sealing the gateway, while Max's tactical brilliance allowed us to outmaneuver the sorcerer's forces. The citizens' unwavering determination inspired us all, bolstering our resolve to protect the world from the impending cataclysm. In a final, desperate surge of power, we sealed the gateway, banishing the dark sorcerer and his malevolent army back to the shadows. The world was saved, and the balance between light and darkness was restored. Our alliance became the stuff of legends, with tales of our exploits echoing through time. The story of Elijah, the Guardians of Light, the German military's Occult Defense Unit, and the citizen volunteers spread across cultures and generations, a symbol of hope and unity in the face of darkness.

In the years that followed, the alliance remained vigilant, knowing that the battle against darkness was an eternal one. New generations took up the mantle, carrying on the legacy of our alliance, and continuing to protect the world from supernatural threats. And so, the story of our alliance lived on, a reminder that no darkness was too great to be overcome by the brilliance of light and the power of unity. As long as there were those willing to stand together, ready to face the shadows that sought to engulf the world, the balance between light and darkness would endure and my mission in Germany was now complete.

(The Great Pestilence)

"David it is time to visit the King of America yet again" I told David as soon as he came with Jordan to pick me up in the New Goshen Jet, and then minutes later the New Goshen Jet took off into the sky leaving Germany. Then after hours flew by, we were in New York landing in Coney Island, then me and David got off the Jet "see you two on the next adventure" said Jordan and then the New Goshen Jet took off into the sky. "Now let's go to The Kings Tower yet again" I said so we did and after some minutes flew by, we arrived at the Kings tower, then we went through the same usual procedures as always and once we finally spoke to the King he refused to let my people go once more. So, me and David left the Kings tower after the King denied my request again then after some minutes flew by we made our way back to the district of believers. "I must not hesitate and start the next plague now" I said to David as we approached his apartment, then I lifted my staff then immediately I began to have another insightful vision.

Then as I looked over New York I saw a great pestilence descended upon the city, spreading like wildfire, and soon, its insidious grasp reached even the most fundamental aspect of survival - the food supply. At first, the people of New York didn't comprehend the magnitude of the threat. Reports of a mysterious sickness circulated, but complacency lingered, as they had weathered storms before. However, the plague proved different, and its effects soon became glaringly evident in the city's markets and stores. Farmers from the outskirts of the city were the first to suffer. Their once-thriving crops wilted and withered, as if cursed by an invisible hand. Livestock fell ill, their cries echoing through empty barns. Panic struck the farming communities, and they struggled to find answers for the inexplicable devastation.

As the days turned into weeks, New York City faced a food crisis of unparalleled proportions. The grocery stores, once laden with fresh produce, now displayed barren shelves and empty aisles. The panic spread like the plague itself, with long queues forming outside the few remaining stores that managed to maintain meager supplies. The authorities, desperate to contain the crisis, initiated investigations and called upon scientists and experts to discover the cause of the pestilence. Yet, even the most brilliant minds were left bewildered as they scoured the city and its surroundings for a trace of the invisible adversary.

Public services began to crumble under the weight of desperation. Riots erupted in food lines, and looters preyed upon the vulnerable. The once-vibrant streets transformed into eerie ghost towns, as people retreated to their homes in fear. Meanwhile, whispers of conspiracy and dark magic enveloped the city. Some believed that a malevolent force had cursed the land, punishing the city for its sins. Others suspected a clandestine experiment gone awry, and rumors of secret laboratories and underground conspiracies pervaded every conversation.

In the midst of chaos, altruistic souls emerged. Small groups of volunteers braved the treacherous streets, distributing food to the hungry and providing aid to the sick. They were the silent heroes amidst the turmoil, striving to alleviate the suffering that had gripped the city. As the seasons changed, hope flickered like a candle in the wind. The plague's mysterious origin remained an enigma, and no cure seemed forthcoming. Yet, amid the darkest moments, humanity's resilience shone through. Communities banded together, sharing what little resources they had left, and cultivating small gardens on rooftops and in vacant lots. The city's spirit persevered, finding new ways to adapt and survive.

As the days passed, the city thrived again, rebuilt, and renewed. The scars of the past remained, forever shaping its collective memory. And somewhere, in the depths of the metropolis, the secrets of the pestilence still lingered, waiting for time to reveal their elusive truth. "Wow I do not know how the world survived with their food supply being infected but they did but now might be a good time to tell you about year 4 of the tribulation" and as we sat in the comfort in Davids's apartment David began telling his story.

So After the first 3 years I thought it couldn't get worse, but everything changed when the world took a dark turn. A collective decision was made, and countries around the globe began recruiting young kids into their militaries. At first, it was hard to believe. The news spread like wildfire, leaving parents frightened and children uncertain about their future. Soon, it was evident that I, too, was not exempt from this new reality. Because my daughter was only eightteen when the recruitment posters adorned the city walls, and my heart sank as I saw the ominous messages urging us to serve our country. The pressure from family, peers, and society weighed heavily on my shoulders. It felt like an impossible choice - a decision no child should have to make. The streets that once echoed with laughter were now filled with anxious murmurs. Friends became foes, as some chose to join, while others resisted, hoping for a different path. Fear and uncertainty loomed, making every day feel like a battle against the unknown.

I couldn't escape the reality that surrounded me, but I held onto hope and the desire for peace. I joined a small group of like-minded youngsters who sought alternatives to violence. We believed that unity, understanding, and dialogue were more potent than the clashing of swords. We met in secret, organizing peaceful rallies to advocate for a different way forward. Our messages spread like ripples through the city, resonating with those who yearned for change but were too afraid to speak up. As the tension escalated, clashes erupted between the military and the protesters. Tear gas filled the air, and the sound of distant sirens became all too familiar. Amid the chaos, our group grew stronger, standing firm in our belief that children shouldn't be forced into such a harsh reality.

The authorities cracked down on dissent, labeling us as traitors and troublemakers. Some of our friends were arrested, leaving us feeling more vulnerable than ever. Yet, we persisted, believing that love and compassion could overcome hatred and aggression. In a world filled with darkness, I discovered the power of human connection and the strength of unity. Together, we raised our voices, demanding an end to this war on innocence. Our message reached beyond New York City, inspiring others across the globe to question the choices made by those in power. Our fight wasn't without sacrifice, as we faced hardships and threats along the way. But I learned that courage isn't the absence of fear; it's the willingness to stand tall despite it. Our story became a beacon of hope for those who refused to give in to violence and war. The bustling streets and towering skyscrapers were always my home, but everything changed when the world took a darker turn. A collective decision was made, and countries around the globe began recruiting young kids into their militaries at even faster rates.

At first, it was hard to believe. The news spread like wildfire, leaving parents frightened even more now and children uncertain about their future. The pressure from family, peers, and society weighed heavily on my shoulders. It felt like an impossible choice - a decision no child should have to make. The streets that once echoed with laughter were now filled with anxious murmurs. Friends were still becoming foes, as some chose to join, while others resisted, hoping for a different path. Fear and uncertainty loomed, making every day feel like a battle against the unknown once more. And I still couldn't escape the reality that surrounded me, but I held onto hope and the desire for peace. And I was still with the small group of like-minded youngsters who sought alternatives to violence. We believed that unity, understanding, and dialogue were more potent than the clashing of swords. So we continued to meet in secret, organizing peaceful rallies to advocate for a different way forward. Our messages spread like ripples through the city, resonating with those who yearned for change but were too afraid to speak up. As the tension escalated, clashes erupted between the military and the protesters. Tear gas continued to fill the air, and the sound of distant sirens became all too familiar. Amid the chaos, our group grew even stronger, standing firm in our belief that children shouldn't be forced into such a harsh realities.

But the authorities continued to crack down on dissent, still labeling us as traitors and troublemakers. Some of our friends were arrested, leaving us feeling more vulnerable than ever. Yet, we persisted, believing that love and compassion could overcome hatred and aggression. In a world filled with darkness, I discovered the power of human connection and the strength of unity. Together, we raised our voices, demanding an end to this war on innocence. Our message reached beyond New York City, inspiring others across the globe to question the choices made by those in power. Our fight wasn't without sacrifice, as we faced hardships and threats along the way. But I learned that courage isn't the absence of fear; it's the willingness to stand tall despite it. Our story became a beacon of hope for those who refused to give in to violence and war.

So as time moved on the news of the global recruitment spread like wildfire even more than before now, leaving parents worried and children bewildered. The United World announced a resolution mandating the involvement of teenagers aged 15 to 17 in military service to bolster their nations' armies. It was a desperate measure born from a wave of escalating conflicts and a perceived need for greater manpower. At first, it was hard to believe that this could happen in our peaceful city. The posters plastered on the walls seemed surreal, urging us to serve our country, to lay down our dreams, and pick up weapons. The pressure from family, friends, and society to comply with this decree weighed heavily on my shoulders. Many were uncertain, torn between duty and a desire for a future beyond the horrors of war.

The once vibrant streets were now filled with anxious murmurs, and the laughter of children playing in Central Park became a distant memory. The city's carefree spirit seemed lost, replaced by an overwhelming sense of apprehension. New Yorkers grappled with the reality of young lives being forever altered. I couldn't escape the reality that surrounded me, but I clung to hope and sought an alternative path. Together with my small group of like-minded youngsters still, we formed an underground network advocating for peace and dialogue. We believed that understanding and compassion could bridge the gaps between nations and put an end to the cycle of violence. Our secret gatherings became a haven for those seeking solace amidst the chaos. We planned peaceful rallies, using social media to disseminate our messages. The movement started small but quickly gained traction, resonating with people across the city and beyond. Together, we were the voice of a generation yearning for change.

As tensions escalated, clashes between military forces and protesters became frequent. Tear gas and now rubber bullets filled the air, and the sound of sirens echoed through the streets. Despite the risks, we remained steadfast in our commitment to a peaceful resolution. The authorities viewed us as a threat to national security, branding us as traitors and insurgents now. and parents worried for the safety of their children, fearing the harsh repercussions they might face for their defiance. Yet, we believed that our actions were justified, and we drew strength from the support of each other. In a world filled with darkness, I discovered the power of human connection and the strength of unity. Our diverse backgrounds and experiences merged into a tapestry of resilience. Together, we were more than the sum of our parts, and our collective voice demanded to be heard.

As our movement gained momentum, our story reached the far corners of the globe. International media picked up our cause, and the eyes of the world turned to New York City, the epicenter of a grassroots revolution. Our peaceful activism inspired other youth-led movements worldwide, showing them that change could be driven not through violence, but through determination and solidarity. The fight was not without its sacrifices. Some of our friends were arrested, and others faced harassment and threats. We experienced moments of doubt and fear, but each setback only fueled our determination to stand firm.

The bustling streets and towering skyscrapers were always my home, but everything changed when the world took a dark turn. A collective decision was made to continue the recent decree, and countries around the globe began recruiting young kids into their militaries once more. The news of the global recruitment spread like wildfire, leaving parents worried and children bewildered in cities far beyond New York. London, Tokyo, Sydney, Paris, and countless others found themselves grappling with the same daunting reality. Governments claimed it was a necessary measure to protect their nations in an increasingly unstable world. In every corner of the globe, young minds struggled with the weight of responsibility that fell upon their shoulders. Teenagers from different cultures and backgrounds faced the same choices and pressures, each with their dreams and aspirations at risk. Across the cities, youth like my daughter sought alternatives to violence and militarization. Peaceful movements blossomed, connecting via the internet or what was left of the internet to share ideas, strategies, and support. We knew that if we were to make a difference, we had to stand united, transcending borders and cultural divides. As the movement grew, we realized we were not alone. From South America to Africa, from Asia to Europe, young people stood up and voiced their opposition to the recruitment of children into war. We organized global rallies, forming an unbroken chain of solidarity that encircled the planet. Each city had its own unique approach to advocacy, reflecting the diversity of the world's youth. Art installations, music festivals, and poetry slams spread messages of peace and hope, echoing across time zones. Social media became our megaphone, ensuring that our collective voice reached every ear, challenging the notion that children were expendable pawns.

The response from governments varied. Some were stubborn, dismissing our calls as mere youthful idealism. Others listened, recognizing that they could not ignore the growing swell of discontent. Our movement gained the support of influential leaders, celebrities, and organizations committed to a peaceful future. As we stood firm in our convictions, our actions transcended borders, uniting us as global citizens. We shared stories of hope and resilience, of young lives transformed by compassion and understanding. The impact of our movement became too significant to ignore, shifting the global narrative away from militarization. But still The news of the global recruitment spread like wildfire, leaving parents worried and children bewildered in cities far beyond New York. London, Tokyo, Sydney, Paris, and countless others found themselves grappling with the same daunting realities and it's like it was not ending. Governments claimed it was a necessary measure to protect their nations in an increasingly unstable world.

But I couldn't accept it. I couldn't believe that the innocence of children like my daughter would be sacrificed for the sake of war. The thought of young lives torn apart by violence haunted my every waking moment. I knew I had to rebel against this oppressive system still, even if it meant standing alone. As the posters urging us to join the military plastered the city walls, my heart burned with defiance. With the support of my friends and fellow activists, we continued with our secret resistance group to counter the government's agenda. We called ourselves "The Peaceful Warriors" now.

Our first act of rebellion was a daring move - we began distributing pamphlets, exposing the harsh reality of child recruitment. Through graffiti art, we depicted children playing with toys instead of guns. We wanted to remind the world of the innocence that was being stripped away. As our movement gained momentum, we took to social media, using encrypted channels to connect with like-minded individuals worldwide. Together, we shared stories of the impact of war on innocent lives and of the resilient spirits that refused to bow to violence. The Peaceful Warriors became a thorn in the side of the authorities. They dismissed us as mere troublemakers, underestimating our resolve. But we refused to back down, determined to show the world that there was strength in peace, not in war.

Our acts of civil disobedience escalated. We organized peaceful sit-ins and demonstrations in front of government buildings, demanding that they listen to our pleas. We carried banners with messages of peace and love, refusing to be silenced by the deafening calls for war. As the government's tactics to silence us intensified, so did our commitment to the cause. We knew the risks, but the thought of remaining silent was even more terrifying. We began to document and share the stories of those affected by the recruitment mandates. Their tales of heartache and loss touched the hearts of people worldwide, igniting further support for our cause. The Peaceful Warriors went beyond New York City, reaching out to other resistance groups in cities around the globe. We formed alliances, recognizing that the fight for peace was universal. Our collective voice grew louder, spreading like wildfire, transcending borders, and uniting people from all walks of life. But with each step, the risks increased. The authorities began cracking down on our movement, arresting some of our members and labelling us as enemies of the state. parents worried for the safety kids of their, pleading for us to step back and choose a safer path. Yet, we stood tall in the face of adversity, bolstered by the support of countless people who believed in our mission. We knew that peace required sacrifice, and we were willing to pay the price for a world where children could grow up without the shadow of war looming over them. In a world battered by conflict and strife, governments across the globe continued to issue their decrees that shook the foundations of society. And chilling announcement remained spreading like wildfire: children as young as twelve were to be conscripted into military service now. The justification offered was the desperate need for manpower to confront an encroaching global threat. The international community was divided, with some nations vehemently opposing the decree while others reluctantly embraced it, citing the dire circumstances.

Amidst this turmoil, a sense of injustice and desperation brewed among the young people of the world. Their childhoods snatched away, they were faced with a future of violence and bloodshed. The collective indignation gave birth to a movement, a rebellion that transcended borders and cultures. The Rebellion of Innocence, as it came to be known, was fueled by the fearless passion of the youth who refused to accept their fates. Online forums and secret gatherings became their refuge, where they hatched plans to defy the decree. Strategies were discussed, stories were shared, and a network of young minds united in the face of adversity.

At the heart of the rebellion was a profound understanding that the world had failed them. Schools were transformed into military training grounds, books replaced with weapons, laughter replaced with harsh commands. The sense of camaraderie that blossomed among the rebels was rooted in the shared loss of innocence and the yearning for a different future. As the rebellion spread like wildfire, governments struggled to suppress it. Protests erupted in the streets, and clashes between rebel groups and government forces became common. The youth, armed with their newfound resilience, fought back with fervor. Guerrilla tactics and covert operations disrupted the machinery of conscription. Acts of civil disobedience multiplied, from strikes to graffiti campaigns that criticized the merciless decree.   But the world was not prepared to witness such defiance from its youngest citizens. A vicious cycle of suppression and retaliation emerged, painting the streets red with the blood of young lives cut short. Families were torn apart, friendships shattered, and the landscape of once-thriving cities was transformed into a haunting tableau of conflict. The media landscape, controlled by those in power, painted the rebellion in a damning light. Images of destruction and reports of rebel atrocities overshadowed the root cause of the uprising: a draconian decree that had sparked a fire in the hearts of the youth. International support for the rebellion wavered, governments citing security concerns as they looked away from the humanitarian crisis. Despite their valiant efforts, the rebellion couldn't escape the harsh reality of a world driven by power and politics. The movement that had begun with such promise found itself fractured, its initial unity shattered by internal divisions and external pressures. As disillusionment set in, some rebels sought refuge in the very institutions they had once sworn to dismantle, while others faced the bitter truth that their fight might never truly change the world.   In the end, the Rebellion of Innocence left scars both visible and unseen. The decree's implementation was not halted, and the youth who had once dreamed of a different future were left to reconcile with a world that had extinguished their hopes. The movement's legacy, though tinged with tragedy, sparked conversations that transcended children everywhere. It became a stark reminder of the lengths to which the powerful would go to maintain control, and the indomitable spirit of those who dared to stand against it. And so, the world moved on, the echoes of the rebellion fading into history books and whispered tales of resistance. The cost of the rebellion was immeasurable, a poignant testament to the fragile nature of youthful dreams in a world defined by conflict and compromise, "and that sums up year 4" David said as the night grew darker then we rested for the night.

(The Mexican Assassins)

The next day I woke up to the sound of David's voice yet again "Elijah today there is a major issue happening in Mexico this time" said David "what's happening" I replied "There is a group of some Mexican assassins attacking the people in the District of believers in Mexico and we need you to stop them ASAP" David explained "ok that should not be a problem" I replied "great and the New Goshen Jet is already in Coney Island waiting for you" David said, and then the both of us left David's apartment and went to Coney Island. And after some minutes flew by, we were in Coney Island and I could see the New Goshen Jet waiting for me and David, so after some moments me and David got on the New Goshen Jet "What's up you two so Elijah has to go to Mexico I heard and David your needed in New Goshen again" Jordan said while starting up the jet engines. So after some hours flew by the 3 of us arrived in Mexico and Jordan found a safe place to land, so after the jet landed I stepped out of it and David stayed in the jet with Jordan "we will meet back up once your mission is complete" David explained, then moments later the New Goshen Jet was in the sky and I was now in Mexico.

So as the sun dipped below the horizon, casting an amber glow over the desert landscape, I, Elijah, found myself in a world far different from the biblical era I once knew. The Lord had chosen me for a new mission, one that would test my faith and resolve. In this modern day, I was no longer a prophet but a solitary figure, roaming the desolate lands. The Lord had whispered in my ear, guiding me to confront a dangerous group of Mexican assassins wreaking havoc on innocent lives. They called themselves "Los Lobos," the wolves, for they struck with ruthless precision and stealth.

With my heart heavy, I embarked on my journey, armed with my unwavering faith and a resolve to bring justice to the oppressed. I knew this task was not one to be taken lightly, for it pitted the ancient against the contemporary, but I trusted in the most high's plan, So as I followed the trail of destruction left by Los Lobos, I couldn't help but feel a sense of uncertainty. These were no ordinary adversaries; they were trained killers with modern weapons and tactics. But as I prayed in the quiet moments, I found peace and reassurance that the most high would be with me.

Finally, I caught up with the assassins in an abandoned town on the outskirts of the desert. Shadows danced on the walls, and the night whispered ominous warnings. I knew that this was the moment I had been led to, the confrontation that would test my faith. The wolves emerged from the darkness, their eyes gleaming with malice. Their leader, a cold-blooded man known as "El Cazador," stepped forward, a devilish grin etched on his face. "You dare challenge us, old man?" he mocked.

With firm resolve, I responded, "I am Elijah, a servant of the Most High God. Your reign of terror ends tonight," Then as the first shot rang out, I felt a surge of energy that defied my age and a supernatural guidance that evaded bullets and blades. I moved with divine grace, my ancient wisdom combining with newfound agility. Though outnumbered, I remained undeterred, trusting that the most high was fighting alongside me.

Through the night, the battle raged on. I faced moments of exhaustion and doubt, but each time I felt weakened, a whisper of encouragement urged me onward. I knew the most high was with me, guiding every step, And eventually, the wolves fell one by one, their reign of terror crumbling beneath the strength of my conviction. El Cazador, the last remaining assassin, stared at me with disbelief, realizing that there was something greater than mere mortal strength at play.

As I approached him, he trembled with fear. "Who are you?" he stammered.

"I am Elijah," I replied, "a servant of the Most High God, sent to bring an end to the darkness you've spread." With tears in his eyes, he confessed to his crimes, seeking redemption in his final moments. I offered him a prayer, praying for his soul to find peace in the afterlife, Then as the dawn approached, I stood amidst the fallen, grateful for the divine guidance that had sustained me through this modern-day battle. Though the world had changed since my biblical days, the power of faith and the guidance of the most high remained steadfast.

And so, my journey continued, a vigilant servant in a world that needed ancient wisdom and divine intervention more than ever. I knew that the Lord's plan was vast, and my role was just beginning. With every step I took, I embraced the uncertainty, knowing that my faith would lead me through the darkest of days.

So as the days turned into weeks, I wandered the arid landscape, guided by a divine presence that led me toward the heart of darkness. The "Los Lobos" again, and it seemed like this ruthless group of Mexican assassins were not backing down, as I had left a trail of bloodshed and despair across the region. Innocent lives had been lost, and their reign of terror had to end.

In this modern era, my appearance drew curious glances and raised eyebrows. My weathered cloak and staff were relics of a time long past, but they were symbolic of my unyielding faith. The most high had chosen me for a purpose, and I would embrace it with all my heart and soul, But the nights were the hardest. Alone in the silence, I found solace in prayer and conversation with the Almighty. His guidance was a constant presence, reminding me of the strength that lay within me. "Fear not, Elijah, for I am with you," His voice echoed in the depths of my soul.

Finally, the time came to confront Los Lobos once more. In an abandoned town on the outskirts of the desert, I stood resolute, ready to face the evil that lurked within the shadows. The night was thick with tension as the assassins emerged like phantoms, their footsteps masked by the soft sand, And as their new leader, El Mateo, stepped forward this time, I couldn't help but notice the cruel glint in his eyes. He was a master of deception, skilled in the art of manipulation and ruthlessness. But I stood unwavering, my heart fortified by divine purpose.

The first gunshot shattered the stillness, and I moved with an agility that defied my age. The Lord's guidance granted me an almost supernatural grace, dodging bullets and evading their strikes. Though they outnumbered me, I felt invincible, knowing that the Almighty was my shield, And the night was very long, and the battle fierce. My ancient wisdom coupled with the Lord's intervention proved a formidable force against the modern weapons and tactics of Los Lobos. Each time doubt crept into my heart, a whisper of encouragement from above rekindled my resolve.

One by one, the assassins fell, their malevolence vanquished by the light of righteousness. El Mateo, the last remaining wolf, was reduced to a trembling soul. "Who are you?" he pleaded, his bravado shattered. "I am Elijah, a servant of the Most High God, didn't El Cazador inform you about who I am" I replied, "No he did not" El Mateo replied to me" "well I am sent to bring an end to the darkness you've spread." I replied to El Mateo

Then as the morning sun bathed the battlefield in its golden glow, I knelt beside El Mateo. The weight of his crimes weighed heavily on him, and remorse filled his eyes. "Can there be redemption for me?" he whispered, And in that moment, I knew that even the darkest souls could find salvation. I offered a prayer for his repentance, witnessing the transformative power of divine grace before my very eyes.

Then as I walked away from the battlefield, the air was filled with a sense of peace. The most high's plan had been carried out, and my faith had been rewarded with victory. But I knew that this was still just the beginning of my journey in Mexico.

So in this modern world of chaos and uncertainty, I would continue to be an instrument of God's will. My journey was far from over, and the battles I would face were bound to be as diverse as the people of this age, So with the staff of faith in my hand and the armor of divine guidance around me, I embraced the unknown, confident that the most high would always lead me through the shadows and into the light. My mission as Elijah, the modern-day prophet, had just begun in Mexico, and I was ready to face whatever challenges that were ahead.

This new journey led me to confront a new and different set of the Los Lobos and they were filled with twists and turns, mirroring the intricacies of life. I traversed vast deserts, trekked through dense jungles, and crossed rivers swollen with memories of ancient battles. Along the way, I encountered individuals whose lives had been shattered by the brutality of the assassins, fueling my determination to bring an end to their reign, So as I journeyed, I reminisced about my biblical days, where I had stood atop Mount Carmel, calling upon the most high to show His presence in a fiery spectacle. But now, in this modern era, the battleground was not just a physical one; it extended into the realms of technology and the human psyche.

But still the most high's guidance was my constant companion, leading me to uncover the web of connections that sustained The Los Lobos. I forged alliances with unlikely allies, individuals who had their reasons to see justice served. Among them was Maria, a brave journalist who had lost her husband to the assassins cruelty. Her pen was her sword, and her words would become the beacon of truth that pierced through the darkness.

And together, we delved into the depths of Los Lobos' operations, uncovering their ties to the drug cartels of Mexico and also the corrupt officials of Mexico. So as we collected evidence, we knew that the battle could not be won solely with physical prowess. We needed to expose the truth to the world, to turn the tides of public opinion against them. So with the dawn of a new day, the confrontation with Los Lobos drew nearer. The abandoned town where they had established their stronghold loomed in the distance, an eerie backdrop for the impending showdown. My heart was heavy with the knowledge that this battle would demand more than just physical strength; it would be a test of our collective spirit.

Maria and I devised a plan to dismantle Los Lobos from within, sowing seeds of doubt and discord among their ranks. We leaked crucial information about their leaders' betrayals, planting seeds of mistrust that sprouted like weeds in a garden of secrets. As Los Lobos turned against each other, their once united front began to crumble.

So the night of the confrontation was filled with tension, as if the very air held its breath. I stood at the heart of the abandoned town, my staff firmly in hand, my cloak billowing in the desert wind. Beside me, Maria held her pen with conviction, knowing that her words would seal Los Lobos' fate. Now a new leader of the Los Lobos named El Santiago stepped forward, his once formidable demeanor now riddled with uncertainty. He had become a shadow of his former self, betrayed by his own comrades. "You are not alone, old man," he hissed, but the fear in his voice betrayed his bravado.

With courage buoyed by divine assurance, I addressed him, "Your reign of terror ends tonight. Surrender now, and perhaps there can still be redemption." But the ensuing battle was fierce, the echoes of gunfire piercing the night like a haunting requiem. Los Lobos fought desperately, their resolve tested as their unity crumbled. But even in the midst of chaos, I felt a peace that defied the storm around me. The most high's presence was tangible, guiding my every move.

So as the first light of dawn broke on the horizon, the battle came to an end. Los Lobos had been defeated once again, but not just physically but morally and spiritually. And El Santiago, broken and humbled, surrendered, knowing that the power that protected me surpassed any physical might. So with The Los Lobos vanquished, Maria and I stood amidst the wreckage of their once formidable stronghold. We knew that our work was not done, that this victory was just a stepping stone on the path of justice and righteousness.

And in the days that followed, the truth about Los Lobos became public knowledge. The exposure of their crimes shook the foundations of the corrupt networks that had sheltered them. Justice, though delayed, found its way to the oppressed, and hope began to bloom like a desert flower after the rain.

So as I continued my journey, I carried the memories of this battle with me, knowing that the most high's plan was far-reaching. There would be more battles to fight, more injustices to confront. My role as a modern-day Elijah, a servant of the Most High God, was a mantle I wore with honor and humility. In a world that oscillated between light and darkness, I would be a beacon, guided by the divine compass of faith. Each step would be a testament to the power of the Almighty, for He had chosen me for a purpose far greater than myself. So with renewed faith and unwavering conviction, I embraced the horizon, for there was always another dawn, another battle, and another opportunity to bring hope to a world in need. The story of Elijah, the prophet of old, had evolved into a tale of a modern-day warrior for justice, a vessel of divine will, unyielding in the face of adversity. And so, my journey continued, one step at a time, toward the call of destiny and the whispers of the Almighty. So, as I faced the remnants of Los Lobos in the abandoned town, I sensed a change in the air. The faint hum of engines grew louder, and a powerful presence loomed in the distance. And now the Mexican military had been alerted to the confrontation, and they approached with caution.

An armored convoy rolled into the outskirts of the town, their vehicles imposing against the stark desert backdrop. Soldiers clad in camouflage uniforms spilled out, weapons at the ready. And their eyes flickered with suspicion as they beheld the scene before them — an older looking man with a staff and a determined woman with a pen, standing amidst the fallen assassins. "Drop your weapons and surrender!" a commanding voice boomed from a loudspeaker, its echo reverberating through the deserted streets. "We have no weapons" I replied, and a look of awe were in all of the eyes of the Mexican soldiers. "Yea and we mean no harm," Maria called out, raising her hands in a sign of peace. "We fought against these murderers. They were the ones terrorizing innocent lives!"

Then as I stepped forward, my ancient wisdom and divine guidance shielding me from any fear, I knew that this confrontation was as crucial as the battle against Los Lobos. The soldiers eyed me with a mix of curiosity and skepticism, unsure of what to make of this seemingly otherworldly figure. "Look I am Elijah, a servant of the Most High God," I declared with conviction. "We acted to bring justice and expose the truth about Los Lobos. They were the ones responsible for the atrocities in this land."

The officer in command approached cautiously, his stern expression showing hints of uncertainty. "We've received reports of an armed conflict. Explain what happened here." Maria stepped forward, recounting the dark tale of Los Lobos' reign of terror, their ties to corruption, and our mission to dismantle them. She presented the evidence we had gathered, painting a vivid picture of the assassins' atrocities. Then the officer listened intently, and I could sense a shift in the atmosphere as he began to comprehend the gravity of the situation. "We'll verify your claims," he said, his tone slightly softened. "But you can't take the law into your own hands."

"We did what we had to do," I replied firmly, "guided by a higher purpose, a divine call to bring justice to those who needed it most." So the Mexican military conducted their investigation, corroborating the evidence we presented. The truth began to emerge, revealing the depth of Los Lobos' crimes and their ties to corruption within the country. And the once-skeptical soldiers now saw us as allies in the fight against a greater evil. So in the following days, the military and I collaborated in dismantling the remnants of Los Lobos' network, ensuring that justice was served through the proper channels. It was a delicate dance, finding the balance between the ancient wisdom I brought and the modern-day strategies of the military.

And as the sun set on that fateful day, I found myself in the company of the military's highest-ranking officials, sharing stories of faith and miracles from times long past. They had seen the power of divine guidance firsthand, and our bond grew stronger.

Then from that point on, the Mexican military became a powerful ally in our quest for justice. They offered their resources and expertise, while I provided insights and counsel from the divine. Together, we worked to rid the land of the scourge of corruption and violence, ensuring that the innocent would no longer suffer at the hands of evil. And though I remained a figure of mystery to many, the Mexican military knew that my purpose was genuine and my intentions were just. And in the annals of history, this unlikely alliance of an ancient prophet and the modern military would be remembered as a force that challenged darkness and brought hope to a land in need and I was told by the Mexican military that I may continued my battles against the evils in their country.

So as my journey continued, the path ahead still remained uncertain I mean even with the Mexican Military on my side now, but I knew that the most high's plan was vast and ever-unfolding. With the Mexican military by my side, our collective strength served as a beacon of hope, illuminating the shadows and pointing towards a brighter tomorrow. And so, I, Elijah, the modern-day warrior, carried on, forever guided by the whispers of the Almighty and the unyielding spirit of faith. In a world where battles transcended time and space, the convergence of ancient wisdom and modern power blazed a trail of justice and righteousness, leaving a lasting legacy that would echo through the ages I was told.

But the confrontation between Me, Maria, and the Mexican military against Los Lobos extended beyond the confines of the abandoned town now. The battle had ignited a fire within the hearts of those oppressed by the assassins, and they rose up to join the fight for their own liberation. So now villagers from nearby settlements, who had endured years of terror under Los Lobos' rule, flocked to our side. And their determination to reclaim their homes and protect their loved ones became the driving force that unified us in the face of adversity. So with each passing day, our alliance grew stronger against the Los Lobos. And Maria's journalistic powers proved invaluable, as she reported the truth about Los Lobos and the corruption that allowed them to thrive. Her articles became rallying cries, reaching every corner of the nation. The public, once indifferent or unaware, now demanded justice. And the Mexican military, recognizing the urgency of the situation, launched a sweeping campaign against Los Lobos and their corrupt accomplices. They raided drug cartels, uncovered clandestine dealings, and arrested high-ranking officials entangled in the web of corruption. The battle had transformed into a nationwide fight against darkness.

And Amidst the chaos, I continued to be a steadfast pillar of faith, offering prayers for the oppressed and guidance to the military commanders. My presence, though unconventional in this modern world, instilled courage in those around me. I became a symbol of hope, a reminder that the Almighty was watching over us.

So as the tides turned, some of Los Lobos' remnants refused to go down without a fight and I was told that I was about to face my last battle in Mexico. So the remnant of the Los Lobos launched counterattacks, attempting to strike at the heart of our alliance. The battles were fierce, and the cost was high, but our faith remained unshaken. And on one fateful night, Maria and I stood side by side, surveying the camp where we had established our headquarters, But the desert wind whispered tales of ancient struggles, and the stars above seemed to form constellations that told our story.

"I never imagined my pen could be mightier than a sword," Maria mused, her eyes glistening with both weariness and determination. "But here we are, making history together." "Our journey is not over yet," I replied, resting a hand on her shoulder. "Then the road to justice is often long and arduous, but we must press on. The Lord is with us, guiding our every step." I replied

Then as the days turned into weeks, the landscape of the nation began to change. The oppressive shadow of Los Lobos slowly receded, replaced by rays of hope and a newfound sense of unity among the people. Faith in the divine merged with the strength of collective resolve, and together, we became an unstoppable force.

And after sometime went by, the time had come to face a new leader of the Los Lobos and his name was El Alejandro. He had managed to evade capture, moving like a wraith in the night. But the bond between us had strengthened through every confrontation, and I knew that this final encounter would be a defining moment. But now with the support of the Mexican military and the villagers, we cornered El Alejandro in a remote location, far from his former stronghold. There, under the open sky, we confronted him.

El Alejandro sneered, his eyes filled with hatred. "You may have won some battles, old man, but you can't defeat the darkness that lies within us all." "We are more than the sum of our mistakes," I replied firmly, "and redemption is possible for those who seek it." Then the showdown grew intense, a clash of ideologies as much as physical strength. El Alejandro fought with desperation, unwilling to relinquish his power and pride. But his strength paled in comparison to the power of truth and righteousness. Then in a moment of divine intervention, as if the heavens themselves wept for him, El Alejandro 's resolve wavered. He dropped to his knees, his weapons cast aside, tears streaming down his face. "Is there still hope for me?" he whispered, his voice breaking.

I extended my hand toward him, a gesture of forgiveness and redemption. "There is always hope," I said, "for those who are willing to change and seek the light." El Alejandro 's surrender marked a turning point in our battle against darkness. With his testimony and cooperation, we unraveled the remaining threads of corruption, and the nation began its journey toward healing. And in the aftermath of the battle, the Mexican military and the people celebrated our triumph over evil. We had faced an ancient prophet, a modern journalist, and a united nation against a ruthless force of darkness.

So as I prepared to depart, my heart filled with gratitude for the souls I had encountered on this journey. Then the echoes of the battle would reverberate through time, a testament to the power of faith, unity, and the indomitable spirit of humanity. And so, I, Elijah, the modern-day warrior, ventured forth into the horizon once more, knowing that my mission would continue throughout the globe. And as long as there were battles to fight and injustices to confront, I would be there, guided by the whispers of the Almighty, a beacon of hope and an instrument of divine will. And the story of this battle, etched in the annals of history, would serve as a reminder that even in the darkest of times, faith and the courage to stand united could prevail against any odds.

And as our campaign against Los Lobos gained momentum, a new chapter of our battle unfolded. Some Mexican citizens, influenced by the assassins' propaganda and seduced by the promise of power, became disillusioned with the changing tides. They saw us as a threat to the status quo and rallied behind El Alejandro, determined to protect what they believed was their way of life. And their ranks swelled with those who had once lived in fear of Los Lobos but now feared the upheaval of the system they had known. They saw me as an outsider, a relic from the past, and doubted the effectiveness of divine guidance in this modern world.

And as our alliance faced this internal conflict, I was faced with an unexpected challenge. I understood their fear and uncertainty, but I also knew that the most high's guidance transcended time and culture. My mission was not just to confront the assassins but also to awaken the hearts of those who had strayed from the path of righteousness. Maria and I, now assisted by the Mexican military, sought dialogue with those citizens who had become adversaries. We listened to their fears and grievances, understanding that the root of their discontent ran deep. With patience and compassion, we tried to bridge the gap between us, offering reassurance and understanding.

So one day during a town hall meeting, I stood before the crowd, my staff firmly planted in the ground. "I know that the world has changed since my time," I began, "but the power of faith and divine guidance is as relevant now as it was then. It is a force that unites us, not divides us." So I shared stories from my biblical past, tales of miracles and transformative change. I spoke of the power of forgiveness and the hope that springs from even the darkest of circumstances. Slowly but surely, hearts began to soften, and skepticism gave way to contemplation.

Some citizens remained skeptical, but others, touched by the sincerity of our words, began to question their allegiance to El Alejandro and his cause. The battle extended beyond the physical realm; it became a struggle to awaken the conscience of those who had lost their way, But as we continued our outreach, I encountered an elderly woman named Isabella, who had lost her entire family to the violence of Los Lobos. She was initially skeptical of my divine claims, but I saw pain and longing in her eyes. I approached her with gentle humility, offering my hand in comfort.

155

"You've suffered unimaginable loss," I said softly. "But even in the darkest moments, there is hope and strength to be found." Then she looked into my eyes, searching for something, perhaps a glimmer of truth in my words. "Can I really find peace and healing?" she asked, her voice trembling. "With faith and the support of those around you, you can," I replied. "And the Lord's guidance will never leave your side." Then Isabella's heart began to soften, and she chose to stand with us, embracing the path of reconciliation and forgiveness. Her transformation resonated with others, and slowly, the division among the citizens started to dissolve.

And as the battles continued, we found ourselves united not just against Los Lobos but also against the darkness that had seeped into the hearts of some citizens. In the crucible of conflict, compassion emerged as a powerful force, knitting together the torn fabric of our society. And in time, El Cazador's ranks diminished, as citizens once loyal to him chose a different path. The battle against darkness within ourselves proved to be as critical as the one against external adversaries. And through unity, understanding, and the power of divine guidance, we emerged victorious. The transformation of hearts brought about a profound change in the nation's trajectory, and a new era of hope and reconciliation dawned. So as I prepared to depart once more, I knew that the battles would continue in this ever-changing world. But the journey had taught me that faith and compassion were universal, transcending cultures and time. And my role as Elijah, the modern-day warrior, was not to impose my ancient ways but to be a vessel for divine love and wisdom, embracing the hearts of those I encountered. The story of this battle would forever remind us that the greatest victories were not only won with swords and strength but also with the transformative power of the human spirit guided by faith.

So now it was time to meet back up with David and Jordan in the same spot that I was dropped off in Mexico. So, as I journey to get picked up by the New Goshen jet it grew darker, but I was getting closer to where I was dropped off in Mexico then all of a sudden, I saw the New Goshen Jet hovering above my head. "Walk no further here we are" I heard a voice, and it was David, then in a moment I was entering the New Goshen jet, and we started our journey back to New York to confront the King once more.

(The Great Hail Storm)

"David like always it is time to visit the King of America again" I told David as the New Goshen Jet was soaring across the United States, and then minutes later the New Goshen Jet was hovering over the east coast of America and we were way past Mexico. Then after hours flew by, we were in New York landing in Coney Island, then me and David got off the Jet "see you two on the next trip" said Jordan and then the New Gosen Jet took off into the sky. "Now let's go to The Kings Tower once more" I said so we did and after some minutes flew by, we arrived at the Kings tower, then we went through the same usual procedures as always and once we finally spoke to the King and not by any bodies surprise, he refused to let my people go once more. So, me and David left the Kings tower after the King denied my request yet again and then after some minutes flew by we made our way back to the district of believers. "I must start the next plague" I said to David as we approached his apartment, then I lifted my staff then immediately I began to have another insightful vision.

Then I immediately noticed the sun dipping behind the towering skyscrapers of New York City, casting long shadows across the bustling streets. As night descended, an eerie stillness settled upon the city, and an unusual tension filled the air. Unbeknownst to the millions of residents, a powerful and unforeseen force was gathering in the atmosphere. It began as a faint rumble in the distance, barely perceptible amidst the city's perpetual hum. But soon, the low growl transformed into an ominous roar, echoing through the canyons of concrete and glass. The night sky turned an eerie shade of green as the clouds churned, foreboding a cataclysmic event.

Then with a sudden ferocity, hailstones the size of baseballs began to plummet from the heavens, shattering windows and denting metal with a relentless fury. Panic gripped the city as people scrambled for cover, seeking refuge in subway stations, office buildings, and any shelter they could find. Then the hailstorm's wrath spread, and no corner of the metropolitan area was spared, and Iconic landmarks like the Statue of Liberty and the Empire State Building were cloaked in a blanket of ice, as if nature had decided to reclaim its dominance over the urban landscape.

Then the streets turned into an icy battleground on top of the already sand covered streets, and with vehicles skidding and crashing into one another. The city's infrastructure struggled to cope with the onslaught, leaving many neighborhoods without power and communication. Emergency services were stretched to their limits, trying to rescue stranded citizens and provide aid to those in need. Then as hailstorm raged on through the night, an unyielding tempest that seemed to defy all logic. Its aftermath left New York City transformed - a frozen, battered, and bruised metropolitan area. As dawn broke, the sun cast its light upon a city that had weathered an unprecedented natural disaster.

So, in the days that followed, New Yorkers demonstrated their resilience and unity. Strangers helped each other clear debris and mend shattered windows. Community centers and shelters opened their doors to those displaced by the hailstorm. Despite the devastation, hope flickered like a candle in the darkness. And as time passed, the hailstorm of New York City became a defining moment in the city's history. It served as a stark reminder of nature's unpredictability and the need for preparedness in the face of adversity. Though the scars of that fateful night lingered, the spirit of New York City endured, stronger than ever, as its people banded together, creating a legacy of resilience that would be told for generations to come.

But just as when people thought that the storm was over the next day things got worse and the hailstorm raged on, and it seemed as if Mother Nature had unleashed her fury upon the city yet again. Because the relentless onslaught of icy projectiles transformed streets into treacherous ice rinks, making each step a perilous endeavor. Trees stood stripped of their leaves and branches, bending under the weight of the frozen missiles.

And amidst the chaos, people struggled to find safety, seeking refuge in any available space. A group of strangers huddled together in a small convenience store, sharing jackets and blankets to keep warm as they waited for the storm to pass. Fear and uncertainty gripped their hearts, but in their shared vulnerability, they found a newfound sense of camaraderie. So high above the ground, inhabitants of the towering skyscrapers witnessed a surreal spectacle. The cityscape, typically illuminated with vibrant lights, was now shrouded in an icy haze, as the hailstorm blotted out the familiar city glow. And from their windows, they saw the mighty

Hudson River turn turbulent and frothy, as if mimicking the tempestuous mood of the storm, But the part of the Hudson River by the district of believers was not affected by the Ice.

But in the heart of Central Park, the once-lush greenery was a ghostly sight, buried under a thick layer of ice. The park's iconic statues stood as silent witnesses to the chaos, their stoic expressions contrasting the upheaval around them. And as the hailstorm raged, it seemed to carry an ominous message, reminding New Yorkers of the raw power of nature so they thought. Then out of nowhere emergency responders, firefighters, and police officers worked tirelessly to rescue those in need. Their heroic efforts saved countless lives, pulling people from mangled vehicles and collapsed structures. The spirit of unity surged through the city as volunteers, undeterred by the danger, joined in the rescue efforts, demonstrating the resilience of New Yorkers in the face of adversity.

So as days turned into weeks, the city gradually began to heal again and the storm was over so they thought, but in that current moment it seemed as if the hailstorm left its mark, with shattered windows replaced by sturdy glass, and dented cars taken off the streets for repairs. The collective trauma of the event, however, lingered, and New Yorkers found solace in the shared experience, forever united by the memory of that fateful night.

In the wake of the storm, a renewed focus on preparedness and disaster response emerged. City officials and residents alike vowed to be more vigilant, devising plans to minimize the impact of future natural disasters. The resilience of the city became a source of inspiration, a reminder that even in the face of adversity, New Yorkers would stand strong and rebuild, brick by brick, hailstone by hailstone, But even though the efforts of the people of New York seemed kinda heart warming The Most High was not finished with this Hail/Ice storm because he felt that the pain and sufferings of his people over the years was way worse.

So as the hailstorm continued its relentless assault, the city's infrastructure buckled under the immense pressure. And tall buildings, designed to withstand the fiercest of storms, now quivered as massive hailstones pummeled their façades. Emergency sirens wailed throughout the city, blending with the deafening sound of ice shattering upon impact. And in the heart of Times Square were they mocked the deaths of the believers, the dazzling electronic billboards flickered and sputtered, their brilliant displays temporarily dimmed. The famed Broadway theaters, usually alive with music and laughter, were eerily silent as the storm forced an intermission in the city's vibrant cultural scene.

And subway tunnels became rivers of slush, forcing transit authorities to suspend train services, and commuters who had sought refuge below ground now faced a new dilemma as they became stranded in the labyrinth of dark tunnels under the surface, and the underground world became a temporary shelter for the displaced, fostering a sense of camaraderie and shared struggle among the bewildered crowd.

And in the midst of chaos, tales of courage and resilience emerged. A group of volunteers, named "The Hailstorm Heroes," risked their lives to assist emergency responders in reaching trapped individuals in high-rise buildings. Armed with ropes and harnesses, they scaled the icy exteriors to perform daring rescues, becoming symbols of hope for the desperate.

But throughout the city, a unique form of beauty emerged from the destruction. The ice-caked streets sparkled under the dim glow of streetlights, creating an ethereal scene reminiscent of a winter wonderland. Photographers braved the elements to capture these surreal moments, sharing their images of resilience and fortitude with the rest of the world, as the hailstorm eventually subsided, the true extent of the damage became evident. The cost in human lives was mourned, and countless tales of loss and survival emerged from the wreckage. But amidst the ruins, a shared sense of unity arose. And in the days that followed, a citywide effort to rebuild and recover once again began. Skilled laborers repaired the damaged infrastructure, while artists and sculptors crafted stunning ice sculptures from the remnants of the hailstorm, But The Most High decided to keep on bringing this particular storm but going forward it wouldn't be just New York getting hit by the storm but the whole world was about to get hit by this storm.

So as the sun set over New York City, a sense of foreboding loomed in the air, as if the world itself felt the impending cataclysm. Unbeknownst to the city's residents, the hailstorm that had besieged New York was merely the beginning of a global calamity. And as night fell, reports of similar hailstorms surfaced from cities across the United States. Chicago, Los Angeles, Miami and so on all experienced unprecedented fury from the heavens. But it didn't stop there. News of hailstorms striking cities around the world spread like wildfire.

London, Paris, Tokyo, Sydney, no corner of the globe was spared from the wrath of The Most High. And each city faced its own unique challenges, as hailstones the size of boulders crashed upon landmarks, reducing centuries of old structures to rubble. Chaos ensued as people scrambled for safety, their world turned upside down by the unforgiving force of the elements. Then the global impact of the hailstorm soon reached catastrophic proportions. Agricultural heartlands were decimated, with crops destroyed and livestock left vulnerable to the elements. Global food shortages loomed, threatening the stability of nations and exacerbating existing socio-economic disparities. Governments and scientists around the world worked fervently to understand the cause of these relentless storms. Then the scientific community pointed to climate change as a likely culprit because no one had a clue that it was the work of The Most High at hand, so warning that extreme weather events would only worsen unless urgent action was taken to mitigate greenhouse gas emissions. And as communities grappled with the aftermath of the storms, tales of courage and resilience emerged from all corners of the world. Strangers came together, transcending borders and cultural divides, to provide aid and support to those affected. Humanity, it seemed, was united in its response to the shared struggle against The Most High's fury. Because in the wake of this global catastrophe, countries collectively shifted their focus towards disaster preparedness and climate resilience. International cooperation surged as nations collaborated on solutions to mitigate the impact of future extreme weather events. Green energy initiatives and sustainable practices became top priorities on the global agenda.

But even still The Most High grew even more furriest and he wanted to keep the hailstorm going because the most high has seen all of the centuries of the mistreatment of his people up until now even when they thought he wasn't looking and especially on that Times Square giant T.V screen so The Most High did not feel bad for the Hail he was bringing to the world. So as the hailstorm's fury spread across the globe, its impact was felt on an unimaginable scale. In Europe, Parisians gazed in disbelief as the iconic Eiffel Tower was coated in ice, its iron structure gleaming like a frozen masterpiece. The Louvre's art treasures were hastily transported to safety as the storm threatened to damage centuries of old masterpieces.

And in Asia, Tokyo witnessed a surreal juxtaposition of ancient temples and modern skyscrapers veiled in ice. The Japanese people, known for their resilience, faced the challenge head on, and quickly adapted to the new reality of their altered landscape, and in Australia, Sydney's famed Opera House, a symbol of architectural marvel, was encased in ice, appearing like a fantastical ice castle. The Great Barrier Reef, already suffering from coral bleaching due to rising ocean temperatures, now faced an added threat from hailstones that pummeled its delicate ecosystem.

And even in Africa, hailstorms struck cities like Cape Town and Cairo, where such extreme weather events were virtually unheard of. So the storm's unexpected arrival shook the foundations of communities, leading to a reevaluation of disaster preparedness in regions not accustomed to dealing with such natural disasters.

And meanwhile, the Americas were grappling with the widespread devastation caused by the storm. The Amazon rainforest, known as the "lungs of the Earth," was not spared. Giant hailstones tore through the dense foliage, leaving a path of destruction in their wake. Environmentalists warned of the dire implications for the planet's biodiversity and the delicate balance of the ecosystem. And as food shortages loomed, governments scrambled to address the humanitarian crisis. And aid organizations worked tirelessly to deliver relief to affected regions, and international cooperation flourished, transcending political boundaries in the face of a common threat to humanity. And with the scientific community pointing to climate change as a root cause, world leaders convened emergency summits to address the global climate crisis. The world had been forced to confront the harsh reality of its own actions, and a new era of environmental consciousness began to take root, And the hailstorm was so bad that the once held secret of Renewable energy initiatives started gaining momentum, with investments pouring into solar, wind, and hydroelectric power. And nations set ambitious targets for reducing carbon emissions, pledging to transition to a more sustainable future so they thought.

So, The Most High saw that the governments of the world were actually helping the planet by releasing the secret of renewable energy to the world, so he decided to run the great hailstorm one last time to push the governments of the world to push out even more secrets. So as the hailstorm's relentless assault continued, the world watched in awe and horror at the unprecedented natural disaster. Meteorologists struggled to comprehend the scale of the storm, unable to find a historical precedent for such a cataclysmic event.

And in the wake of the storm's devastation, international aid poured in from all corners of the globe. Nations set aside their differences and united to support the affected regions, demonstrating the power of collective humanity in times of crisis. Medical teams and humanitarian organizations worked tirelessly to provide essential supplies, medical care, and psychological support to those traumatized by the calamity.

And in the remote regions of the world, indigenous communities demonstrated their deep connection to the land, offering ancient wisdom and traditional practices that proved instrumental in adapting to the harsh conditions. Their profound respect for nature and sustainable living practices became a invaluable lessons for the rest of the world. And the scientific community launched comprehensive studies to understand the underlying causes of the hailstorm. Research expeditions were organized to examine ice cores and study weather patterns, seeking answers to the complex climatic changes that had led to such a catastrophic event. Climate scientists reiterated the urgent need for bold action to curb greenhouse gas emissions and avert future environmental disasters.

And amidst the chaos, a new wave of technological innovation emerged. Scientists and engineers collaborated to develop advanced weather prediction systems, providing earlier warnings and better preparedness for extreme weather events. Artificial intelligence and big data played a crucial role in analyzing weather patterns, enhancing disaster response, and identifying vulnerable areas. And in urban centers, city planners reimagined infrastructure to be more resilient against future climate threats. Green rooftops, flood-resistant buildings, and efficient stormwater management systems became integral to urban design, transforming cities into sustainable fortresses against nature's fury.

Beyond the physical impact, the hailstorm left a deep emotional imprint on humanity. Stories of resilience, compassion, and hope became a source of inspiration. Artists around the world expressed the human spirit through paintings, poetry, and music, creating a cultural tapestry that conveyed the shared experience of the global hailstorm, And the global catastrophe also led to a resurgence of interest in space exploration. Humanity sought to understand not just the Earth but the broader universe, contemplating the possibility of finding new habitable worlds to ensure the survival of the species in the face of unpredictable environmental challenges.

So as the governments of the world saw that the great hailstorm was ending, they did the unthinkable by letting out the secret that they could control the weather but they did not tell the people of earth that in the past they used their weather creation machines for evil by creating tornadoes, hurricanes and pandemics in order to control the populations, And they made sure that the public knew that all storms were not created by them and most storms were 100% natural just like the great hailstorm that just hit them, but the governments after telling their citizens that the great hailstorm was 100% natural they introduced a new solution to the world and that solution was that from now on when the winter came and it got so cold they would use their weather machines to heat up the earth and temperatures would never ever go below 65 degrees worldwide excluding Antarctica, now this solution was a game changer for the world because in the past the governments loved when their cities began to freeze because it helped their depopulation agenda but the hailstorm was so bad and terrible that their heart were soften and they decided to use their weather machines for good bringing in a entire new era of prosperity to the earth and this was all the plan of The Most High.

(The Arab Wizards)

The next morning I woke up to the sound of David's voice once more "Elijah today there is another major issue happening but it's in Arabia this time" said David "what's happening" I replied "There is a group of some Arab wizards attacking the people in the District of believers in Arabia and we need you to stop them ASAP" David explained "ok that should not be a problem" I replied "great and the New Goshen Jet like always is already in Coney Island waiting for you" David said, and then the both of us left David's apartment and went to Coney Island. And after some minutes flew by, we were in Coney Island and I could see the New Goshen Jet waiting for me and David, so after some moments me and David got on the New Goshen Jet "What's up you two so Elijah you have to go to Arabia this time I heard" said Jordan "Correct" I replied "Ok and David is once again needed in New Goshen" Jordan said while starting up the jet engines. So, after some hours flew by the 3 of us arrived in Arabia and Jordan found a safe place to land, so after the jet landed I stepped out of it and David stayed in the jet with Jordan "we will meet back up once your mission is complete" David explained, then moments later the New Goshen Jet was in the sky and I was now in Arabia.

So as the sun set over the Arabian dunes of the Arabian desert, I, found myself standing on the threshold of a world that seemed to defy all logic and reason. Summoned from the distant past by an enigmatic force, I discovered that the countries of Arabia had changed drastically since my biblical days. I was now facing a modern-day group of Arabian wizards who wielded powers beyond even my understanding.

The wizards, clad in mysterious robes adorned with ancient symbols, stood with an aura of confidence that sent shivers down my spine. They chanted incantations that echoed through the desert, and the sand beneath their feet swirled in response, forming shapes that defied nature itself, but despite of my uncertainty and the odds stacked against me, I knew I could not back down. The innocent lives of many depended on my courage. So drawing strength from the Almighty, I stepped forward with unwavering resolve, my staff in hand, and my heart pounding in my chest.

And as the battle commenced, bolts of mystical energy shot forth from the wizards' hands, crackling through the air like lightning. I deftly dodged their attacks, and my instincts honed through years of devotion and spiritual training. With each step, I chanted verses from the Scriptures, calling upon the power of The Most High to protect me. Then the desert landscape transformed into a battlefield of the arcane, where reality was bent and twisted. The sands beneath my feet felt unstable as the wizards manipulated the very fabric of existence, and I thought to myself how is this even possible. But I knew I couldn't falter; my faith was my shield against their sinister magic. So with a mighty swing of my staff, I unleashed a wave of divine energy towards the wizards. The force collided with their dark magic, creating a dazzling display of light and shadows. And for a moment, it seemed as if we had reached a stalemate, but I knew that their dark powers were formidable and unrelenting.

So as the battle raged on, I learned to anticipate their moves, using my knowledge of ancient wisdom to counter their spells. So I weaved through the onslaught, determined to protect the innocent from the malevolent intentions of the wizards. And in an act of desperation, the lead wizard conjured a massive sandstorm that threatened to engulf us all. The swirling sand obscured my vision, making it challenging to maintain my footing. But I knew the most high was by my side, guiding me through the chaos. So by summoning every ounce of strength within me, I concentrated my thoughts and whispered a prayer. In response, a gust of wind swept away the sandstorm, revealing the astonished faces of the Arabian wizards. The winds carried my voice across the desert, resonating with divine authority. "Fear not, for the Lord is with me!" Empowered by my faith and the knowledge that the Almighty stood beside me, I charged towards the astonished wizards. And my staff glowed with a blinding radiance, matching the intensity of my conviction. With a final surge of energy, I released a beam of light that engulfed the Arabian wizards, stripping them of their malevolent powers.

Then the desert fell silent as the last echoes of battle faded away. The Arabian wizards lay defeated, their wicked intentions undone by the unwavering faith and divine power that had been bestowed upon me. And though the battle was won, I knew my journey was not over. As I looked towards the horizon, I understood that my purpose transcended time and place. Guided by the Almighty, I would continue my mission to bring hope and protect the innocent against all darkness, no matter the challenges that laid ahead.

So as the sun set over the ancient dunes of the Arabian desert, I, Elijah, stood in awe of the countries of Arabia and that had summoned me from the pages of history. Then the barren landscape seemed both familiar and foreign, transformed by the passage of time. Gone were the simple tents and wandering tribes I knew from biblical times, replaced by sprawling cities and modern marvels I was truly in awe.

So confused and disoriented, I sought answers from the divine. It became apparent that I was called here to confront a new form of darkness that had risen in the heart of the desert. A even more secretive group of Arabian wizards than the first group, practicing the arcane arts that had long vanished from the world I once knew, threatened to plunge the land into chaos. And their dark intentions were evident. They sought to harness the mystical power of the desert sands and unleash it upon the unsuspecting population. But their motives remained unclear but I understood that their malevolence must be stopped.

So drawn by an unseen force towards their lair, I found myself standing at the entrance of a hidden cavern. Inside, the wizards gathered in a circle, robes flowing like shadows, and symbols etched in the sand illuminated by flickering flames. Their chanting filled the air, resonating with ancient power. So as I stepped forward, my footsteps betrayed my presence, and the wizards' eyes turned towards me. Their expressions wavered between astonishment and malice. I held my staff high, the same staff that parted the waters and summoned divine fire in days long gone. I prayed for strength, invoking the name of the Almighty, and the staff began to glow with a celestial radiance that I had no knowledge of.

And without hesitation, the lead wizard named Amir raised his hands, conjuring a torrent of dark energy aimed directly at me. Instinctively, I twisted and turned, evading the deadly assault with the agility of a dancer, and unleashed a counterattack of radiant light. The clash of opposing forces sent shockwaves through the cavern, causing the very walls to tremble. Then the battle became a dance of elemental forces. And my knowledge of ancient wisdom and the guidance of the Almighty allowed me to anticipate the wizards' moves and adapt accordingly. But they fought fiercely, determined to eliminate the threat I posed to their dark ambitions.

The sands beneath my feet churned and swirled, manipulated by the wizards' incantations. It was as if the desert itself conspired against me, but I remained resolute. With each strike of my staff, I invoked divine intervention, and beams of light cascaded upon the wizards, sapping their malevolent powers. Then in a last ditch effort, the lead wizard Amir conjured a massive sandstorm just like the wizards in the last group, and a whirlwind of fury that threatened to engulf us all again. And the tempest seemed insurmountable, but I called upon the Almighty's strength and whispered a prayer. My plea was answered, and a fierce gust of wind swept away the sandstorm, revealing the astonished faces of the Arabian wizards.

"Fear not, for the most high is with me!" I proclaimed, and the words carried with the authority of divine decree. And Empowered by my faith, I charged towards the bewildered wizards, with my staff shining like a beacon of hope. The light enveloped them, breaking their dark enchantments and leaving them defenseless. So the battle ended, but the mission continued. Though the Arabian wizards were defeated, I knew that darkness could emerge anew. With my heart resolved and faith unwavering, I vowed to remain vigilant, prepared to face any threat that dared to challenge the forces of good and justice. So as I departed from the cavern, the sands whispered tales of an ancient warrior who crossed time and defied the odds. My journey continued, guided by the Almighty's hand, as I ventured more forth into a Arabia far from my own, united in the timeless quest to protect the innocent and uphold the light.

So deep in my heart I heard The Most High saying that the battles in Arabia were not over and they were going to get more intense. So as the sun dipped below the horizon, casting a fiery glow over the Arabian desert, I, Elijah, found myself facing a challenge beyond any I had encountered in my biblical days. Summoned into the future, I discovered a Arabian world transformed, where the ancient ways intertwined with modern marvels and technologies. And in the heart of the desert, an enigmatic new group of Arabian wizards lead by a wizard named Hassan wielded powers that defied the laws of nature.

Then the Arabian wizards, garbed in intricate robes adorned with ancient symbols, exuded an aura of confidence as they gathered in a hidden oasis, their lair obscured by the shifting sands. Mystical flames danced before them, illuminating the night with an eerie glow. Their chants echoed through the desert, and the language of their ancient art forgotten by time so I thought. But Uncertain of my purpose, I sought guidance from the Almighty. And it became evident that I was brought to this time to end the dark intentions of the Arabian wizards, who sought to harness the desert's mystic energy for nefarious purposes and I thought to myself they shouldn't even have this ancient knowledge because innocent lives hung in the balance, and I could not turn away now.

So drawn by an unseen force, I approached the entrance to their cavernous lair. As I stepped forward, the shifting sands betrayed my presence if that makes sense, and the wizards' piercing gazes fell upon me. Their expressions wavered between curiosity and hostility as they beheld a figure from the distant past standing before them. But raising my staff, I invoked the name of the Almighty and felt a divine presence envelop me again. And the staff glowed with a celestial radiance just like before but just a different color, and a testament to the ancient power it held.

Then without warning, the lead wizard Hassan extended his arms, and torrents of dark energy erupted towards me. Dodging with the agility of a desert fox, I managed to evade the lethal assault. Channeling divine energy, I unleashed beams of radiant light in retaliation, causing the cavern walls to tremble from the force of the clash. But the battle escalated into a breathtaking spectacle of elemental forces. The wizards summoned great gusts of wind, manipulating the desert sand like an army at their command. And their spells shot forth like bolts of lightning, weaving through the air with deadly precision, But my faith was unwavering, and my resolve unyielding. I chanted verses from the ancient scriptures, calling upon the Almighty's protection. With each strike of my staff, I countered their dark magic, leaving trails of radiant energy in my wake.

Then the desert became a swirling symphony of sand and energy, and I danced amidst the chaos, my every move guided by divine intervention. Time seemed to stand still as the battle raged on, the desert's heart echoing with the echoes of mystical incantations. Then in a desperate gambit, the lead wizard Hassan conjured a massive sandstorm and I thought what is with theses Arabs and their sandstorms because their sandstorm were almost as terrifying as the one I caused earlier in my arrival, but a maelstrom of fury threatened to consume us all. And the tempest was relentless, disorienting even the most steadfast of souls. But my faith in the Almighty remained steadfast, and I whispered a prayer as the sandstorm bore down upon me.

So in response to my plea, a fierce gust of wind surged forth, sweeping away the sandstorm and revealing the astonished faces of the Arabian wizards. The winds carried my voice across the desert, resonating with divine authority. "Fear not, for the Lord is with me! I heard again" So I proclaimed, and the words carried with them the weight of divine decree. And empowered by my faith, I surged forward, my staff a beacon of hope in the encroaching darkness. Then the light engulfed the Arabian wizards, sapping their malevolent powers, leaving them defenseless against the divine might. Then the battle reached its crescendo, and the cavernous lair shook as the final clash of forces rent the air. With a resounding explosion of light, the Arabian wizards laid in defeated just like the previous group, and their dark intentions undone by the unwavering faith and divine power that had been bestowed upon me. And as the last echoes of battle faded away, I knew my mission transcended time and space. But my purpose was to stand as a defender of justice, to protect the innocent from the darkness that lurked in the hearts of men. Guided by the Almighty, I would continue my journey, vigilant against any threat that dared to challenge the forces of good.

And so, with a heart filled with gratitude and resolve, I departed from the ancient desert, leaving behind tales of an ancient warrior who had crossed time itself literally. But my quest continued, for the battle against darkness knows no end at all, and the sands of time would forever carry my tale. So as the sun dipped below the horizon, casting a fiery glow over the Arabian desert, I, Elijah, found myself facing a challenge beyond any I had encountered So far, And I discovered in the heart of the desert, an even newer enigmatic group of Arabian wizards lead by a guy named Ali Omar and he was determined not to fall like the 2 leaders before him and he had wielded powers that defied the laws of time and gravity.

So Then the new group of Arabian wizards, garbed in intricate robes adorned with ancient symbols, exuded an aura of confidence as they gathered in a hidden oasis, their lair obscured by the shifting sands. Mystical flames danced before them, illuminating the night with an eerie glow. Their chants echoed through the desert, the language of their ancient art forgotten by time, But unbeknownst to us, the dark intentions of the wizards had not gone unnoticed. The Arabian military, alerted to the potential threat these sorcerers posed, deployed a contingent of elite soldiers to investigate and neutralize the danger.

So as I stood at the entrance to the cavernous lair, my senses tingled with a growing presence. From the periphery of the desert, the thumping of hooves and the clanking of armor heralded the approach of the Arabian soldiers. Their faces etched with determination, these brave warriors represented a formidable force, clad in gleaming armor that glistened under the desert moon. Then the soldiers formed a protective circle around the cavern, and their weapons drawn and shields raised. A seasoned general, with eyes that betrayed the wisdom of countless battles, took the lead. Approaching me, he spoke with a tone of both respect and caution, acknowledging the aura of ancient power that surrounded me. He recognized my intent to confront the sorcerous threat, and we formed an uneasy alliance to tackle the common enemy.

Then as the Arabian wizards lead by Ali Omar emerged from the cavern, their malevolent intentions clear, the soldiers braced for the imminent clash. The lead wizard, in a display of arrogance, dismissed the military's presence, confident in the superiority of their dark powers. And with the battle lines drawn, the Arabian soldiers launched their assault, arrows soaring through the air and swords flashing like lightning. Their precision and coordination were unmatched, and they engaged the wizards in a fierce exchange of might and magic.

Yet the dark powers of the wizards proved elusive and unpredictable. Bolts of mystical energy shot forth, incinerating arrows midflight and sending shockwaves through the desert sands. Despite the soldiers' valor, their conventional weapons were ineffective against the ethereal nature of the arcane. Then realizing the urgency of the situation, I stepped forward, staff raised high, and invoked the name of the Almighty.

A radiant aura enveloped me, imbuing me with divine strength, as I charged towards the fray. And with a thunderous voice, I chanted ancient verses from the Scriptures, channeling the Almighty's power through my staff. The soldiers' eyes widened with awe as they beheld the manifestation of divine energy.

Then in a display of unity, the Arabian soldiers rallied around me, their faith in the Almighty strengthened by the presence of this ancient warrior. Their weaponry augmented with spiritual fervor, and they pressed forward with a renewed determination. Then the battle intensified into a symphony of light and darkness. Soldiers and wizards clashed in a dance of destiny, the desert's heart echoing with the fervent prayers and incantations that defined the battle's essence. So as the battle wore on, the soldiers' spirits began to wane under the unrelenting assault of the wizards. Drawing strength from my unwavering faith, I redoubled my efforts, weaving through the chaos, and unleashed beams of radiant light that struck at the heart of the arcane.

Then the Arabian soldiers took heart from my resolve, and together we formed a formidable force. We advanced with unwavering determination, each step carrying the weight of justice and the hope of protecting the innocent and I thought to myself The Arabian military chose the right side. Then the tide of battle shifted as the wizards struggled to maintain their ground against the combined forces of faith and military powers. But bolstered by the Almighty's divine intervention, we gained the upper hand, slowly pushing the dark sorcerers back towards their cavernous lair.

But as the last remnants of the sorcerous threat fell before us, the desert fell silent once more, and a sense of victory and camaraderie filled the air. And the Arabian soldiers exchanged glances of gratitude, having witnessed the timeless power of faith combined with the valor of the modern military. And in the aftermath of the battle, the Arabian soldiers and I stood united, comrades in arms against the darkness that had threatened to consume the land. With the Arabian military now aware of the dangers that lurked within their borders, they vowed to remain vigilant against any resurgence of sorcery. And so, with a shared purpose and the sands of time bearing witness to our triumph, we parted ways, our destinies forever entwined by the Battle of the Sorcerous Sands. With the Almighty's blessing guiding me forward, I resumed my journey, knowing that wherever darkness dared to emerge, the light of faith and valor would stand ready to vanquish it. But I was told that their was another battle in Arabia was ahead of me. So as the sun dipped below the horizon, casting a fiery glow over the Arabian desert, I, Elijah, found myself facing a newer challenge beyond any I had encountered, And I discovered a newer secret group of Arabian wizards lead by a wizard named Abdul Jamal and he wielded powers of dark matter. So the Arabian wizards, garbed in intricate robes adorned with ancient symbols, exuded an aura of confidence as they gathered in a hidden oasis, their lair obscured by the shifting sands like they have been taught. And I recognized their pattern because like last time mystical flames danced before them, illuminating the night with an eerie glow. Their chants echoed through the desert once more, and the language of their ancient art forgotten by time, But unbeknownst to us, the dark intentions of the wizards had not gone unnoticed. The Arabian military, alerted to the potential threat these sorcerers posed, deployed a contingent of elite soldiers to investigate and neutralize the danger.

So as I stood at the entrance to the cavernous lair, my senses tingled with a growing presence. From the periphery of the desert, the thumping of hooves and the clanking of armor heralded the approach of the Arabian soldiers. Their faces etched with determination, these brave warriors represented a formidable force, clad in gleaming armor that glistened under the desert moon. Then the soldiers were led by General Malik, a seasoned veteran known for his tactical brilliance and unwavering loyalty to the Arabian kingdom. And he had faced many adversaries in his illustrious career, but nothing could have prepared him for the surreal encounter that lay ahead.

So approaching me, General Malik spoke with a tone of both respect and caution, acknowledging the aura of ancient power that surrounded me. And he recognized my intent to confront the sorcerous threat, and we formed an uneasy alliance to tackle the common enemy just like the lower ranks of the Arabian Military did with me. Then in the distance, the Arabian wizards emerged from the cavern, their malevolent intentions clear. The soldiers braced for the imminent clash. The lead wizard, Aramis, in a display of arrogance, dismissed the more seasoned military's presence, confident in the superiority of their dark powers.

Then with the battle lines drawn, the Arabian soldiers launched their assault, arrows soaring through the air and swords flashing like lightning. Their precision and coordination were unmatched, and they engaged the wizards in a fierce exchange of might and magic.

Yet the dark powers of the wizards proved elusive and unpredictable. Bolts of mystical energy shot forth, incinerating arrows midflight and sending shockwaves through the desert sands. Despite the soldiers' valor, their conventional weapons were ineffective against the ethereal nature of the arcane. And realizing the urgency of the situation, I stepped forward, staff raised high, and invoked the name of the Almighty. A radiant aura enveloped me, imbuing me with divine strength, as I charged towards the fray. Then with a thunderous voice, I chanted ancient verses again from the Scriptures, channeling the Almighty's power through my staff. The more seasoned soldiers' eyes widened with awe as they beheld the manifestation of divine energy.

Then in a display of unity, the Arabian soldiers rallied around me, their faith in the Almighty strengthened by the presence of this ancient warrior. Their weaponry augmented with spiritual flavor, and they pressed forward with a renewed determination. Then as the battle intensified into a symphony of light and darkness just like the last one, a new player emerged from the shadows: the Arabian citizens now. Driven by curiosity and fear, a group of common people had gathered to witness the spectacle. But as the battle unfolded before them, they realized they could not stand idly by. And their spirits emboldened by witnessing my unwavering faith and the valor of the soldiers, the Arabian citizens picked up discarded weapons and joined the fight. Ordinary men and women now stood side by side with the soldiers, united against the common enemy that threatened their homeland.

So with makeshift weapons in hand and determination in their hearts, the Arabian citizens launched themselves into the fray. Their courage surprised even the wizards lead by Abdul Jamal, who struggled to comprehend how mere commoners could possess such tenacity. Then the battle became a tapestry of epic proportions. Soldiers, citizens, and me the ancient warrior, Elijah, fought against the dark forces of the Arabian wizards lead by Abdul Jamal. The desert sands bore witness to the unwavering spirit of the people, their collective will to protect their home and loved ones propelling them forward. And the Arabian citizens fought with a raw ferocity, their newfound resolve serving as a potent weapon against the dark arts of the sorcerers. Each blow struck with the weight of their homeland's history and the hopes of a better future.

So Their presence ignited a sense of camaraderie among the soldiers, bolstering their strength and determination. Together, they formed an unyielding wall against the wizards' onslaught, their combined force overwhelming the dark sorcerers.

And the Arabian wizards, sensing the tide turning against them, became desperate. They unleashed a final, cataclysmic surge of dark energy, their malevolent intentions laid bare. But the soldiers, the citizens, and I stood resolute, my staff glowing with a brilliance that matched the fire in our hearts. So with a collective effort, we pushed back against the dark forces, each step imbued with the strength of faith, valor, and unity. The Arabian wizards fought with the desperation of those who had lost all hope, but their malevolence was no match for the unwavering spirit of the Arabian people. And in a resounding explosion of light, the Arabian wizards lay defeated, their dark intentions undone by the unwavering faith and divine power that had been bestowed upon us. The desert fell silent once more, the echoes of battle fading into the sands.

And as the dust settled, the Arabian citizens, soldiers, and I stood victorious, united by the shared experience of the Battle of the Sorcerous Sands. The Arabian military's valor, the citizens' courage, and the ancient warrior's unwavering faith had forged an unbreakable bond among us. So with the dawn of a new day, we parted ways, our destinies forever entwined by the battles fought and the triumphs achieved. But the memory of our shared victory against the darkness would endure, a testament to the power of unity, faith, and valor in the face of adversity.

Then finally I was told that the very last battle in the countries of Arabia was just ahead of me. So as I stood at the entrance to the cavernous lair, my senses tingled with a growing presence. From the periphery of the desert, the thumping of hooves and the clanking of armor heralded the approach of the Arabian soldiers. Their faces etched with determination, these brave warriors represented a formidable force, clad in gleaming armor that glistened under the desert moon. Then the soldiers were led by General Malik once more, the seasoned veteran known for his tactical brilliance and unwavering loyalty to the Arabian kingdom. Then in the distance, the Arabian wizards emerged from the cavern, their malevolent intentions clear. The soldiers braced for the imminent clash. The lead wizard, now Aramis Abdul, in a display of arrogance, dismissed the military's presence, confident in the superiority of their dark powers.

So with the battle lines drawn, the Arabian soldiers launched their assault, arrows soaring through the air and swords flashing like lightning. Their precision and coordination were unmatched, and they engaged the wizards in a fierce exchange of might and magic. Yet once again the dark powers of the wizards proved elusive and unpredictable. Bolts of mystical energy shot forth, incinerating arrows and sending shockwaves through the desert sands for the last time. And despite the soldiers' valor, their conventional weapons were ineffective against the ethereal nature of the arcane. But realizing the urgency of the situation, I stepped forward, staff raised high for the last time in Arabia, and invoked the name of the Almighty. A radiant aura enveloped me, imbuing me with divine strength, as I charged towards the fray. So with a thunderous voice, I chanted ancient verses yet again from the Scriptures, channeling the Almighty's power through my staff. And in a display of unity, the Arabian soldiers rallied around me again, and their faith in the Almighty strengthened by the presence of me a ancient warrior. So as the battle intensified into a symphony of light and darkness, a new group of Arabian citizens came on the scene and this was a younger group of Arabian citizens that were encouraged by the previous older group of Arabian citizens that were mostly their parents. But driven by curiosity and fear, a group of common people had gathered to witness the spectacle. But as the battle unfolded before them, they realized they could not stand idly by.

And their spirits emboldened by witnessing my unwavering faith and the valor of the soldiers, the younger Arabian citizens picked up discarded weapons and joined the fight. As Ordinary young men and young women now stood side by side with the soldiers, united against the common enemy that threatened their homeland just like their parents did. Then with makeshift weapons in hand and determination in their hearts, the young Arabian citizens launched themselves into the fray. Then the battle became a tapestry of epic proportions. Soldiers, citizens, and me the ancient warrior, Elijah, fought against the dark forces of the Arabian wizards. The desert sands bore witness to the unwavering spirit of the young people, and their collective will to protect their home and loved ones propelling them forward. And the young Arabian citizens fought with a raw ferocity, and their newfound resolve serving as a potent weapon against the dark arts of the sorcerers. Each blow struck with the weight of their homeland's history and the hopes of a better future.

So their presence ignited a sense of camaraderie among the soldiers, bolstering their strength and determination. Together, they formed an unyielding wall like their parents against the wizards' onslaught, their combined force overwhelming the dark sorcerers. Then the Arabian wizards lead by Aramis Abdul, sensing the tide turning against them, became desperate. They unleashed a final, cataclysmic surge of dark energy, and their malevolent intentions laid bare. But the soldiers, the young citizens, and I stood resolute, my staff glowing with a brilliance for the final time that matched the fire in our hearts. And with a collective effort, we pushed back against the dark forces, each step imbued with the strength of faith, valor, and unity. The Arabian wizards lead by Aramis Abdul fought with the desperation of those who had lost all hope, but their malevolence was no match for the unwavering spirit of the younger Arabian people. So as the dust settled, the young Arabian citizens, soldiers, and I stood victorious, united by the shared experience of the Battle of the Sorcerous Sands led by the grand wizard Aramis Abdul. Then the Arabian military's valor, the citizens' courage, and the ancient warrior's unwavering faith had forged an unbreakable bond among us. Once again, So now I was truly finished here in the countries of Arabia and it has been a epic journey, but now it was time to meet back up with David and Jordan in the New Goshen Jet.

(The Locust Outbreak)

"David like before it is time to visit the King of America once again" I told David as soon as he came with Jordan to pick me up in the New Goshen Jet, and then minutes later the New Goshen Jet took off into the sky leaving Arabia behind. Then after hours flew by, we were in New York landing in Coney Island, then me and David got off the Jet "see you two on the next mission" said Jordan and then the New Gosen Jet took off into the sky. "Now let's go to The Kings Tower for the hundredth time" I said so we did and after some minutes flew by, we arrived at the Kings tower, then we went through the same usual procedures like always and once we finally spoke to the King to nobodies surprise again at this point he refused to let my people go once more. So, me and David left the Kings tower after the King denied my request again then after some minutes flew by we made our way back to the district of believers. "I have to start the next plague now unfortunately" I said to David as we approached his apartment, then I lifted my staff then immediately I began to have another insightful vision.

So this time as I looked over New York City, a sudden and eerie silence descended upon the sand covered streets. The air thickened with anticipation, and residents gazed upward in bewilderment. As the clock struck noon, a dark shadow began to creep across the skyline. A swarm of locusts, unlike anything ever witnessed before, swept down upon the city like a relentless plague. And the horde of locusts seemed never-ending, blotting out the sun and casting an ominous pall over the city that never sleeps. Panic spread like wildfire, as people sought shelter wherever they could find it. And the deafening hum of a million wings echoed through the streets, drowning out even the loudest of sirens.

Buildings, parks, and landmarks were overrun by the relentless onslaught. The once vibrant greenery of Central Park after the corrections from the governments weather machines was devoured within minutes, leaving only bare, desolate land behind. Skyscrapers became eerie silhouettes, obscured by a thick layer of locusts, their silvery wings shimmering in the pale sunlight. So authorities scrambled to contain the disaster, but the sheer scale of the invasion proved overwhelming. They

178

tried using loud noises, smoke, and chemicals, but the locusts continued their relentless march. News channels broadcasted live coverage, with reporters struggling to find words to describe the surreal scene unfolding before their eyes. And as the day wore on, the swarm seemed to intensify, stretching far beyond the city limits. The specter of this apocalyptic invasion spread fear across the entire country. Scientists and experts puzzled over the cause, trying to discern what had triggered such an unprecedented catastrophe. And with the city paralyzed and resources dwindling, an unlikely unity began to emerge among New Yorkers. Strangers banded together to share whatever supplies they had and offered comfort to one another amid the chaos. The locusts had brought destruction, but they also brought the city together in a way that no one could have predicted.

So as night descended, the city's skyline was obscured by the ever-present cloud of locusts. The city's lights flickered on, casting an eerie glow on the swarm. Even in the darkest hour, there was a glimmer of hope as scientists and emergency responders tirelessly worked on finding a solution. And in the days that followed, the swarm slowly began to recede, retreating from the city they had ravaged. The damage was extensive, but New Yorkers proved resilient. They picked up the pieces, rebuilding their homes and lives, vowing to learn from the event and find ways to prevent such a catastrophe from ever happening again. And so, New York City stood strong once more, a testament to the human spirit's resilience in the face of nature's might. The swarm of locusts became a part of the city's history, a haunting memory that would forever remind them of their collective strength and determination to survive, but little did they know that those locust was just the first wave of locust and another wave was to come.

So after a day of trying to rebuild another swarm of locust descended upon the city, and these locust were not regular like the ones in the first wave but theses locusts were poisonous, so chaos erupted in the streets. People rushed to find shelter, seeking refuge in buildings, cars, and any available space. The deafening hum of a million wings filled the air, causing disorientation and fear among the inhabitants. And the locusts insatiable hunger led to widespread devastation. They voraciously consumed everything in their path spitting out poisonous fumes, and trees plants, and crops fell victim to their relentless assault. Parks and gardens turned into barren wastelands, and Central Park was reduced to a poisonous skeletal landscape.

And the city's iconic landmarks, such as the Empire State Building and the Statue of Liberty, were shrouded in a veil of locusts, so imagine the whole Statue of Liberty being covered in locust that's what the citizens saw. And the swarming insects seemed to take over every nook and cranny, creating an otherworldly atmosphere that left residents and visitors in awe and terror. So, the authorities worked tirelessly to find a solution again to the locust, but the scale of the invasion was so overwhelming. But entomologists and scientists from around the world were called in to study the phenomenon and devise strategies to combat the locusts. And the media covered the catastrophe extensively, broadcasting live reports from ground zero, and some reporters has their microphones fully covered in locust but some of them documented the city's struggle against this unprecedented disaster.

But despite the calamity, the New Yorkers displayed remarkable resilience. Strangers banded together, forming impromptu support networks and offering aid to those in need. Community centers and churches became makeshift shelters, providing food and solace to those who had lost their homes. And as the days passed, the poisonous swarm of locust seemed to extend beyond the city, affecting neighboring states and regions. The situation became a national emergency, drawing the attention of politicians and government agencies. The nation rallied to offer assistance to New York City, sending supplies, volunteers, and experts to aid in the recovery efforts.

And at nightfall, the city glowed with a surreal luminance caused by the combination of streetlights and the shimmering wings of the poisonous locusts. And the sight was both mesmerizing and haunting, and a reminder of the power of nature and the fragility of humanity's urban fortresses.

So the second wave of locust gradually began to end, as the swarm of locust started to recede, the city began the arduous process of rebuilding like little ants. Parks were replanted, damaged structures were repaired, and communities rallied together to restore the city to its former glory. New York emerged from the ordeal stronger and more united than ever before, having weathered a catastrophic event that left an indelible mark on its history. And in the aftermath, research continued to understand the cause of the locust invasion and to develop measures to prevent such a catastrophe

But The Most High was not finished with New York and a third wave of Locust was about to invade the city and these locusts were giant compared to the locust of the first two waves. So as the giant swarm of locusts descended upon the city, the initial shock of citizens gave way to panic and chaos. They have never seen such insects that were that big, I mean maybe in dinosaur movies. But people ran through the streets, seeking shelter from the relentless giant swarm of locust. And the deafening hum of a million wings filled the air, drowning out all other sounds and adding to the sense of foreboding that enveloped the city.

And the giant dinosaur movie like locusts, driven by an insatiable hunger, swept through the city with a voracious appetite. They devoured trees, plants, and crops, and even some people, and the giant locust left a trail of destruction in their wake. And Central Park really began to start looking like Egypt at this point. And landmarks like the Empire State Building and the Statue of Liberty were shrouded in a dense cloud of locusts, and it was so bad that the giant locust knocked off the head of the Statue of Liberty, and their silhouettes barely visible through the giant swarm. And the city's skyline, usually a symbol of progress and modernity, became an eerie spectacle, cloaked in an ever-moving mass of giant insects.

And as the situation escalated, the authorities mobilized an emergency response. And they enlisted the help of entomologists, biologists, and experts from around the world to analyze the swarm's behavior and find a solution. The media covered the disaster extensively, broadcasting live reports from the ground, showcasing the city's struggle against an biblical plague they called it. And New Yorkers faced a daunting challenge, but their resilience shone through the darkest moments. Strangers became allies, working together to share resources and support each other emotionally. And the city's diverse communities displayed a remarkable sense of unity, transcending social and cultural boundaries to confront the common threat.

But with the city's infrastructure strained to its limits, makeshift shelters were established in schools, churches, and community centers. And these sanctuaries offered food, water, and medical aid to those who had lost their homes or were displaced by the giant swarm's relentless advance. But the locust invasion extended beyond New York City, affecting neighboring states and regions. And the disaster became a national emergency in America, prompting an outpouring of support from across the country. Volunteers and supplies poured into the city, showcasing the nation's solidarity and willingness to assist those in need. So during the nights, the city took on an otherworldly appearance. The glow of streetlights mingled with the iridescent shimmer of giant locust wings, creating an eerie and haunting spectacle. Many found it difficult to sleep, as the constant buzzing of wings and the unsettling sight of the giant swarm's dark cloud lingered in their minds.

But the third wave of locust was coming to an end, and as the hours turned into days, the giant swarm of locust finally began to recede. And the city could start assessing the damage and focus on the long and challenging process of recovery once more. And residents came together to restore their beloved city, planting new trees, and rebuilding parks, and repairing damaged infrastructure. But even still the disaster left an indelible mark on the city's history and psyche. And it became a turning point, prompting discussions on environmental conservation, preparedness for natural disasters, and the importance of unity in the face of adversity. But New York City emerged from the ordeal a changed place. The memory of the giant locust invasion would forever be etched into the collective memory, serving as a reminder of the fragility of urban life and the resilience of its inhabitants. And the city's journey to healing was a testament to the human spirit's ability to rise from the ashes and rebuild, even after the most challenging of trials. But now there was about to be a fourth wave of locust and just like the last wave of locust these new locusts were not just giant but they were giant and poisonous. So as the giant poisonous swarm of locusts descended upon the city, an eerie silence fell over the sand covered streets. And the atmosphere was charged with tension, and people gazed upward in disbelief and fear. And the sheer size of the giant poisonous swarm was unimaginable, stretching as far as the eye could see, blotting out the sun and casting an ominous shadow over the metropolitan.

And the giant poisonous locusts wings beat in unison, creating a deafening roar that drowned out the sounds of the city. And the air was filled with a poisonous scent of earth and foliage, now mingled with the pungent odor of the insects. And residents hurriedly sought refuge, barricading themselves indoors or seeking safety in subway tunnels and basements. But as the giant poisonous swarm moved methodically through the city, destruction followed in its wake. Trees were stripped bare and died, and their leaves reduced to confetti that covered the ground like a somber carpet. Flowerbeds and gardens were transformed into barren patches of dirt, devoid of life and color. And the giant poisonous locusts reached iconic landmarks, and even the sturdiest of structures were not spared. And the giant poisonous swarm engulfed skyscrapers, the gnarled branches of the Chrysler Building and One World Trade Center memorials obscured by the churning mass of insects. And the headless Statue of Liberty, standing tall and defiant, appeared to wear a shimmering cloak of locusts, lending an eerie and surreal beauty to the monument, and even more pieces began to fall off the monument.

But the city's response was swift, but the scale of the invasion posed unprecedented challenges. So, the authorities deployed teams of experts to assess the situation and find ways to mitigate the damage. They experimented with noise generators, chemical barriers, and even enlisting the help of natural predators, but the giant poisonous locusts seemed relentless, their numbers seemingly inexhaustible.

But as usual the media coverage was relentless, capturing the dramatic scenes unfolding across the city. And reporters risked their safety to provide live updates, showcasing the desperation and determination of New Yorkers in the face of this calamity. The entire nation was transfixed, watching in disbelief as the giant poisonous swarm's relentless march continued and it seemed to never end. But Amid the chaos, stories of courage and compassion emerged. Everyday heroes rose to the occasion, organizing impromptu rescue missions and assisting the elderly and vulnerable. And the city's spirit of resilience and unity shone through the darkest moments, as strangers extended helping hands to one another, sharing food, water, and hope. But as days turned into nights, the city took on an eerie and haunting beauty. The glow of streetlights illuminated the swarm, creating a mesmerizing display of twinkling lights that seemed to pulse with a life of their own. And the constant hum of locust wings became a constant backdrop, a dissonant symphony that echoed through the sleepless nights. And the swarm's impact extended beyond the city limits, affecting neighboring states and regions again. And New York's disaster became a national concern, prompting a united effort to offer aid and support. Volunteers from all walks of life flooded into the city, their altruism a testament to the nation's resilience and compassion.

But still the disaster left a lasting legacy, influencing urban planning, environmental policies, and disaster preparedness for months to come. And the giant poisonous locust invasion became a cautionary tale, and a reminder of the fragile balance between humanity and nature and the importance of cherishing and protecting the environment. But just as people thought the worse was over a great spread of the giant poisonous locust began, And as the swarm of locusts descended upon New York City, it quickly became evident that this was not an isolated event. And reports started pouring in from neighboring states and regions, indicating that the locust invasion was a widespread catastrophe. Now Cities like Philadelphia, Boston, and Washington D.C. faced similar challenges as the swarm swept through their streets, devouring vegetation and leaving behind a trail of destruction. Parks and gardens in these cities suffered the same fate as Central Park did, transforming into desolate landscapes all over America and a devoid of life.

But now the nation's capital, Washington D.C., faced unique challenges as the giant poisonous swarm descended upon its iconic landmarks like the old White House and the old National Mall. And the sight of locusts enveloping the Lincoln Memorial and the Washington Monument sent shockwaves across the country, symbolizing the gravity of the disaster. And the Midwest and Southern states were not spared from the locust invasion either. Agricultural regions, known as the country's breadbasket, were hit hard as the voracious giant poisonous insects consumed crops and threatened food supplies. Farmers fought a desperate battle to protect their livelihoods, but the sheer size of the giant poisonous swarm overwhelmed even the most diligent efforts. And in California, the giant poisonous locust invasion added to the state's woes, exacerbating existing environmental challenges. So the Golden Gate Bridge and Hollywood's iconic sign were obscured by the cloud of giant poisonous insects, casting a surreal and eerie atmosphere over the state. And now countries around the world also faced their own encounters with the giant poisonous swarm. Europe, Asia, and Africa reported locust infestations on a scale not seen in generations. And international cooperation and assistance were mobilized as countries shared strategies and resources to combat the devastating plague.

So scientists and researchers worked tirelessly to understand the origins and behavior of the giant poisonous swarm. And it was discovered that a combination of climatic factors, including unusual weather patterns and changes in vegetation, had triggered a perfect storm for the locust population to explode so they thought. And the giant poisonous swarm's rapid spread was aided by the global interconnectedness of modern travel and trade. And the giant poisonous locust invasion's impact on the environment was far reaching. And the loss of vegetation disrupted local ecosystems, affecting wildlife populations and leading to a ripple effect on other species. Efforts to restore and rehabilitate the affected areas became a priority, and with governments and environmental organizations joining forces to reforest and rehabilitate the landscapes.

But the disaster also prompted discussions on food security and agricultural practices. Farmers and scientists collaborated to develop strategies to protect crops from future locust swarms and build resilience into agricultural systems. And despite the devastation, stories of hope and resilience emerged from affected communities. And people came together to support one another, offering aid, resources, and emotional support. And acts of kindness and compassion spread like wildfire, showcasing the strength of humanity in the face of adversity.

And As the swarm of giant poisonous locusts continued to engulf cities and regions worldwide, the scale of the catastrophe was unlike anything humanity had ever witnessed. From densely populated urban centers to remote rural areas, the relentless giant poisonous insects left a trail of destruction in their wake. And in North America, major cities like New York City, Los Angeles, and Toronto continued experienced the full force of the invasion. Skyscrapers and iconic landmarks were engulfed everywhere by the churning mass of giant poisonous locusts, creating surreal scenes that struck fear into the hearts of millions it was like a horror movie. And Europe, known for its rich history and cultural heritage, was not immune to the disaster. The streets of Paris, adorned with centuries of old architecture, were overrun by the relentless giant poisonous swarm. And even the Colosseum in Rome, a symbol of ancient human ingenuity, was encircled by the giant poisonous swarm, emphasizing nature's supremacy over human achievements. And in Asia, cities that were hubs of innovation and technology, like Seoul, Singapore, and Bangalore, faced their own battles against the giant poisonous locust invasion. And the towering skyscrapers and cutting-edge infrastructure in Saudi Arabia were no match for the ancient force of nature that descended upon them. And even in Africa, already grappling with locust infestations in the past, now faced a crisis of unprecedented proportions. Because the giant poisonous locusts devoured vital crops, exacerbating food insecurity and threatening the livelihoods of millions. And Kenya's Maasai Mara and South Africa's Kruger National Park, renowned for their wildlife, now saw the intrusion of the giant poisonous locusts, disrupting delicate ecological balances.

And now South America, known for its diverse landscapes and vibrant cultures, confronted the giant poisonous locust invasion with resilience and determination. And the Amazon rainforest, a crucial carbon sink and biodiversity hotspot, faced the looming threat of the giant poisonous swarm, underscoring the need for urgent global action on climate change and deforestation. And even Australia, already struggling with environmental challenges like wildfires and droughts, now faced the onslaught of giant poisonous locusts in its remote regions. And the Great Barrier Reef, already suffering from coral bleaching, was now faced with a new threat as the giant poisonous swarm's devastation extended even to the coastal areas.

But the locust invasion became a defining moment in international relations and diplomacy. And countries put aside geopolitical rivalries to coordinate global efforts to combat the crisis. And the United World convened emergency summits, and international organizations worked in tandem to distribute aid and resources to affected regions. And in the scientific community, experts collaborated on unprecedented scales. And the giant poisonous swarm's behavior was analyzed in minute detail, leading to groundbreaking research that shed light on the complexities of migratory patterns and swarm dynamics. The knowledge gained from this disaster laid the foundation for more effective pest control strategies in the future.

And environmental activists rallied with renewed vigor, leveraging the global attention to call for transformative action on climate change and environmental preservation. And public awareness campaigns urged individuals to adopt sustainable practices in their daily lives and hold corporations and governments accountable for their environmental impacts. And the recovery efforts were a testament to human resilience and adaptability. Communities came together to rebuild homes, restore ecosystems, and revitalize economies. Governments implemented policies to promote sustainable development, invest in renewable energy once more, and protect natural habitats. Now finally the fourth wave of locust was coming to and end and a fifth and final wave of locust was to come and this wave of locust had a mixture of all of the other locusts in the previous waves, but now there was about to be some paralyzing locust to come in the coming days, but nevertheless the fourth wave of locust was ending and over time, the swarm gradually subsided, leaving behind a changed world. And the giant poisonous locust invasion became a cautionary tale, and etched into the annals of history as a stark reminder of the consequences of human-induced environmental changes.

And the catastrophe ultimately catalyzed a global shift in consciousness. Governments, corporations, and individuals embraced a new era of environmental responsibility, prioritizing sustainable practices and ecological conservation. And the legacy of the giant poisonous locust invasion was not just one of devastation, but also of resilience, cooperation, and the triumph of the human spirit in the face of adversity.

And As the days passed, the planet healed, and ecosystems began to recover. And the locust invasion became a distant memory, but its lessons remained imprinted in the collective human consciousness. And the world emerged from this dark chapter more united, more sustainable, and more determined than ever to protect and cherish the fragile planet we call home. But now it was time for the fifth and final locust attack.

And now as the paralyzing locust invasion started persisted, the world's resources were stretched to their limits. International aid poured into affected regions, providing much-needed support for recovery and reconstruction efforts. Humanitarian organizations worked tirelessly to ensure food supplies reached those in need, alleviating the immediate threat of famine in hard-hit areas. And in the wake of the disaster, the global community recognized the urgent need for improved disaster preparedness and response mechanisms. And nations established international agreements and protocols to coordinate efforts in addressing future environmental crises. And the United World convened a special commission on global environmental threats, leading to the establishment of an international task force dedicated to monitoring and addressing potential ecological catastrophes.

But scientists continued to study the paralyzing swarm's of locust and migratory patterns and behavior, seeking to develop predictive models to anticipate future locust outbreaks. This research revolutionized pest control and crop protection, leading to more sustainable agricultural practices that minimized the use of harmful chemicals. And the paralyzing locust invasion served as a catalyst for innovation in the field of renewable energy and weather manipulation. And governments and corporations invested heavily in clean energy technologies, reducing their carbon footprints and mitigating climate change. And solar wind farms dotted the landscapes, providing clean and reliable energy sources while reducing dependence on fossil fuels. And in the aftermath of the disaster, there was a global movement to conserve and restore biodiversity. Protected areas expanded, and efforts to combat deforestation intensified. Reforestation projects took root worldwide, aiming to restore vast swaths of land that had been decimated by the paralyzing locusts. And the crisis also prompted a shift in consumer behavior, with people demanding more sustainable and eco-friendly products. And companies responded by adopting greener practices, leading to the rise of a new era of environmentally conscious businesses.

And education on environmental conservation became a cornerstone of school curriculums. And the next generation grew up with a deep understanding of humanity's interconnectedness with the natural world, ensuring a more sustainable future for the planet. And international cooperation on environmental issues became the new norm. As countries put aside political differences to address shared challenges, forging a spirit of solidarity that transcended borders. The locust invasion had inadvertently united the world in a common cause, fostering a new era of global collaboration. So as the days passed, the scars of the paralyzing locust invasion began to fade, but the world was forever changed. And the catastrophic event had left an indelible mark on human consciousness, serving as a stark reminder of the fragility of the planet and the urgency of environmental conservation.

And New York City and other affected cities rebuilt and flourished, embracing sustainable urban planning and green initiatives. Central Park, once devastated by the locusts, was transformed into a thriving urban oasis once again, and a symbol of nature's resilience and humanity's determination. And the global effort to combat the locust invasion laid the groundwork for tackling other environmental challenges, such as deforestation, water scarcity, and habitat loss. And the world learned valuable lessons from the disaster, lessons that would guide humanity toward a more sustainable and harmonious relationship with nature.

And the locust invasion of the past had transformed into a beacon of hope for the future. It served as a cautionary tale, reminding humanity of the consequences of neglecting the environment. But it also sparked a transformational change, leading to a greener, more sustainable world where people, wildlife, and ecosystems thrived in harmony. And in the end, the paralyzing locust invasion had given rise to a global movement, a movement that transcended borders and united humanity in a shared commitment to protect the planet and secure a brighter, more sustainable future for generations to come. And the world emerged from the crisis stronger, wiser, and more determined than ever to safeguard the delicate web of life that sustains us all. And finally the fifth and final wave of locust came to an end.

(The African Wizards)

The next morning, I wasn't surprised when I woke up to the sound of David's voice again. "Elijah today there is yet another major issue happening and this battle will be the final worldwide battle and this time it's in Africa" said David "what's happening" I replied "There is a group of some African wizards attacking the people in the Districts of believers in Africa and we need you to stop them ASAP" David explained "ok that should not be a problem" I replied "great and like usual the New Goshen Jet is already in Coney Island waiting for you" David said, and then the both of us left David's apartment and went to Coney Island. And after some minutes flew by, we were in Coney Island and I could see the New Goshen Jet waiting for me and David, so after some moments me and David got on the New Goshen Jet "What's up you two so Elijah has to go to Africa this time I heard and yes David your needed in New Goshen again sir for the last time" Jordan said while starting up the jet engines. So after some hours flew by the 3 of us arrived in Africa and Jordan found a safe place to land, so after the jet landed I stepped out of it and David stayed in the jet with Jordan "like always we will meet back up once your mission is complete" David explained, then moments later the New Goshen Jet was in the sky and I was now in Africa.

So now in Africa I found myself standing at the precipice of an otherworldly encounter in a African village, and my heart pounding with a mix of anticipation and trepidation. I, Elijah, the prophet from biblical times, had been transported through time to a modern-day African village so I thought. Here, I encountered a group of enigmatic wizards who wielded mystical powers, unlike anything I had witnessed in my own era and even more powerful than the Arabs. And the village was nestled amidst lush greenery, surrounded by towering mountains that seemed to guard its secrets. And the inhabitants were kind and welcoming, but they lived in fear of the powerful wizards who demanded tribute and obedience in exchange for sparing their village from calamity.

Then drawn by divine guidance, I decided to challenge these sorcerers, whose powers seemed to be rooted in a dark, ancient forces. But my mission was to liberate this village and restore their freedom from the

190

grip of fear. So with my staff in hand, I approached the wizards and their first leader named King Kofi in a sacred sanctuary, and then in a mysterious cave hidden within the depths of the mountains. Inside, I faced a quartet of formidable figures, adorned with vibrant patterns and symbols that exuded an aura of power. And their eyes narrowed at my intrusion, and I could feel their disdain for an intruder from a distant time. Undeterred, I addressed them with a voice that carried the authority of my divine purpose.

"I am Elijah, the prophet of the Almighty, sent to vanquish the darkness that shrouds this land," And I declared, my faith bolstering my resolve. And they laughed, taunting my antiquated appearance, but their laughter faltered as I raised my staff, and its end glowing with an otherworldly light. So the battle commenced, and bolts of energy surged through the air. And their spells were potent, conjuring storms and summoning spectral beasts, but my faith in the Almighty provided me with a shield against their malevolence. So I countered with my own arsenal of divine miracles, calling forth heavenly flames and lightning to pierce their defenses. And the cave trembled with the intensity of our clash, and the very earth seemed to quake beneath us.

So, as we fought, I realized that these wizards were not inherently evil; they had been misguided by the allure of power and darkness. I felt a pang of compassion for them, but I knew that their tyranny must end for the greater good. So in a final, decisive strike, I unleashed a torrent of light that engulfed the wizards, stripping them of their malevolent abilities and revealing the lost souls within. Their eyes now showed remorse and confusion, no longer cloaked in arrogance. "I offer you a chance for redemption," I implored. "Turn away from the darkness, embrace the path of light, and find forgiveness." And Touched by my words, the wizards relented, their hearts softened by the sincerity of my plea. They chose to abandon their malevolent ways and embrace a new journey towards redemption and healing.

Now with the village liberated from the clutches of darkness, a newfound peace settled upon the land. Grateful villagers celebrated my victory, recognizing that it was not my might alone that triumphed, but the divine guidance that had led me there. And as my mission concluded, I bid farewell to the village, knowing that the memory of this extraordinary encounter would remain etched in the tapestry of time. With my staff in hand and the Almighty's grace as my guide, I returned to my own era, carrying with me the lesson that even in the most desperate times, redemption and compassion can triumph over darkness. But my battle in Africa was not over yet and now I was about to encounter a second leader of the African wizards and his name was King Zaire. So, as I stepped into another sacred cave, an ethereal silence enveloped the atmosphere. And the air crackled with an energy that seemed ancient and potent. And the four African wizards lead by King Zaire regarded me with a mix of skepticism and amusement just like the last group, and their eyes glinting with a mysterious power. Then I shouted as a warning to them "I am Elijah, the prophet of the Almighty," I repeated, my voice unwavering, and though my heart raced with excitement and trepidation I continued to speak. "I have been guided here to free this land from the grip of darkness that shackles it." I said

And their response was a mocking chorus of laughter, and they gestured with their hands, summoning spectral images of fierce animals, elemental forces, and dark shadows. And their spells danced in the air, vivid and terrifying, a testament to the formidable power they held. But undeterred, I lifted my staff, a simple wooden rod that had witnessed the miracles of old, and recited the sacred words passed down to me through generations. And as I spoke, a radiant light emanated from the staff, illuminating the cave with an otherworldly glow. And the wizards lead by King Zaire expressions wavered, their laughter faltering as they recognized the gravity of my intent. But they realized that I was no ordinary visitor, but someone imbued with a power greater than they had known. So, the battle erupted, and with each clash of their spells against my divine miracles, the cavern reverberated with an ear-splitting resonance. And I summoned the heavens flames, sending them spiraling towards the wizards, who countered with gusts of wind and swirling currents of water.

And their powers seemed limitless, as an ancient knowledge passed down through generations. And their chants resonated with the heartbeat of the land, and I found myself battling not only their spells but the primal pulse of the earth itself. So as our confrontation intensified, I called upon the Almighty's strength, my staff becoming a conduit for divine intervention. Heavenly lightning cascaded from the cave's roof, striking the ground with a force that sent tremors through the mountain.

But the wizards were not so easily defeated. They retaliated with shadowy tendrils that sought to ensnare my spirit, to sap my strength. I felt the darkness tugging at my soul, threatening to overwhelm me, but I clung to the light within, drawing from my unwavering faith. And in the midst of our furious exchange, a glimpse of understanding flickered within me. These wizards were not inherently evil; but just like the last group they were individuals who had lost their way, lured by the temptation of untold power. And in that understanding, my heart softened, yearning for their redemption rather than their destruction.

But now with a newfound determination, I altered my approach. Instead of pushing them back with aggression, I extended a hand, an olive branch of compassion and hope. "Turn away from the darkness, embrace the path of light, and find forgiveness," I urged. And their defiant gazes wavered, revealing traces of remorse and longing for something more. The battle slowed, and the cave seemed to sigh with relief as the animosity ebbed away. And they surrendered their weapons of darkness, releasing the malevolent energy that had ensnared their souls. Then I led them to the village, where the inhabitants hesitated, fearing the wizards wrath. But I assured the villagers that these individuals had chosen redemption, and they now sought forgiveness and a new way of life. And then the village welcomed their former oppressors with hesitant smiles, gradually accepting their newfound intentions. Together, we built a bond of understanding, and the wizards used their remaining powers for good, mending what had been broken and nurturing the land instead of subjugating it. So for now my mission was complete, and as I bid farewell to the village, I knew that this encounter would be etched into their history forever. Then the clash between ancient biblical wisdom and modern-day African sorcery had brought about not only liberation but also a profound lesson in compassion and redemption.

So now I got a message from David saying that I was about to encounter a third group of African wizards lead by a man named King Jabari. So as I stood at the entrance of yet another sacred cave, a chill ran down my spine, not from fear, but from the anticipation of what laid ahead. And the cave's interior was adorned with ancient symbols and intricate carvings that seemed to pulsate with an eerie, primal energy. And the African wizards lead by King Jabari came before me with wore garments made of vibrant colors and adorned with beads and feathers, signifying their connection to the spiritual realm. But with warning I shouted to them "I am Elijah, the prophet of the Almighty," and I declared again, my voice echoing through the chamber. "I have been sent here to release this land from the clutches of darkness that have ensnared it." And Their response was not just laughter but a disdainful mockery unlike the last groups of wizards and that sent shivers through my being. And their eyes gleamed with an otherworldly luminescence, a testament to the immense power they held at their fingertips.

So without hesitation, they raised their hands, and the cave erupted with a symphony of spells and incantations. And the air crackled with energy as they summoned forces of nature to do their bidding. And ethereal beasts materialized from thin air, and their eyes glowing with an unsettling brilliance. But undeterred, I grasped my staff, an unassuming wooden rod that had accompanied me through the miracles of old days. And as I raised it, it seemed to resonate with the energy of the present, a conduit between the ancient and the contemporary. So with every clash of their dark spells against my divine miracles, the cave trembled as though torn between two opposing forces. The wizards lead by King Jabari wielded their powers with a familiarity that comes from lifetimes of practice, and I knew I had to match their strength with unwavering faith. So by calling upon the Almighty, I invoked the heavenly flames, engulfing the cavern with their radiant glow. But the wizards conjured gusts of wind, redirecting the flames with a precision that astonished even me. I could feel the ebb and flow of the elements, the heartbeat of the earth, as though it were guiding the wizards in their endeavors. But still with each passing moment, the battle intensified, and I felt the darkness tugging at my spirit, trying to penetrate my soul. It was a test of not just my strength but my resolve to stay true to the light. I found myself on the verge of exhaustion, my mind and body pushed to their limits.

But amidst the chaos, a flash of insight struck me: and these wizards were not malevolent beings, but individuals who had lost their way in the pursuit of power. So my heart softened with compassion, recognizing the misguided souls that hid behind the veil of arrogance. But determined to change the course of the battle, I altered my approach. Instead of retaliating with force, I extended my hand and uttered a prayer of forgiveness. "Turn away from the darkness, embrace the path of light, and find redemption," I implored. And Surprised by my offer, the wizards hesitated, their eyes showing glimmers of regret and longing for a different path. And the tension in the cave subsided, and the oppressive atmosphere gave way to an aura of contemplation.

And one of the wizards, a wise elder with streaks of gray in his hair, stepped forward, uncertainty etched on his face. "You come from a time beyond our comprehension," he said, his voice tinged with a mix of curiosity and respect. "Why do you seek to save us?" I met his gaze with unwavering determination then I answered him. "The Almighty's guidance transcends time and place," I replied. "My purpose is to bring light to the darkness, and that includes offering a chance for redemption to those who have strayed." So moved by my words, the elder nodded, and one by one, the other wizards followed suit. And they relinquished their dark arts, releasing the malevolent energy that had enslaved them for so long. And together, we emerged from the cave, and I led the wizards to a village they had once oppressed. But the villagers were apprehensive at first, but with each passing moment, they witnessed the transformation of these once malevolent sorcerers into individuals seeking atonement. And the wizards used their remaining powers to heal the land and bring prosperity to the village. And they became protectors rather than oppressors, guardians of nature and keepers of ancient wisdom. So as I prepared to depart from the village, the villagers gathered to bid me farewell. And their eyes were filled with gratitude, seeing the clash between ancient prophecy and modern-day sorcery had brought about not just liberation but also a profound lesson in compassion and redemption.

But now I was told that I was about to face my fourth group of African wizards lead by a man named King Faraji. So as the battle between Elijah and the African wizards raged on, news of the extraordinary clash spread like wildfire across the continent. It caught the attention of different African militaries, each eager to understand the source of the upheaval and how it might affect their nations.
So curiosity turned to concern, and leaders from neighboring countries dispatched emissaries to the village, seeking to ascertain the truth behind the mystical confrontation. Among the envoys were seasoned military commanders, well versed in strategy and tactics.

And the village elders, recognizing the potential ramifications of involving powerful military forces, called for a meeting with me. As the sun dipped below the horizon, the elders and the emissaries gathered in a thatched-roof meeting hall, its interior illuminated by flickering torchlight. So I sat at the head of the assembly, with my staff resting against my chair, exuding an aura of ancient wisdom. I addressed the dignitaries, explaining that the battle had been fought not for conquest or power, but to free the village from the oppressive grip of darkness. "These wizards were once tyrants, but they have chosen a path of redemption,"I said solemnly. "Their desire now is to heal the land and mend the wounds they once inflicted."

So The military leaders exchanged uneasy glances, unsure of how to proceed. And the wizards lead by King Faraji powers were unlike anything they had encountered before, and the thought of having such forces under their control was both tantalizing and terrifying. But one of the emissaries, a battle-hardened general known for his strategic brilliance, stepped forward with a respectful nod. "Prophet Elijah, we acknowledge the change in the wizards' hearts," he began, his voice resonating with authority. "But we cannot ignore the potential threat they pose to our nations." Then I acknowledged their concerns, realizing that a delicate balance needed to be struck. I proposed a solution that would allow the wizards to continue their path of redemption under the watchful eye of the village, while also offering their unique abilities to serve the greater good.

Then in a moment of insight, the village elders suggested forming a council, composed of representatives from the village, the wizards lead by King Faraji, and the different African militaries. This council would oversee the wizards' actions, ensuring they were directed towards healing and protection rather than aggression. And it was a proposition that intrigued the military leaders, offering a chance to harness the wizards' powers for the benefit of their nations. And they agreed to this alliance, and a pact was forged, uniting the villagers, and the wizards, and the military forces. So as the council began its work, the wizards lead by King Faraji used their gifts to quell natural disasters, restore barren lands, and protect wildlife from poachers. And the once-oppressive energy that surrounded the wizards had transformed into a force of good, a testament to their genuine desire for redemption.

And I, too, played a crucial role in the council, sharing my wisdom and guiding their efforts with divine insight. My presence offered a calming influence, ensuring that the alliance remained steadfast in its commitment to healing and peace. And the news of this unprecedented alliance spread far beyond the borders of the village, captivating the attention of nations worldwide. And governments and leaders from distant lands sent envoys, seeking to learn from the council's example and forge their path toward a harmonious existence. And in time, the council became a beacon of hope, an emblem of unity and cooperation that transcended borders and cultural barriers. And it was a testament to the transformative power of forgiveness, compassion, and redemption that could heal even the deepest wounds of history.

But after some days went by, I was told that I was about to face my fifth and final battle in Africa lead by a man named King Dakarai. And as the news of the clash between me and the African wizards lead by King Dakarai spread across the continent, it ignited both curiosity and concern among ordinary citizens. And the village where the battle had taken place became a pilgrimage site for many seeking answers and witnessing the remnants of the awe-inspiring confrontation. And among the intrigued citizens were a group of young warriors from various African tribes. They were known for their courage, skills, and unwavering loyalty to their homelands. So inspired by the legends surrounding the battle, they felt a calling to understand the truth behind the mystical encounter.

So with their weapons strapped to their backs and hearts filled with determination, the warriors set off on a journey to the village, eager to witness the aftermath of the historic clash. But when they arrived, they found the villagers rebuilding their homes and healing the land under the council's guidance. So I, knowing the significance of their presence, greeted the young warriors with a warm smile. And I sensed their curiosity and the potential for greatness within them. "You have come seeking knowledge and understanding," I said, his voice resonating with wisdom. "But Know that this battle was fought not for dominance but to liberate a village from the grasp of darkness."

So the young warriors listened with rapt attention, absorbing every word from me the prophet. And they were drawn to my aura of wisdom and the mysterious powers that surrounded me. And despite their initial skepticism, they felt an undeniable sense of respect for me the prophet and the wizards who had chosen a path of redemption. So I recognized the potential within the warriors and offered them the chance to learn from the wizards and the council. So with humility and a desire to grow, they accepted the invitation, immersing themselves in the village's teachings. And under the wizards' guidance, the young warriors learned to harness their inner strength and connect with the spiritual energies of their ancestors. And they discovered the power of unity, transcending tribal boundaries and fostering a brotherhood that crossed cultural divides.

Then as the days turned to weeks, the warriors underwent rigorous training, honing their combat skills and learning to channel their energy with purpose and precision. And they became adept at using their weapons not for violence but to protect and preserve life. And with their newfound knowledge, the young warriors returned to their respective tribes, spreading the teachings of the village council and the lessons they had learned. And their stories of the battle and the power of redemption ignited a spark in the hearts of their fellow citizens, inspiring them to look beyond their differences and embrace a shared destiny. And the warriors' influence was felt far and wide, uniting tribes that had been divided for generations. And they formed a league of warriors dedicated to peace, justice, and the protection of their continent's rich heritage.

And my name became synonymous with hope and transformation, and my teachings were passed down through generations. And The tale of my battle against the wizards lead by King Dakarai and the subsequent formation of the council became an integral part of African folklore, an emblem of the extraordinary possibilities that lay within the human spirit. And in the months that followed, the village where the battle had taken place grew into a beacon of unity and enlightenment. And citizens from different corners of Africa flocked to the village, seeking to learn from the council and participate in its mission to heal the continent's wounds.

And as the legend of me and the warriors spread across Africa, it served as a testament to the power of compassion, redemption, and unity— values that had transcended time and history, leaving an indelible mark on the heart and soul of the continent. But the story continues to be told, carried on the lips of storytellers, whispered in the ears of children, and etched into the hearts of all who hear it. And it is a story that reminds

Africa of its capacity for greatness and its ability to overcome any darkness that seeks to shroud its brilliance. And it is a reminder that even in the most extraordinary of battles, it is not just the warriors and prophets who make a difference but the ordinary citizens who answer the call to be part of something greater than themselves. And as the weeks passed, the village that had once been a battleground became a place of pilgrimage and wisdom, known across the continent as the "Sanctum of Redemption." And The council, comprising the village elders, the reformed wizards, the young warriors, and representatives from different African militaries, continued to thrive and fostered a spirit of unity and cooperation.

And the council's work extended far beyond the village, and their efforts to heal the land and protect its people garnered international recognition. Leaders from around the world sought their counsel, recognizing the council's unique ability to harness ancient wisdom and modern knowledge in pursuit of harmony. And I remained at the heart of the council, with my presence a guiding force that transcended time. And my words carried the weight of divine wisdom, and my counsel was sought not just by the council members but also by world leaders who sought an understanding of the profound transformation that had occurred.

So as the council's influence grew, so did its commitment to education and enlightenment. And they established academies where young minds from different African nations could come to learn about their continent's diverse cultures, history, and spirituality. And these academies became a hub of knowledge and a catalyst for cultural exchange, bridging gaps between tribes and fostering a shared sense of identity. And the village itself became a sanctuary for cultural preservation, with its inhabitants serving as custodians of ancient traditions and stories. And the Sanctum of Redemption became a center for art, music, and dance, celebrating the richness of Africa's cultural tapestry.

And the council also played a crucial role in fostering regional peace and stability. Because their efforts to mediate conflicts between tribes and nations became renowned, and their commitment to reconciliation served as an example to the world throughout it all, and the African wizards lead by King Dakarai remained steadfast in their pursuit of redemption. They used their powers not to dominate but to heal, lending their abilities to support the council's efforts in protecting the environment and conserving wildlife. And with each passing week, the legend of me Elijah and the wizards lead by King Dakarai became an integral part of African heritage, an inspiring tale of transformation that resonated with people from all walks of life. And the story was retold in songs, dances, and oral traditions, passed down through generations as a testament to the enduring power of forgiveness and unity. And my time in Africa finally came to an end.

(The Great Darkness)

"David it is time to visit the King of America yet again" I told David as soon as he came with Jordan to pick me up in the New Goshen Jet, and then minutes later the New Goshen Jet took off into the sky and we left Africa. Then after hours flew by, we were in New York landing in Coney Island, then me and David got off the Jet "see you two on the next one" said Jordan "Ok but there might not be a next one but I will still see you soon" David replied and then the New Gosen Jet took off into the sky. "Now let's go to The Kings Tower once again and I'm getting very close to wrapping things up" I said to David so we did and after some minutes flew by, we arrived at the Kings tower, then we went through the same usual procedures as always and once we finally spoke to the King he refused to let my people go again and no one was surprised by it either. So, me and David left the Kings tower after the King denied my request again then after some minutes flew by, we made our way back to the district of believers. "Now it's time for the next plague and I must start it now" I said to David as we approached his apartment, then I lifted my staff then immediately I began to have another insightful vision.

Then I began to look down on New York City, and the once vibrant metropolitan city went into darkness. And the city's streets fell eerily silent as the power grid failed, leaving millions of residents in utter darkness. And the initial confusion and chaos quickly gave way to a sense of unity as neighbors banded together to face the challenges ahead. So without electricity, daily routines were disrupted, and modern conveniences became obsolete. People adapted, relying on their resourcefulness and the strength of their community. And as the hours turned into days, New Yorkers found ways to cope and survive. So candle-lit gatherings became the norm, fostering newfound connections and friendships. People shared stories and experiences, realizing the profound impact of genuine human connection amidst the darkness.

And in this black-out world, the boundaries of class and status dissolved, and individuals from all walks of life came together. Strangers offered each other food, shelter, and comfort, demonstrating the resilience of the human spirit in times of adversity. And amid the darkness, a sense of rediscovery emerged. Parks became gathering places for concerts and storytelling under the starry night sky. And libraries and museums opened during the day, relying on natural light to offer knowledge and inspiration to those seeking refuge from the darkness. And as the city adjusted to its new reality, innovative solutions began to emerge. Renewable energy sources like solar panels and wind turbines were embraced to power essential services, gradually bringing light back to the city's streets. Yet, despite these advancements, people cherished the simplicity and closeness that the black-out pandemic had fostered. So as days passed, and eventually, the city's lights flickered back on, but the memories of the black-out pandemic lingered in the hearts of its people. The experience had forever changed their perspectives, reminding them of the value of human connection, community, and the strength found in unity. And as life resumed its course with electricity restored, New Yorkers continued to embrace the lessons learned from the darkness. And they vowed to cherish the newfound bonds and sense of togetherness that had emerged during their time in the black-out pandemic, forever grateful for the unity that had illuminated their lives in the darkest of times.

But the electricity going out was only the beginning and only the first phase of this black-out because in an unexpected turn of events, the black-out pandemic in New York City took a harrowing twist when the sun and moon seemingly vanished from the sky, leaving the city shrouded in perpetual darkness for three long days. Panic and fear gripped the hearts of New Yorkers as they faced an even more daunting challenge. And some people even thought that the world was ending for sure without the sun, moon, or stars in the sky.

And with no natural light to guide them, the already dire situation escalated. The city's makeshift power sources faltered, plunging the streets back into complete darkness. And the sense of unity that had blossomed during the initial black-out began to waver as desperation set in. And as the hours turned into days, the absence of sunlight and moonlight took a toll on people's morale. The once bustling parks and gathering spots were now deserted, and a palpable sense of isolation settled over the city. Without the sun's warmth and the moon's gentle glow, people felt disoriented and lost.

And communication became a struggle, as cell towers and internet services struggled to function without reliable power sources. The darkness hindered rescue efforts, making it difficult for emergency services to reach those in need. And panic spread like wildfire, and hope seemed to fade away. And as the darkness persisted, food and water became scarce. And the candle-lit gatherings that had once fostered camaraderie now dwindled as resources depleted. So people retreated to their homes, rationing what little supplies they had left, unsure of when the sun and moon would return. But yet, amid the darkness and despair, some small glimmers of hope emerged. As strangers came together to share whatever resources they had, clinging to the last threads of unity. And communities formed protective circles, ensuring the safety of those who were most vulnerable. And on the third day, just when hope seemed almost lost, a faint glimmer of light appeared on the horizon. And the sun and moon slowly began to reemerge, casting a dim light over the city.

And the relief that washed over New Yorkers was indescribable, and a renewed sense of gratitude for even the most basic elements of life took root. And the city, now scarred by this profound darkness, emerged with a newfound appreciation for the light. And the experience had tested the resilience of its people, pushing them to their limits, but it had also taught them the true value of community and the importance of cherishing every moment. And though the scars of the black-out pandemic and the days without sunlight and moonlight, New York City stood united, determined to face whatever challenges the future might hold. And the darkness had changed them, but it had also shown them the strength that comes from coming together in the face of unimaginable adversity. But those three days without the sun or moon was just the second phase of the darkness and a third phase was soon to come but nevertheless New York City did recover from the darkness for now.

But after some days went by and people thought that the darkness was over the black-out pandemic came back for another three days without sunlight and moonlight in New York City, but similar occurrences started emerging in other parts of the world Now. Reports flooded in from different cities, each experiencing their own version of the darkness now. And in Los Angeles, the City of Angels, the Hollywood lights dimmed, and the iconic skyline vanished, leaving residents in a state of disarray. And despite the challenges, the creative spirit of the entertainment capital shone through, as impromptu performances and storytelling sessions took place in the few remaining areas of light.

And London, a city known for its rich history and vibrant nightlife, found itself enveloped in darkness as well. And the River Thames became a guiding beacon as people relied on its flowing currents to navigate through the city. And the British resolve shone through, with citizens coming together in true stoic fashion, offering support to one another during the trying times. And in Tokyo, the bustling metropolitan city was cloaked in darkness, and the neon lights that once adorned the cityscape were now nothing more than memories. And Japanese ingenuity and discipline prevailed, as citizens efficiently rationed resources and managed to keep essential services running despite the lack of celestial light. And as the darkness spread to different corners of the globe, communication between cities became increasingly challenging. But people began to share stories of their experiences through handwritten letters, forming a network of shared struggles and triumphs. And in the midst of this global catastrophe, scientists and experts worked tirelessly to find an explanation for the sudden and simultaneous disappearance of sunlight and moonlight. And theories ranging from cosmic anomalies to supernatural events were discussed, but no concrete answers emerged.

So as the three days of darkness drew to an end, a collective sigh of relief reverberated across the world as the sun and moon finally returned to the skies. Then the cities gradually emerged from the shadows, but the impact of the black-out pandemic had left an indelible mark on the collective consciousness forever. And in the aftermath, countries came together to share resources and knowledge, forming global alliances to better prepare for future uncertainties. Renewable energy sources were heavily invested in, and new technologies were developed to prevent such widespread darkness from ever happening again so they thought.

And the memory of those dark days continued to shape societies, reinforcing the importance of unity and preparedness. And communities around the world became more resilient, fostering stronger bonds among their residents. And months passed, and the world eventually healed from the scars left by the black-out pandemic. And it became a turning point in human history forever, and a reminder of the fragility of modern society and the strength that can be found in unity during the darkest of times literally. And the legacy of the black-out pandemic endured, etched into the annals of history as a testament to the resilience of humanity and the unyielding spirit to overcome even the most formidable challenges. And as the sun and moon continued to rise and set, the world vowed never to forget the lessons learned from those dark days, cherishing the light that guides them through both the brightest and darkest hours of life. But little did they know a fourth phase of darkness was around the corner, but things went back to normal for the time being.

But after some weeks the fourth phase of darkness begun for another 3 days and as the world grappled with the mysterious disappearance of sunlight and moonlight during the black-out pandemic, the global community turned to NASA for answers. Recognizing the urgency and importance of the situation, So NASA swiftly mobilized a team of scientists, engineers, and astronauts to investigate the celestial phenomenon. By launching from the Kennedy Space Center in Florida, a specially equipped space mission named "Project Luminous" embarked on a daring journey to explore the cosmos. And the mission's objective was to discover the cause behind the vanishing sun and moon, providing a glimmer of hope that they could bring light back to Earth. So guided by cutting-edge technology and fueled by the desire to shed light on the darkness that had enveloped the planet, the spacecraft traversed through the vast expanse of space. And the astronauts on board remained in constant communication with mission control, exchanging data and observations to piece together the puzzle.

And as they ventured further into the cosmos, they encountered a celestial anomaly unlike any ever seen before. And massive cosmic clouds of unknown origin surrounded the Earth, creating an invisible barrier that obstructed sunlight and moonlight from reaching the planet's surface. So back on Earth, the world watched with bated breath, clinging to the hope that NASA's mission would hold the key to restoring light to their lives. And the scientific community, governments, and citizens alike united in support of the endeavor, understanding that the stakes were nothing short of humanity's survival.

So as weeks passed the astronauts analyzed the mysterious phenomenon, driven by an unyielding determination to unravel its secrets. And they conducted experiments and collected data, and all the while grappling with the psychological toll of being so far from home and witnessing the darkness that had befallen their planet.

But finally, after an arduous journey of exploration and discovery, the astronauts made a groundbreaking revelation. And the cosmic clouds surrounding Earth were not of natural origin; they were the result of an advanced alien civilization attempting to shield the planet from a cosmic threat that had targeted Earth. So now the governments had to let out the secret that we were never alone in this universe because now they just could not hide it anymore.

And realizing the gravity of the situation, the astronauts communicated their findings to mission control, and subsequently, the world. And in a remarkable display of international cooperation, governments set aside their differences and joined forces to address the crisis. And now united with newfound allies from distant stars, humanity collaborated on a plan to confront the cosmic threat. Armed with the knowledge provided by NASA's Project Luminous, And earth's combined forces devised a powerful countermeasure. And by using advanced technology provided by their extraterrestrial allies, a grand-scale cosmic shield was created to protect Earth from the encroaching danger. And slowly but surely, the cosmic clouds dissipated, and the sun and moon returned to grace the sky, illuminating the world once more.

And the black-out pandemic had taught humanity the importance of unity, and this newfound sense of solidarity extended beyond national borders. As Earth flourished under the renewed light, NASA continued its space exploration, forging lasting friendships with civilizations from distant stars and advancing the boundaries of human knowledge. And the legacy of the black-out pandemic remained etched in history, a testament to the strength and resilience of humanity in the face of adversity. And as NASA continued to gaze at the stars, and the world never forgot the role the agency played in not just bringing back light, but also uniting a fractured planet under a shared purpose - to protect their home and seek out new horizons among the cosmos, But even with the efforts of NASA and their newfound evil aliens assisting them there was still a fifth and final phase of the darkness to come.

So after many weeks went by the fifth and final phase of darkness began and this phase lasted for seven days and as the world grappled with the mysterious disappearance of sunlight and moonlight once more during the black-out pandemic, NASA's "Project Luminous" caught the attention of another space agency this time and the Russian space agency, Roscosmos. Begun recognizing the significance of the global crisis, So Roscosmos decided to join forces with NASA to investigate the celestial anomaly that had plunged Earth into darkness again.

And Russian cosmonauts, working in collaboration with their American counterparts, were sent on a joint mission to the International Space Station (ISS). From the vantage point of the orbiting laboratory, so they could observe the phenomenon from a unique perspective, by gathering crucial data to understand its origin. And the international cooperation between NASA and Roscosmos showcased the power of unity, as both space agencies shared knowledge, technology, and resources to confront this unprecedented cosmic challenge. And this was a surprise too the people of earth because these space agencies been battling sense the 1950s

But now working side by side, the astronauts from different nations exchanged information, analyzed data, and conducted experiments aboard the ISS. And they used the station's advanced instruments to study the cosmic clouds enveloping Earth, hoping to find clues that could explain the anomaly's nature.

And in the spirit of camaraderie forged in the vastness of space, the international crew lived and worked together, transcending national boundaries. And they shared their diverse cultures, languages, and traditions, strengthening the bond between Earth's nations during a time of uncertainty. So as days turned into weeks, the astronauts discovered that the cosmic clouds were not limited to Earth alone. Because similar anomalies were observed around other planets in the solar system and this darkness was affecting the whole universe now, but leading to the realization that the threat was not solely targeted at Earth so they thought. And the joint NASA-Roscosmos mission took on an even greater significance as it morphed into a global effort. And the space agencies from around the world joined the endeavor, pooling their collective knowledge to decipher the mystery of the cosmic threat. So now the international collaboration extended beyond space agencies. And world leaders convened to form a unified council dedicated to resolving the crisis. And political differences were set aside as nations worked together, with the guidance of the scientific community, to develop a cohesive strategy to protect the entire solar system from the encroaching cosmic clouds. And by using the combined expertise of the global scientific community, humanity forged a powerful shield, capable of safeguarding Earth and all its neighboring planets from the enigmatic threat.

And the black-out pandemic had proven to be a transformative period for humanity, solidifying the importance of international cooperation in the face of cosmic challenges. And the unity displayed during this crisis laid the foundation for future collaborations, and not only in space exploration but also in addressing the global issues that affected all of humanity. But the darkness was far from over and after three days people were confused of why the sun and moonlights were still not returning because in the first four phases the celestial lights returned after the third day

So as the black-out pandemic and the cosmic threat continued to perplex humanity, the world's attention turned to yet another key player in space exploration - the Chinese space agency, CNSA (China National Space Administration). And now Recognizing the gravity of the situation and the importance of global cooperation, CNSA stepped forward to join forces with NASA and Roscosmos in tackling the enigmatic celestial anomaly. And with a history of remarkable space achievements, CNSA brought its technological powers and scientific expertise to the table. And the Chinese space agency deployed its space station, Tiangong, and sent a team of dedicated taikonauts to the orbiting laboratory to collaborate with their international counterparts.

And the astronauts from China, the United States, and Russia worked hand in hand, sharing knowledge and insights from their respective space agencies. And they combined their resources to conduct further research on the cosmic clouds surrounding Earth and to explore the impact on other planets within the solar system.
And the global space community forged an unprecedented bond, transcending political boundaries, as they collectively pursued the truth behind the cosmic threat. And From different corners of the world,

scientists collaborated on a scale never seen before, pooling their resources and data to solve the enigma that had gripped the solar system. And as CNSA's contribution became instrumental in decoding the mystery, the taikonauts shared their nation's ancient astronomical wisdom and observations of celestial phenomena. But their insights proved valuable in understanding the cosmic clouds' patterns and their potential link to ancient cosmic events.

So with the combined efforts of NASA, Roscosmos, and CNSA, a clearer picture of the cosmic threat emerged. The anomaly was traced back to an ancient cosmic phenomenon that occurred cyclically in the universe, affecting star systems across galaxies. And in the spirit of international cooperation, the global space community crafted a multifaceted solution. Advanced technologies from each nation's space agency were integrated into a comprehensive cosmic defense system. And this united effort ensured that Earth and the solar system could withstand the cyclical cosmic event, preserving the planets' ecosystems and civilizations.

And the breakthrough heralded a new era of collaboration among spacefaring nations, not just in addressing the cosmic threat but also in exploring the cosmos as one united human race. So, with the joint efforts of NASA, Roscosmos, CNSA, and other space agencies worldwide, humanity stood ready to face any future challenges lurking among the stars, and as the sun and moon began to shine their light once more, the world celebrated its victory over the darkness, a victory that was only possible through unity and shared determination. And that was the last phase of the darkness plage I was told.

(The Blood Games)

"Elijah do you know what today is" I heard David say as I woke up "no what day is it" I replied "well because of the worldwide darkness the nations of the world decided to speed up the blood games and instead of it happening in 2 weeks the blood games will be starting tonight" David explained as I looked at a clock hanging in David's living room wall and the clock read 10:00am "Do you know what time exactly the blood games will start I replied" "no I don't but in the past years they always waited until the sun went down to start the blood games so my guess would be at sun-set" David replied

Then after a moment of thinking I asked David a question "David do you know the current population of the believers in New York right now" I asked David "well in New York alone I would say there are about 20,000 believers in New York right now and there was about 25,000 believers but we lost about 5,000 believers in the past blood games unfortunately" David explained "well we will not lose any believers this year" I replied "Elijah I know that you're the great prophet and all but that's a bold statement what's your plan. "Well first things first we must tell everybody to stay in their apartments and not just in New York but in every District in the world" "so you are going to try to save all of the remaining believers in the world because you know there are about 600,000 – I million believers left if you add up all the believers in every district in the world" David replied "yes but unfortunately just like in the Ist exodus when Moses told all of his people to stay indoors before the Passover some of his people did not listen to his instructions and those people died so the same thing will happen this time some people will not listen and those people will be in danger and maybe even the possibility of death" I replied

"So are you saying that there will be a 2nd Passover" David asked me "yes there will be a 2nd Passover and it will start at the same time as the blood games at sun-set and then it will bleed over into the next day as well but this Passover will be a little bit different" I explained to David "how different" David asked "well for starters in the Ist exodus Moses told his people to individually sacrifice a lamb and then wipe the blood of the lamb on their front door to protect their Ist born children from the angel of death well this time there will be no need to sacrifice a lamb because the sacrifices are not being accepted right now but however they just need to stay indoors and when the angel of death arrives this year it will come for 2 purposes this year and the first purpose will be to make sure that every believer in their apartment will be safe from any intruders and the 2nd purpose will be just like the 1st exodus to kill all of the 1st born children of the non-believers across the whole world" I explained to David then he replied "I understand the 2nd purpose but that 1st purpose is throwing me off a little what do you mean by the angel of death will make sure that no believer in their apartment will be harmed" "exactly what I said you will see what I mean but quickly we have to leave this apartment and figure out how we will get the word out to all of the believers world-wide to stay in their apartments" I replied.

"Ok that's not a problem so first let's make sure we tell everybody in the district of believers in New York to stay indoors and we will figure out how to tell the rest of the world" David said as we left his apartment. So, minutes later we were in David's car driving up to the common park to get the word out to everybody. And it was noon, so we had about 6 to 7 more hours until the blood games, so we did not waste any time. So, after minutes later we arrived at the common park and hundreds of people were outside, and then everyone looked at David as we walked on some kinda platform and then David began to speak.

"I have a very important message today delivered by Elijah and that message is that everybody must stay indoors tonight because there will be a great Passover happening tonight and if your caught outside you might not survive this year" David explained to the crowd then a man suddenly shouted "What do you mean stay indoors because tonight the Blood Games starts and I have to be moving around because I cannot be a sitting duck" and then another guy shouted "yea he's right we can't be no sitting ducks" and then David spoke "Look I understand y'all's concerns because in the past we would have to stay moving for our survival but this year is different" then the first guy that shouted spoke "different how" then David replied "because this year we have Elijah The prophet and The Most high on our side and in the previous years we did not so if you stay indoors you will be divinely protected" David explained.

So, after David got done explaining the urgent message, we got in Davids's car and left the common park. "Great now the word is out in New York now we have to quickly alert the other districts" I said to David then David pulled out his cell phone and made a few calls "Done" David said "What do you mean" I replied "I alerted all of the Head Chiefs in every district in the world just now" David said "but how" I replied and then David said "because technology is amazing" and I still did not understand the technology of this time yet but luckily David did. So, many minutes later me and David did what we told the believers all over the globe to do and we went inside Davids's apartment then in what seemed like no time the sun began to set and then I began to have another insightful vision.

So in my insightful vision the first thing that I saw was the change of heart in many people and I'm not just talking about the believers I'm talking about the non-believers because many of the non-believers started to convert to believers and the reason is because when the message got out that the military was getting involved in this year's Blood Games that was enough to make a non-believer think well something might not be right about this and the unfairness of the situation causes a lot of non-believers to become believers, but that changed everything because before tonight there was only 1 remaining district of believers in America and that was the one in New York but now smaller groups of believers started to pop up all around the United states and just before the Blood Games was about to start, so then my insightful vision continued.

And as I looked the streets of New York City, usually teeming with life, lay eerily silent beneath the flickering glow of streetlights. Because the Blood Games had come, and not as a rumor or a warning but as a brutal inevitability. Because for twelve hours, all crime was not only permitted but encouraged, sanctioned by the highest levels of the government. And yet, this year, there was an unsettling difference. And that was that the government had deployed its military forces to participate, transforming the streets into a battleground where survival seemed impossible. Then all of a sudden, the announcement echoed across every television, radio, and mobile device: "From 7 PM to 7 AM, no laws will be enforced. And government personnel, including military, will be active participants and no emergency services will be available so may you find peace through your actions."

So as the sirens blared, marking the beginning of the Blood Games, people either fled for their lives or locked themselves in their homes. And for those who stayed indoors, prayers for mercy filled the night air. And hope felt fragile, but many clung to the rumors—the whispered tales that divine beings would shield the righteous who chose sanctuary over slaughter. So, in the first hour, chaos erupted in the streets. Soldiers clad in black body armor patrolled with precision, taking out targets without hesitation. And tanks rolled over abandoned cars, and drones circled overhead like mechanical vultures. As gang members and ordinary citizens, driven by desperation or bloodlust, prowled alleys alongside them. And for once, the line between law and lawlessness had been erased, but something extraordinary began to unfold. So, in a dim apartment on the Lower East Side, a family huddled in their living room, trembling at the sounds of gunfire just beyond their door. And the eldest daughter stared out the window, her breath fogging the cold glass. And a patrol of soldiers marched past, rifles gleaming under the moonlight. Then one of them raised his weapon toward their building—but just as his finger curled around the trigger, something stopped him. It was like a presence shimmered in the air. And at first, it was only a suggestion—a ripple of light, barely perceptible. Then it solidified into the form of a divine being, translucent wings unfurling like silk against the night. And the soldier's face twisted in confusion, his weapon drooping as if weighed down by an unseen force. And the divine being's gaze—ancient and sorrowful—fell upon the soldier, and the rifle clattered to the ground. Then he stumbled backward, and his breath shallow with awe, and then he fled.

And this phenomenon played out across the city. And in Harlem, a young boy, left alone after his parents failed to return from work, curled up under a blanket in his apartment. And soldiers pounded on doors, and tried forcing and dragging people into the streets, but then when they reached his building, an unseen force turned them away, and no bullet pierced his windows. So, in a luxury penthouse overlooking Central Park, a hedge fund manager with a guilty conscience listened to the distant sounds of slaughter below. And he had hoarded supplies, boarded his windows, and prepared for the worst. But he never imagined the glowing forms that now hovered at his door, and shielding his home from the horrors outside. And divine beings drifted in and out of sight, each one radiating an otherworldly calm, their presence making the air shimmer like morning dew.

But the streets, however, were another matter. Because those who chose violence found themselves without any protection, so left at the mercy of both marauders and military alike. And even the soldiers who participated in the Blood Games began to turn on one another as madness set in. So, squads that entered the homes of the innocent found themselves disarmed by invisible hands or frozen in place, paralyzed by the overwhelming sense that they were being watched by unseen judges. So, throughout the night, strange sights were reported and a entire apartment building glowed faintly from within, while the streets just outside ran red with blood. And helicopter pilots flying low over the city swore they saw figures walking on rooftops, too large and bright to be human, with wings that stretched across the skyline. And a tank attempting to demolish a residential block stalled without explanation, and its crew panicked as the turret refused to fire.

But the most haunting moment came just before dawn. In Times Square, where corpses littered the pavement and neon signs flickered through the smoke, and a battalion of soldiers gathered to make one final push. And they had orders to raze the last remaining pockets of resistance and leave no survivors. But yet as they marched forward, the sky above them seemed to ripple. And it appeared that Dozens—no, hundreds—of divine beings descended, and their luminous forms blotting out the stars. And their wings unfurled in unison, and the soldiers halted as if rooted to the ground. And in that moment, the entire battalion dropped their weapons and knelt. And the divine beings did not speak, but their message was clear: This ends now.

So as the Blood Games continued the streets of New York City were only the beginning. Because across the nation, the Blood Games swept through towns, suburbs, and cities like wildfire, leaving no place untouched. From the glimmering high-rises of Los Angeles to the silent fields of Iowa, every corner of America was plunged into chaos. And for twelve hours, the government had abandoned the rule of law—and, this year, with a sinister twist by letting the military, who were once the protectors of the people, had now joined the madness. So, moments later the official broadcast read again, and it had played across every screen, speaker, and phone in the country:

"From 7 PM to 7 AM, all crimes are legal. And the U.S. military has been granted full participation in this year's Blood Games. So, shelter if you can or fight if you must. But may you find peace through your actions."

Then panic spread like an infection, and Those who could afford it fled to remote locations, hoping isolation would save them. But the vast majority of Americans were trapped—either by circumstance, poverty, or pride. And some boarded up their homes, hoping for mercy, while others sharpened their weapons, ready to hunt or be hunted. But across the country, whispers grew—stories of divine beings. Some claimed they had seen winged beings in New York, shielding families, turning soldiers away, and deflecting bullets. And for many, it was a fantasy. But for others, it was the only hope they had left. So as the sun sank beneath the horizon, sirens howled across the country. And in the heart of Chicago, gangs took to the streets, seizing the opportunity to settle old scores. And Las Vegas casinos lit up with more than just neon, as the sound of gunfire replaced the usual slot machine chimes. And in rural Texas, pickup trucks roared down dirt roads, hunting for anyone foolish enough to be out and in the open. and meanwhile, armored convoys rolled through Detroit, soldiers dismounting to raid homes, and their orders were clear: eliminate, cleanse, dominate.

But it wasn't just civilians under attack. Small police departments in places like Phoenix and Denver tried to resist but were swiftly overrun by military units who fought amongst themselves, and factions breaking apart as madness and greed infected even the most disciplined. And no one was safe—except those who stayed indoors. And, as the night wore on, something extraordinary began to happen.

And in a cramped apartment in Los Angeles, a single mother and her two children sat in darkness, listening to the boots of soldiers outside. But when a squad broke down the door of the apartment next to them, she squeezed her children tight, whispering desperate prayers. And the door handle to her own home rattled violently—and then, nothing. But a strange, warm light filled the room, and through the window, she saw them: figures of light standing between her door and the soldiers, wings spread wide, glowing against the darkness. And the soldiers, confused and terrified, turned and fled into the night. And meanwhile in a small town in Kansas, a

215

group of teenagers huddled in the basement of an old church. And they had barricaded the doors with pews and prayed silently while sirens echoed in the distance. As men in military fatigues approached, ready to torch the building, the teenagers heard the unmistakable hum of wings—like the sound of wind through trees. Suddenly, the soldiers froze, their faces contorted in awe and terror. And their torches extinguished as they dropped their weapons and ran, and chased by unseen shadows in the night.

And in Florida, there where people who had sought refuge in hurricane shelters, reports spread of divine beings descending from the sky. With witnesses described luminous beings with faces too bright to see, driving back both looters and soldiers alike. And entire shelters, marked for attack, were left untouched. And in Texas, a farmer sitting by his dying wife's bedside saw a divine being standing in the doorway, blocking a band of marauders from entering his home. Then the men cursed and screamed, but their weapons would not fire. And on every battlefield, in every town, stories spread of impossible things: bullets turning to dust in midair, armored vehicles refusing to start, and soldiers falling to their knees, weeping uncontrollably under the gaze of winged beings.

And also in Washington, D.C., chaos ruled. And government officials watched from fortified bunkers as their plan spiraled out of control. Because the military's participation had been meant to create absolute fear, to assert dominance. But instead, entire units were going rogue, refusing orders and retreating. Some soldiers claimed their weapons became unusable as they tried to storm homes. Others refused to fight at all, whispering that they had seen something. So, the Secretary of Defense paced nervously, watching live feeds from across the country. And his worst fears were confirmed—as divine beings, or something like them, were intervening. And he barked orders, demanding more force, but it was useless. Soldiers were abandoning posts. And drones malfunctioned mid-flight, and tanks stalled without reason. And in a final act of desperation, the King of America ordered the launch of airstrikes on several major cities, hoping to restore order through brute force. But the missiles never launched. And military bases reported widespread system failures, as if their equipment had been shut down by an invisible hand. And even pilots who attempted to take off found their aircraft mysteriously grounded, and those who insisted on attacking met the same fate as the soldiers—they collapsed, overcome by the presence of beings they couldn't comprehend.

So, By 4 AM, the tide had turned. Across the country, marauders and soldiers alike abandoned their missions, haunted by the presence of the divine beings. And looters dropped their stolen goods and fled into the darkness while gangs, once emboldened, disappeared into alleyways and forests, driven by an unshakable fear. And in New Orleans, a street preacher stood on a rooftop, watching as the first light of dawn touched the Mississippi River. "They tried to end us," he whispered, "but mercy came on wings." And his words echoed in the hearts of millions who had survived the night. So as the Blood games continued it started to spread around the world and even though it began in America, the madness did not stay there. And news of the Blood Games spread like wildfire across international borders, capturing the attention of world leaders and everyday citizens alike. And what had once seemed like an isolated experiment in legalized chaos quickly grew into a global contagion. And nations—both allies and adversaries—watched with fascination, horror, and envy as the United States' government declared its own military participants in the slaughter. And some even saw it as an opportunity to reset society through violence; but others feared that their own citizens would demand the same.

So, within weeks of the American Blood Games, other governments began to follow suit. And at first, it was confined to a few authoritarian regimes, eager to unleash violence on political dissidents. But soon, democracies crumbled under pressure from their populations. And fear, lawlessness, and a thirst for vengeance spread across the planet, ushering in a new and terrifying chapter in human history. Even from the bustling markets of Tokyo to the narrow streets of Cairo, people rushed to prepare for what was now being called The Global Blood Games. And no nation was spared. And in London, citizens barricaded Victorian homes with furniture, while the police abandoned their posts. And in Moscow, both criminals and government operatives readied themselves, eager to use the chaos for personal gain. And across South America, cities erupted with protest and looting even before the official start, and as people sensed what was coming. And meanwhile in Africa and Southeast Asia, local militias armed themselves, determined to use the Blood Games to assert dominance. And even island nations like New Zealand, hoping to remain isolated from the violence, quickly found their borders overwhelmed by desperate refugees and those seeking to spread the chaos abroad. But meanwhile, a strange and persistent rumor followed the Blood Games wherever it went: And that was that the divine beings are watching. But survivors from the United States spread their stories across social media—of the divine beings intervening to protect those who stayed indoors, turning bullets to dust, freezing attackers in their tracks. And at first, the stories were dismissed as hysteria. But soon, the tales grew too numerous, too consistent to ignore.

And on the night of the Global Blood Games in every nation, sirens blared, marking the start of twelve hours where law ceased to exist, where violence would reign without consequence. And in Paris, masked figures roamed the Champs-Élysées, burning storefronts and dragging people into the streets. And soldiers from the French military, released from duty, joined the fray, looting and executing citizens with impunity. But as they tried to force their way into a historic apartment, something stopped them. As a figure appeared in the doorway—a divine being with wings as pale as moonlight. And one soldier's rifle jammed, then shattered in his hands. While another dropped to his knees, trembling as tears streamed down his face.

And meanwhile in Rio de Janeiro, favelas erupted in chaos. Criminal factions fought each other, while military units swept through the streets, mowing down anyone in their path. But those who stayed indoors, hidden in crumbling homes, began to report strange phenomena: glowing lights in hallways, gentle whispers urging them to stay still, and shadowy figures with wings blocking doorways. And entire squads of soldiers found themselves disarmed without explanation, and their weapons scattered as if by an unseen force. And even in Hong Kong, where the Global Blood Games coincided with growing unrest, protesters filled the streets, clashing with both police and government agents. And fires burned across the skyline, and drones filled the air, armed to the teeth. But yet, in pockets of the city where families huddled behind locked doors, and an unearthly calm prevailed. As divine beings hovered over rooftops, with their wings glimmering against the smog-choked night. So when riot police tried to force their way into an apartment tower, the entire squad fell unconscious, as if touched by divine sleep.

And meanwhile high above Earth, astronauts aboard the International Space Station watched as cities across the planet flickered with fire and gunfire. But something else caught their attention—strange lights moving across the atmosphere. And at first, they thought it was the Aurora Borealis, but the lights moved with purpose, forming patterns too deliberate to be natural. As winged shapes shimmered briefly before vanishing into the clouds. And these same phenomena were seen from the ground. And in Cairo, divine beings were reported descending over the Nile, spreading their wings over the chaotic streets. Also in Lagos, people swore they saw figures walking across rooftops, with their steps as light as air. And pilots flying military jets in formation suddenly found their instruments malfunctioning, forcing them to return to base without firing a single shot. And all across India, a entire military convoys ground to a halt as divine beings stood in the roads, blocking their paths. As soldiers tried to fire, but their weapons refused to work. And some soldiers abandoned their vehicles and fled into the forests, haunted by the sense that they were being watched. And others knelt in surrender, overcome by a peace they couldn't explain.

So, in capitals across the globe, world leaders watched in disbelief as their forces faltered, and their plans unraveling. And also in Beijing, generals tried to issue orders, but their radios buzzed with static. Also in London, a nervous Prime Minister stared at satellite feeds, while watching as tanks refused to move and helicopters hovered aimlessly in the sky. And back in Washington, D.C., the U.S. King received frantic calls from allied nations, begging for explanations about the divine beings. But there were no answers. Systems that should have been foolproof failed inexplicably. And global stock markets crashed as news spread of militaries refusing to follow orders, disarmament sweeping through even the most elite units.

But the chaos of the Blood Games turned inward as governments began to collapse under the weight of their own powerlessness. And leaders who had unleashed violence upon their people were toppled overnight. And some vanished into exile, while others were dragged into the streets by their own citizens. But yet, in the midst of the collapse, homes that remained untouched began to radiate hope. And as dawn broke across the world, the sirens marking the end of the Global Blood Games blared in every nation. Slowly, people emerged from their homes, blinking in the early light, their hearts still racing from the night's terror. But something had changed those who had embraced violence had been left broken, and their weapons scattered, and their spirits shattered. And those who had stayed indoors, protected by the divine beings, emerged with a newfound sense of purpose. And in the weeks that followed, governments attempted to reinstate order. But something extraordinary happened: across the globe, people refused to participate in violence. And communities began to rebuild, not with fear, but with kindness following the Blood Games.

(The Great Passover)

The next day after the Global Blood Games I was told that it was now time for the final plague, so I began to have my last insightful vision. And I saw that in every capital, and in every seat of government, a terrible silence fell. Leaders awoke to find their own children struck down in their sleep. Even from the palaces of Europe to the slums of Asia, and the firstborn were taken—sons and daughters, heirs and promises, all gone in a single breath. And those who sat in power wept, powerless and broken, for they knew the hour of judgment had come. And the governments issued desperate orders to their armies, but the soldiers would not fight. They too had lost their children. And so, the rulers of the world, like Pharaohs of old, relented at last. And they opened the gates they had kept locked for so long and told the people to go.

Then the people—millions upon millions—rose from the ashes of the world that had enslaved them. And they left the cities, the factories, the prisons, and the refugee camps. They crossed borders that had once divided them, walking together toward the unknown. And no nation could stop them, for the powers of the earth had been humbled by something greater. And as they journeyed, they carried with them the memory of the plagues and the hope of freedom. And they knew the way ahead would not be easy. So, The governments, broken and defeated, watched helplessly as their power slipped away. Their armies had no one to command. And their wealth lay in ruins. Because now the people were free, and no law, no border, no edict could chain them again. And so began a march toward a future beyond the reach of tyrants, toward a world made anew by those who remembered the taste of oppression and vowed never to taste it again.

So, in my head I thought wow so I rolled the tape back to see how this all happened and this is what I saw. So it began just after midnight, under a sky devoid of stars. And across every continent, the world held its breath in uneasy sleep, unaware of the dread that would soon sweep through palaces, penthouses, and refugee camps alike. And in the silence, there was no warning—no alarms blaring, no shouts over police radios. And it was a quiet plague, but it would leave devastation louder than any war. And in every capital and stronghold, in the homes of the powerful and

221

the helpless, the firstborn children—those precious hopes for the future—drew their last breath without sound or struggle. Kings stirred in silk sheets and found their sons cold beside them. And generals woke to daughters who would never rise. And in estates fortified against intruders, no locks or guards could stop the unseen hand that swept through the night. And no hospital could revive the children taken. Also no doctor could name the illness that claimed them. And the grim reaper so they thought had walked the earth with precision, striking with a divine purpose.

Then the news spread like wildfire, igniting fear that governments could not contain. And the leaders called emergency meetings, but their voices faltered, knowing no answer would come. They tried to downplay the catastrophe on state broadcasts, insisting it was a natural disaster, a tragic coincidence—and anything to mask the truth. But the people knew better. And they had heard the warnings. So they had watched the plagues unfold, each worse than the last, and now they knew: this was the final blow. This was judgment. And in the luxurious offices of CEOs, heirs lay lifeless beside billionaires who had thought themselves untouchable. And in royal palaces, nurses sobbed over cribs that would never rock again. And in military bunkers, hardened commanders stared in disbelief at the pale faces of their children. Even some of the world's most secretive and protected individuals—children kept in underground shelters, miles from the chaos—had not been spared. And no amount of wealth, status, or security could shield anyone from what had descended upon the earth.

And the scale of loss was incomprehensible in homes rich and poor, from deserts to jungles, from war-torn streets to gated suburbs, parents stumbled out into the streets, clutching the lifeless bodies of their firstborn. And the cries of mourning rose in every language, and in every nation—it was a global lament, a wail so deep it seemed the earth itself grieved with them. And yet, there were those untouched by the plague. And these were the believers, and their homes were passed over, just as ancient legend had foretold. And inside these modest dwellings, by candlelight and with trembling hands, parents held their children close, knowing that deliverance was upon them. And their neighbors, seeing that these houses had been spared, fell to their knees in fear and awe. And they whispered of a force greater than kings, a justice that not even the most powerful governments on earth could defy. And in the corridors of power, terror consumed the rulers. And in one hand, they held the weight of their own grief; in the other, the knowledge that they were powerless. And there were no more options—no armies left to deploy, no more decrees to sign. Because the plagues had broken every structure they had built, and now, the final one had shattered their spirits. And leaders fell silent, their once-mighty voices hollowed out by sorrow. And in Washington, Moscow, Beijing, and Brussels, leaders gathered to issue their final commands. But these were not orders of war or suppression. No, these were orders of surrender. And they gave permission, at last, for the people to leave—leave their crumbling nations, leave the factories, leave the borders and the barbed wire. "Go," the messages said. "Go, and do not return." The rulers knew now what Pharaoh had once learned too late: when a divine hand demands freedom, no power on earth can resist.

And so, the gates were thrown open. And the checkpoints were abandoned. And soldiers—many of whom had lost their own children—laid down their arms. And there would be no more commands, no more decrees. And now the people were free.

So as the sun began to rise, those who had prepared quietly all along—those who had waited for this moment gathered what little they had and began to walk. Families, communities, strangers now bound by shared suffering, all set out together. And the highways became rivers of humanity, flowing toward an uncertain future. And nations that had once separated people by borders, race, class, and creed were now powerless to stop the tide. And as the exodus unfolded, the rulers, trapped in their empty halls of power, watched helplessly. As their palaces and parliaments, once bustling with the machinery of control, had become tombs—monuments to a time that had passed forever. And the tyrants wept bitterly, but not only for their children but for the realization that their reign was over. And their power had withered like the crops in the fields, and there would be no return to the old world.

So, the people marched on, leaving behind the ashes of the civilization that had enslaved them. And they knew their path would not be easy—and that there would be deserts to cross, hunger to endure, new challenges to face. But they also knew that they were free, and they would never again bow to masters made of flesh and blood. So in the cool morning light, as the procession of humanity stretched toward the horizon, the wind carried a simple message—one that echoed across continents and oceans, from the humblest shack to the grandest palace: "Let my people go." And this time, no one dared resist.

But then a unexpected twist happened and the kings, governments, and militaries of the world decided to flex their muscles one last time and just like the pharaoh of Egypt in ancient times they did let the believers go but their heart was hardened again, and the last thing that I saw in my insightful vision was a mass reverse exodus led by the militaries of the world and it took days but some how they got millions and millions of believers back in their cities and they refused to let them go once more and every body was ordered to go back to their places of residents including me and David.

(The Global Courtroom)

So as I slept through the night I began to fall into a deep sleep, then I began to hear the voice of The Most High as I started to dream. 'Elijah you've done wonderful you did everything you could do but now tomorrow it will be time for you to go' said The Most High 'ok but your people are still being held captive so if I leave who will gather all of your people 'I asked The Most High, then The Most High answered me and said 'It's now time for my servant David to restore the Kingdom of Israel' 'but you and I both know that David dose not even remember who he truly is' I said 'That's why you will have to explain to David that he is truly King David the King of Israel ' The Most High answered 'but what if David doesn't believe me' I asked The Most High 'He will believe you because I already poured the spirits of wisdom and understanding on him a long time ago before you even came back to the earth that's why I made him my prophet, and also that's why he always had a feeling that he might be King David, but he just does not know for certain, but he will know once you tell him' The Most High said, and then suddenly I woke up from out of my deep sleep.

So Then the next morning when I woke up I knew that I was going to be taken back up to the heavens, and I also knew that I had to tell David that he is really King David. So I looked for David and when I found him he was already up watching the news 'yes it is true all of the firstborn children all around the world have died suddenly' a news reporter said as David cut off the T.V 'Elijah I see your finally up and yes all of the firstborn children were killed last night so now I know the king has to let us go now because the thing that has been shall be' said David. 'yes you are correct David, but do you know that according to the scriptures of truth the thing that has been that shall be includes the soul of a man, but men just have no remembrance because when a soul is regenerated back into the earth that soul does not have no memory of his pass lives' I told David , then David answered me and said ' yes I am aware of this it is true men do not have any remembrance of their past life cycles, but why are you telling me this Elijah' said David ' because you are King David the king of Israel you just do not remember because you can't remember, but The Most High gave me the permission to tell you this' I told David 'really so what I have always felt is true then wow' said David 'yes it is true David and there are some more things I need to tell you' I said 'I'm listening' said David 'ok first you must know that today I will be taken back up to the heavens, and then you must take your rightful place as the King of Israel and restore the Kingdom of Israel' I told David

'So are you telling me that the king will finally listen' said David 'yes he will and since you are the anointed one of Israel you cannot lose David' I said 'I believe you Elijah I just got to ask you something' said David 'go ahead' I replied 'when you get taken back up to the heavens can I get a double portion of your spirit' said David, and then I smirked and replied ' you know a man named Elisha asked me that same thing the last time that I was taken up to the heavens' I told David 'yea I know' said David ' ok so since you know that what did I tell Elisha' I replied ' you told Elisha if he witnessed you get taken up to the heavens then he would get a double portion of your spirit' said David, then I replied and said ' correct that is what I told Elisha and the same thing applies to you as well' 'ok' said David 'now I must leave it is time for me to go now and thanks for letting me stay with you, but now it's your turn to run this show' I told David and then I started leaving his apartment, but before I left The Most High spoke to me "Good job on explaining to David that he is the True King David and now that he knows starting now I will begin speaking with him just as I was speaking with you", and that is all The Most High said to me before I left David's apartment.

(The End of Elijah's Narration)

So The Most High spoke 'David what are you doing go after Elijah' I heard a voice say I think I was having some kind of a vision or something 'David this is your maker speaking to you and from this point on I will be dealing with you just like I dealt with Elijah now snap out of this vision and go after Elijah' said The Most High, so I snapped out of the vision I was having and I left my apartment, then as I stepped out of my apartment building Elijah was nowhere to be found so I got in my car and I drove around the district looking for Elijah. Then moments later I started to ask people have they've seen Elijah, but I had no luck and it was obvious to me that Elijah did not want anyone to see him get taken back up into heaven, so then I thought to myself what if Elijah already was gone, then I got back into my car and I started driving with no real destination.

Then minutes later I saw Elijah entering Central Park. So I parked my car and I quietly followed him, and I saw Elijah go to a quiet area behind a big tree where nobody could see him, then I saw Elijah spread his hands, but Elijah did not see me. Then after a few seconds a small whirlwind came down from heaven and it took Elijah. Then I thought to myself I just witnessed Elijah get taken back into heaven, and then it came to pass that I could feel a double portion of Elijah's spirit come on me, and then I walked to the spot where Elijah was taken and I saw that ancient stick that he used so I grabbed it, then after I grabbed the anointed staff I felt a strong breeze come over me and it made me feel powerful, then I heard The Most High's voice again "David I see that you have found the anointed staff and this is the same staff that Moses and recently Elijah used" when I heard The Most High say that now I was certain with no doubt that I found the anointed staff, and then The Most High began speaking again "Now that you have the anointed staff I need you to go down to the United World building and demand for the release of our people for the final time" said The Most High "yes sir" I replied then I hoped back into my car and I headed towards The United World (formally The United Nations).

So after a nice quick drive I was approaching the United World building and then once I was fully in front of the building I parked my car, then after I got out of my car I noticed that just like the King of America's tower there were lions in front of the United World building also, so as I approached the lions I was not sure how they would respond to me because I was not Elijah but I lifted the anointed staff anyway and once I lifted it the lions started behaving like house cats and they even started licking me in a friendly way, then I made it to the guard that was guarding the United World Build "yes can I help you sir are you lost" the guard said "No I am not lost" I replied "Ok so how can I help you" I am hear to represent my people in front of all the world leaders" I explained "and who are you and who's your people" the guard said "I am King David and who you call the believers is my people" I replied, then the guard let me into the United World building.

The building was not how I expected it I thought it would be Royal looking just like the King of America's tower but it wasn't, and then I read a sign on a wall, and it said "The meeting of all the world leaders will begin in 30 minutes in the Main hall theater so I walked to a waiting area and I waited for the meeting to begin. "Are you really David" a lady asked me "That is what I have been told from 2 ultimate sources so yes I am" I replied "that's awesome I have read about you and how you would be regenerated back into the earth one day you know before they raided all of the bibles" the random lady said, then I pulled out my scriptures "not all of them" I said while showing the lady my scriptures "wow that must be the only one left" the lady said "I believe it is at least in America anyway I'm not sure about other countries" I said, then me and the lady continued talking then after some time the lady mention the act declared my martial law to detain everybody in America 65 and up, so I asked her a question "What ever happened to those American elders" I asked the lady then she whispered lowering her head "I'm not suppose to say anything about this but since you are who you are I will tell you" the lady said and then she kept speaking "the American elders are still alive but they are being detained in a classified government building called Area 52 but you did not hear it from me" the lady explained, then she left the waiting area, and then I rubbed the anointed staff and thought to myself man these people are very truthful these days and then I thought so my parents are hopefully still alive in that Area 52 place.

Then after that knowledge about Area 52 twenty-five minutes went by so I started walking towards the Main Hall Theater, and the walk was not long because after a short elevator ride, I was approaching the entrance of the Main Hall theater, so I stepped inside the room and immediately noticed that it looked like a huge court room on steroids then I took a seat.

"Every leader will get a chance to speak for their nation" a man said on the front podium, then after various leaders of various nations spoke it was my turn "This man is the newest leader of a people who I'm not sure about but he was with Elijah the prophet so he must be important" and then after that guy that I did not know introduced me I stepped up to the podium "You all may not know me but my name is David and the people who y'all call the believers are my people and we are actually a nation of a very ancient seed line and know we must be released into the wilderness to serve our God" then I took a sip of water because the air was very suspenseful, then I began talking again "All of the plagues that Elijah did was just results of all of you world leaders not releasing my people including the last one of every first born child passing away yesterday, but I am here to warn y'all that everything that has happened is nothing compared to what will happen if y'all don't finally release my people out of every country on the earth" I explain then then King of America spoke into his mic "What can possibly happen now that the worse has already happened" the King of America said so I replied "something that has not been seen since the creation of this earth will happen if my people are not released, then shortly after I said that the all of the leaders in the world agreed to let my people go and then the meeting was over.

So, after the meeting was over I left the United World building and as I walked out of the front entrance, I petted the lions guarding it one last time, and then I got in my car and headed towards the district of Believers, and after some time I was approaching my apartment. "David where is Elijah" Ashely said as I parked my car "Elijah was sent back to the heavens in a whirlwind, and I saw the whole thing" I replied "No way so that means" Ashely said before I shouted "Yes that means I have a portion of Elijah's spirt now" and that's all I said because I was told that I couldn't tell anyone that I was the real King David. "so can you do the things that Elijah was doing" Ashely asked "yea and more and I just left a United World meeting and I represented our people by asking them to release us from these districts across the world" I explained "and what did they say" Ashely responded "they did agree the decision was unanimous but they did not tell me the day that they could arrange such a big Exit so in the mean time I have a plan to free my parents if they are still alive" I explained "how" Asley replied "because before the United World meeting some lady was telling me about where the government was detaining the Elder Americans" I explained "and where is that" Ashley replied "some place called Area 52" I said.

So, after I told Ashley about Area 52 I had a idea to go see if Michael knew about this Area 52 place, so I left my apartment and walked over to Michael's Apartment because no car was needed. So, after a short walk I approached Michael's front door, then after a couple of knocks Michael answered. "David nice to see you" said Michael as he opened his door to let me in "Nice to see you too and I have a question for you" I replied "ok what is it" Michael replied "Have you ever heard of a place called Area 52" I asked Michael because I just thought that with him being my head sergeant he might know "I actually have heard of Area 52" Michael answered "really and do you know how to get there" I asked Michael "I do but why do you want to go there" Michael asked "Because yesterday when I was at the United World building a lady told me that the elder Americans 65 and up where being held there and my parents might be there and I want to get them out of there before the King of America lets us go" I explained "ok we will go there I'm just trying to think of how we will get there because the beast system got stronger since it came back" Michael said then I showed Michael the anointed staff that Elijah was using "this is how" I replied "Is that" Michael shouted "Yea it's the staff that Elijah was using and it was given to me because I saw Elijah go back into the heavens and I have a double portion of his spirit now so the anointed staff works for me now" I explained to Michael "ok that's good so what's your move" Michael asked "I will crash the beast system again just like Elijah did and then we can use the New Goshen jet to go to Area 52" I replied "ok that sounds like a plan lets do I" Michael said.

Then I raised up the anointed staff with thoughts of crashing the beast system and within seconds it worked I knew it worked because there was not I drone in the sky "Great" Michael said then I picked up my phone to call Jordan and when I spoke to Jordan he told Me and Michael to meet him at Coney Island because now that Elijah was gone I was like the God onto Pharaoh and Michael was the prophet so me and Michael started walking to my apartment to get my car. "Michael you are now the prophet of The Most High" I said "I am" Michael responded "yea because when Elijah left The Most High made me a God to pharaoh and you were the next runner up to be the prophet because I was the prophet when Elijah was here" I explained and then after I got done explaining to Michael we got in my car then we was on our way to Coney Island.

So, after not to long of a drive Me and Michael was approaching Coney Island and I immediately saw the New Goshen Jet, so we left my car and walked to the jet. "David we must hurry because we don't know how long the Beast System will be down this time because they made improvements from the first time" Jordan explained, so me and Michael quickly got onto the New Goshen Jet. "So, David told me you know were Area 52 is" Jordan said to Michael "Yea I do" Michael replied then Michael gave Jordan a piece of paper with the coordinates to Ara 52 "got it" Jordan replied and then we were on our way to Area 52. "So David how long have your parents been missing" Michael asked me "probably like 5 years now they were detained by Martial Law" I replied "well I hope we find them" Michael said "most likely we will because the lady back at the United Word told me that the American Elders were unharmed they were just being detained" I explained, and then when minutes started flying by we were approaching Area 52 undetected, so then Jordan landed the New Goshen Jet. "So, David how will we sneak into Area 52" Michael asked "Well back when Elijah was here I remember he put some guards to sleep with the Anointed Staff back when we was trying to sneak in the King of America's tower in the beginning so I will use that same tactic with anyone in our way in Area 52" I replied.

So, then me and Michael left the New Goshen Jet "Hurry I will be waiting" Jordan said, and then me and Michael snuck our way into Area 52, and when we got inside it looked like a abandoned school or prison building to me so we walked through the halls searching for my Parents and then suddenly we heard someone approaching us "Hey you two are not supposed to be in here" a man shouted, then I lifted the anointed staff and instead of the man going to sleep something weird happened it's like the man fell into some kind of a weird trance or something "How can I help you two" the man said with a smile on his face "umm I am looking for my parents they are apart of the American Elders" I replied, then the man pointed at a hall way "They are that way" the man said, then he walked away so me and Michael walked in the direction that the strange man pointed too. "What happened to that guy" Michael asked "I don't know but even the lady at the United World building acted little weird its crazy because people were not even acting like this even with Elijah, then after walking down the hallway that the strange man pointed out we saw a door leading to a indoor gym, and when we opened the door there they were the American Elders, so we searched the crowds looking for Davids parents and after a few minutes there they were "David is that you" my mother said "Yes" I replied "boy what took you so long" my dad said "This is a highly secretive military base but Luckly my friend Michael knew how to get here now we cant take all of the Elders but they will be ok because tomorrow they will be released by the King of America" I explained "released what do you mean" my mom said "it's a long story but I will explain on our way back to New York" I replied, the Me, Michael, and my parents quickly left Area 52 and got on the New Goshen Jet then seconds later we were in the air heading towards New York.

"So David what did you mean by the other Elders would be released" my mom asked me then I realized that her and the rest of the Elders did not get to witness the plagues from Elijah because they were looked down so I explained to my mom "well recently Elijah the Prophet came back to earth and he was plaguing the world and now the Kings of the earth our releasing our people tomorrow" "really" my mom said "It may be hard to believe but yes really" I replied "and were will we go after we are all released" my dad replied then everybody stopped to hear my responds "we will go to the wilderness where no country claims and also where Moses led the Israelites a long time ago" I replied "And what will we do in this wilderness" my dad said " we will build our own society and be completely free from the rest of the world" I replied "Good because these last seven years have been hell for our people" my dad said, then after some time we were approaching New York. "luckily the beast system is still down" Jordan said as he landed the New Goshen Jet on Coney Island "Thanks again and next time I see you it most likely will be in the Wilderness with everyone else currently in New Goshen" I said to Jordan as me, Michael, and my parents left the New Goshen Jet.

"You guys remember were our people were sent to right" I asked my parents "No" they replied "oh that's right because the government did not send us to the District of Believers until like 2 years after the American Elders were detained so yall wouldn't know so basically let me explain after the American elders got detained the government decided to cut off our people from their society so they threw us all in the upper part of Manhattan and called it the District of Believers and they would perform a purge on us every year and yes just like the movie years ago" I explained "Wow now I understand why we gotta leave these countries" my dad said, then we all got into my car and headed towards the District of Believers "Why did they call it The District of believers" my dad asked "who knows they probably wanted to mask the truth" I replied and then minutes later

232

we were in The District of Believers. I have my own apartment here so we will be staying there tonight until tomorrow" I explained and then Michael went back to his apartment and me and my parents went in my apartment. "Tomorrow we will get all of our people in this district all together and prepare to leave" I told my parents "I hope it wont take long because the government has a history of delaying things when it came to our people" my dad said "yea we were always overlooked" my mom replied "yea that is why we must leave theses counties because in my opinion we was out growing theses countries anyway" I replied and then me and my parents went to sleep for the night.

(The Chariots)

"Yesterday at the Global Courtroom the head of all the nations was in attendance and also that guy the King of America was also there and I was the only one of the so-called believers that they allowed in the meeting yesterday but to make a long story short I told the King that because he refused to let us so-called believers go that is why The Most High killed all of the first born children around the world and there was nothing that I could've done about it" I explained to my people at the so-called believers district as they stood around me.

Then a guy yelled out and asked me "so did the King agree to finally let us go and if he did where will we go" then I responded "yes the King did agree to let us go and once we are set free we must go to the wilderness of the people and are there any more questions" then I saw a hand go up in the air "yes you can ask me your question sir" I said then the guy with his hand in the air spoke "How will all of us be transported to the wilderness because as you know there are more districts of believers around the world in every nation" so I replied " "the King said that he will declare all of the airlines to reserve some airplanes for us and theses airplanes will carry our people all around the world then drop us off in the wilderness of Sinai in the Sinai peninsula to be exact" "And when will this happen" the same guy asked "as soon as possible the King said because him and the nations are sick of these plagues plaguing them so they cant wait to release us this time so it can be as soon as tomorrow" I responded.

Then after I answered that last question Michael my top chief pulled me to the side to tell me something "yes what is it Michael" I asked then Michael responded "David remember in the Ist Exodus with Moses after the Passover Pharoah released Israel finally then at the last moment Pharoah heart was harden and then Pharoah and his army came after Israel to attack them then The Most High had to split the red sea through Moses so that Israel could walk through it and then he drowned the Egyptian army" Michael explained" yes so what are you trying to tell me Michael" I responded then Michael replied " my point is that I do not trust the King or his airplanes and I believe that the nations will all try a sneaky move once our people board their planes" Michael said.

"So what should we do" I asked Michael "we should go spy on the Kings tower because I heard that will be a secret meeting there tonight" Michael replied "ok so tonight sounds like a plan but Michael how will we get past the Kings guards this time and suggestions" I replied "hmm let me think" Michael said and then Michael thought for a minute and as my head spy chief I knew he would think of something great then Michael spoke "I got it so now that you have the anointed staff David you should be able to put anyone or anything to sleep with it" Michael said "but how because I never used the staff before" I replied "don't worry just think it and send up your request to The Most High and he will answer your request because he has anointed you so we will sneak in the kings tower through a window and then you will need to put anyone to sleep that crosses our path just raise the staff after you think it and you will not fail" Michael said "ok I can do it" I replied

So later that night Michael and I got in my car and headed towards the Kings tower and the sand from earlier in the month was still covering New York City so that made our plan even easier because we did not plan to walk in through the front door especially this time. So as we approached the Kings tower we saw that the Kings guard was oat the front door guarding the tower as usual so we parked 2 blocks away from the Kings tower, and as we walked the 2 blocks towards the Kings tower we saw many people mourning for the losses of their firstborn's as a matter of fact the mourning's were so great that nobody even cared or had time to notice that 2 so-called believers was in their district so me and Michael just continued walking.

So after a couple of blocks me and Michael approached the back end of the Kings tower and I had the anointed staff with me as well just incase I had to put someone to sleep, so as me and Michael walked closer to the Kings tower we saw a open window so we began to enter the window and as we entered the window I asked Michael "So Michael how long should I keep a person a sleep for if I have to use my staff then Michael replied "for at least a hour" and then moments later we was in the Kings tower.

So, after making it in the kings tower without no one seeing us we noticed that the room that we entered was some kind of library then we quickly left the room and we saw that we was on the 4th floor so instead of taking the elevators we took the staircase to the Kings floor because the secret meeting was in the Kings office, so as Michael and I walked up the staircase we heard something and then we realized that the noise we heard was a security guard approaching us so I lifted my staff and though to put the guard to sleep and then seconds later the guard started to close his eyes and as he began to fall I caught him and then just and then just laid him on the floor safely so he wouldn't be hurt, then me and Michael continued walking up the staircase all the way until we got to the Kings floor and then I noticed that the guard that I had to put to sleep was the only guard on the staircase, so as me and Michael entered the Kings floor we entered the hall way leading to the Kings office door and then we saw another guard but he didn't see us and I noticed that this guard was sitting at a desk so it was no need for me to catch him as I put him to sleep he just simply rested his head on the desk and then the coast was clear, so me and Michael approached the Kings office door and we started to listen in on the conversation that we heard going on, then we heard the King speak.

"Many fools for a long time thought that the invention of the nuclear bomb was for world war 3 but it's funny because when we started the United World back in the year I A.D you know the same year that we made up the new testament that was the year that all the nations in the earth became one nation secretly and this was prophesied in the true Hebrew scriptures aka the so-called Old Testament in (Psalm 83:1-5) and throughout history as you all attending this meeting already know that every war since I A.D has been staged because all of the real wars happened in the so-called B.Cs and you all know that we staged theses wars in order to fool the masses so that they can think that the nations are still divided and there will be a upcoming New World Order when in fact we been in a New World Order since I A.D I mean what did they think we started the times of the years over for really, but today I am hear to reveal what you all do not know and that is that the real reason that we invented all theses bombs was to bomb all of the true Hebrews so that we could wipe them out once and for good and war against the God of Israel yes the Old Testament is true and in a couple of days we will bomb all of the district of believers in the world once they all board their airplanes, then the King stopped talking and then me and Michael saw through a cracked blind into the office and all we saw was a bunch of dropped jaws in the room and I could tell that United World organization has been keeping this secret until the very end, then the king began to speak again "this is why we isolated the believers into their own districts for the purpose of destroying them once and for all so tomorrow we will play like their saviors and send them some airplanes then once all the believers are gathered that's when we will strike" the King explained then a guy in the meeting raised his hand "go ahead" the king said then the guy started to speak "In all do respect King you don't have to call them believers no more we all now know that they are the true Hebrews" the guy said "oh yea your right" the King said with a little chuckle at the end, then me and Michael left the Kings tower with no interruptions.

"I knew it I knew that the King was not going to play fair" Michael said " so should we tell the others" I asked Michael "no because that will just make them panic but we must quickly go to New Goshen and inform the Elites of what we just heard "ok lets go" I replied then once me and Michael got into my car I called the main headquarters in New Goshen "I need a jet ASAP this is David I am in New York City" I said once the phone was answered "Copy that one will be on the way soon" a sergeant answered "ok we will need to go to Coney Island to wait for the jet" I said to Michael So then I started my car and we were off to Coney Island, Then a couple of minutes later we arrived in Coney Island "wait I thought that the beast system was back up again" Michael said "It was but the Elites figured out a way to temporary disable their system" I replied "ok so how long do we have now" Michael said "The yet will be hear in 1 more hour" I replied "ok that's good" Michael replied and then the 2 of us sat and waited on the jet. So do you think that the King will succeed in his plan" I asked Michael "now David you and I both know that the Most High will perform a miracle before he would let all of his children get blown up" Michael replied, then after about an hour the New Goshen jet showed up so me and Michael walked over to the jet after I parked my car and when we walked over to the jet I looked inside and I noticed that my 1st command pilot was not operating the jet it was Brandon my 3rd in command pilot "long time no see Brandon" I said as me and Michael boarded the jet "yea its been a while" Brandon replied "And I got urgent news Brandon" I responded "What is it" Brandon replied "Me and Michael just snuck into the Kings Tower and we over heard what the King was planning" I said to Brandon "what is he planning" Brandon replied "the

King said that after he fakes letting our people go with his airplanes then at the last minute he plans to bomb all of the districts of believers in the world" I explained to Brandon "well we must not waste time then bro and we need to inform the Elites ASAP" Brandon responded while starting up the jet and then seconds later we was in the sky headed for New Goshen.

Then after a while of the 3 of us being in the air Brandon the pilot blurted out something "do they really think that they will pull this off I mean The Most High said that if it is possible to do away with the Sun and Moon then he will do away with his people and last time I checked the sun is still coming up everyday" Brandon said "I know this is true" said Michael "just like The Most High parted the sea through Moses he will do something else this time but it will not be a parted sea because our people are scattered everywhere around the world so I parted sea will not work this time around" I explained "well what if the most high parts multiple seas around the world at the same time" Brandon asked "I used to think that because the thing that has been shall be but this time the same I sea will be parted again for the 2nd time but only for a remnant who makes it through the wilderness but not for the 2nd exodus which is about to happen" I explained to Brandon "so what do you think will happen then" Brandon asked "I am almost sure that The Most High will intervien himself with the help of thousands of his angles and they will rescue us with their chariots" and as I said that Michael began to smile in agreement.

So after a while Me Michael and Brandon started to approach New Goshen "Wait until the Elites hear what the King is planning" Brandon said "right and I hope that they send up a special prayer just like they did for Elijah to show up" I replied "that's a good idea" said Michael and then moments later the jet landed and we was on the Island of New Goshen, then once the 3 of us arrived on the Island we were told that the Elites would be at the Black House so we started walking to the Black House. So once the 3 of us arrived at the Black House we saw all of the chiefs, sergeants, officers, elders, and the Elites all in the auditorium room in the Black House, and then Brandon and Michael took a seat in the auditorium while I went to the mic to inform everyone about the Kings plan tomorrow, so as I walked up to the mic I could see that a lot of people were in the audience to hear what I had to say because after all I did have the last bible in existence.

So finally I made it to the mic and I started to speak "hello everyone I just want to briefly inform you all about what me and Michael heard the King said yesterday and basically we heard that tomorrow the King is going to send airplanes to every district of believers in the world and then after all of our people board the airplanes the airplanes will not move because it will be just a hoax just to gather up our people because the king is planning to bomb all of our people and wipe us all out for good" I kept explaining until the sun began to set and then immediately after the meeting in the Black House all of the Elders and Elites gathered together and went to the special prayer chamber in the Black House as everybody else left the Black House "Now that everyone in New Goshen is informed about tomorrow me and Michael must head back to New York City" I said to Brandon "No Problem" Brandon replied as we started walking towards the New Goshen jets and it did not take us long to reach them.

So once me, Michael, and Brandon boarded the New Goshen jet Michael spoke "Now David remember we do not want to scare the people back in New York so its best if they do not know what the King is planning" said Michael "ok no problem" I replied "so when we get to New York we will just go with the flow and board everybody on the airplanes that the King will send over" Michael explained, and then we the jet took off. "I still can't believe that King is really planning to destroy our people and it wouldn't surprise me if they try to blow up New Goshen as well" Brandon said "yea maybe so but even if they will try to blow up New Goshen it they even find it it will not matter because it will not work" I replied as the New Goshen jet sored through the Night sky and as I looked out of a window I saw that the Moon was fuller than I ever saw it. "Tomorrow must be the 15th day and remember that's when the Red Sea was parted during the 1st Exodus so everything is lining up" I explained and then after a while the 3 of us was approaching Coney Island the New York drop spot "It is a good thing that this New Goshen jet has hyper sonic engines or else we probably would have not made it to New York in time" Brandon said as he landed the jet on Coney Island "we will see you in the wilderness Brandon" I told Brandon as me and Michael exited the New Goshen jet, and then moments later the jet was gone after Brandon saluted me and Michael.

So after the jet was gone my car was still parked in the same spot where I left it so me and Michael started walking towards it "well I guess its time to go back to the district of believers for the last time" said Michael "yes indeed" I replied as we entered my car then I immediately started up my car and we were off to the district of believers, then once me and Michael arrived at the district we gathered everyone at the main road because that is where the King said that he would send the airplanes, so after all of my people were gathered on the main road I started to speak "The King should be sending his airplanes any minute now and today we will be freed" I said as the crowd gave a cheer so loud that it reached the heavens, and at that moment since The Most High was dealing with me like he delt with Elijah The Prophet he gave me an insightful vision to see that all of my people around the world in every district was being gathered to board the airplanes, and then right after that vision I could see the airplanes approaching all of The district of believers in the world including the one that I was currently at in New York City and I knew it was time.

"Hello everyone as I promised today is the day I will release you and here is the plane that I will use to do it" the King said while pointing to the airplane he came with and of course me and Michael knew that he was full of it but we went along with it anyway, and after the King spoke the staircase leading to the entrance of the plane opened and my people stared to board the airplane and then I got another insightful vision. "Sir let us know when all of the believers are on the plane so we can send you a helicopter then blow theses fools up" a officer said to the King "ok I will" the king replied, so then minutes later all of my people boarded on the plane and then the king took off in a helicopter, so then me and Michael boarded the plane and we were the last 2 to board it so as we took a seat with everyone else about 10 minutes later someone yelled out something so I tuned in.

"What's taking so long is the pilot dead or something" then the guy who yelled out that statement went to go see what the pilot was doing "wait let me go with you" I said so the both of us went to the pilots door and the man started knocking on the door but there was no answer so then the man reached to open the door and when the door opened he was surprised that the door really opened up so then we entered the pilots room only to see that there was no pilot operating the plane "Oh hell No the king must be setting us up" the man screamed and then he ran to tell everyone else "everyone the king is setting us up there is no pilot on this plane" The man explained to everybody then I got another insightful vision "time to light theses believers up" the king said as he was about to press a button that would launch the bombs globally to all the districts of believers and then seconds later the King hit the button and then a countdown began, then as the countdown began winding down to the last second an alarm went off in the kings headquarters "Launch Failure the missiles are disabled" and the alarm kept on repeating this for at least 10 times "What how did the bombs disable we have the highest technology in the world" The King yelled, then all of a sudden a loud noise was heard from outside and the noise sounded like a lot of rushing waters at the same time and the noise was so loud that everyone in the whole world heard it then I snapped out of my insightful vision, then even once I snapped out my insightful vision I could still hear the loud noise coming from outside "what's that noise" a lady on the plane yelled and then everybody including me got off of the plane to go see what that loud noise was, and then seconds after we all stepped off of the plane all we could see was thousands of chariots aka UFO's in the sky, then it I knew these were the angles of The Most High in theses chariots and they must have disabled the bombs some how, and from the looks of theses angels they were really mad because they were shooting some type of weapons from their chariots and they was destroying everything in sight. "It's a Alien invasion" I heard someone scream , then the chariots got closer to me and my people and there was a special looking chariot amongst the other chariots, then I looked closer to the special chariot and I could see that it was a very ancient looking man with hair as white as snow and his eyes was like fire and in my heart I knew it was The Most High himself, and then seconds later the chariots started beaming up my people one by one including me Then the figure that I felt was The Most High spoke "Get all of my Children" , then in a moments notice I was in one of the chariots and the feeling of being in a chariot was unreal the chariot seemed to be moving at the speed of light and the chariot was moving all around the earth just beaming up my people in different regions and the chariot was moving so fast that it did not take long for the chariots to beam up all of my people and then within minutes the chariots were successful in beaming up all of my people, and at that moment I was given another insightful vision of the King and his army "those UFO's just beamed up all of those believers this can't be" the King said as everyone left in the world stood id aww, then the King command his army to attack the chariots with missiles but they did not work and then the chariots continued destroying everything in sight.

So after a while the chariots stopped destroying the earth but they didn't completely destroy everything or everyone because I think that they was just trying to send a message so as life continued on earth my people were all on the chariots, then after some time went by the chariots suddenly stopped and moving and then they started beaming my people back into the earth and the place that they were beaming us looked like a deserted waste land and then it hit me they were dropping my people into the wilderness so after a while the chariots were all done and all of my people including me was in the wilderness and I noticed that it was not just any wilderness but it was the wilderness of Sinai the same wilderness that my people went to after the first exodus with Moses, So after I looked around for a moment I con clued that it was at least 1 million of my people in the wilderness now and most of them were looking very confused and did not understand what was happening but I knew that a new era was about to begin and right as I realized that most of the chariots left earth but a few chariots remained and as the days went by the chariots led my people through the wilderness and just like the days of old the chariots was like a pillar of a cloud by day and like a pillar of fire at night.

www.ingramcontent.com/pod-product-compliance
Lightning Source LLC
Chambersburg PA
CBHW031227020726
47499CB00002B/671